ANATOMY
OF A
CROSSWORD

ANATOMY
OF A
CROSSWORD

NERO BLANC

BERKLEY PRIME CRIME, NEW YORK

ANATOMY OF A CROSSWORD

A Berkley Prime Crime Book
Published by The Berkley Publishing Group,
a division of Penguin Group (USA) Inc.
375 Hudson Street, New York, NY 10014

First edition: July 2004

Library of Congress Cataloging-in-Publication Data

Blanc, Nero.
Anatomy of a crossword / Nero Blanc.—1st ed.
p. cm—(Crossword mysteries)
ISBN 0-425-19620-8
1. Graham, Belle (Fictitious character)—Fiction. 2. Polycrates, Rosco (Fictitious character)—Fiction. 3. Private investigators—Massachusetts—Fiction. 4. Crossword puzzle makers—Fiction. 5. Television programs—Fiction. 6. Crossword puzzles—Fiction. 7. Married people—Fiction. 8. Massachusetts—Fiction. I. Title.
PS3552.L365A53 2004
813'.54—dc22

2004041125

PRINTED IN THE UNITED STATES OF AMERICA

10 9 8 7 6 5 4 3 2 1

Greetings from Nero

Anatomy of a Crossword gave us the wonderful opportunity to revisit Los Angeles and the entertainment industry. Prior to becoming Nero Blanc, we were actors; in fact we met in an acting class, and it wasn't long before we were involved romantically as well as artistically. When our careers segued into writing rather than performing, our theatrical training proved invaluable; and we continue to "improvise" our scenes and act out the various parts when searching for inspiration.

Allowing Belle and Rosco to experience the excitement of Hollywood was irresistable—especially its balmy climate when their hometown of Newcastle, Massachusetts is locked in an icy New England winter. And for you long-time film and stage buffs, there's a special treat in store at the novel's end. We urge you not to peek.

We dearly love hearing from fans, so please write us at www.CrosswordMysteries.com where you'll find original puzzles and info on other Blanc books. We promise a speedy response.

Happy sleuthing!
Nero (aka Steve and Cordelia)

For Flo Allen
Who has forever outshone the brightest stars.

Acknowledgments

The authors would like to acknowledge the generosity of
David O'Hara
and
The Marquis de Sod Landscaping of Los Angeles, California.

The authors also wish to thank
Grace DeVito
for her magnificent artwork that truly does
"grace" the Nero Blanc covers.

CHAPTER

1

To use the old Hollywood vernacular: Back in April, Chick Darlessen "couldn't get arrested." Of the six pilot scripts he'd submitted to various television studios the previous fall, each and every one had been "shot down" by some twenty-eight year old "suit," a person literally half Chick's age, with comments that had ranged from insensitive to downright abusive.

". . . Chick, baby, honey, nobody's doing Westerns anymore. Who knows from horses these days? Horses-smorshes. They shoot them, don't they? Har. Har . . . We're thinking fresh, here, innovative. You want animals, they gotta be *cute* animals . . . Small animals . . . A talking weasel. Now *that* might be something *new* . . . And remember, it's the gal-pal market we're selling to. Maybe a *mother* weasel . . . A nag, yes, but no horses. Please."

". . . Darlessen, sweetheart, extraterrestrials in the Nevada desert? Been there, done that. Everyone has. Give us something that'll grab the viewers and won't let go. I'm talking figuratively, of course . . ."

". . . The concept? Too pricey, Darlessen. It's also a big

fat downer. You want a mature audience, you don't peddle death. No one likes a hero who croaks. No one needs a history lesson . . . Who's this Patrick Henry guy, anyway? 'Give me liberty, or give me death.' Who talks like that? Nobody. Think interactive, Chick. We're selling corn flakes here. Oat squares. Fiber for a healthy diet. Give us something we can put in a box and you're gold, baby . . .!"

And so the litany had gone, all winter long and well into spring. Every studio "pitch" meeting Chick Darlessen's agent had arranged ended with a brush-off more callous than the last, sending the screenwriter further and further into the depths of depression, and deeper and deeper into debt. He needed work so desperately, and was so broke, he'd taken a part-time job with a phone-sales bank—a job at which he was spectacularly ill-equipped. While he watched his fellow "marketing consultants" sweet-talk their way into endless sales and commissions, Chick only heard the angry click of receivers dropping back into their cradles. Often he didn't even get a chance to name the product, and by the Fourth of July he was three months late on his rent.

But then, on August 19, something just short of miraculous had happened—his uncle, Bartann Welner, unexpectedly dropped dead. Chick was Uncle Bart's sole surviving heir; and although Bart had just turned ninety, they'd been close, living only a few block from one another for the past twenty years and taking lengthy walks into the Hollywood Hills on an almost daily basis. Until his sudden demise, Uncle Bart had been as healthy as an ox. In fact, the joke between uncle and nephew was that the old man might well outlive the younger.

Initially, the thought of financial gain from Bartann Welner's estate seemed slim. Uncle Bart had been no more affluent than Chick, living on Social Security and a modest Screen Actors Guild pension he received from doing film stunt work in the 1940s and 1950s. The funeral costs alone could have put Chick in the poorhouse, but two weeks prior to his untimely death, Bart had been the Grand-Slam Winner of one million dollars on the TV program *Down & Across,* a crossword puzzle–themed evening game show.

Uncle Bart had been a crossword "junkie" for as long as Chick could remember. He was born on the same day the first puzzle appeared in a newspaper: December 21, 1913, and could complete the Sunday *Times* puzzle in less then fifteen minutes—in ink. Bart was born to be the Grand-Slam Winner, and as Gerry Orso, the host of *Down & Across,* had said at the show's close, "Let's hear it, folks—despite his age, Bart Welner has kicked butt here tonight!"

The check for the million dollars had yet to arrive, but Stan McKenet, the producer of *Down & Across,* had informed Chick that it was "in the works", and "not to worry. As soon as that show airs, the check is in the mail."

And Chick wasn't worried. The payment would appear; an estate lawyer would perform his magical legal mumbo jumbo, and Chick would would have the lucre in his hands. But the real pot of gold, as far as Chick was concerned, wasn't the promised inheritance; instead, it lay inside a manila envelope he had found while clearing out his uncle's refrigerator. At first he'd assumed the envelope had been placed there to prevent something from leaking into a half-eaten bowl of moldy peanuts. But there were no apparent stains on the paper, and when Chick turned it over, he was intrigued by what Uncle Bart had handwritten on the outside: ANATOMY OF A CROSSWORD. Inside the envelope, Chick had discovered a neatly typed treatment for a TV movie of the week, and accompanying crossword puzzle, and a handful of articles clipped from newspapers published in Massachusetts and Vermont.

Chick never had any use for crosswords. He'd once tried to tackle one in the back of *TV Guide* but found he'd had no flare for word games. He was only able to wrangle two answers after studying the thing for forty-five solid minutes— and if he hadn't been a Larry Hagman fan, he wouldn't have solved the *Genie* clue. His mind just didn't move in a lateral direction. It had always been full steam ahead. But, after perusing Uncle Bart's treatment, Chick realized he'd hit the jackpot.

Less than a minute later, he was on the phone, punching in the numbers to his agent, Lee Rennegor. Given the screenwriter's current deplorable status, however, he was asked to "hold" for a considerable period of time before the great Rennegor himself got on the line. And even then, Chick wasn't permitted to speak.

"No more animals, Darlessen . . . No more monsters. No more messages. No more dead people—"

"Lee, this is good. This is the money concept. I'm talking possible series here. No, make that a *definite*."

There was an audible sigh on the other end of the line. "You've never heard the term, 'six strikes and you're out'? It's over. I can't get you in another door. The Chick Darlessen keys have been thrown away."

Chick's lie number one: "Lee, I've come up with a fabulous story concept. Movie of the week—or pilot . . . you call it. Get me into FOX, ABC, CBS, I don't care. A cable network? Showtime? That's all I'm asking, and I'll sell this baby in twenty minutes. Ten . . . Five, even."

"It's over, Chick."

"Lee, Lee, Lee, what are you saying?"

"I'm saying it's over."

"I don't believe I heard you say that."

"If you were listening closely, you would've heard me say it three times."

"Lee, I can wrap this up in one word: *Crossword . . . Puzzle*."

Lee groaned; no one said writers could count. Counting was the agent's job. "This doesn't have anything to do with your dearly departed uncle, does it?"

Lie number two: "Nothing. Nothing at all. I came up with this completely on my own." Chick silently nudged Bart's handiwork under the couch with his foot, somehow suspecting that Lee might be able to spot the envelope through the phone line. "This is hot, Lee. Just what the studios have been asking for. Interactive, smart, a cast you can identify with, people you can *feel* for . . . sexy, even . . . It's the whole nine yards."

"Okay . . ." Another sigh. "Let's have it."

Lie number three: "I've been doing some research. I spent all day yesterday at the library, and I pulled up some very interesting articles from a number of newspapers in the Boston vicinity."

"What library? There's a library in L.A.?"

"Doesn't matter. The point is, the concept is based on a true story. A true crime."

"I'm all ears, Chick." Lee almost sounded as if he meant it.

"Okay, last winter in Vermont . . . That's in New England. Snow, pretty scenery, and dynamite product placement for the automotive industry . . . Four-wheel-drive heaven, if you get my drift . . . Anyway, four couples get themselves snowed in at a country inn . . . They're stuck. The phone lines are out. Plows can't get through for an entire weekend, and guess what? This really happened. You're gonna love this—"

"I've got another call. Hold on."

While Lee attended to a more important client, Chick retrieved Uncle Bart's work, then studied the answers to the crossword. "Ahh, Uncle Bart. What the heck is this?" He shook his head. "You can't do this—"

"Can't do what?" Lee was back on the line.

"Nothing. Nothing. Just talking to myself."

"So what happened in Vermont?"

"One of the eight snowbound people turned up dead in the middle of the night."

"We're back to dead again?"

"This is solid stuff, Lee," Chick pleaded.

"Okay, okay, I'll bite, murder or accident?"

"Murder, of course. The straight skinny, too. I've got newspaper clippings to prove it—"

"You stole newspapers from the library?"

Lie number four: "Ahh, no. They're photocopies."

On the other end of the line, Chick could hear Lee light

a cigarette—a good sign. He was interested. "So, where's this crossword fit in?"

"It seems one of the guests at the inn was a puzzle editor from a Massachusetts newspaper; a babe by the name of Annabella Graham. She was there with her husband, who just happens to be a private eye. His name is Rosco—is that great or what? Who names their kid Rosco? Anyway, the rest of the couples were foodies—you know, amateur chefs . . . They worked together as well as socialized together. Taking a yearly trip to the inn was a tradition, but—and here's the kicker—one of the original couples was a no-show. Instead, the wife sent a special dessert recipe, a sort of 'sorry, we're missing the fun,' and hid it in a crossword puzzle—"

"I'm fuzzy on this, Chick. Where's the connection between death and a puzzle . . .? Oh, and before you go any further, who was killed: a male or a female?"

"Male."

"Good. No one's buying dead dames right now."

Chick made mental note of the fact. "It was a he . . . The victim was one of the husbands. At first, no one knew how he died. Was it poison? Strangulation? Ordinary heart attack? Suffocation?"

"Nobody had a cell phone?"

"Sure. But what difference would it make? No one could come in or go out."

"So who did it?"

"That's where the crossword comes in. It seems there was a secret message in the puzzle, and this Anna Graham babe figured it out, and then fingered the guilty party."

"So who did it?"

"Who cares. Don't you see, Lee, that's the pitch."

"To be honest, no, I don't see. What pitch?"

Chick took a deep breath. "Okay, follow closely." *Lie number five:* "I've worked out a fictionalized treatment based on the research I've done. What we have is a mystery story with everything hanging on the puzzle . . . And here's the kicker—we cobroker a deal with a network *and* a magazine publisher, so the show's crossword appears on airdate. That way the viewer gets to solve the crime right alongside Miss Annabella Graham!"

"I thought you said she was married?"

"Mrs., Miss, what difference does it make?"

"According to my divorce lawyer, quite a bit."

"Okay, Lee, fine. But can't you see this? We publish the puzzle in *TV Guide* or something—"

"They already have a crossword."

"Okay . . . okay . . . We put it in a magazine that needs a circulation boost. They'll love it. The show sells the mag— the mag sells the show! I think *Playboy*'s circulation has been down lately."

"*Playboy?*"

"Okay, maybe not *Playboy*. But I'm telling you, *anyone* would jump at this. It's a great hook. It's a *money* hook." Chick looked at a note Bart had scrawled in the margin of his treatment. "Did you know that forty million Americans do crossword puzzles every single day?"

"Where'd you get that?"

Lie number six: "I'm a professional, Lee. I do my homework. You check the numbers if you don't believe me."

"Humm." Lee was thinking it over. "Maybe you have something."

"Have something? *Have something?* Call Stan McKenet. He produces *Down & Across*. He'll eat this up."

"It's a game show, Chick. Stan doesn't produce nighttime drama."

"Call him. Call him right now. I'll stay on hold. Dollars to doughnuts he eats this up in a second—game show or no game show."

"You got a title?"

"You're going to love this." *Lie number seven:* "I was up all last night working on it. *Anatomy of a Crossword.*"

"I like it."

"I told you. I *told* you. Call Stan. I'll hold."

While Chick was on hold, he once again glanced over Uncle Bart's treatment and puzzle. It was all there. All he had to do was create the working script. However, there was one slight problem; Uncle Bart's puzzle contained the true identities of the people involved in the true crime. He knew full well that any network legal department would balk on using real names. Chick needed to get a new puzzle for his pitch to fly.

Lee came back on the line and said one word. "Pass."

"What?"

"Stan McKenet passed."

"Get out of here. No way. You didn't pitch it right."

"I told you, Stan doesn't do nighttime. He's strictly game show." Lee lit a second cigarette—he was still thinking. A good sign. "You've got a puzzle you can serve up with the treatment, right?"

"Ahh . . . Yeah. But here's the thing . . ." *Lie number eight:* "I created it, and I'm not real happy with some of the clues. It needs a little tweaking here and there. We're marketing to a savvy audience, a clever audience—"

"I'm going to call Lew Groslir, in Culver City, for you. He's looking for something. This may be it."

Lie number nine: "Lew Groslir. Right. Tell Lew I've contacted Anna Graham to make an original crossword for the show—if he bites. She's got a solid following among puzzle fanatics—a built-in audience. How's that for a hook?"

"You spoke to her? You have this all set up?"

Lie number ten: "Would I lie to you? We talked last night. I phoned all the way to . . . Ahh . . . Ahh . . ." Chick shuffled through Bart's news clippings. "All the way to . . . Newcastle, Massachusetts. That's where she lives. It's back East. She's on board. Can't wait for the go-ahead. And I can tell you, she'll be thrilled to work with Lew."

"Obviously she's never met him . . . Okay, hold on, let me see if I can get him on the line."

"Lee?"

"Yes?"

"I've got one word: Forty million people."

A brief sigh emanated from the receiver. "Right."

For Chick, it felt like an eternity before he heard his agent's voice again; it was quite obvious Lee was already on his third cigarette. "You're in," he said, dispensing with a more traditional greeting. "Tomorrow morning at eleven. It's 10411 Culver, third floor . . . And, Chick?"

"Yes?"

"Don't blow this one."

All that was back in August.

CHAPTER

2

Gray enveloped the windows of Belle Graham's home office: *leaden* gray intermingled with spurts of sleet and frozen rain that spattered hard and dismally against the panes. Simply trying to peer through the murky glass into the small garden made her feel cold and miserable. This spirit of hopelessness seemed to extend outward. The three yew bushes she could see had lost their usual buoyant elan, while the lack of bird life normally clustered around the squirrel-proof feeder was the *coup de grâce,* turning the frigid and sodden day even more woebegone and cheerless. *Welcome to late January in coastal Massachusetts,* she thought. *Welcome to ice-covered roads, grizzled, somber skies, snow and more snow—and more snow after that.* Spring seemed a long, long way away.

Belle put down her pencil, shoved aside the sheet of graph paper upon which she'd begun constructing a new crossword for Newcastle's *Evening Crier,* shivered, and gazed at her dog Kit. The lanky, multicolored mutt lay curled in happy, puppy dreamland near the base of an overworked space heater. The electronic device was struggling in vain to keep the house's converted rear porch at a temperature that could be deemed remotely habitable and pleasant. Studying both the dog and the heater, Belle momentarily considered stretching out on the floor beside Kit and borrowing a little of her furry warmth. Instead, Belle sighed, pulled the long cuffs of her bulky cable-knit sweater over her hands, hunched her shoulders, and wondered whether she should search for her down vest—and then whether the interminable dark days of winter were ever going to depart.

The phone rang, interrupting her gloomy reverie. She reached for it, forgetting to peel back her sweater-mitten. The combination of clenched fingers and wool sent the receiver spinning to the floor, where it clattered sharply against the painted wood floorboards. The sharp noise woke Kit, who immediately sprang to her feet and began barking at the garden door.

"It's okay, Kitty. It's just the phone," Belle said as she bent to rescue the receiver. "Nobody's outside . . . Nobody would *want* to be outside . . . Shhh . . ."

". . . I can't believe Legal didn't set this up! They should be shot!" a male voice bellowed when she finally lifted the chilly plastic receiver to her ear. "I mean, I can't do everything, can I? And if you consider how fast they got contracts out to the others . . . They'd never pull a stunt like this with a cast member, I'll tell you that much. In a word, the show's technical consultant should at least be awarded the same courtesy as the *actors!*"

Belle squinted in confusion while her eyes drifted back to the crossword on her desk. "Pardon me? Who's calling?"

"Chick Darlessen, of course." The voice on the other end of the line sounded outraged—more than outraged. Belle couldn't detect whether it was a result of her query or his own personal problem. She was about to inform her irate caller that he'd gotten the wrong number when he blurted out an aggrieved, "This *is* Annabella Graham, isn't it? The crossword editor? The crossword *sleuth,* I should say?"

Belle took a moment to answer. To say, "You have the wrong number," seemed a tempting response, but she realized he would only call her back. So she reluctantly admitted, "Yes . . ."

"Well, my idiot secretary got something right! Glory be! She assured me she had you holding on the line, Ms. Graham . . ."

Belle looked at the spot on the floor where the phone had fallen, as if it might yield some vital piece of omitted information: words on paper, or perhaps individual letters scattered across the wood forming the missing link in this peculiar conversation.

". . . As I was saying, I can't believe Legal made such a heinous blunder. I'll take it upon myself to apologize for them. Yours should have been one of the first contracts issued, instead of waiting for the word from me—the creator." It was said as if he had a direct line to the real *Creator*.

Belle ran a hand through her blonde hair; it was a habitual gesture when she was perplexed. Her frown of incomprehension increased. "I'm afraid I really don't know what you're talking about Mr.—"

"The M.O.W., of course"

"M.O.W.?"

"Movie of the week . . .? *Anatomy of a Crossword!* The TV movie." He sighed audibly and ferociously. "Okay, here it is—the M.O.W. I'm the screenwriter . . . more significantly, the *creator* of the show . . . And you're going to be our technical consultant? Yes? No? Yes? Right? At least, you're *supposed* to be—if Legal hadn't *totally* screwed up and failed to contact you two months ago . . . And, please, please, *please* don't tell me you're unavailable. I'll just shoot myself in that case . . . I mean, we need you on the set, like yesterday. Look, Anna—"

"It's, Belle . . . My name is, Belle. Not Anna."

Belle's eyes returned to the streaked, frosty window panes. A number of thoughts raced through her brain: first, April Fool's Day was a long way off; second, although this Darlessen person was obviously upset, he didn't sound *completely* irrational or necessarily dangerous, that is, he didn't seem typical of one of the prank callers she had become accustomed to; and third, "Legal." That was always a potent word as far as she was concerned. As a constructor and an editor of a newspaper's daily crossword, as well as the creator of a number of puzzle collections, she knew about deadlines and what was or was not binding—contractwise.

"I'm going to have to ask you to step back a moment, Mr. Darlessen. Whoever was supposed to contact me from Legal, didn't, and in reality, I haven't a clue as to what you're talking about. Sorry."

Another aggravated sigh greeted Belle's response. "I'm going to personally murder those morons at the studio. I am! I swear I am . . . This is the last time I sign on to do anything with Groslir, I swear . . . Look, we've got Shay Henlee, Dan Millray, Andy Hofren—"

"To do what?" Belle asked. She recognized the names: all famous actors whose monikers had appeared numerous times in Bartholomew Kerr's *Evening Crier* gossip column.

"To do what?! Why, to film your story, of course!" Darlessen groaned.

"My—?" Looking at Kit, who was now circling around as though creating a nest in a bed of leaves before lying down, Belle realized she was as out of sync as her dog. There was Kit, acting out some stone-age memory of caves and campfires, while her human companion, ensconced in a chilly rear porch of an eighteenth-century New England town house, was coping with impossibly glamorous names—*movie stars'* names—and the disembodied voice of a man who claimed he'd written a TV show about—*Her*?

"You know! The one where you solved the crime at that snowbound country inn . . . remember, the suspicious recipe . . . and the crossword . . .? And the husband who woke up dead the next morning . . .?"

Belle didn't answer for a long minute. She couldn't, although she vividly recalled the situation to which Chick Darlessen was referring: the secret and unsettling alliances and animosities of the couples involved, as well as the startling amount of media attention the murder had received. The wealth and notoriety of the victim and his erstwhile friends had insured that. But to imagine anyone wanting to make a television movie . . . Belle shook her head while her glance drifted across her office—a puzzle motif run rampant. There were black and white captains chairs, the wood floor was painted to resemble a crossword grid, curtains were hand-blocked with a similar scheme, and a lamp whose rectangular shade held four of her most clever word games. There was nothing remotely *glamorous* in sight.

"Are you still there, Ms. Graham?"

"Yes. Yes, I am."

"So, when can you get out here? I assure you I'll make . . . Look, Legal can scramble up all the necessary—"

"Out where, Mr. Darlessen?"

"To Hollywood! Well, Culver City, really. That's where the studio is. We'll have a limo pick you up at LAX . . ."

Belle took another breath. "Mr. Darlessen, you're going to have to bear with me because I'm not really sure what you need, or want, from me."

There was another groan on the other end of the phone as well as a sound like a yelp of despair before Chick Darlessen painstakingly began to explain the situation to Belle. His pitch had been "gobbled up" by heavyweight producer Lew Groslir; Shay Henlee and the other actors had jumped at the chance to do something innovative, something breakaway and interactive; Groslir had wooed megabuck director, Dean Dilva, from another project in order to work on *Anatomy* . . .

He concluded in a suddenly honeyed tone. ". . . Look, with all the screw-ups here, I can certainly understand your hesitation, Anna, Ms. Graham, Belle . . . Consultant's get paid, of course . . . hotel, first-class airfare, you name it. But if you want to negotiate for a higher salary, or perhaps a buy-out, my agent, Lee Rennegor, is your man. Blood from a stone, that's the type of guy he is—"

"Well, Mr.—"

"Chick, sweetheart. Call me Chick, please."

"Chick . . . This is all so new. I'm going to have to talk to my husband—"

"Rosco Polycrates, right. I got a bio worked up: ex-cop, now a P.I. . . . But I couldn't get a pix on him. What is he, camera-shy? The invisible man? How would you describe him? From a Greek-American family, right? Maybe a *Magnum* type?"

"Magnum?"

"We've had a little problem with that part, too . . . Lance diRusa's going to be testing—"

"Lance diRusa?!"

"You disagree with the choice? We can talk. I like your thinking—he's never been one of my favorites, and nothing's inked yet—you want someone beefier? I hope we're not talking a guy with a gut? A Raymond Burr–type . . . You know what I mean . . . You remember him? Perry Mason? Nah, you're probably too young for that."

"No, it's not that—"

"Lance is a buff chunk of male, no doubt about it. He turns on the fem viewers big time, but it's all smoke and mirrors with him. I've been thinking Quinton Hanny. Major audience, there . . . Maybe the biggest. The demos—that's demographics—are positioning the show to be a hit with the gals . . . Twenty-five to forty-six, that's our money market . . . Of course, Shay's a total fox, so the Annabella Graham part's gonna have its sexy side . . . You know, bod and brains. That's why we can't go too . . . eh, large . . . with Rosco."

Belle stared at the phone. *Shay Henlee,* she thought, *the Annabella Graham part, paid consultant, limos, Hollywood agent* . . . It was all too much to consider. "I'm going to have to call you back, Mr.—"

"Chick, honey . . . Please . . . ! 'You, Belle . . . Me, Chick,' But, what's to call back? You and me can make a deal right now . . . Verbal, that's what we call it in L.A. terms, you know, like a spoken agreement . . . Verbal's binding in this biz; save's on ink, know what I mean . . .? But, hey, I can type up a deal-memo and fax it to you in twenty minutes if you want a little something on paper." His voice speeded up, blipping though the phone line in an unnatural and un-nerving rush. ". . . And if you're worried about how many hours this gig is gonna chew up, 'cause let's face it, who isn't under pressure all the time, I got great news for you. One week! That's it! 'Course, Dean needs four to shoot this baby, but all I'm asking from you is one! A mere seven days away from home and hubby . . . and dog, too, right? You got a dog . . .? Sure, everyone in the East has a dog."

"I—"

"Wait, wait, I got another news flash: weather."

"Weather?"

"As in: What's the temperature in Newcastle, Massachusetts right now? 'Cause here in So-Cal, it's a sunny seventy-eight degrees. You could be poolside as we speak, palm trees swaying, private cabana, the whole nine yards . . . You got snow back there?"

"Yes."

"How long's it last? I mean, when's it all *kaput*? March? April . . .? Actually, that's gonna work in our favor, 'cause we may have to do some second-unit pick-ups. Snowy hill-sides, quaint country inn, snow plows, that sort of thing."

"Second unit?"

"Forget it, Annabella. No need for you to worry your pretty little head . . . I'll bring you up to speed later. But my point is this; you could be outta there and livin' the high life. Sunny Malibu, T-shirts, sandals . . . in-line skates down at Venice Beach . . . You like to skate? And without ice? 'Cause you could be on a plane tomorrow, if you want. You talk to Rennegor, he'll get Groslir to throw in a pair of Rollerblades."

"I don't know . . . I think you are going to have to write this information down and fax it to me. I want to talk it over with my husband. I need to consider what you're asking me to do."

There was a long, anxious pause on the line's other end. "Sure, sure . . . gab with your hubby . . . Sara, too, and all your buds back East. Whatever . . . Dynamite characters, each and every one . . . believable, but quirky, you know . . . New England, Katherine Hepburn, Wilford Brimley, all that, cute but no pushovers . . . The 'suits' just ate up your folks . . . But while you're deliberating, maybe you could do me just the smallest favor?"

"Yes?"

"That crossword that proved who done it? You know, the one you found at that country inn, with the recipe?"

"Yes, I remember."

"Well, I'm gonna need you to make a new one for the show. One without the real folks' names in it."

"I—"

"Don't say a word. We'll talk tomorrow. Brainy gals like you gotta *think*, I know. I'll shoot off that fax to you pronto. Oh, and one other little item . . . If you call back with a big, fat 'Yes'—and I'm sincerely praying you will—I'll need to dispense our design team to Newcastle ASAP. Get some snaps of the police station . . . Your happy home . . . Sara Briephs's digs . . . That coffee shop where you all—"

"Lawson's?"

"Righteroonie! Lawson's! Love, love, love it! My team should take an hour per locale—max."

"I'll need to—"

"Don't say another word! Just think, think, think while I fax, fax, fax!"

After supplying her fax number, Belle replaced the receiver and leaned back in her chair. Staring across the room, she began to wonder whether to believe anything she'd heard during the past several minutes. While Chick, three thousand miles away, also sat brooding, although his body, unlike his would-be "technical consultant's," remained rigid and fearful.

And here was the crux of the problem: Chick was stuck in another stupendous lie. What he hadn't bothered to tell Belle, what he hadn't told anyone, producer, director, cast, or more important, the studio legal department—was that he'd barreled full steam ahead on the project, insisting he had everything under control, all the pieces in place, everything sewn up. In fact, he'd been using Belle's name as well as large chunks of her personal history—somewhat modified, of course—without ever speaking to her or obtaining permission. He hadn't considered the effort important. *A dame from some burg in Massachusetts—what's to worry?* he'd told himself. *Hollywood calls? Who says no?* But his innate laziness or his conscious scheming had finally caught up with him. And to make matters worse, the pivotal crossword that he'd "hired" a neighbor/friend to create for the show was a total bust. The "friend" had stiffed him, opting to spend the last few weeks in a marijuana-induced stupor that showed no signs of abating.

Now here it was a little over a week before principal shooting was scheduled to start, and Chick Darlessen's career was on the line—maybe even over before it had begun. To say that he was sweating bullets would have been a major understatement.

CHAPTER
3

"Nan DeDero's playing *who?*" Martha Leonetti, head waitress, all-around queen bee, and presiding martinet of Lawson's Coffee Shop in downtown Newcastle, couldn't conceal her disbelief. Her shellacked, bottle-blonde hairdo quivered, which was a highly unusual occurrence; even during a serious nor'easter, it was almost impossible to make those processed locks stir.

"Sara," Belle mumbled as she looked across the pink formica tabletop at Sara Crane Briephs, doughty dowager empress of the city's social set. "Nan DeDero's playing Sara."

Martha almost spilled her carafe of coffee. "That is the most inane piece of casting I have ever heard! Nan DeDero's got a mouth like a sailor—and probably as many guys in as many ports. *The Globe* had three pages on her just last month. She wouldn't know a lady from a leprechaun. Even if you told her one of them was real short." In a lifetime full of surprises, Martha never ceased to amaze her regular customers when it came to her various fields of expertise. In this case, she displayed an almost encyclopedic knowledge of the complex and often steamy existences of film and television personalities.

"Are you going to stand there pontificating, Martha, or are you going to give me some java?" This was Al Lever speaking; Lieutenant Al Lever, chief homicide detective of the Newcastle Police Department. Along with Sara and Belle and her husband Rosco, Al was part of Lawson's informal Saturday Morning Breakfast Bunch. The numbers swelled on occasion, but this was the core group, including Martha, of course, who was always on hand for service, gossip, and endearing comments, although not necessarily in that order.

Naturally, the relationships of these five people stretched beyond the confines of the antiquated eatery with the scarred but well-loved pink countertop, the time-worn linoleum tiles, and the plate glass windows into which LAWSON'S had long ago been etched in a bold and florid script. Sara, regal and with a private heart of platinum, served as Belle's adoptive grandmother, mentor, and dearest friend. Rosco had been Al's partner before he'd quit the NPD to become a private eye. "Albert," so styled by Sara, had served as best man at Rosco's wedding to one Belle Graham; who'd met her husband because he'd once been hired, sight unseen, by a certain domineering *grande dame* named—Sara Briephs. And the wisecracking and proudly blue-collar Martha? Well, in true small-town-in-the-middle-of-a-big-city fashion, she and Sara were fond and loyal members of their church's sewing circle.

"Keep your shirt on, Big Al." Martha sloshed coffee into a thick restaurant cup that sat atop a cherry-colored paper placemat, while Al, accustomed to running his own show, merely opened and closed his beefy fingers in a gesture of hopeless submission. "And don't even think about lighting up here, Al. New rules . . . No smokes."

"But I wasn't—"

"I saw you. Sara saw you. My man, Rosco, saw you."

Al affixed his former partner with a grim stare.

"Oh, surely you can make a small concession for Albert, Martha, dear. If we don't mind his cigarettes . . ."

Martha looked at Sara. That single "dear" melted her every time, probably because Martha realized the term was truly and affectionately meant. "I can't, Sar . . . It's not my decision. I don't own the joint."

"I've given up the habit anyway," Al interjected.

Four heads spun toward him in surprise.

"New Year's resolution . . . for the wife."

"But I was with you yesterday, Al," Rosco chuckled. "Down at the station? You were smoking like a—"

"You haven't heard of breaking resolutions on occasion, Poly-crates?" Nettled, or simply because he enjoyed ribbing his ex-partner, Al Lever took pains at mispronouncing the Greek name, turning the four syllables, po-lick-ra-tees, into a heavy-handed three that sounded like an order to a parrot.

"Have you kept this resolution even *once* since you made it, Al? Come to think of it, you quit last New Year's, too, didn't you?"

"Har har, Poly-crates . . . You won't be acting so smug when your sweetie's off in La-La-Land doing the rumba with Lance diRusa!" Lever took another slug of coffee; Martha immediately refilled the cup, uttering "I assume you'll all be ordering the usual today: cheese omelet, extra fries for Big Al, there; a single poached egg for Sara, rye toast, no butter . . ." The list trailed off as Martha returned her concentration to Belle. "And you're sure this Darlessen guy's on the up-and-up?"

"I've got his fax right here. The address is a studio in Culver City. I called the number listed. It's the real deal."

"Wowie . . ." Martha cooed. "Belle Graham in a movie."

"Well, not me, Martha."

"I know. You said. Shay Henlee's doing you. And Greg

Trafeo's playing Rosco? He's cute, but he's not Rosco . . ."

"Chick Darlessen said there was a bit of hitch with Greg Trafeo," Belle cautioned. "I don't know what that meant."

"Yeah, but look at you Belle, you're gonna be the show's technical consultant—fancy salary, first class digs, one glorious week of all-star treatment."

"According to Chick Darlessen."

"Trafeo and Henlee . . ." Martha repeated in quiet awe while Rosco beamed at his wife. His pride in having an obvious talent like Shay Henlee play the part of Belle Graham was written all over his face.

"She's not nearly as pretty as Belle, but still . . ."

"She's *tons* prettier, Rosco." Belle returned his loving gaze and the two were momentarily lost to the group, to the muffled shouts of Kenny the fry cook, to the clink of the cash register, the loud and soft voices of the other patrons, the comforting morning aroma of bacon and sausage, hash browns, eggs sizzling on a griddle, local maple syrup warming, and the soothing cinnamon scent of French toast browning in butter in a pan.

The three other members of the group allowed this intimate moment to pass before Martha spoke up again. "Let me see that fax, Belle."

Belle handed it over. It was the cast list of *Anatomy of a Crossword*.

Martha's shrewd eyes ran down the names. "Louis Gable . . . who knew that pompous old coot was still around? Plus he's one of DeDero's exes, too. Number four, I think, maybe . . . or is it five? I get so confused with that dame's amours . . . Anyway, having Gable around will probably make things real dicey on the set. Nan's not one to appreciate having her leftovers around when she's on the warpath for her new soul mate . . . Dan Millray plays the victim? That's sure a waste of his talent and looks, if you ask me . . . Carol Von Deney . . . Oh, she was *to die for* as the rich witch on that nighttime soap that folded last year . . . Andy

Hofren. Now, he's a *curious* choice for her husband—or anybody's husband, if you ask me . . . Ginger Bradmin. What an absolute sweetheart! Too bad her marriage to Quinton Hanny didn't work out . . ."

"Actually—" Belle tried to interrupt, but Martha was on a roll.

". . . On the other hand, she's definitely better off without Quint, especially now that he's taken up with . . . No, wait, that fling's over, too." A sudden gasp put an end to Martha's monologue. "Jes Nadema's doing Big Al!"

Four pairs of eyes regarded her without comprehension. Unlike Martha, the rest of the Breakfast Bunch had not educated themselves regarding either personal relationships or performance credits of Hollywood's current talent pool.

"Jes Nadema, the ex-pro wrestler . . .! Mr. I-take-off-my-shirt-in-all-my-close-ups! You guys must know who he is! He does all the 'muscle man' ads on TV . . . You've seen the jackhammer one? Where he gets a headache? Boy, did they ever goof on that particular bit of typecasting!" Martha pointedly moved her gaze to Al's less-than-trim waistline while her laughter rose in a gleeful hoop.

"Very funny, Martha," Al muttered.

Sara murmured a conciliatory, "Well, I think you should take the choice as a compliment, Albert. After all, the studio or whomever it is out there wouldn't have—"

But Sara's kind effort was also interrupted as Martha gulped back her own hoots of amusement. The sound she made was similar to someone choking on a large and dangerous object. "Me! I'm in it, too! I'm Madeline Richter! Madeline 'Gorgeous Legs' Richter! Hey, everyone, listen up!" Martha turned to the company at large, brandishing the fax as she did so. "Listen up, you all! Guess who's playing yours truly in a TV movie? Madeline Richter, herself!"

At that moment, Belle who had taken Rosco's hand, realized there was no stopping this particular train.

Hollywood—or, in this case, Culver City—had apparently appropriated not only her life but everyone with whom she shared it. How could she possibly bring herself to disappoint her friends?

CHAPTER

4

True to Chick Darlessen's promise, the invasion of the Polaroid People took place a mere thirty-six hours after Belle's tenuous and apprehensive "yes" to the screenwriter's request. The design team's "one hour max" visit was heralded by the arrival of a luxury-size rental car. It roared up historic Captain's Walk and lurched to a halt in Belle's and Rosco's narrow driveway. A second later, the vehicle's four doors flew open, and five people of indeterminate gender spilled forth. Obviously, they ascribed to Darlessen's credo that time was of the essence. All five members of the team wore tight black jeans; tight, black, quilted jackets; and rose- or blue-tinted glasses, and sported short, dark hair streaked mustard-blond, or vice versa. Opening the front door, Belle hadn't a clue which person before her was male or female—or if, perhaps, the group was of a single sex. But she couldn't have ventured a guess as to which sex. The hasty introductions didn't help, either: Miso Lane (the only one to reveal a double name), Omagh, Chris, Randi, and Bret, each of whom proceeded to swarm into and through her house as if she were not the owner and resident but some insignificant being hired to turn a key in the lock of an uninhabited building.

It was unsettling to hear their comments as they began to either deride or coo condescendingly over the winter-battered wicker settee and table on the front veranda, the living room with her favorite secondhand-store treasures, the kitchen where they burbled about outmoded chrome appliances, mismatched cookware, and a refrigerator to which magnets actually stuck. "Sub-zero outside, but not in here, hee, hee. Oh, so quaint." But it was in Belle's office where the critique rose to new heights.

"A fantasy in black and white," decreed Miso Lane, while placing palms to cheeks and bending backward slightly. By now, Belle had labeled him as male and the leader of the group. He concluded this authoritarian opinion with a loud and world-weary sigh that indicated he found the word-game motif more of a nightmare than a dream. On his orders, the others fanned out across the room, pulling reference books from the shelves, clucking over Belle's various collections of poetry, her foreign language dictionaries, and her two sets of encyclopedias, then muttering about while rearranging her desk. Ogling and discussing the crossword she was constructing for Chick Darlessen, he was popping so many photos that the air whined with the sound.

Then the team rushed upstairs, snapping away in the bedroom and bath while Belle trailed behind, worrying if the sink was clean enough, if she'd succeeded in vacuuming all of Kit's fur from the rug, and, if someone decided to open a closet, how many haphazardly stored items would come tumbling out.

"Oh, look!" she heard one of the five squeal (Belle thought it was Randi). "A double bed! Isn't that the cutest thing?"

"Well, a *king* would never fit up that weensy stairway, darling."

"How do two people sleep in something that tiny?" It was Bret this time, Belle guessed.

"With a whole lot of cuddling, I'd say." The comment

(maybe it had come from Omagh) produced universal snickering in all but Belle, who stood in her bedroom's doorway with a sick and unhappy ache growing in the pit of her stomach.

Then the cameras disappeared into black bags, and the crowd scurried back downstairs. "Who's got the MapQuest info on Lawson's?" Miso Lane demanded.

"I thought we could GPS it. Hello OnStar, it's Batman!"

"I'll take you there," Belle offered. "After all, I'm the tech—"

But her suggestion was cut short by Miso's brusque "Let's get moving, then. We're on the red-eye back to L.A. tonight. And Chick wanted me to be sure to—" The words vanished beneath the stamp of feet and the slamming of the front door.

"I'll be back soon, Kitty. Be a good girl," Belle barely had time to whisper before she hurried after them.

The photographic inspection and cataloging of Lawson's interior was followed by an equally diligent examination of the Newcastle Police Department's main facility—Al Lever's office, the holding cells, forensics, the morgue. In each location, the design team members repeated their performance: snapping away at rooms, doorways, and objects as if they'd never seen a restaurant-size stove or the venting ducts in a forensics lab or a station house basement painted institutional green. The cops on duty, sturdy men and women with jelly doughnut—enhanced waistlines and blunt chop-shop hair styles, regarded the lithe and black-clad troop as if they were watching the exploratory foray of some potentially malevolent alien force.

Belle tried to ease the tension of the situation, repeating Darlessen's explanations concerning designers and second-unit camera men, but her words were greeted by apprehensive and sometimes antagonistic stares. "They're coming back?" was the most oft-repeated comment.

"Maybe," Belle would answer. "But not this group . . . And they'll only be shooting exteriors."

"Shooting?"

"Filming. For the movie."

"Right . . . Shooting . . ."

But Belle could sense this was no reassurance. As far as NPD was concerned, the only "shots" came from guns. And Miso Lane and crowd were none too happy when Al Lever insisted on going through every single one of their Polaroids and removing the photos he deemed *sensitive* to security or *compromising* to critical undercover personnel.

As for Lawson's'—aside from Martha, who clucked tenderly over the band and tried, unsuccessfully, to insert herself in their photos—it was clear that the group was disrupting the local customers, and that any "second-unit" types would find themselves on shaky ground if they wished to return.

And then the team and Belle raced on to Sara Briephs's impressive and ancestral home, White Caps, where the whirlwind of activity suddenly ceased.

"I'm simply delighted you could come," Sara pronounced. She was "receiving" her visitors in her downstairs sitting room. Here the fireplace was aglow with birch logs, sending warmth and light spilling across the antique oriental carpet and the polished ball-and-claw feet of the Chippendale chairs and tables, over the silk-shaded alabaster lamps, the Chinese export porcelain, and the crystal vases filled with greenhouse flowers, and finally up into the proud face of the house's invincible owner.

"You'll take tea with me, I hope. Or something stronger on this dreary winter's day. Sherry, perhaps?" Seated in a high-backed wing chair, her cane discreetly hooked on an armrest, Sara motioned to her elderly and stouthearted maid, Emma, who disappeared to return a few moments later pushing a laden tea trolley. A plate of warm shortbread cookies rested beside a stack of fresh scones, the traditional clotted cream and homemade strawberry jam resting in matching Wedgwood bowls close by. And yes, there was a decanter of dry sherry along with the requisite slim-stemmed glasses, as well as bottles of aged port and *vin santo*. "Belle, dear, will you do the honors?"

Miso Lane and his team were slack-jawed. Not a camera was in evidence.

"So lovely to have you here, Mr. Lane," Sara continued in her modulated and aristocratic tone. "Although our chilly temperatures must seem quite an abrupt change from Southern California. I've only been to Los Angeles once, I must confess, but I was greatly taken by a panorama from the bluffs in a place called Pacific Palisades. A village, it was then, with charming little bungalows . . . I expect it's gotten bigger since. But it did have the most spectacular views looking out over the ocean. I remember the blue seemed as sublime and shimmering to me as the Bay of Naples. I refer to Italy, naturally. The other Naples, the Floridian town, is pleasant, of course, but what can compare to *la bella Italia?* And then, I don't fish or play golf." She graced her speechless guests with a glowing smile while Emma proceeded to pass around the tea that Belle had poured. "Don't forget to offer sherry and so forth, Belle dear. Oh, and Emma, be good enough to fetch something salty to accompany our fortified wines . . . perhaps, those herbed pecans and the cheddar wafers? I regret to say that we don't have any Stilton at the moment. That and a glass of aged port is a custom I know you gentlemen are fond of. At least, the Anglophiles among you—" She nodded in Miso Lane's direction who finally found the courage to interrupt.

"Mrs. Briephs . . . ma'am . . . With your permission, would it be acceptable for us to take a few photographs of your home?"

"But, of course, young man! That's why you're here, isn't it? Snap away! But tell me first, are you intending to replicate White Caps on your studio set?"

Miso looked to the others who returned his dazed gaze.

"I don't know if it's possible, ma'am. All these beautiful, old things—"

"Oh, come now!" Sara laughed. "The next thing you know, you'll be telling me I'm also too much of an antique to be duplicated."

"Oh, no, ma'am. Nan DeDero's playing—"

"So I've heard," was Sara's acerbic response. "I've also been informed that she is less than ladylike in her off-stage demeanor." Then the doyenne of White Caps waved the team ahead with a gracious smile. "Don't let me detain you. You have an assignment, I realize. Emma will conduct any of you who wish it to the second floor. Although I believe you'll find have sufficient material downstairs."

Miso's response was an unexpected, "We'll just finish our beverages, ma'am, if that's acceptable?"

"Of course! Of course! Take all the time in the world. My home is yours," Sara replied while the other members of the team turned startled eyes toward their leader who continued to slowly sip at his tea as if he had all the time in the world. It was quite obvious none of them had witnessed such peaceable behavior before.

Accompanying the group to their car at the conclusion of the visit, Belle had a strange and not altogether comforting experience. Miso Lane's canvas bag slipped from his shoulder and fell on the broad, marble entry steps. The cameras were already packed for travel, but his photographs went flying: shots of her home, of Lawson's, of Al Lever's office, of the morgue, and holding cells. In none of these pictures was there a human face or torso, not even one half-glimpsed or out-of-focus. But within this cache, Belle suddenly caught sight of a large number of Polaroids of Sara, all quite obviously taken when the subject was unaware of being photographed. "What are these for?" Belle began as the team's leader bent to scoop them up.

"A great face. You don't see many like that."

"But you didn't ask her." Belle wasn't sure why she said this. Given Sara's expansive personality, she would have readily acquiesced to a request to pose for candid portraits.

"Hey, we gotta get a move on," Miso said by way of a reply. He dumped the photos in his satchel and gestured to the others who jumped into the car.

"But you—" Belle repeated.

"But I what?" Lane turned to her, his features suddenly hostile and tense.

Belle didn't answer. The words that came to mind would have made Sara sound enfeebled, in need of protection, old.

"A face is a face. You don't own it. I don't own it."

"Such lovely young people," Sara said when Belle reentered the house. "Curious names, however. I expect they may have invented them themselves. Don't you agree? Omagh is an Irish town, of course, so it's conceivable that parents might call a child after a place . . . But Miso is a type of soup . . . Japanese, I believe . . ."

Belle nodded, distracted and still curiously uneasy.

"He looked like someone, didn't he, Belle? The Lane boy? Other than himself, of course. I can't think who . . . Oh, well, my poor old brain isn't always as sharp as I'd like." With that, she turned on her cane and began walking with cautious grace back into the depths of her house. But before leaving her guest, Sara offered a final word of advice. "Take good care of yourself out there, Belle dear. Remember, we want you home safe and sound."

CHAPTER

5

Belle was in the midst of preparing a plate of deviled eggs when Rosco came home that evening. In times of crisis, this was her favorite therapeutic food. She was so engrossed in the soothing chore of scooping hard-cooked yolks into a mixing bowl, adding a pinch or so of dried English mustard, and popping in some healthy dollops of mayo and a couple of spoonfuls of capers that she didn't hear the front door open or Kit's delighted yips as she greeted her favorite male companion of the two-legged, we'll-go-for-a-walk-in-a-minute variety.

It took a concerned, "Everything go alright with the visitors from Los Angeles?" from Rosco before Belle realized she was no longer alone.

She jumped. "You scared me."

"That's what you get for having such a sotto voce watchdog." He walked over to her, circled her waist with his arms, and kissed her neck.

His wife's brain was elsewhere. Ordinarily, Belle would have turned to face him and continue the embrace, then asked him how his day had gone. This time, she stood still, gazing at, without fully seeing, the fluffy yellow mixture in the bowl before her. "Maybe Kit was asleep . . ."

"Ah . . . Actually, she wasn't. I was kidding with the 'sotto voce' bit. Her nibs was her usual chatty self." Rosco gently shifted his wife's stance until he was looking down into her pensive face. "Was there a problem with the design team?"

"Well . . ." Belle's reply was drawn-out and hesitant.

"I assume they weren't rude to you, or out of line?" Gorilla-style, he facetiously pounded his chest. "A Greek-American like myself doesn't like to see women insulted. Especially one I happen to love a lot."

"No one made a pass, Rosco, if that's what you mean."

"Well, they should have." He put on a Bogey accent, "Gorgeous dame like you?"

Belle smiled, but the expression was as rueful and uncertain as her tone. "The visit went according to schedule, but I felt very uncomfortable with them snooping around our house, so I decided to accompany them on their rounds."

"NPD, Lawson's, and Sara's?"

Belle nodded.

"Let me guess . . . The folks at NPD didn't cotton to having ordinary civilians around? Especially ones with cameras?"

"No, everyone at the police station was okay . . . Well, pretty much okay."

"Big Al, too?"

Belle shrugged. "A little cranky, I guess . . . But, then that's how he likes to present himself. Tough cop. No nonsense. He did some editing before he let them leave with their photos."

Rosco laughed briefly. "I'm not hearing a heck of a lot of enthusiasm for the invading guys and gals from outer California." He tried for a lighter tone, which on other occasions would have brought a quick grin to his wife's face. This time it did not.

Belle looked up at him, her troubled gaze growing. "The

leader of the team, Miso Lane, took a lot of Polaroids of Sara."

"She's quite a character. I can't say I blame him."

"But he didn't tell her, Rosco! Or ask her permission."

"He probably simply wanted candid snaps, Belle. Shots that would be considered more artistic and immediate rather than posed."

"But there was something secretive in his behavior. Something . . . well, not nervous, really, but kind of sly. And his entire approach shifted the minute he set foot in White Caps. Up until then, he couldn't stand in one place longer than a minute. But when he saw Sara, he looked as if he'd been shot with a stun gun. It was almost as if he was suddenly fixating on her."

"That's a strong term—fixate."

"I know it is, and I'm not really sure why I use it, but there was a weird quality about him." Belle let out an elongated sigh. "I can't believe this; I haven't even asked you how things went in court today."

He shrugged. "The usual. Sit around and wait. Wait around and sit." Rosco was in the final phases of a lengthy fraud case and had been asked to testify by a team of insurance company lawyers who believed a client had bilked the company out of two million dollars by submitting phony claims on "stolen" merchandise. Rosco had collected evidence that supported the company's position, determining that goods were simply being moved from warehouse to warehouse and then being shipped overseas by a subsidiary business under a different name. The job had required a substantial amount of undercover work, something Rosco enjoyed and had a knack for. And these initial hearings were only to determine if cameras would be allowed into the courtroom. Since he held a vested interest in not wanting his mug spread throughout every media outlet in eastern Massachusetts, he'd opted to attend the proceedings.

"It's odd," he said, "that we should both have our pea-brains focused on cameras. In retrospect, I'm glad I put my foot down when the Polaroid clan asked to shoot my office. I'm a little too fond of my anonymity. Though, in Sara's case, she must have known Mr. Miso Lane was taking pictures of her. A flash goes off every time someone fires one of those Polaroids."

"You didn't see them at work. The five of them took so many photos, it was like being in the middle a summer lightning storm. Who knew what was in their sights?"

As Rosco thought, his arms returned to holding his wife close, sending a silent message of caring and concern. "And did you pick up on those same peculiar vibes when this Lane guy was here?"

"No, not the vibes, but they snapped as many pictures—none of me, though . . . And none of Martha when they were at Lawson's." Belle frowned. "Then the odd thing was that when I returned home from Sara's, I noticed that the crossword I was constructing for Chick Darlessen was missing. Not that losing it is the end of the world. I just need to draw another grid and put in the words I still remember, which, fortunately, is all of them. The puzzle most likely got swept up among all the photos the team was taking of the office."

Rosco was silent. Belle also was silent, while their two bodies, accustomed to fitting together in mutual and loving support, remained intertwined and interconnected.

"You don't have to go out there, Belle. If you're getting cold feet—"

She tried for a second smile. "Well, they're not really cold. They're more tepid."

"I'm serious, Belle. You don't have to go. Darlessen et al will work it out."

She sighed and attempted another small jest. "Martha would never forgive me."

"Martha would get over it."

Belle pressed her face against Rosco's shoulder. "You know what I love about you?"

"My sexy bod."

"Very funny. What I love about you is that you're level-headed."

Rosco chuckled. "There's a recommendation for you! 'Levelheaded,' that is, *boring guy* available for advice or snuggling or whatever. Only *serious* women need apply."

"That's not what I mean, and you know it. What I'm trying to say is that you're centered. You don't let yourself fly into a tailspin. You don't let your imagination get the better of you."

"There's nothing wrong with imagination, Belle—and everything *right* with following your instincts. Which, by the way, have gotten us out of hot water on more than one occasion."

"Hmmm, they've also managed to get us *into* hot water from time to time . . ."

He chuckled and then repeated his previous suggestion. "Look, you don't have to go to California. You can overnight the crossword and stay home. Or fax it to them and call it quits."

"But I gave my word."

"Tell Darlessen your plans have changed. After all, it's his studio's fault for not giving you more advance notice . . . Or, *I* can phone him and say you fell on the ice, broke your leg . . . No, wait . . .! You were knocked unconscious, and have amnesia. They'll love that story line."

"That's nothing to joke about."

"Who's joking? Isn't that how all those soap operas work? Folks get hit on the head and end up shipping out on tramp steamers, wandering the globe for years and years, completely unaware that they're really the wealthy scions of some blue-blood family from Boston or Philadelphia . . ."

"Forget what I said about levelheaded." This time Belle

truly smiled while Rosco looked at the concoction on the countertop, noticing it for the first time.

"That's what we're having for supper? Deviled eggs?"

"For starters," Belle said.

"And for finishers?"

"I was thinking maybe the Athena Restaurant."

"How did I know you were going to suggest that?"

They kissed, all worries momentarily banished. When they pulled apart, Rosco looked down into his wife's smiling face. "You don't have to go to California, Belle. Think of Kit being without you for an entire week? Who's going to entertain her all day long? Toss balls, give belly rubs?"

"I work around here, in case you hadn't noticed."

"Not according to Kit, you don't."

Belle smiled again. "Everything's going to be fine, Rosco. It is."

M aybe it was the *taramosalata* at the Athena Restaurant, or the spinach and feta pie or the moussaka or the honey-drenched baklava. Or perhaps it was a result of indulging in all four highly spiced delights, but Belle's sleep that night was disrupted by odd and disquieting dreams.

She saw Sara's house—but only as a series of doors and windows—all the places of entry and exit Miso Lane and his crew had so deliberately recorded.

Then her sleeping mind visited her own home, although she and Rosco were not living there. Instead, the place was inhabited by a band of brigands who remained locked inside during daylight hours and crept about at night to ransack the neighborhood, returning to the kitchen before dawn to gloat over their new-found loot. The actress Shay Henlee appeared suddenly among this unsavory group, cautioning a stern, "Nan DeDero is quite upset with each of you!" while Kit, who also made a surprise visit, began alternatively growling at the startled thieves and cringing in terror.

Belle awoke to find the dog truly growling. Curled at the foot of the bed, Kit was sound asleep and snarling at her own imagined enemy for all she was worth.

"Kitty," Belle soothed. "It's only a dream."

Then Belle sat up and stared at the night-dark windows, and began to wish she'd never heard of Chick Darlessen or his movie.

O ver the next few days her dreams came full circle, so that the notion of balmy weather, royal palms waving in a languid breeze, and sun rather than Massachusetts' incessant gray began to seem like a very welcome respite. And as those days flew by, her friends in Newcastle became more and more excited for her, more envious of her chance to window-shop on Rodeo Drive, cruise along Sunset Boulevard, and star-watch at hot spots like, Liana by the Sea or String. The downside, of course, was spending a week away from Rosco, something Belle mentioned more than once as he drove her to Boston's Logan Airport on a blustery and frigid Wednesday morning, and something she reiterated after they shared one final kiss in front of an airport security sign that read TICKETED PASSENGERS ONLY BEYOND THIS POINT.

"I'm going to miss you, too," he admitted. "A lot. But don't worry, everything's going to be fine. It's only a week, and I'm sure you'll return bronzed and loving every minute of it." He kissed her again. "Just don't fall for any movie actors."

Belle smiled. "I'll try not to."

"I'm serious."

"Okay, I'll do more than try."

"That's better. Uh oh, I almost forgot." Rosco pulled an envelope from his jacket and handed it to her. "This is a little going away present from the Breakfast Bunch. It's a ticket to that crossword puzzle game show—*Down & Across*. It was Martha's idea."

Belle opened the envelope. "But the show's tonight. In Burbank. How am I going to—?"

"Get from your hotel in Santa Monica to the San Fernando Valley?"

Belle nodded.

"For starters, I guess you'd better shake a leg and board that plane." He kissed her again. "See you in a week."

CHAPTER

6

"Whoever wrote 'It never rains in Southern California' sure didn't have a night like this in mind, did he?" The cab driver gave Belle a broad smile through the rearview mirror as he swung through the cloverleaf that connected the number 10 Freeway to the 405 Freeway. His question seemed rhetorical, so she simply returned the smile and suppressed a weary, jet-lagged yawn.

How many hours had it been since she'd seen Rosco? Belle wondered as she counted on her fingers: one transcontinental plane trip, one on-time arrival at LAX, a forty-minute cab ride to her hotel in Santa Monica, half an hour to shower and change, and then back into another taxi that would take her to Burbank and the studio for *Down & Across*.

She stifled another wrong-time-zone yawn as she listened to the wipers slap noisily against the framework of the taxi's windshield. The blades were doing very little, if anything, to squeegee the torrents of water that were cascading from the charcoal-black Los Angeles sky. The driver was young, possibly twenty-three or -four, with sandy blond hair hanging down to his shoulders. He reminded Belle of pictures of the Beach Boys from a mid-1960s' record album cover.

"Yeah," he continued, "the rubber on these dang blades gets all dried and crackly sitting in the sun day after day . . . Then when it does rain, it's like you're rocketing through a fish tank—blind."

Belle watched the speedometer's needle jump to seventy-five miles-per-hour as they headed north toward the San Fernando Valley. Given the horrendous driving conditions, she was shocked to see cars flying by on their left, while other drivers moved at a snail's pace to her right.

"And it's always the same old story," the cabbie added. "These hotshots in Vipers and 'Vettes out in the left lane . . . sooner or later meet up with the toads in the Volvos and VWs in the right. Next thing you know, you get a chain reaction and a ten-car pile-up. Yep, that's why I like to take it nice and easy when the weather's like this. 'Get there in one piece,' that's what I always say. Call me a weather wimp, it's okay by me."

As far as Belle was concerned, seventy-five in a driving rainstorm didn't pass for "nice and easy," even by Massachusetts standards. She checked to be certain that her seat belt was secure, as though the vehicle's pilot had just announced that he expected some major turbulence up ahead.

The taxi climbed up through the Sepulveda Pass, approaching the summit. Belle could see a sign for Mulholland Drive through her rain-splattered window. The words were illuminated only by the glare of the oncoming headlights, like a scene out of a 1950s' black-and-white Robert Mitchum movie.

After another quarter of a mile, the cab reached the top of the hill, where the rain suddenly and miraculously stopped, revealing a handful of stars twinkling in the night sky to the north. Below them, a carpet of luminescence stretched as far as the eye could see, the city blocks delineated in perfect rectangles by streaks of red and white automobile lights. The freeway's surface was bone dry. Not a drop of rain had touched the San Fernando Valley.

"Is this your first time to a TV studio?" the driver asked.

"Yes. I just flew in. I've never been to Los Angeles before. It's certainly an intriguing city."

He laughed. "Yeah, that it is . . . Intriguing. Every day I'm more *intrigued*. But . . . You gotta call it 'L.A.' Nobody says Los Angeles except the mayor, and nobody listens to him. And technically Burbank, where you're going tonight, isn't even part of L.A. It's a city within a city, with its own police force, its own school system, et cetera. Just like Santa Monica, where I picked you up? Same thing. Its own city. Its own police, yada-yada."

"Why is that?"

"Beats me." The cabbie pulled off the 405 and headed east on the 101 Freeway. "So, what show are you going to see? A sitcom? Don't they shoot *Gilbert's Gondola* at the McKenet Studios?"

"Gee, I don't know. Do they?" Belle said. "I hope I've got the right address. Some friends back home gave me a ticket to a game show. It was a going-away gift . . . The show's *Down & Across.*" She pulled the ticket from her purse and held it to the window for more light. "Yes, it says it's taped at the McKenet Studios in Burbank."

"Yeah, that's right. *Down & Across* is one of Stan's babies. Big hit."

"Stan?"

"Stan McKenet." The driver said this as if he and "Stan" had been best of friends in high school, or perhaps surfing buddies.

The response prompted Belle to ask "Do you know him? The producer?"

"No. No. But he's done that show for a while. My mom watches it all the time . . . But hey, she lives in Indiana, what do you expect?"

"Is something wrong with Indiana?"

"I grew up there." He gave Belle no time to fathom what the remark was intended to mean; instead, he continued. "So, you're into crosswords, huh? One of them puzzle junkies."

Belle wasn't certain what prompted what would become her first lie of the evening; it simply popped out of her mouth almost before she was aware of speaking. "Not really, but my friend thought I'd enjoy seeing a game show, with a live audience . . . get a behind-the-scenes look." Then she added a bit of truth to the mix. "I don't watch much TV. I'm more of a book person."

"The show's pretty good."

Belle couldn't resist saying, "Did you hear that from your mother?"

"Er . . . Ah . . . No. Well . . . I've watched it once or twice myself." He swerved the cab quickly and passed three cars on the right side. "So, you don't know how *Down & Across* works, then?"

Lie number two. "Not really."

"But you know the host, Gerry Orso, right?"

"Ummm—"

"I mean, everybody's gotta know Gerry Orso. He used to be in that sitcom about the polo team . . .? I loved that when I was a kid."

"The polo team?"

"Great show . . . really dynamite . . . Anyways, so Gerry's hosting *Down & Across,* and each night there are two contestants. You know what a tic-tac-toe grid looks like? Or that little pound sign on the telephone? Two lines across and two lines down? And they intersect each other? Some people call it a hash mark . . .? Well, that's what the playing grid looks like on *Down & Across,* except there are *six* lines going down and six lines going across on the show, instead of two. Get it?"

Throughout this brief monologue, the driver kept his

eyes fixed on Belle in the mirror. She nearly screamed, "Yes, yes. I get it! I get it!" in an effort to force him to concentrate on the road ahead.

"Okay. The way the show goes is like this: In the first round there are six words, all the same length, three letters—three words across and three down and they crisscross symmetrically. The words always have an odd number of letters as Orso expands the grid round by round; that's the only way it works. So the two words in the center always share a middle letter. Now, Gerry Orso gives you the letter in the middle of the grid at the start of each round . . . You with me so far?"

"Yes." Belle was greatly relieved to note the cabbie had finally returned his concentration on the traffic patterns before him.

"Okay. Now, if you can visualize all this on the back wall of the studio set . . ." He lifted both hands from the steering wheel in an attempt to paint a picture in the air. "What you have up there are spaces for the six words . . . In the case of the two center words, you already know what the middle letter will be. Okay, Gerry—by the way, he's from Indiana, too. So's David Letterman . . . Okay, Gerry Orso then reads a clue; then, one of the contestants hits the buzzer, gives the answer, and tells Gerry where to place the word. The first two clues are always for the two center words; and natch, the correct answers need to include the center letter Gerry's already supplied . . . Then the contestants guess the other four words from Gerry's clues and place them correctly—either north, south, east, or west on the grid."

"I follow that . . . You can put your hands back on the steering wheel if you like."

"Okay. When the grid expands, and you get to the third, fourth, fifth, and sixth words it gets harder because the grid fills in and you need to match more of the letters, just like in a crossword puzzle."

"But you win more money as it get harder, is that it?"

"Right. And, of course, the length of the word changes with each round. The first is three-letter words, so the grid looks something like a Rubik's Cube; then the pressure mounts as you get your seven-letter words, et cetera . . ."

"I see," Belle answered, but the cabbie didn't need any prompting.

". . . Gossip has it that some old coot was a million-dollar Grand-Slam Winner a while back . . . But Stan McKenet hasn't aired that show yet, so no one knows who the old geezer is . . . well, the studio audience, I guess, but they have to sign waivers that keep them from blabbing until the show's aired."

"You seem to know *Down & Across* fairly well for someone who's only seen it once or twice."

"Ahh . . . Yeah, well, my mom keeps me filled in from time to time. Me, I'm like you. I don't spend too much time in front of the TV."

"So, you do a lot of reading?"

"Nah, surfing. On water."

"I see," Belle repeated, then suddenly wondered what was it about this city—or cities—that prompted people to lie. Because the cabbie obviously had not been telling the truth about how familiar he was with *Down & Across*. And neither had she. She found it very curious.

The remainder of the trip passed in silence. The freeway changed from the 101 to the 134, from which the cabbie exited onto Pass Avenue in Burbank. About eight blocks north on Pass Avenue, the car reached the corner of Magnolia Boulevard and the entrance to Stan McKenet Studios. It was highlighted by a drive-through archway blocked off by a pole-gate marked with reflective spiral orange-and-white stripes and a flashing red light. There were pedestrian walkways on either side of the gate, each with a turnstile. A uniformed guard ensconced in a booth presided over all three entry points. The driver stopped and turned in his seat to face Belle.

"Generally they don't let cabs onto the lot, but I'll give it a try."

A second security guard approached the car. The cabbie rolled down his window and said, "*Down & Across*. We're running a little late, so if you could just raise the gate we'll be outta your hair . . ."

The guard looked at Belle. "Do you have a ticket, ma'am?"

Belle produced the ticket, which he glanced at and retuned. "Thank you. You'll need to walk onto the lot and take the shuttle over to Studio Twenty-six. Security's tightened. We don't let taxis in any more."

"Is there a terrorism threat?"

"No, there's a fear that the taxis may be driven by desperate actors." He checked his watch. "You've got plenty of time."

Belle paid the driver and stepped from the car.

"Take a left after you pass beneath the arch," the guard said, pointing. "If you want your cab driver to pick you up here, he'll have to get in line fifteen or twenty minutes early."

"Oh, that's okay. I'll just hail a taxi when the show's over."

Both the guard and the driver reacted as if she'd told them the joke of a lifetime. When they settled down, the guard said, "You're not from L.A., are you?"

Belle shook her head.

"Well, you don't *hail* taxis in L.A., ma'am. You'd be here a month of Sundays before one passed this gate. If you want to get home tonight, I suggest you have this young man pick you up . . . at say . . . eight-thirty. Taping should be done by then."

Belle said nothing. The cabbie tooted his horn twice, gave her a thumbs-up signal and called out, "Catch you at eight-thirty." He then backed into traffic.

"You don't drive?" the guard asked as they walked toward the pedestrian entry together.

"Yes."

"Do yourself a favor, rent a car. Taxis are murder around here."

"Starting tomorrow, I have someone who'll be driving me around. I'm only here for a week."

The guard shrugged. "Suit yourself. Show your ticket to Artie there. The shuttle is just on the other side of the gate. It should be leaving in five minutes. Studio Twenty-six. Don't miss the stop."

CHAPTER

7

The McKenet Studio shuttle bus resembled the average airport courtesy van. Ten rows of seats, two on each side of a center aisle, enabled it to hold forty people. The bus was nearly half-full when Belle stepped on, and as she worked her way toward the rear, she noticed a seventy-something woman with pink-white hair sitting alone. This woman was petite, almost child-sized, and dressed in a silky pants ensemble in soft shades of peach, coral, and gold; a chiffon scarf, knotted at her neck; and large hoop earrings intended for a younger wearer. Beige sandals constructed to support aging and falling arches added the only jarring note to the ultrafeminine garb, but the wearer kept the shoes locked together in a ladylike pose, tucked away from sight. She was also in the midst of fastidiously filling in spaces in a Charles Preston giant crossword collection——in ink. Deciding the passenger was probably well-acquainted with *Down & Across,* Belle asked if the seat beside her was taken.

"Why, not at all, dearie." The response was a birdlike warble. "I'd love some company." She slid her small but surprisingly agile legs into the aisle, and Belle took the seat next to the window.

"Sorry, hon, but I just can't sit in the outside seat," the woman said. "I know Herbert is an excellent driver, really the best on the lot, but I feel trapped on the outside . . . Ever since that one fellow drove the courtesy van into the lake where *Sea Demons* was filmed and that poor man drowned . . . Of course the driver on that run was always high as a kite. I don't think Herbert smokes too much pot. At least, I hope he doesn't. You never do know nowadays, do you? Well anyway, I just believe it's better to be on the aisle in case there's a problem. At my age, I don't like problems."

"I'm fine with the window," Belle said as she settled in.

The woman's round, black eyes scrutinized Belle. "Haven't I seen you before? Well, not in person . . . but I'm sure I recognize your face . . . and that blonde hair . . . Maybe from a story in a magazine . . .?"

As Belle scrambled for a response that would ensure her anonymity, the woman gasped suddenly.

"I know! You were Richard Perry's partner's ex-girlfriend in the TV movie about the crooked cop! Are you currently filming something on this lot?"

Belle blushed a bright red. "No, no. I'm not an actress. I'm just here to watch a taping of *Down & Across*."

"Well, you certainly could be an actress. You have that *look*. I'm a pretty good judge of who has the *look* and who doesn't. It's all in the cheekbones. A person will never become a movie star if they don't have high cheekbones like you. And I'll bet you have no trouble getting the boys, either, do you?"

"Actually, I'm married." Belle held up her wedding ring as evidence.

The woman laughed. "Yes, but how many times? I've had five husbands." This was said with much pride, as if each mate represented a notch on a gun handle. "Of course, none of them were able to keep up with me. A weak constitution, to the man. You'd think I could have picked them better, but I've always had a soft spot for a pretty face." She laughed again. "But, they all drop dead sooner or later, don't they? You get yourself a good life insurance policy on that man of yours, young lady. You don't want to be left out in the cold." She extended her hand to Belle. "My name is Harriet Tammalong. I'm going to the *Down & Across* taping, too."

Belle shook her hand and immediately realized that the woman, being quite obviously a puzzle fiend, would undoubtedly recognize her name, and that the last thing she wanted in her weary state was undue attention. So she said, "It's nice to meet you, Harriet . . . I'm Gale Harmble." It was the name of one of her best friends in grade school.

"G-A-I-L or G-A-L-E? Like Gale Storm. I've always loved that name."

"Yes, it's G-A-L-E."

"And are you tempestuous, dearie?"

Belle laughed. "I'd suppose you'd have to ask my husband about that."

"Oh, I can tell by looking at you that he has his hands full." Harriet gave her a suggestive wink, then said, "This is your first visit to *Down & Across,* isn't it?"

"Why, yes . . .?" Belle answered quizzically as the bus began to pull away from the pickup area.

"Oh, I'm not clairvoyant, hon; it's simply that I never miss a show. I'm the most *regular* of the regulars, so if there's a new face in the crowd, I'm the first to spot it." Harriet patted Belle on the leg. "Well, you'll just have to sit with me, then, won't you Gale?"

Belle again held her ticket up to the light. "I'm not sure where my seat is. I don't see any numbers here, just the date."

"It's general admission, but an usher always saves a special seat for me. And if the seat next to me is taken today, I'll ask one the boys to give the person the boot. I'm in the third row."

"That's very nice of you."

"I sit on the aisle . . . In case there's an emergency. I don't like to be in a place where the exit is difficult to reach. If you're my size, you have to be extra careful. Gerry Orso always gives me a big hello and a kiss before the show starts. If I were thirty years younger, I'd snap him up for hubby number six, I swear. He's such a dreamboat, don't you think?"

Unbidden, another falsehood rose to Belle's lips. "Actually, I've never seen the show."

"Well, then, you must be the only woman on earth who isn't in love with Gerry Orso. *Orso* it would seem." Harriet cackled at length over this bit of witticism. "Oh, don't mind me," she finally said, "that's a running gag with Gerry and the regulars."

"I see. Well, I'm looking forward to seeing all this—how a game show is filmed, I mean."

As the bus worked its way through the maze of studios, outbuildings, and the mostly darkened trailers of the TV and movie stars, Belle explained how she'd just arrived from Massachusetts and had been given the ticket to *Down & Across* as a going-away gift from friends back East. On a hunch that her seatmate might have information about a future TV movie whose denouement involved a crossword puzzle, Belle avoided using real names. Instead, she continued in her disingenuous vain, explaining that she was taking a short vacation out West while her husband was fishing in Minnesota. She smiled to herself, thinking that fishing in Minnesota was the last thing Rosco would dream of doing. After a ten-minute ride, the shuttle came to a stop, and the driver called out, "Studio Twenty-six."

"This is us," Harriet said excitedly. She jumped to her feet like a ten-year-old. "Stay close. Don't get lost on me now. I want you to get a good seat."

Belle followed as Harriet authoritatively pushed her way off the bus and trotted toward the studio door. The evening air had cooled down to a pleasant seventy degrees, but clearly many of the "natives" considered this near to freezing, and quickly pulled on sweaters and jackets. Belle found their behavior amusing, but as soon as she stepped into the studio,

she, too, slipped into her denim jacket. The cavernous building appeared to be the size of an airplane hangar; the chill
made it seem as if the hangar were somewhere in northern
Alaska.

"Oh, don't worry, hon," Harriet smiled, "things'll get
warmer as soon as they kick up these lights." She pointed up
to the colossal black metal framework that hung from the
ceiling and seemed to support a thousand studio lights.

"Good evening, Mrs. Tammalong." The greeting came
from a burly man wearing a plaid shirt; faded, but well-
ironed jeans; and wide orange suspenders that gleamed neon-
bright across his paunch. He looked to be nearing sixty,
mostly bald with a salt-and-pepper beard that was trimmed
in a surprisingly elegant and precise fashion.

"Good evening, Matthew," she responded. "I have my
niece with me tonight, so I hope the seat next to mine is free?"

Belle raised bemused eyebrows while Matt craned his neck
to look past the crowd of people. "Tsk, tsk, tsk, someone's in
those seats, but I'll take care of it right now, Mrs. Tammalong." He moved down the aisle.

"Niece?" Belle asked.

"For your own protection, dearie. Besides being an absolute dreamboat, Gerry Orso is also a world-class letch.
He'd be all over you otherwise."

"Well, I *am* married."

"Don't make me laugh. When would that stop a man
like Gerry? Follow me."

Harriet again shoved her small body into the crowd, ordering a brisk, "Coming through, coming through," while
Belle tagged along like a gangly and awe-struck child. When
they reached the third row of seats, they found Matthew
standing guard over Harriet's chosen places.

"Thank you, Matthew, you're such a sweetheart." She
handed him a twenty dollar bill. Belle raised her eyebrows
slightly as the cash exchanged hands. "Oh, it's only money,
dearie. . . . I mean, what's it for, anyway? I say, if you have
it, share it."

Belle smiled, and the two women sat down.

"Besides, like they say . . . You can't take it with you. Look at all those husbands of mine." She sighed, but the sound was more disapproval than regret. "That Matthew is such a nice man. He's new. Well, new to his current job; he had a lesser position and was just moved up last week. He's now the key grip. It's a very good promotion. Although he's done it before."

"Key grip?"

"The number one stagehand . . . ? He basically runs the whole shooting match. Don't let anyone tell you anything different. You think it's the director, right? The producer? Forget it; not in a million years." Harriet paused, looking to see if her new friend Gale was keeping up. ". . . Years ago Matthew was the key grip on that drama . . . You know the one . . . What was the name of that show . . .? The one that whats-his-name starred in? Set in Hawaii? Or was it Chicago? Well, it makes no difference. But he's only here on trial basis for a month, *Orso* I'm told . . . Then they decide if he stays on. I don't watch dramas, myself. People are always getting killed on them . . . And they call that entertainment? You can keep it . . ." Harriet pointed to a smoked glass window high above the lighting grid. "That's where all the head honchos are— up in the booth."

" 'Head honchos'?"

"The show's creator, and so forth." Harriet hesitated for a moment. "Huh, well I'll be, I never looked at it like that until this very minute . . . The creator. Up there in the heavens? That sure gives you pause for thought, doesn't it? Anyway, the fellow who dreamed up *Down & Across* is in the booth with the director, the staff writers, and the producer—Stan McKenet. Stan's father, old Stan, started this studio forty years ago." Harriet opened her purse and removed a package of black licorice and offered Belle a stick. "This is my absolute favorite snack," she said.

"Mine, too." Belle answered without thinking, "Well, actually deviled eggs are the top of the list, but right below them is licorice." It was less than a millisecond later that she realized that Belle Graham's addiction to deviled eggs was a well-documented fact. *Gale Harmble* would have to be a little more careful if she wanted to keep her alias intact.

But before Harriet could respond, there was a commotion at the rear of the studio. They turned to see Gerry Orso arriving to applause, banners, and placards proclaiming his fans' enthusiasm, as well as excited whoops and hollers. Everyone wanted Gerry to grace them with a special nod. The show's host walked forward greeting his audience, supplying kisses for the women nearest the aisle and convivial hand shakes for the men, although it was clear that the female members of the group received superior attention. Orso was slender and handsome, in his mid-forties—or made to look that age— with wavy, brown hair and a tan that appeared to have been applied chemically rather than acquired in the normal, lazing-poolside manner.

Gerry worked his way down the aisle, and finally stopped next to Harriet. He bent down, kissed her on both miniature cheeks and said, "Ah, the ever faithful Mrs. Tammalong." But like a savvy politician, his eyes had already moved to the next potential admirer—who was Belle. "Well, hello! And who have we here? A new visitor to *Down & Across? Orso* I'd guess. And who might *you* be?" He took Belle's hand, kissed it, then nearly crawled over Harriet in an attempt to plant a smooch on her lips.

Belle recoiled instinctively, while Harriet shoved her purse into the host's ribcage. "That's my niece, Gerry! You stay away from her."

He straightened, rubbing his ribs, then extended his hand to Belle. "So nice to meet you, will you be visiting Harriet long, Miss . . . ?"

"Not really. And it's *Mrs.* . . . Mrs. Harmble."

"You look familiar . . . Have we met? Or have you accompanied your aunt before? I pride myself on remembering faces."

"That's because Gale looks just like that actress who was

in that movie with Richard Perry," Harriet said. "The one about the crooked cop. Everyone tells her that's who she looks like."

"Ah-hah . . . But you're not in the entertainment business, I take it, Gale?"

Belle pondered the question. *Could the business of entertainment encompass constructing crossword puzzles? Maybe. And what about being a technical advisor on a movie set? Definitely.* Another fib seemed called for, but this time, it was Harriet who supplied the latest piece of deception.

"Gale's in town staying with me while her hubby's away on a fishing expedition with his buddies . . ."

Buddies? Belle thought. *Did I say that? I don't think so.*

". . . In Minnesota? Isn't that right, Gale? The land of 10,000 lakes. The boys are at a very exclusive wilderness camp."

"Not Lake Winnibigoshish?" Orso beamed. "I go there every summer."

"Ahhh, no, he's farther north than that."

"So he's an ice fisherman?"

Belle gulped. Ice fishing, of course! Who else but devotees of the sport would frequent northern Minnesota lakes in January? "Sort of . . ." She felt her brain growing more and more jumbled. Soon it was going to be impossible to keep track of the many facets of her invented persona.

"Well, enjoy the show, *Gale*," Gerry Orso murmured intimately as he moved away. Belle decided it was only her now over-taxed imagination that supplied a shrewd and all-knowing tone to her assumed name. The host passed the first two rows of seats, crossed the stage, placed his arm over Matthew's shoulder, and whispered something in his ear. They were then joined by a third man wearing a three-piece suit and two-toned wing tips on his feet.

"That's Stan McKenet, there." Harriet scowled at the three men. "Now, I told you, didn't I tell you? I knew Gerry'd try to rape you. He's just like my third husband; can't let a pretty girl pass without attacking her."

Belle laughed. "I'd hardly use those words . . . But thank you for saving the day."

"Think nothing of it, Gale." Again, Belle was struck by an eerie echo in the way Harriet said the name, but she pushed those peculiar suspicions from her brain, thinking, *My puzzles are syndicated, but my photo is printed only in New-castle. And, after all, why would Gerry Orso or Harriet Tamma-long imagine me to be anyone other than out-of-town-visitor Gale Harmble—despite the "niece" and "exclusive fishing camp" refer-ences? Rosco and ice fishing—wouldn't that be a sight?*

Belle turned her concentration to the set, gazing at the giant grid of TV screens: seven across and seven down, a to-tal of forty-nine TV monitors, each capable of displaying a single letter. At the moment, they spelled out WELCOME TO *DOWN & ACROSS* WITH GERRY ORSO. To the left of the TVs stood a navy-blue-and-gold podium, its front decorated with a fleur-de-lys, and Orso's name scrolled across the top in scarlet lettering. To the right of the TVs were two smaller podiums for the contestants. Above their stations were elec-tronic readouts designed to post each player's winnings.

"I don't see an APPLAUSE sign," Belle said. "My friend back home said there'd be one to tell us when to clap."

"Oh, they went out years ago, hon. Rolly Hoddal takes care of all that now."

"Rolly Hoddal?"

"Rolly's a stand-up comedian. He'll be out in a minute *orso* to warm us up. He'll tell us some lame jokes to get us in the mood for fun, and then when it's time for applause, he'll walk up and down in front of the audience waving his hands like a frightened chicken—except chickens don't have hands . . . It's an embarrassing sight, really; I liked the AP-PLAUSE sign much better, myself."

Belle watched with fascination as the grips began prepar-ing the stage for the taping. They positioned thick, black cables, dusted off TV monitors, and checked microphones and sound levels. Three cameramen were perched atop large camera cranes that were capable of dipping down to floor

level or rising twenty feet in the air with remarkable ease
and quietude. Fat rubber tires permitted each crane's crew
to rove across the polished floor and "hit marks" that had
been "flagged" on the floor with reflective tape. The crews—
hefty types in comfortable-fit jeans—worked in total silence
while the cameramen sat aloft reading sports magazines and
displaying total indifference to the free ride they were receiving. Both crew and camera operators wore headsets,
which received instructions from the invisible group in the
control booth. Belle found it curious that only a few had
mouthpieces that would allow a response.

"Okay, folks, weee'rrre getting ready for shooowtiiime!"

Without any help from Harriet Tammalong, Belle surmised that this was Rolly. He was a squat, bow-legged man
with a poorly fitting toupee that looked like caramel-colored
rabbit fur. Belle wasn't sure if Rolly intended the hairpiece
to be an amusing addition to his act, or if he thought he
looked pretty snappy in it. The comic ran through three or
four rather tired jokes that brought far more laughter from
the audience than Belle expected, while the two contestants
arrived on stage and took their places. Each player was accompanied by a sound technician and a make-up artist who
dabbed at their faces with soft fluffy brushes and powder.

Harriet leaned into Belle and whispered, "The taller guy
is yesterday's winner and the tubby fellow's the challenger.
He looks a little nervous, don't you think? You can always
tell by their eyes . . . that kind of crazy-horse stare."

"I heard the contestants win a lot of money playing this,"
Belle said.

"A million bucks . . . Well, a million if you're a Grand-
Slam-Winner." Harriet proceeded to explain the intricacies of
the competition. "The way it works is this: At the end of each
taping, there's a winner, and that person is *Down & Across*.
There's a garden-type bridge the grips roll out; the winner
steps over it and 'across' to the next day's show. The loser is
'Down and *Out*,' as Gerry Orso likes to say. He loves to laugh
at the losers, you know, really rub it in . . . Sometimes

it surprises me that they don't just up and belt him . . .
Anyway, if a contestant wins five shows in a row, he—or
she—becomes undefeated champion. Once there are sixteen
champions, there's a round-robin tournament. Eventually,
one person comes out the Grand-Slam Winner. The payoff is
a cool million."

"Wow."

"The last time that happened was back in August. A man
named Bartann Welner. Everyone called him Bart, though.
A really classy old gent. I could have taken him for hubby
number six in a heartbeat, though he must have been
ninety, if he was a day. He dropped dead . . . just like that!"
Harriet snapped her fingers for emphasis. "Less than two
weeks after he won the big pot."

"Oh, that's so sad."

"That's not the half of it, hon." Harriet leaned in closer
and covered her mouth as if she expected the people in the
control booth to be able to read lips. "They've never aired
the show. And it's my guess they never will."

Belle made no attempt to hide her confusion. This time
her reaction was genuine. "So?"

"The contestants don't get a cent if the show doesn't air.
It's in their contracts. It's the same with all the game
shows. The producers don't have to make a payout if they
keep a show in the can and don't release it . . . Of course,
I'm not supposed to be talking about this . . . Every member of the studio audience signs a waiver promising to keep
mum till after air date. You'll get one, too."

"But if the man, Welner, died, then the producers
wouldn't have to pay—"

"Indeed, they would! His heirs would be entitled to his
winnings because the money was earned before his death. So
if I *had* married Bart Welner—not that I came close, you
understand—I'd still be waiting for my dough . . . Just between you and me, Gale, I wouldn't be surprised to learn
that skin-flint Stan McKenet killed the poor old geezer
himself just to save the million bucks. You know, make it

look like natural causes like they do on those detective shows?" Then Harriet sat back in her seat and patted Belle's leg. "Don't mind me, Galie, I was just kidding about Stan. Things like that don't happen in Hollywood. Aside from what goes on in screenwriters' brains, we're much too ordinary." Then she added a sunny, "Too bad your hubby's missing all the fun. I don't like fishing, myself. And through that ice and everything? Forget it. I'm a Southern California girl all the way."

CHAPTER

8

The next morning, Belle half-awakened to the sound of a very strange clock-radio buzzing insistently in a room that didn't smell remotely like her own bedroom. She gave her ears and nose a moment to arrive at some conclusions, but when they failed her, she called upon her sense of touch. Her left hand reached for Rosco while her toes dodged through the cold sheets toward the foot of the bed where Kit should have been snoozing peacefully. But the antiseptic-smelling bed was devoid of those loving bodies.

Belle drowsily slapped at the radio. The buzzing stopped only to be replaced by an irate talk-show "caller" who couldn't get over the fact that the Lakers had "blown a fourteen-point lead" the previous night and lost to the Trail Blazers—"of all people!"—in double-overtime. She slapped the radio once more, and the room returned to silence.

Then her gray eyes opened a crack. "Rosco?" she murmured. "Kitty?" She stretched across the sheets, lifted her head slightly to stare at the heavily curtained window. Sunlight burned through the cracks where fabric failed to meet corresponding fabric.

California, Belle remembered all at once. A hotel in the beachside community of Santa Monica, a town surrounded by the sprawl of Los Angeles . . . And last night she'd been at a studio in Burbank watching the taping of . . . Suddenly, memory crashed into full and alert comprehension. Today was her big day! Her introduction to the cast and crew of *Anatomy of a Crossword*. The screenwriter, Chick Darlessen, would be picking her up at 7:30. It was now a terrifying 6:45. *I should have set the alarm for 6 A.M.; when will I learn?!* Belle barreled out of bed; her feet were in the shower two minutes later.

It was not until she was dressing that she became fully cognizant of how lonesome she was: no Kit prancing back and forth, short tail twitching, fetching her leash from the downstairs hall, then racing back upstairs to shake it in gleeful anticipation of her morning romp; no yips, no puppy "talk," no paws to trip over. And without Rosco, there was no one to talk to. Talk *at,* Belle corrected herself with a wry smile. Her husband wasn't chatty in the mornings; he needed a fair amount of coffee to jump-start his vocal cords, but he was a pro when it came to *pretending* to listen. Belle sighed; she couldn't quite believe how much she missed him already.

She picked up her comb and gazed at the mirror. "It's only been twenty-four hours . . . Get a grip!" she said to her reflection. She tried to change her mopey face into a cheery one, then realized her clothing choice was all wrong for the big event. She looked frumpy, mismatched, and starchily academic—too New England, by far. She'd stand out like a sore thumb in style-conscious Los Angeles. She shucked off her skirt and top, grabbed another selection, decided that was no better, remembered Rosco cautioning her to "just be herself," then groaned aloud in disgruntled frustration. How could she meet an entire cast of famous people when she was just *herself*? She was supposed to be the show's technical consultant, not some dopey-looking, star-struck hick.

She dove for the closet again, grabbed her best silk shirt and paired it with her jeans. The outfit was definitely not one she would have tried at home, but it gave her a sense of daring and bravado. She topped this off with her "good" earrings—cameos that had belonged to her long-gone great-great aunt.

When Chick Darlessen pulled his brand new vermilion Porsche convertible up to the hotel's curb at the allotted time, Belle was ready. Hungry, yes, but satisfactorily attired. Choosing her wardrobe, and then trying to "style" her pale, blonde hair had chewed up every minute. She hadn't even had time to bolt down a swallow of coffee. Rosco would have nagged her into eating something. Yet a another reason to miss him.

"This morning, Dean's conducting auditions to replace Greg Trafeo, our original 'Rosco,'" Chick said as he ushered her into a Porsche so highly polished that even its chrome wheels showed no sign of roadway grime. "And before I say another word—thank you, thank you, *thank you* for that crossword puzzle you faxed to us last Friday. Talk about a lifesaver. Dean Ivald loves it, I love it, Lew Groslir— the producer—loves it, everyone loves it . . . I mean, what's not to love, right?" There was a manic quality to Darlessen's behavior, almost a sense of desperation as he rattled off the words. For a moment, Belle wondered whether the man was concealing something, or whether his behavior was indicative of all screenwriters with a script in production. ". . . To say nothing of you dropping everything to get your tush out here . . . Like I said, a lifesaver . . . and I don't mean the lime or lemon kind . . ."

Belle watched as he darted around the hood of the car and

nearly leaped in behind the steering wheel. "Buckle up . . .!" Twisting the key in the ignition, Darlessen smiled, deepening the long creases in his bronzed cheeks while his low brow melded into curly black hair whose few tell-tale white streaks were the only indication that the screenwriter was no longer a young man. The smile grew; strangely, it aged him, making him look gaunt and anxious rather than the reverse. Belle found herself questioning just how old her companion was. In a place where youth was a commodity, being sixty— or even fifty or forty—might be considered a serious detriment. ". . . One thing I'm strict about—seatbelts. Too many fatalities in L.A. No one's strapped in. That's why we're in the mess we're in. Too many joy riders misjudging 'Dead Man's Curve.' "

Belle turned sideways in her seat. "You make it sound like the place actually exists."

" 'Dead Man's Curve'? You bet it does. Up on Mulholland Drive. Would you like to see it?"

"Maybe some other time."

Chick spun the convertible across the street in a quick U-turn, giving Belle a view of azure-blue ocean, wide white beach, and a cliffside line of palms trees she hadn't noticed during her arrival. "If you take a walk on the esplanade," the writer continued in his jittery tone while he cocked his thumb over his shoulder and then hastily shifted gears, "pay attention to the signage. The ground up here is none too stable. Basically, it's just dirt. No bedrock like you have back in Massachusetts. We wouldn't want you plunging down into the P.C.H. accidentally, now would we?"

"P-C-H?"

"Pacific Coast Highway. Runs through Malibu to points north. Route One, technically. A pretty road, but subject to rock and mud slides."

The Pacific, and its crumbling mountainsides and gorgeous vistas, were left in the dust as the convertible sped onto the number 10 Freeway heading east. The scenery was considerably altered from Belle's rainy cab ride the previous night. "Should be interesting for you to watch our director, our own in-house *Napoleon,* casting a new 'Rosco,'" Darlessen continued. "A little odd, maybe, but interesting."

"What happened to Greg Trafeo?"

"Ah . . . I'll get to that in a minute."

"Okay . . ." Belle said somewhat suspiciously. Then added, "I guess it will feel pretty strange to see 'myself,' as well."

"Not to worry there. Shay Henlee's gonna do a bang-up job as the show's 'Belle.' The make-up people made her a glowing blonde, just like you. You probably remember her as a brunette from that Scorsese film." Chick gave another over-bright smile while the Porsche made a leap that Belle equated with a rocket leaving Earth. Her body jolted backward in the leather seat.

"What did happen to the first 'Rosco'?" she asked after a moment. "Your fax indicated that Greg Trafeo was playing that part. I've always thought he was a pretty good actor."

"I think Dean wanted to be the one to brief you on that . . . But," Chick sighed. "I'll tell ya: working in Hollywood's not for sissies. Just when you think you've got everything sewed up: ducks in a row, actors, agents, everybody happy . . . *Bam!* Everything blows up in your face! Like your situation with Legal. A case in point . . . With Greg, it was a little problem over the weekend. We figured it best not to tell you until you got out here, but like I said, no seatbelt. It's a big mistake . . . Greg was rear-ended on Sunset Boulevard . . . He'll be okay in a month or two, but production couldn't wait—not with our *brilliant* director on his way to Paris to shoot a major film in four weeks with Gerard D . . . A prima donna of the highest order this director, but aren't they all? Anyway, Greg's face did a number on the steering wheel—or should I say vice versa . . .? He also lost a nice little MGA roadster in the bargain. 'Course those babies didn't come with shoulder belts to begin with, and a purist like Greg wouldn't *think* of adding them. Oh, no, not our boy Greg." As he spoke, Chick zoomed around a truck, slalomed across two—then three—lanes of speeding cars. Each maneuver appeared to Belle to leave only inches to spare.

"We're not late, are we?" she managed to ask.

Chick laughed too loudly. "My girlfriend's always wondering the same thing. You need to air these Porsches out, blow the carbon off the valves every now and then. They thrive on this kind of action."

"I'd just hate to end up like the 'nice little MGA roadster,' or Greg Trafeo."

"Not to worry," was the blithe reply.

Belle nodded, but her hands on her knees were clenched and wet.

Nothing could have prepared Belle for the scene she encountered when she and Darlessen entered the soundstage. In front of her was an exact replica of her home office: a wood floor painted in vivid black and white squares, curtains with hand-blocked puzzle grids, crossword-motif lamp shades, even a puzzle-themed ceramic plate holding her cherished nibble—deviled eggs.

There were her beloved books, too: her foreign-language dictionaries, her encyclopedias, her much-thumbed OED—and all housed, as they were in Newcastle, within what appeared to be the converted exterior porch of an eighteenth-century town house, which, at the moment, faced a garden enfolded in a deep and tranquil layer of snow. Part of the exterior scene was painted on a flat scrim; eerily, it seemed more "real" than real life.

Belle gasped in wonderment. So this was what Miso Lane and his crew were "documenting." She gazed from one corner of this fantasy to another. For a moment, she was unsure whether she'd even left home.

"Welcome, welcome, welcome! I can see by your expression that our set designers and carpenters have outdone themselves. Miso is a genius with that little Polaroid of his. His snaps were a boon, an absolute prize. We've duplicated your home, your friend Sara's handsome demesne, that quaint, little downtown coffee shop—as well as the country inn where the vile and dreadful deed was done . . ." The man striding toward Belle was tall, lean, almost cavalier in his understated elegance. With his British accent and an imperial cast to his light-blue eyes, he looked like a retired member of Her Majesty's Home Guard. "You are the one and only Annabella Graham, I take it? Of course you are. I am filled with gratitude that we at last meet face-to-face. The telephone is such a poor substitute for a genuine rendezvous; ergo, I avoid them at all costs. Rather un-L.A. of me, I believe, but I much prefer to leave room for surprises in my life. It pleases me to imagine that secretaries throughout Hollywood spend their days telling their bosses that Mr. Ivald is unavailable."

"And you're Mr. Ivald." Belle put out her hand, which was swooped into his while his long frame bent in a courtly bow.

"Dean, my dear. Simply, Dean. We're all chums here—" But the director's commanding words were interrupted by a shattering crash, and then a female voice shouting angrily, a male swearing mightily, and the jitter of hurrying feet.

"What is it *this* time?" Ivald spat out the words. The cords of his neck tightened, and his easy and aristocratic demeanor changed abruptly to one of barely restrained rage. "One more delay on this bloody project and I swear I'll be packing it off to the great 'director's home in the sky.' I don't have time to muck around with this wretched—"

"A sound boom fell, Mr. Ivald," came a cowed reply. "Sorry, about that . . . I guess it wasn't secure. I don't know who put it—"

The female voice interrupted. Her tone was shrill, demanding, operatic in its intensity. "Dean, I simply *cannot* work when pieces of equipment *insist* upon tumbling down around me. I might very well have sustained serious—"

"Nan, darling, sweetheart . . . I'm on my way." Ivald spun on his heels, leaving Belle forgotten and deserted.

"Nan DeDero," Chick murmured. "She plays your 'Sara.'"

"Yes," was Belle's immediate response. "Everyone back home was thrilled to hear that I would meet her." As soon as the words were out of her mouth, Belle quietly cringed inside, thinking, *Yeeesh, do I sound like a hick or what?*

Darlessen laughed in his brash and brittle way. "The one and only child star turned superstar, turned fiery, aging diva." He added a facetious, "Oops, did I say 'aging'? Where on earth did that come from?"

"I kind of wondered . . ." Belle began. She couldn't reconcile the woman with the flock of ex-lovers, the titanic ego, and the temper to the true Sara, a lady whose ancestors had founded Newcastle, and who remained the city's arbiter of correct—if old-fashioned—behavior.

As if he'd been reading her mind, Chick's reply was an amused, "Don't worry. Nan's wearing a white wig. The cane was another matter, altogether. The world would come to an end long before any camera caught the great DeDero using a 'walking stick.' Reality is one thing . . ."

They moved toward the racket created by Nan berating both the director and sound technician, leaving behind Belle's "office" and entering the fabricated "sitting room" of White Caps. Through a crush of cameramen, stagehands, props people, and makeup artists, Belle saw another exact reproduction: Oriental carpets, mahogany end tables, chairs upholstered in chintz, and an antique marble mantle gracing a fireplace ablaze with flickering light. While standing in the midst of this familiar haven, Belle noticed a white-haired and steel-spined autocrat who she knew and loved as Sara.

"Oh—" Belle said, instinctively moving forward to greet her friend "Sara." Clearly Nan, or the makeup people, had studied Miso's Polaroids at length. Sara's exact double had been created. But Nan fixed Belle with a gaze that was at once withering and dismissive before returning her irate attention once again to director and crew.

Belle stepped back in chagrin, then looked across the soundstage from "White Caps" to her own "home" and was filled with a swift and terrible sensation. It felt if she'd died, as if she were now watching what had once been her earthly existence from some unremembered netherworld.

CHAPTER

9

Belle's discomfort and loss of equilibrium was compounded when she came face-to-face with "herself" in the form of Shay Henlee. This "Belle" was decked out in green corduroy slacks that had gone soft and baggy with age, a loose beige turtleneck, and a lumpy, threadbare gray cardigan. But except for the clothes, the true Belle and the actress portraying her were nearly identical. As Chick had indicated, the blonde wig and gray contact lenses had completely transformed the show's star.

"Yikes . . ." Belle murmured with some dismay. It was clear that the costume designers had decided the lead character was a frowzy New England frump.

"For crying out loud . . ." Shay muttered simultaneously. She looked at her outfit and then at Belle's. She frowned and shouted, "Wardrobe!" without turning her head to see if anyone was there to heed her call. Then, just as precipitously, she grinned, extended her hand, and uttered a pleased, "You must be the *real* Annabella Graham. I'm Shay. I'm *you*. Well, for the next four weeks, anyway."

"Yes," Belle said. She felt unexpectedly tongue-tied in

the presence of so famous a person. Rosco would never have recognized her—Belle Graham lost for words?

"I'm you except for those crosswords, of course. I couldn't finish one, let alone create one, if I was paid—Wait, I *am* being paid! I should work on that, I guess." Shay gave Belle a sly wink and a breezy laugh. It was the serene sound of someone at the top of their game. "I can't even fill in one measly square, I swear. I tried the puzzle you sent out, but jumped to the answers immediately. By the way, the message is really a sneaky one."

"Crosswords take practice, that's all—" But the effort at a mutual friendship was interrupted by the arrival of "wardrobe" bearing new costume selections for "Miss Henlee," leaving Belle, once again, forgotten and ignored.

She strolled toward the "office" that the production people had set up for her. It consisted of a battered steel desk pushed up against the painted cinder block wall of the studio. There was a folding metal chair; when it was pulled out, there was only a two-foot walkway between it and the back panel of the Lawson's Diner set. Attached to the wall above the desk was a blackboard, where someone had scrawled MS.GRAHAM, TECHNICAL CONSULTANT, and under that, another person had ornately lettered WELCOME BELLE in red chalk with fancy orange shadowing. On the desk was a telephone and an in-out box distressingly—or perhaps fortuitously—devoid of papers. Having no idea what to do, Belle sat in the folding chair and began to open the desk drawers where she found nothing but a handful of empty Burger King and Dunkin' Donuts wrappers.

"Okay, people, we'll do Lance diRusa's screen test first," she heard Dean Ivald call out. "Then Quinton Hanny's this afternoon—whoa . . . Damn! Quinton's in this morning, too? Who scheduled these two madmen so close together . . .? Someone's trying to give their favorite director a heart attack, is that it?"

A script girl hurried past with a panicked look on her face, and Belle decided to follow along. Within a matter of seconds, a battery of stage lights switched on, illuminating the crossword-motifed room with an intensity equal to a home game at Fenway Park on the darkest of summer nights.

". . . I'm not going to be responsible if the fur flies between those two boys," Dean continued. "Get me Nils."

"Not to worry, Dean," a distant Shay sang out. "I'll have your 'Roscos' eating out of my hand in no time . . ."

"Not good enough, my dear . . . Nils! Nils Spemick, front and center. Nils, I want to *see* you. Pronto!"

Belle gulped, found an empty chair, and disappeared in the shadows while a phalanx of cameras, sound booms, and dialogue boxes began closing in on Shay, who was now perched upon "Belle's" untidy home-office desk.

A disembodied voice rang out in a stentorian tone reminiscent of the Wizard of Oz—if that autocratic being had owned a Scandinavian accent. "I'm up here, Dean." The words obviously emanated from the PA system.

"Get your butt down here, Nils. Now! On the double!"

"I'm with *Lew Groslir,* Dean."

A tall man with broad shoulders, a thick mustache, and sandy brown hair that flowed evenly over the tops of his ears pulled up a chair and sat next to Belle. He wore a dark-green polo shirt, jeans, and scuffed cowboy boots. "And so the pecking order is established," he said in a low voice. "Lew Groslir is the producer."

"I know," Belle responded. "But who's Nils?"

"The casting director . . . or *Star Wrangler* would be more like it. He's got his hands full if he plans to act as referee between Lance diRusa and Quinton Hanny. There's no love lost there."

Belle extended her hand. "I'm Belle Graham. I'm the . . . Technical Advisor."

He chuckled slightly. "You're more than than that; you're reason we're all here . . . I'm the key grip on the set, Don Schruko."

"Oh . . . No . . . Really? I know you." They shook hands, and Belle could tell from his crinkled brow that she'd definitely confused him. "I mean, I don't really know *you,* but I know what you do. I was at a taping of *Down & Across* last night and I met a woman who told me that the key grip 'runs the whole shootin' match.' "

"Don't I wish." Don laughed aloud and shook his head. "I'd say I'm a little more like a lion tamer—I keep the big cats from scratching each other up too much."

"That still sounds like it could be a pretty tough job to me."

Don chortled again. "You don't know the half of it. But I enjoy myself, and as they, say, Mr. Groslir made me an offer I couldn't refuse . . . So, here I am."

"And aren't you supposed to be moving things around? You know, doing 'grip' stuff?"

"Nah, this is just an audition . . . Lights up lights down. That's it. As long as I'm within earshot, they can find me. But if we're doing an actual take, don't get in my way. People have been known to get trampled to death when I get my Jekyll and Hyde thing going . . . Auditions? Half the time they're done in an office somewhere on Wilshire Boulevard, but Dean's running late with this production since losing Rosco Number One. Wants to get this recasting finished today and start rolling. Time's weighing real heavy on his shoulders."

"Nils!" Dean bellowed. "Get your skinny little butt down here!"

The deep voice returned to the loudspeaker. "Dean, I'm going to remain up here and keep Quinton company. I think that's best . . . Lance is on his way down to you. Divide and conquer, Dean, divide and conquer."

A woman's voice then came on the PA system saying, "Lance diRusa to the set, Lance diRusa, to the set, please," but the actor was already boldly walking forward, pausing only to share a few convivial words with a man attired in a business suit, who'd arrived with him. A make-up artist near

Belle murmured to a colleague, "Must be important if Lew Groslir comes downstairs," and then they both giggled.

Dean Ivald greeted Lance, draping an arm around his shoulders and leading him toward Shay, who puckered her lips in an airy smile. Belle felt her stomach churn in a peculiar combination of regret, envy, and helplessness. Lance wasn't quite the spitting image of her husband, but he carried himself with the same self-confidence. Seeing him standing so close to Shay gave Belle the odd feeling she was watching Rosco make a pass at her twin sister—except that she didn't have a sibling.

"Ready when you are, lover-boy," Shay cooed at the actor while the director began moving back behind the cameras.

"Lance, sweetie," Dean started, "this is the scene where you're trying to persuade your wife to leave the criminal investigation to you and you alone. You're worried about her safety. You're also more than irritated at her pigheadedness . . . But remember, you love your dizzy dame . . . Got it? Fear. Anger. Adoration . . ."

The scene began and the cameras rolled. Belle watched, but the actors' speech and mumbled delivery were nearly inaudible from where she sat. Then, all at once, Chick Darlessen bolted to his feet while Lance diRusa's face turned an outraged and self-righteous red. This time, Belle heard every syllable in the exchange.

"Just say the words as they're written, will you? How hard is that?" Chick growled.

"I'm not a trained monkey, Darlessen. I don't do word-for-word. I go with what works, and this," Lance slapped the script, "doesn't work. It's not written in a way that—"

"This is a show that *revolves* around a word game and exact usage, diRusa. Every one of these lines has a precise reference to—"

Dean stepped between the two of them. "It's only an audition, Darlessen. Lighten up. I'm sure Lance understands the value of your . . . literary effort . . ."

"Literary?" Lance queried, contempt underpinning the tone. "That's a new one."

"If you had half a brain, diRusa," Chick spat back, "you'd recognize the importance of the lexical clues—"

"Lexical? Aren't we getting fancy?"

Belle then heard the director's voice murmuring phrases of conciliation, but neither actor nor screenwriter seemed prepared to relinquish the argument. Shay stalked away with a irritable toss of her head while Chick and Lance moved closer. Rage seemed to ripple around the men. Belle had the sudden intuition that the battle wasn't about dropped or improvised lines. She leaned toward Don Schruko and whispered, "It doesn't seem like Lance has a shot at getting this part if he's going to criticize the writer."

"The writer?" Don answered with a laugh. "Nobody cares what the writer thinks. If the writer wants a particular actor for the part, that's the kiss of death for the poor sap. No, Lance only needs to impress Dean Ivald and Mr. Groslir. You watch. If Dean hires Lance to play Rosco . . . and things get tense, he'll kick Darlessen off the set long before he'd even consider canning diRusa."

As if Dean had been reading the key grip's mind, he called out, "Shay, get back in here. We're going to take this from the top." He then walked Chick toward the edge of the set closer to Belle and Don. "Look, Darlessen, this is only an audition. I want to get these two guys on tape so I can make a decision this afternoon. We're under a lot of pressure here. I want a new Rosco on the set tomorrow . . . Now, I understand you and Lance have some issues, and I understand the cause, but do me a favor . . . Take a hike until I get finished with him, okay? Just step into the parking lot for twenty-five minutes."

Chick gritted his teeth. "I don't have any personal problems with diRusa. He's the one with the ex-girlfriend—"

"Do me a favor, Darlessen. Take your macho I-got-the-dame-and-you-don't attitude for walk. I need to see Lance work—"

"Hey—his loss, my gain . . . Debra is *not* an issue, as far as I'm concerned. If he doesn't know how to hold onto a woman, that's his fault. Besides, if he wants her back, he knows where to look." As if he'd divulged confidences he hadn't wished to, Chick abruptly changed tack. "What I'm trying to point out, Ivald, is that the guy is a no-talent, hack actor and shouldn't have been auditioned in the first place. You want to get this over with quick? Send Lance home, hire Quinton Hanny, and let's get rolling right now."

Dean pushed Chick farther from the set. "Are you going to leave pleasantly, or do I have to ask Mr. Schruko to—"

"I'm not going to be tossed off my own—"

"*My* set, Darlessen. *Mine.* I'm the director, remember? And what I say, goes."

"If it weren't for—"

"Don? Could you come over here a moment?" The director looked in the direction of his key grip.

Chick raised his hands in swift and hopeless frustration. "Okay . . . Okay . . . It's your call, Ivald, but remember one thing; I'm also the creator of this show, and if you go with diRusa, there's going to be repercussions. Count on it." Then he turned on his heels and stormed off toward the exit.

Dean ran his fingers through his hair and stared down at Belle and the still-seated Don Schruko. "Do you know why Shakespeare wrote 'Let's kill all the lawyers'?"

In unison they shook their heads.

"Because he was a *writer,* that's why. Anyone in their right mind, anyone else in the world, would have said, 'Let's kill all the damn *writers.*'" Dean strode back to the center of the set, again placed a conspiratorial arm over Lance's shoulder, and began reiterating directions on how he wished the scene to be played.

"So, what happens now?" Belle murmured to Don.

"Beats me . . . But it's going to be interesting." He paused, watching Dean put Lance through his paces. "This is how directors apprise the writers of who's in charge—by hiring the actors *they* want. On the other hand, Chick's also the creator and seems ready to duke it out . . . I guess you deduced he's

now bedding down Lance's ex-flame, one Debra Marcollo—
though the little birdies who flap through our sunny air say
that may *not* be a match made in heaven, either."

Belle raised an eyebrow at these casual references to what
was obviously an intimate relationship. She didn't know
how to respond, so instead nodded toward the producer who
was standing on the opposite side of the set. "I noticed that
Lance diRusa and Lew Groslir are pretty friendly."

He smiled mirthlessly. "You've got a lot to learn, Belle.
Lew's going to make both Quinton and Lance think he's
their very best friend on earth. And you know why? Because
he's going to have to negotiate a contract with one of their
agents tonight. And whoever gets the call is going to stick
it to him for every perk in the book, because they know
Lew's trapped between the proverbial rock and a hard place.
This is a situation every talent agent in Hollywood would
kill for." Don laughed quietly. "Hell, I wouldn't be surprised to learn that it was Lance's agent who rear-ended
Greg Trafeo's MGA."

Belle didn't respond, and the two sat quietly as Lance
worked his way through the audition process. Then he was
asked to leave by the south door of the studio, while Quinton
Hanny approached through the north entrance. Again, the
new actor bore an eerie resemblance to Rosco, although the
impression was of gentler and less volatile man than Lance.
True to Don Schruko's prediction, Lew Groslir greeted Quinton as if he were a long lost son.

Don nudged Belle. "I didn't put two and two together
until just now, but it's going to be a real hoot if Quint gets
this part. He was married to Ginger Bradmin seven or so
years ago."

"I don't know who she is," Belle responded.

"She's been in a bunch of stuff . . . baby-doll voice like
what's-her-name in that Jeff Bridges flick . . . Anyway, she's
playing the wife at the country inn. The one whose husband
gets murdered? I forget the gal's name."

"Annie?"

"Right . . . So, if Quinton gets this part, he's going to have a few choice scenes with his ex-wife . . . and she ain't no Georgia peach, despite the cutesy diction." Don chortled. "I'll have to be sure all potentially lethal objects are bolted in place. What those two went through during their divorce proceedings was the stuff of Hollywood lore."

A stagehand passing quietly behind them stopped and crouched down to their level in order to hand Belle an envelope. "This is for you Ms. Graham. It just arrived by messenger."

Belle said, "Thank you," opened the envelope, and removed a crossword puzzle. She smiled as she turned to Don, a sense of happy accomplishment spreading across her face. "Here it is . . . the puzzle I constructed for the show . . . typeset and ready for its close-up." She began to refold it and slide it back into the envelope when she noticed something was wrong. "This is odd . . ."

"What's odd?" Don asked.

"Well, it's the same grid that I created for the show, but all the clues are different. This isn't my puzzle, at all."

Across

1. Classic roadster
4. Wolfed down
7. Mr. Guevara
10. Stargazer?
13. Mr. Brynner
14. Film speed
15. Parking area
16. Film speed
17. Greeting; part 1
20. ____to the stars
21. ____la Douce
22. No Way____
23. Greeting; part 2
24. Mr. Sinatra
26. Ambulance wkr.
27. Slippery one
28. Sunset, poetically
29. Inc. cousin
31. Greeting; part 3
34. Exodus author
36. Return
37. L.A. film sch.
40. Greeting; part 4
42. Korean soldier
43. Roger Miller hit
45. A Great Lake
46. Greeting; part 5
47. "The Greatest"
48. ____of Innocence
51. Mr. Chaney
52. Space
54. Dipped out
56. Greeting; part 6
58. Guiness or Olivier
59. Cat call?
60. The____ Commandments
61. Greeting; part 7
65. Brain wave recorder; abbr.
66. Layer
67. Long____Tomorrow
68. Geom. Fig.
69. Kildare & Casey; abbr.
70. Horse fodder
71. It's often inflated
72. One of D.C.'s 100

Down

1. Take____, please
2. War in France
3. Super hero
4. Much____About Nothing
5. Mr. Conway
6. Hollywood to Pasadena dir.
7. Hollywood power
8. Jack, Tim or Jennifer
9. LAX info
10. "You look____"
11. PDQ
12. Sonoma neighbor
18. When repeated, a Porter hit
19. Mr. Selleck
23. Belgrade native
25. Quincy star
26. Cut film
27. Al Bundy portrayer
30. Elm, oak, or pine
32. Sgt. or cpl.
33. Hooded org.
35. Request enc.
36. Andrea___, of The Perfect Storm
37. Security Co.
38. LAX overseer
39. Hints
41. The Parent__
44. H.S. Sub.
48. Wards off
49. Mr. Clooney
50. Winner of the first Emmy Award

GREETINGS!

52. George Steven's Oscar Winner
53. Mr. Carney
55. Latin love
56. Flower part
57. Garden annoyance

58. Mets' home
61. ___ *Framed Roger Rabbit*
62. Miss West
63. 66-Across output
64. Seduce

CHAPTER

10

The sun beat down on the asphalt pavement outside the studio's main door. The ultraviolet rays and intense heat seemed to pulse from the concrete walls of every box-like building on the lot, from the burning metal of each parked minivan and studio courtesy car, from the glass windshields, the dented trash receptacles, the terracotta tubs of panting flowers that emitted steam—if they'd been watered—or, if not, a parched dryness that smelled like death. There was nothing in the entire smog-laden arena that seemed remotely hospitable, or even slightly seductive or glamorous, to Chick Darlessen. He wondered why on earth he'd chosen his career, and the next second, pondered what he would to do if this final stab at The Big Time failed. *Thrown off the set,* he thought in disgust. *Sent packing while some preening prima donna put a no-talent piece of beefcake through his sorry paces . . . a hack, like lover-boy Lance diRusa, whose only "motivation" seemed to be how many starlets he could bed down.* Anatomy of a Crossword *belonged to Chick Darlessen! It was his creation! (Well, sort of . . .) And no one was going to take it away from him*. Turning the corner, while fury, frustration, and fear made his eyelids jitter and his palms sweat, the reality of the situation—as well as the sight of a certain Wanda Jorcrof—stopped Darlessen cold in his tracks.

For a long moment, he simply couldn't speak. Neither did Wanda. Instead, she glared at him, her pigeon-toes planted firmly in blunt, stridently trendy thick-soled shoes, her bowl-cut hair almost bristling in its steely straightness. She crossed her arms over her ample chest and stood her ground, unaffected by the scorching heat beating down upon her boxy shoulders, or Darlessen's pointed stare.

"How did you get on this lot?" he finally demanded.

"Told the guard I needed to see you, Chickie. Told him we were working together—we were partners, and you were waiting for these rewrites." She flapped a few sheets of paper in the air. "You needed these PDQ, ASAP, right?"

Chick opened his mouth, closed it, swallowed, and tried again. "No one phoned the set to say I had a visitor." His throat felt as dry as sand.

"That's your problem—and their problem. Security a-round here isn't in my jur-is-dic-tion." She pronounced the word carefully, sounding out each syllable as if she were questioning its etymology.

Darlessen looked her over while he kept his distance. His manner seemed to indicate that he half expected Wanda Jorcrof to suddenly leap forward and knock him to the ground, a concept that would have made him laugh out loud on any other day.

"I'm busy. What do you want, Wanda?" As Chick asked the question, his eyes ducked furtively toward the door he'd just exited. Wanda was becoming a major pain in his neck.

"Only what I've always wanted. My share of the take. The twenty-five thousand I was promised . . . that I *earned*."

Chick's glance dodged back and forth between the studio door and Wanda. "Why don't we find another place to talk? Somewhere out of the sun."

"You don't want to be seen with me? Is that it—?"

"No . . . no . . . Wanda . . . It's just that it's so hot standing here."

"It's gonna get hotter if I don't get my cash."

"There's nothing I can do—"

Her fiercesome expletive stopped the words in Darlessen's
throat. "You can call McKenet!" she all but screamed. "Like
you promised!"

"But it's not really his—"

"We're in this thing together, Darlessen! Whether you
like remembering it or not!"

"Look, Wanda—"

"I need that twenty-five thou, Chickie. Not next week or
next month. I need it now. I've been waiting since last friggin' August. Half a damn year."

Darlessen ran his dry tongue over his even dryer lips.

"I don't want any more games from you, Chickie. I don't
want any more *word* games, either." She gave him an evil look.

"What do you mean by that?"

"I think you know. Mr. Crossword Puzzle. Mr. Fancy
Screenwriter . . . If it weren't for—"

"Look, Wanda . . . This isn't a good time or place to discuss—"

"It is for me."

Darlessen, in his nervousness, kept talking as though she
hadn't spoken. "But I want to help you, Wanda. I do. I
know that money's important to you. Look, I've been there.
I understand. I do . . . And I know you've had a longer wait
than you should have had—"

"You can friggin' say that again—"

"But right now I've got to focus on potential script
rewrites, and replacing an actor, and—"

"And a crossword—"

"That, too, Wanda . . ." Darlessen clenched and un-
clenched his sweaty hands. Again, he shot a worried glance
toward the studio door.

Wanda Jorcrof followed his gaze; her expression turned

even more merciless and malevolent. "If you want to get out of the heat, I'll step inside the studio with you—"

"No! Not there . . . What I mean is, we're in the midst of auditions right now. It's very hectic, and—"

"Did you get the Graham dame?"

Darlessen watched Wanda's mouth move. Coral-colored lipstick stuck to her teeth; her lips were as thin as razors. "Yes . . ." he finally admitted.

"So the impossible isn't impossible after all." She stared at him with an expression he couldn't interpret, and he gazed numbly back. "I'll expect you to get me that money, Chickie. By this weekend. Whatever you have to do. Whether McKenet comes clean or not . . . It's in your hands. I want my twenty-five thou. Whatever it takes . . . *Whoever* it takes . . ." And then, Wanda miraculously turned around and walked toward a distant car.

In her wake, Darlessen was left panting for air. His new silk shirt was soaked through with sweat; his new Italian loafers, his new silk socks, the gabardine slacks that still retained the perfumed scent of the fancy shop on Rodeo Drive—everything felt dank and dirty and old. He turned to retrace his steps to the studio door, but as he did, Lance diRusa came barreling out, his auditioning script still clutched in his hand, the tweed jacket he'd worn as a "Rosco costume" clenched heavily in his fist.

He made an angry beeline for Chick. "You ruin this one for me, Darlessen, and you're toast," he snarled. "*Anatomy* will be your swan song in this town."

As with his previous confrontation, Chick was stunned into momentary silence.

"Toast, Darlessen," Lance repeated while Chick at last found his voice.

"Don't threaten me, diRusa. I call the shots around here. *Anatomy* is my—"

"You're the writer, Darlessen, and that's it. Creator means nothing. You're a nobody. And if you get in my way, you're gonna be a very, very sorry nobody."

CHAPTER

11

After unceremoniously dumping Belle off at her hotel in Santa Monica, at the end of what seemed an interminable day, Chick Darlessen opted to take out his many frustrations on the Porsche's gearbox and the asphalt of the Pacific Coast Highway, leaving a set of parallel black tire marks at each and every stop light along his way home. The early winter twilight had already darkened into night, and the exclusive beachside community in Malibu, where he and his current girlfriend were now renting a multimillion-dollar bungalow, was awash in pale, flickering lights that shone from the houses like beacons of welcome against the vastness of the inky ocean. It should have been a lovely scene, a picture-postcard scene. But Chick Darlessen scarcely noticed it; and if he did, it only produced more spasms of terror in his already jumpy stomach. How much were he and Debra shelling out per month for this quaint little shack? Correction: How much was he shelling out to keep the two of them in fancy digs and fancy togs? Debra Marcollo wasn't a woman to waste her days fretting over the disparity between income and expense.

Chick clenched his teeth. *Wanda Jorcrof,* he suddenly thought, *Wanda and her twenty-five thousand.* What was he supposed to do about that particular time bomb . . . or her weird reference to Belle Graham . . .? What was she getting at? What had she discovered? The questions made Darlessen's clenched teeth ache in his jaw and his forehead knot in pain. And what was he supposed to do about the McKenet situation? What did Wanda expect him to do? And Lance? What about that particularly sorry piece of work? The thought of having to work with that "yo-yo" only made Chick's teeth hurt more.

Careening along the sand-blown lane that led to his garage, and thence into his ocean-front rental, Darlessen's bouncing headlamps picked up a female form dodging into the shadows of a neighboring property. He nearly screamed aloud in his shock and dismay. Instead, he pounded the horn, slammed on the brakes, and hit the automatic lock button that shut down exterior access to his car with a series of pinging thunks. In the next second, he recognized the "prowler." It was none other than his Debra, too scantily clad for the cold of a Malibu night, and by every appearance, three sheets to the wind.

She weaved up to the car, her eyes red and swollen, her mouth puffy from tears. "Someone's in the house, Chick," she managed to gasp out. "They broke in . . . I got home from the gym . . . well, I had a couple of stops to make first, and then I, well, when I drove up, I noticed . . . 'cause I know I beeped the garage door closed before I left, but it was open when I . . ." Her words disappeared into a fresh spate of crying—added to which were a couple of unladylike hiccups.

Darlessen swung open the car door and stepped out. He didn't want to. Instead, he wanted to drop the Porsche into reverse, take off, straight up the Pacific Coast Highway and never look back. Not deal with Debra Marcollo or Lance diRusa or Wanda Jorcrof or Dean Ivald or Don Schruko, or his own maxed-out credit cards, or Belle Gra-

ham or Stan McKenet or Lee Rennegor or any of the tur-
moil and trouble that seemed to bubble up out of every
studio and every project in L.A. For a moment, Chick even
cursed his dead uncle Bart, the gander that had left what
had appeared to be the proverbial golden egg, but was now
seeming more and more moldy and rotten.

"You're drunk, Debra," Chick said. His tone was weary
and unkind. "You promised me you were quitting all that."

"I'm not drunk," she insisted. "I'm upset, is all." She
clutched a fashionably short aqua sweatshirt against her
shoulders. The remainder of her costume consisted of a matching sports bra and tights with lavender thong panties
underneath. Her designer cross-trainer shoes were the only
substantial part of the outfit. "And I'm cold . . . and I'm
scared." She looked up at the house's rear windows, an unlit
room above the garage. "Someone's in there, Chick, I
swear."

"Did you call the cops?"

"I couldn't find my cell phone . . ." She sniffled and
tugged at her sweatshirt.

"Not another one—"

"I'm sure it's in with my exercise stuff. Or back at the
gym."

"It's the third one this month, dearest." It was not said
with kindness.

"I'll find them Chickie, honey . . ."

Darlessen looked at her, shaking with chill and fear. He
knew he should put his arms around her and warm and
comfort her, but that was the last thing he wished to do.

"You can call nine-one-one from your car, Chickie."

As soon as Debra voiced the suggestion, Darlessen recognized it for another situation he wanted to avoid. If someone
had indeed broken into the house, he needed to determine
why that person was there. Screenwriters who'd just gotten
their first big break didn't possess anything worth stealing—
except, perhaps, a new car and clean socks.

He turned to stare into the garage, dark and empty without Debra's 4x4, which she'd probably left farther up along the road once she saw the open door. From what little Chick could see, the garage looked unviolated and blank, as if Debra had merely sped off to her exercise class—or whatever else she did to occupy her days—and forgotten to beep the dang thing closed. *Like the lost cell phones,* he thought bitterly, *like the promise to lay off the booze and attend meetings.*

He stifled an angry sigh, and began walking toward the steps that led up to the front deck.

Debra clutched at him. "You're not going in there, are you, Chickie?"

He shook her off. "It merely looks like you forgot to close the garage door—"

"But I'm sure I—"

"Right." Chick pounded up the stairs. Despite his prior statement, his heart was racing. He had a half-formed notion that if he were about to disturb a burglar, noise was imperative. The sound of approaching feet would give the person time to run away—probably down the garage stairs. "Go stand on the beach," Chick yelled down to Debra, then paused on the deck until she wavered nervously into sight. "Near the overhead lamp, where you're easily visible. If there's a problem, just go down the beach until you find someone who's home." Then he shouted at her again. "I'm going in!"

He twisted the knob. It was locked. He cursed, yanked his keys from his pocket, then turned the key until the door swung open. "Oh, Chickie, be careful . . ." he heard Debra moan from the beach, but he ignored her and whatever she was trying to say. He then strode into the bungalow and switched on every light as he walked along.

All appeared in order—as orderly as Debra habitually left it: the sitting/dining room, bedroom, kitchen, bath, the small rear alcove he used as an office. Nothing had been removed, nothing rearranged.

Chick found his level of irritation rising. He tromped down the rear steps and into the garage, flipped on the wall switch, and stared at the empty space. Then he methodically walked outside to his car and slowly drove it to its parking place. His heart was fluttering painfully, and his face felt engorged with misery and loathing.

Debra chose that inopportune moment to wander down the stairs. "I thought you'd driven off, Chickie. I heard the Porsche start up . . . I thought you'd left me . . ."

He climbed out of his car and slammed the door. "I should have I should have let you run back to Lance—or whomever his predecessor was." He felt like striking the silly woman, and her cowed and now awkwardly sobered-up pose did nothing to diminish the intensity of the sensation.

Debra didn't respond. Instead, she climbed back up into the house, squaring her shoulders and lifting her head in an attitude Chick recognized as spoiling for a fight. "My 4 x 4's down the lane. The keys are in it."

"Brilliant." Darlessen stormed out and returned five minutes later.

With both vehicles now safely ensconced in the garage and the door closed for the night, Chick mounted the interior stairs. Sure enough, Debra was waiting for him, still in her gym clothes, still blue-white with cold. "I'm not stupid," she said.

Chick didn't answer.

"I'm not stupid, and I'm not drunk."

Again, Chick didn't reply, which was unwise because his silence clearly indicated his rejection of her opinion.

She glowered at him while standing taller, straighter, and more entrenched in her own defense. "And I don't care anything about Lance . . . not any more."

"Well, he seems to think otherwise—"

"You've started hanging around with him all of a sudden? What do you know about Lance?"

Chick's second mistake, mentioning diRusa's name, was

compounded by a third. "He was auditioning for *Anatomy* today." The words were out before Darlessen recognized the trap he'd set himself.

Debra grew deathly still, her pallid face turned whiter and then flared pink with fury. "You gave Lance an audition and not me!"

"Let's not go through the same old gripes and problems again, Debra."

"You didn't let me audition!" she repeated. "You didn't even let me see the casting director, or submit a picture or anything!"

"There were no parts you were right for, Deb." Too late, Chick's tone had become conciliatory. "Besides, Nils Spemick does the casting, not me."

"Shay Henlee's 'right' for your show, though? Ginger Bradmin's 'right.'" Debra's voice was choked and challenging. "You didn't tell *them* they couldn't audition!"

"Shay Henlee's a star, Debra. She's a major talent. So's Ginger. They sell SUVs to soccer moms; demographics love them—"

"As opposed to me?! As opposed to me? I have no talent . . . or . . . or *demographics?*" Debra's clenched fists flew into the air while Chick, on the other side of the room, found himself ducking reflexively. "That person who called today said you were a skunk; a slime that went back on his word. And you are, Chick! You are!" Debra was now close to tears, but Darlessen was immediately on the alert.

"Who? Who was this who called?"

"Someone . . . I didn't write the name down. They said they'd been working on a project with you . . . I told them you were at the studio." Debra flounced away and nearly threw herself into the bedroom. "What'd you do? Stiff someone else? Cut them out like you did me? And I bet you did, too! You're a creep, Chick Darlessen . . . What have you got going this time?"

Chick pursued her. "A man or a woman?" he demanded,

but before Debra could reply, he piled on another question: "When did the call come in?"

"Sometime this morning, I guess . . . Maybe noon, I don't know . . ."

Chick grabbed Debra's shoulders, and spun her around until she was facing him. "And you said where I was?"

Looking into his face, Debra saw anger mingled with an emotion she recognized as terror. "What's wrong, Chickie?" she murmured. "Can't keep your lies in place? Who is this person?"

"Look, I don't want this house left unlocked or the garage door—"

"It was an *accident,* Chick. Accidents happen."

"Well, I don't want any more *accidents* to happen. Ever!" Darlessen's palpable fear created a comparable sensation in his girlfriend.

"Is he dangerous?"

"So, it was a man?"

"Maybe . . . I don't know . . . Maybe it was a guy . . . a guy trying to sound like a girl, or maybe it was the other way around . . . I couldn't tell!" Debra all but shrieked. "But whoever it is, is dangerous, right?"

"No." Chick's tone was commanding, but Debra paid no heed.

"And you're going to let me sit out here at the beach while some crazy witch—"

"So, it was a woman?"

"A babe would make more sense than a man, wouldn't it? Given your history."

Chick grabbed at his hair. The entire situation was driving him crazy. All he wanted was an end to it. "She's not ticked off," he said.

"So, yes! It is a babe! Some dish trying to sound like a guy . . . I should have known . . . How come she said you owed her money? What's that all about?"

"That's what she said?"

"That's what the call was about! Money!"

Chick watched Debra's face wrinkle in concentration as she struggled to recall the conversation. *Wanda,* he thought, *it must have been Wanda.*

"I didn't want to move all the way out to Malibu," Debra screamed at him. "I was happy staying in the Valley . . . There's lots of people around . . . shops and places I knew . . . I had friends . . . You're setting me up for some loony walking in here with a grudge, aren't you? Get rid of me and take up with a 'major talent' like Shay Henlee! Or this other one. What is she, some Hollywood madam? Is that why you owe her money?"

"Stop it Debra." Chick's voice was loud and forceful: Debra obeyed at once.

"I'm not 'taking up' with anyone else, and I don't expect you to, either. As far as this person is concerned, she's just a sad little friend of my late uncle's. She thinks they had a 'romantic attachment.' They didn't. If you saw the woman, you'd know why." Chick put the finishing touches on what seemed like an excellent set of lies. "She's confused on a number of issues. She also believes Uncle Bart should have left her something in his will—"

"So, she's just nuts, huh?" Debra's worried face was slowly opening, although a strong residue of mistrust remained.

"Basically, yes."

"How nuts?" Debra studied Chick. She knew she wasn't a stupid person, but she also realized she didn't always pay close attention to the facts; and there was something in Chick's current attitude regarding this woman that didn't gibe with his previous behavior. "She's not dangerous, huh?"

Chick thought. His facile brain began to note a number of options he hadn't seen before. "Tell you what, Deb," he said, dropping his hands from her shoulders to encircle her still-icy back. "If it would make you feel better about security—being all the way out in Malibu and everything—I'll show you how to use the pistol I keep in my office . . . That way, if you hear a strange noise, and I'm not around, you'll be armed."

"But—" Debra protested.

"I'm not saying anyone's out to hurt either of us. I'm just saying I want you fully protected. In fact, I'm angry with myself for not considering the problem before. You're a pretty girl, and this can be a lonely place. I should be thinking of your safety. You're right to be upset with me, Deb."

Her resistance beginning to flag, Debra offered a breathy, "I can always call nine-one-one."

Darlessen chuckled; it was an indulgent sound. "Not if you can't find your cell phone, sweetheart."

The endearment melted the last of Debra's suspicions. "Okay," she offered.

"There's my girl." Darlessen draped an arm around her shoulder, then proceeded to lead her to his desk and the drawer where he kept his revolver.

"I didn't know you had a gun."

"Everyone has a gun. This is L.A."

"Chick?" she asked as he retrieved the pistol, "why can't I play a part on *Anatomy of a Crossword?*"

"I'll tell you what I'll do, Deb. First thing tomorrow, I'll talk to Nils Spemick. Better yet, I'll talk to Nan DeDero. She plays this rich, old aristocrat named Sara, and she's got a maid named 'Emma'—"

"I don't want to play a maid—"

"Emma's more than a servant, sweetheart . . . She's really Sara's trusted advisor and friend. It could be a good role for you . . . show you to advantage against an older woman. I'll write you some extra lines." Chick was spinning the story out of whole cloth, but he didn't care. He put the pistol in Debra's hand. *If Wanda Jorcrof dared to show her face in Malibu over the weekend, she'd be in for a nasty surprise.* The thought brought a smile to his lips. "Let's take the gun outside, so you can practice loading it. Then, we'll blow a few rounds into the ocean."

"And I can do 'Emma'?

"I think you'd be just right. But you gotta promise me to cut out the booze."

"Oh, I will. I will."

CHAPTER

12

"I'm your murder victim. A dead man walking." The voice near Belle's chair was melliflous and soft, a gentle buzz as peaceable as it was amused. Belle's head jerked up from the strange crossword puzzle she'd just been studying. She had a fleeting and peculiar impulse to hide it in her *official* desk, and her fingers wavered indecisively.

"Dan Millray, here." A slow and relaxed chuckle accompanied his introduction. "And it looks like I caught our illustrious technical assistant trying to make off with the goods. The plot thickens." He laughed again as he peered over Belle's shoulder at the word game still in her hands. "That *is* the crossword that proves whodunit, isn't it? The famous puzzle that the real flesh and blood Belle Graham—well, you, in fact—used to track down my despicable killer . . . correction: the killer of the ornery and unloving cuss I'm portraying. I'm glad to welcome you to the set, Ms.—"

"Belle." She smiled. "It's just Belle." There was something immediately likable and genuine in the actor who'd been cast as the doomed man. Of middling height with a rumpled and unprepossessing build, he looked as if he would have been completely at home dispensing advice about stove bolts, brass hinges, or deicers in Newcastle's family-owned hardware store.

"I don't know how you can make up those things," Millray added. "I can't even fill 'em in, let alone . . . But then I've always been a terrible speller . . . And dyslexic, on top of everything, . . . So, tell me how the message thing works. I am right, aren't I? Chick said you—or Shay, in this case—nabs the villain because of words spelled out in the puzzle." Dan took it from Belle's hands. *"Greetings!"* he read. "Well, that doesn't seem too sinister to me."

"This isn't the actual crossword for the show," Belle answered.

"It sure looks like the one the prop department has."

She frowned, although she couldn't have explained why, as the message in this anonymous puzzle proclaimed an innocuous, even cheery: WELCOME TO L.A. SIP A DRINK. GET A TAN. TAKE A SWIM. WHAT ME WORRY? But its lack of identifiable authorship confused and disturbed her; since receiving the crossword the previous day, Belle hadn't been able to shake away those small and amorphous clouds of apprehension.

As if Dan had intuited her concern, his expression also turned serious. "So, I gather it's not—?"

"No. It's the same *grid* as the one I created for the show, but the clues, and therefore the answers, are entirely different."

Dan frowned as well. "Someone's playing a trick, you mean? Well, that's no surprise, we've got a lot of practical jokers on the set. That's for sure. Even I get into the act every now and then."

Belle read the puzzle's central message aloud.

"Sounds like a clever, new form of greeting card," Dan offered."

"I guess . . ." Belle said. Shared with another person, the mystery crossword seemed more innocent and amusing than perplexing. ". . . a greeting card. I like that . . . That makes sense."

"Looks like you've got yourself a competitor, then. Oh, hey, that wasn't very polite. You're supposed to be the best in the biz. At least, that's what everyone on the set's been saying."

Belle shrugged. She wasn't a person who was comfortable with compliments. "So you're 'Annie's' husband?"

" 'Annie'?" Dan asked, then caught himself and shook his head in self-rebuke. "First thing you learn as an actor is to start getting into character by calling yourself—and all those around you—by their names in the script . . . Well, in the theater anyway . . . That method doesn't always fly in TV-Land. Yup, 'Annie'—or Ginger Bradmin—is my wife . . . My long-suffering wife, I should say."

Belle raised an eyebrow. " 'Annie's' husband really was a reprehensible person . . . That's not to say he deserved to die . . ." Belle scratched her head. "I just can't get used to the names Chick has selected for this script. 'Annie' of course wasn't your wife's real name; then he's named your character 'Edison,' and the woman 'Edison's' having the affair with is now 'Deb', after his girlfriend, Debra Marcollo, I guess. But I don't think I'd ever confuse you with 'Edison,' you don't seem at all—"

"Dastardly?"

Belle laughed. "I was going to say conniving and manipulative."

"Appearances can be deceiving . . . Take Ginger . . . Looks like America's sweetheart, but she's really hard as nails—"

"Exactly like the original widow—"

"I don't know about that. But I do know Ginger. She's a top-notch professional and all that, but she can sure give Nan a run for her money in the temperamental department—"

"Typecasting." Belle smiled. "The original woman screamed bloody murder when she found her husband's body . . . Normal behavior given the situation, but in that instance, the wife was so *overly* distraught that her reaction started to seem unnatural to Rosco and to me, which was why—"

"Ahh . . . I'll have to remember that the next time I bump someone off. Wouldn't want to tip my hand to the cops by overreacting."

"No," Belle agreed, "you'd better be careful there. Subtle shock and remorse followed up with an 'I'd rather be left alone' attitude throws the cops off the trail every time."

"Got it." Dan Millray chuckled as he changed the subject. "Well, just you wait till you see the fit Ginger's going to throw when Quinton Hanny makes his appearance. I don't know if Dean Ivald's told her yet."

This was the first Belle had heard that the part of Rosco had been cast. Chick Darlessen had obviously won his battle—Quinton Hanny had been chosen over Lance diRusa.

"Quint is Ginger's ex, you know," Dan continued to explain. "And there's not one drop of good blood between them. I'm going to need to remind myself to keep my head down, and hightail it when fuses start to melt."

"Oooh," Belle said, "that's not going to make the scenes where 'Rosco' is interviewing and/or accusing 'Annie' of murder very pleasant—"

"You can say that again. Lucky thing for me, I'll already be long since dead—"

At that moment a hellish noise engulfed the sound stage. A scene being prepared for Nan and Shay in the sitting room of "White Caps" erupted in the deafening sound of crashing metal and splintering wood, while a high-pitched female scream reverberated long and horribly, and feet began thudding toward the site as grips and actors were galvanized from every section of the enormous sound stage. "Is she dead?" Belle heard Shay shriek. "Is she dead . . . ? Is she? She is! Tell me she's not dead!" Hysteria made the actress's voice rise in decibel and speed.

Hurrying to the spot, Belle and Dan saw chaos. A wall of "White Caps" had collapsed onto Nan. Made of flimsy stuff, one-by-two-inch slats and canvas, it would probably have inflicted no more than several unpleasant bruises. But among the debris sat what appeared to be a section of steel beam, and beneath that, face down, lay a bloodied and motionless Nan.

"Out! Get out! Everybody out!" Dean Ivald shouted. "All unnecessary personnel, move! Now! Schruko, get your people in here, A-S-A-P."

His orders went unheeded. Instead, everyone, as a herd, bundled closer to the stricken figure. A few people gasped, some moaned softly, but mostly there was a stunned and terrified silence. Then all at once, each person present went into noisy action, lifting the lethal weight from Nan's back, pulling away the fallen wall, calling for an ambulance, covering Nan's body with a blanket ripped from a stage "bedroom in Vermont," helping the still-kneeling and still-weeping Shay to her feet and leading her away. In what seemed, again, to be mere seconds, Don Schruko ushered the studio EMTs through with a wheeled stretcher and requested space in which they could work.

The group fell back, watching as the unconscious Nan was gently placed on the stretcher, strapped in and whisked away. Seeing the ashen face, the white hair, the bloodspeckled clothes of a proud, old New England lady, Belle began to weep, although she knew it wasn't Nan she was frightened for, but Sara. Sara who, though indomitable, would not—could not—live forever.

"That's it," Dean announced above the uproar that followed Nan's eerie and solemn exit, "no more shooting today. It's Friday; that's it . . . Get yourselves plenty of sleep over the weekend, boys and girls, we're packing it in. And be here on time Monday morning. We're going to finish this film if it kills every last one of us.

CHAPTER

13

Dean Ivald sat in leaden silence in his canvas director's chair. The strips of fabric that made up the seat and back seemed to be sagging more than usual under his unhappy weight. His long spine sagged, and his neck bent crookedly as he held his face in his hands and stared at the blackened screen of a teleprompter, as if in a near-comatose state. Once in a while his eyes flickered, suggesting that his misery might find an end and that he'd somehow miraculously discover a solution to his problems. Techies and make-up people tiptoed by as if they were edging their way through a minefield; they glanced at his defeated form but kept moving, as they shut down the set for the weekend. Eventually Ivald looked up at Don Schruko and mumbled, "Get me Nils."

The key grip remained quiet, frightened, or perhaps unwilling to supply the next piece of bad news.

"Nils Spemick!" Dean bellowed, "Get down on this set immediately!"

"He's not here, Mr. Ivald," Don Schruko said in almost a whisper.

"What do you mean he's not here? He's the casting director, for Pete's sake. Where the hell is he?"

"After Quinton Hanny's contract was negotiated, Nils decided to leave early for the weekend. I believe he said he was going to San Francisco."

A bitter groan escaped Ivald's angry chest. "I am not waiting until next week to replace this old bat. I promise you I'm going to be rolling film on Monday morning—come hell or high water . . . with a new actress. I'll get my own mother in here from England if I have to. Phone Nils Spemick in San Francisco and tell him he's fired. Tell him never to return to Los Angeles, or I'll wring his scrawny neck."

"That's my call, Dean," Lew Groslir said as he approached the two men. "I hire, and I fire," He was the picture of serenity and calm and was closely followed by a sleep-deprived Chick Darlessen.

"And nobody's firing Nils Spemick, not yet," Lew continued. "We're going to need a little powwow. Bring us a couple of chairs, will you, Don? And a production schedule."

"You got it, Mr. Groslir."

Schruko retrieved two more canvas-backed chairs along with the schedule and placed them beside Dean. Then, knowing that these "powwows" never intended to include lesser personnel, he moved away and proceeded to patrol the perimeter like a sentry, keeping anyone from disturbing the lordly trio.

"I don't know if I can take much more if this," Dean said. "What else can go wrong? My actors are dropping like flies."

"Worse things could happen," Lew offered as he glanced at the schedule. "Hmmm . . . It looks like those scenes at 'White Caps' need to be in the can next week so we can strike that set and replace it with the barn set at the country inn." Lew handed the production book to Darlessen. "Know any old ladies, Chickie?"

"Well . . . now that you mention it, and this may be a stretch, but I'll bet with enough make-up and a gray wig, my girlfriend could probably—"

"Debra Marcollo?" Dean said incredulously.

"It's worth a shot."

"A shot to the head, maybe." Dean ignored Chick altogether and spoke directly to Lew Groslir. "No. No. No. A million times, no, and I mean that. I let him have his way when he blackballed Lance diRusa. I hired Quint instead. Okay, I can live with that. Quint can act and he's solid. But I draw the line with Marcollo—doing anything! She's a lush, and she can't act her way out of a paper bag. I worked with her two years ago on a Chevy commercial and she ran a damn Tahoe over the craft services table . . . food everywhere . . . lunch ruined . . . We had to get an emergency 'roach coach' sent onto the lot . . . Plus, she'll jump into bed with anything that moves. That's all I need—to have all my stage hands sniping at each other. Sorry, Chick, no offense meant."

Darlessen's response was subdued; it wouldn't have pleased his girlfriend. "It was only a suggestion."

"Well, we've got to move fast on this. Lew's right, we need to start rolling on the 'White Caps' stuff Monday. What about your agent, Chick?"

"Lee Rennegor?"

"Yeah, have you seen his client list? Does he have any old battle-axes?" Lew tossed in.

"Forget it. His list of actresses is very short. And Lee's idea of an ancient woman is twenty-five. After that, he puts them out to farm."

The three said nothing for nearly ten minutes, instead, making small clicking sounds with their mouths, tugging at their earlobes, chewing the insides of their lips, and drumming their fingernails on the wooden armrests of their chairs.

"Coffee?" Chick finally said, and stood.

Lew and Dean answered a simultaneous, "No," and Chick sank back down in his seat. Another ten minutes of heavy thinking passed before Don Schruko advanced timidly.

"Excuse me, Mr. Groslir, but Miso Lane would like to show you something."

"What is it?"

"He didn't say."

The producer sighed impatiently. "Send him over, then. But tell him I only have a minute."

Permitted into this embattled circle, Miso crouched on the floor between them. He then opened a large D ring notebook, which contained the numerous Polaroid photographs he'd taken in Massachusetts. They'd been organized as to location and placed in clear plastic sleeves.

"Listen, Miso," Lew Groslir said in a slightly distracted manner, "the sets are set, so to speak. If anything needs to be added or changed, talk it over with Mr. Schruko or the prop master or scenic, but right now, this is crisis control central."

Miso began waving his hands, and frenetically flipping through the pages of his notebook. He never said a word, giving Chick the impression he was watching a silent Harpo Marx routine. Finally Miso reached his many snapshots of Sara Crane Briephs. He glanced up to make certain he had the full attention of the three men, then turned the next six or seven pages very slowly. Each sheet had a half a dozen pictures of Sara.

"Okay, Miso," Lew sighed irritably. "We've seen these. We know what she looks like. The point is, every actress her age is dead, gaga, or has a one-woman show on Broadway."

"Wait!" Dean shouted. He stood and circled the others twice. "Wait, wait, wait. Miso's right . . . We just fly the real person out here. It's simple."

Miso stood as well. He then slammed his notebook closed, said, "Bingo," and left the set.

"She's not an actress, Dean," Chick said, but at the same time he was thinking, *Hey, this might work.*

"Actress, schmactress, did you see my Kitty Krunchies commercial?"

Lew said, "No."

Dean was flabbergasted. "I won a Clio for that one. Everyone saw it."

"What's the point, Dean?"

"The point is, my good man, if I can get a performance out of a friggin' cat, I can get a performance out of that old babe." He pointed toward the exiting Miso.

"If you think about it, it's not a bad PR hook, Lew . . ." Chick added.

"I'm very uneasy about this. I like working with professionals. You can count on them."

Dean laughed. "Count on them for what? To put their face into a steering wheel? To hang out under falling stage equipment? It's not that big of a part, Lew. Believe me, I can coax a performance out of her. The right words . . . The encouraging gesture. And if we need to have Nan loop the voice in later, so be it."

Groslir sighed again and glanced at the production schedule once more. "Okay, let's give it a shot. What have we got to lose?"

"Of course, she could say, 'No,'" Dean offered. "Then we're right back where we started."

"This is TV. Nobody says, 'No' to TV."

"Just in case . . ." Chick pulled his cell phone from his belt and tapped a number into the autodial. "Time to call in the big guns. I don't want to lose this one."

The phone was answered after two rings, and Chick said, "Yeah, let me speak to Lee Rennegor."

CHAPTER

14

"That's a crying shame about Nan DeDero. She's a real trooper, and she'll be missed, big-time. It's going to take a very, very, and I mean *very* special person to replace her." Lee Rennegor said this with so much sincerity that even he was surprised at how genuine and sympathetic he sounded. "More than special . . . it's going to take a unique individual with truly unique gifts. Unparalleled, you might say." No linguist, the agent was quickly running out of accolades with which to impress Belle. "An original, even."

Seated at the metal desk of her makeshift studio office, she'd been penning a card to Rosco when Rennegor started his spiel. Belle would have left the set with one of the cast members, but Chick had insisted that he be the one to drive her back to Santa Monica, placing her now in the agent's direct line of fire.

"Lee Rennegor, here," he said. "We haven't met yet. Please call me Lee."

Looking up from the Kodachrome-bright picture-postcard of a red 1965 Mustang convertible sitting on the boardwalk of Venice Beach, Belle was surprised at the agent's wheedling tone, which simply didn't match his physical presence. He was a six-foot-eight man with a lean and fit body that cried out "personal trainer," dark hair carefully combed into a ponytail, eyes semi-hidden behind azure-tinted glasses, and a pale blue Italian suit that probably cost well over two thousand dollars. When he sat on the edge of Belle's desk, his black alligator shoes remained firmly planted on the studio's concrete floor. Rennegor extended his hand to her and smiled. His teeth were almost too perfect to be true.

Belle shook the proffered hand, wondering whether or not to stand. In her cramped metal chair, her head was a good two feet below the agent's. He continued to grin down at her while Belle gazed upward, uncertain what had prompted the visit. "I'm waiting for Chick to finish his meeting with Mr. Groslir," she said.

"Great kid, Chick. One of my best writers. A clever, clever guy. I've always known he'd go far." Then, not being one to waste time on small talk, Rennegor got straight to the business at hand. "Like I said, a crying shame about Nan DeDero. That type of thing never, never, *never* happens on a Dean Ivald set; he's a consummate professional. My actors adore working with him. Would kill to work with him, in fact."

Belle only nodded in response. She had no idea where this conversation was heading.

"Of course, they're going to have to replace her before the weekend is out." Rennegor folded his arms across his chest. "And Nils, the casting director, has disappeared into the steamy depths of San Francisco . . . You know," he continued, looking up at the lighting grids as if he were recalling some quaint event from the distant past, "when Chick first brought me this idea, or this *concept,* if you will, the very first words out of my mouth were: 'Hey, why don't we get the Real McCoy? Why not get Belle Graham to play herself? She's a very attractive woman, and what a hook! The networks'll love it.' I still think the idea would have flown very well. Very well, indeed."

Belle laughed aloud. "Oh, please. I'm not a performer by a long shot . . . Although I did act the part of Shylock in a high school play once—"

"I knew it! I knew it! I can always spot natural talent. That's why I'm the best agent in the business—bar none." Lee clapped his hands twice, and gave her another toothy smile. *The Merchant of Venice* right . . . ? And, uh . . . your drama teacher decided to do an experimental, cross-gender thing? Talk about a high concept approach!"

"No," Belle admitted, "the boy cast in the role dropped out, and I knew all the lines from working backstage, so . . ."

"I'm sure you were *wonderful,* Belle. Brilliant, probably . . . A teenaged girl playing an old, embittered man . . ." Words failed him; to compensate, he poured on the charm. ". . . I would have given anything to see that." Rennegor pointed his finger at her. "And originally, that was exactly my point with Chick; often amateurs can deliver a far more convincing performance than the professionals—especially if they look the part. It's done all the time in L.A."

"I don't know if I looked that much like Shylock."

"I'm back on *Anatomy of a Crossword* now."

"Ah." Belle glanced down the narrow walkway that separated one studio wall from the "Lawson's Diner" set. At the far end, she saw Dean Ivald, who appeared to be ordering the crew not to walk in her direction or disturb her conversation with Lee. "I'm . . . Not sure what . . . Do you need me for something?"

"Funny you should ask . . . As I said, they've got to replace Nan DeDero, and I couldn't help but notice that your friend Sara Briephs—who our dear Nan was merely *attempting* to replicate—has an unlisted telephone number."

All at once, Lee's motives became crystal clear. "What!" Belle nearly shouted. She slid her metal chair from the desk and slammed into the back of the "Lawson's" set. The wall began to rock slightly, and Rennegor placed a hand on the edge of the scenery flat to steady it.

"Look, Belle . . . I see this, ah, *suggestion* has taken you by surprise . . . But, trust me, everyone concerned believes Mrs. Briephs would do an excellent job with the part. Better than excellent—"

"You called Sara? At home?" Belle was still in a state of shock, mingled with an uneasy sense of dread—as if Sara, like Nan, were about to fall victim to a horrible accident.

"Well, no . . . I tried, but I don't have her phone number. It's a private line . . . I was hoping you could help me out there."

"This is ridiculous. Sara's not an actress."

"No, she's not. You're absolutely right about that. More than right. You've hit the nail on its proverbial head . . . But look at how popular these reality-based TV shows are, Belle. Are those people actors? Of course not. They're just everyday folks. One doesn't have to know the craft of acting to be a TV star anymore. Look at all those stand-up comedians with sitcoms. And besides, with a world-class director like Dean Ivald, what's not to like? Your wonderful friend, Sara, would be in the most capable hands in L.A. She could even get an Emmy Award out of this."

Again, that intimation of fear. "I don't know . . ."

Rennegor raised his voice and said, "Folks, can I get a chair back here?" It materialized in a matter of seconds. The stagehand who brought it vanished just as swiftly. Rennegor left his desk-side perch, moved close to Belle, and sat, lowering his voice to create a mood of utmost confidentiality. "Okay, Belle, I didn't want to have to say this, but these clowns . . . ? I'm talking about Dean, Lew, and Chick, now. They're desperate. Groslir's got his back up against the wall. Mrs. Briephs can wring some very heavy dollars out of Lew, if we play our cards right."

Belle smiled at him. "Sara could probably buy this entire studio three times over and turn it into a zoo if she wanted."

He chuckled loudly—too loudly. "It already is a zoo . . . Okay, fine, Belle, but we're in the driver's seat here. I say, let's get some perks out of this. What do *you* want? Is there anything you're unhappy with? How about I rework your contract for you?"

"Well, I'd like not to be staring at the back of a stage-prop wall for the next week."

Lee smiled and snapped his fingers. "You got it. As of Monday morning you're up in the booth with Lew. Consider it done."

But the more Belle thought on the situation, the more uneasy she became. "I don't know . . . If Nan DeDero was injured so easily . . . I'd never forgive myself if something like that ever happened to Sara."

"Belle, honey . . . it was an accident. A freak accident . . . Nothing like that has ever happened on one of Dean's shoots, ever . . . Just this once . . . Okay, I'll tell you what; we'll get Groslir to put a man on her 24-7. I'm telling you, the sky's the limit. These guys are up a creek. What do you want? A car and driver for Mrs. Briephs . . . ? Stretch Lincoln? Cadillac? Hummer? You got it."

"Well . . ."

"What did they give you to drive?"

"Actually, Chick's been chauffeuring me around so far."

Rennegor rolled his eyes. Obviously he was dealing with a real hick. "Man, who negotiated that deal for you?"

"Chick said you did."

"Ouch . . . That hurt, Belle . . . Okay, you've got your own car starting tomorrow . . . What else?"

But Belle still wasn't convinced. Obviously, Sara would love to do the show; she'd be in seventh heaven, thrilled to come out to Los Angeles and test her mettle with Dean Ivald and the gang. But how safe would she be? When was the next object going to drop or fall onto the set? On the other hand, it would be wonderful to have company. The city was proving to be a very lonely place with no friends, and no Rosco. Then, as if some little devil with a piece of candy had gotten inside of her mouth, Belle said that one word, "Rosco?"

"Rosco? Rosco? Is that all you want? You want your husband? You got him . . . I could get you Leonardo if you wanted him. Hey, I have a better idea! We fly Rosco out here, and we get him on the payroll. He can be Mrs. Briephs's bodyguard. He can be her twenty-four-seven guy. You want it? You got it. Why give the gig to one of these local goons, right? Especially when we have one of our own. He'll be on a plane by Sunday. Just say the word."

Belle wanted to say "No," but that sneaky, little devil took hold of her and made her say, "Okay."

"You won't regret this, Belle. What's the number?"

"Number?"

"Mrs. Briephs's phone number?"

"Oh, right . . ." Again Belle's doubts began to resurface, "I don't know; maybe this isn't such a good idea . . ."

"Belle, honey, this is like a done deal. Don't go back on me now. You can't just say you'll do something and then back out of it. Besides, this is quick stuff, these scenes. Sara will be on the same plane heading home with you and your hubby in one short week. One tiny, little week! Think of all the wonderful stories you'll have . . . all the laughs you'll share . . . When I consider how my own mother would have jumped at the chance . . ." For once, Lee was telling the truth. If his mom had been alive, she would have clobbered him if he hadn't handed her the part. "Why, the notion of being of service to a lovely, older person just makes me choke up, that's all. Think of the opportunity! Think of the gift you'll be giving your dearest friend!" He took a deep breath. "What's that number?"

Belle also drew in a long and hesitant breath, then slowly released it. "It's five, zero, eight, five, five, five, seven, nine, zero, eight."

Rennegor stood. "You're a doll. You won't regret this, not for a minute, believe me."

"Aren't you going to write the number down?"

He tapped his index finger to his temple. "Mind like a steel trap."

As Lee Rennegor turned to leave, Belle said, "Oh, and another thing, Rosco's going to need a car."

"You got it."
"A Mustang."
"You got it."
"Red."
"You got it."
"Convertible."
"You got it."

CHAPTER
15

Max Chugorro should have been a happy camper. Three of his scripts were now in development: *Border Deals, White Like Snow,* and *Tijuana Traffic.* He was a good screenwriter, having graduated from the UCLA film school with an award-winning short—all of which came just after a brief stint in the army and some unpleasant experiences during the first Gulf War. Max had a keen eye for life in the barrio and an ear for Hispanic machismo dialog, and was handy with a variety of firearms. He knew how to weave an action tale better than half the yo-yos who currently boasted Hollywood production deals.

But that single word, *development,* was his problem. It was a long, long way from a *production deal,* which could be even further away from *casting* and *lensing. Development* contracts often didn't put a lot of money into the pockets of new-kid-on-the-block screenwriters. And although the future should have looked bright for Max Chugorro, he was smart enough to realize that the time was not yet right for him to dispense with his small landscaping business.

So Max toiled away in the evenings honing scripts, while

during the day, he worked over the lawns, gardens, and sprinkler systems of those people in the hills who couldn't quite afford a private gardener. His black-and-gold pickup truck had become a near fixture on Doheny, Hillcrest, and Beverly Drive. He wasn't rolling in dough, but the fairly steady work kept him afloat, and many homeowners thought it quaint to have their lawns redone by Max Chugorro, THE MARQUIS DE SOD, as his business card read.

But this particular sunny Saturday morning didn't find Max doing his usual—trudging behind some twenty-two-year-old trophy wife while she decided *precisely* where she wanted him to place the seventy-five pounds of potted agapanthus he'd been lugging around in his hands. No, this Saturday found him at the Garden Depot on Roscoe Boulevard in the San Fernando Valley doing a little pro bono work for his elderly aunt, none other than Harriet Tammalong. Harriet had wanted to replace her concrete patio with a brick one for as long as Max could remember, but his schedule had never been able to accommodate her wishes—until today, which placed the two of them on Roscoe Boulevard in the midst of the "hardscaping" section of the emporium as Harriet rattled off an array of questions concerning cinder blocks, mortar, slate, blue stone, statuary, and terra-cotta planters.

". . . I want it to look like it's always been there, Maxie," she said for the tenth time. "None of these shiny red ones." She pointed to a pallet of bricks. "Oh, and not those brown ones, either. They're disgusting. They remind me of those tacky office buildings on Ventura Boulevard. Don't they have any old bricks here?"

"We can get used ones at another supply center, but they're expensive. Plus, if they're too soft, there's no telling how long they'll hold up."

"There's no telling how long *I'm* going to hold up, Maxie. They don't need to last into the next century."

"Right, but the other problem is, they're uneven. They make attractive walls, but they're hard to walk on. I think we should be considering tumbled bricks. They're uniform in size and easier to work with."

Max took a step toward the pallet of tumbled bricks, but Harriet stopped him by grabbing the back of his tank top. "How's the movie business treating you, Maxie?"

"Er . . . fine, I guess. I've got a few things in development at Fox and another at Universal."

"Hah, I know what *development* means. How's your money holding out?"

"I'm okay. There's still a lot of sick lawns in Beverly Hills."

"Don't make me laugh. I know how cheap those muckety-mucks are. How many of them owe you money?"

"Ah . . . Not many?" He smiled at her.

Aunt Harriet was nobody's dummy; she'd been around, and she guessed that her dear nephew Maxie wasn't forceful when it came to demanding payments. "I want to pay you for your work, and I mean that. I have plenty of cash, Maxie . . . Not from your shiftless Uncle Harvey, though. Sheesh, he was the worst of the lot."

Max laughed. "I wouldn't hear of you paying me. I'm sorry it's taken me so long to get around to it, that's all." He tugged his shirt from her hand and walked over to the tumbled bricks. Harriet followed.

"See," he said, "they take brand new bricks, slop a little paint on them, place them in a huge drum, and roll them around for a while. That way, they become distressed and have that used look."

"Humph," Harriet said with a frown. "Speaking of distressed and used looks, whatever happened to that girlfriend of yours? What was her name? Daisy? Dotty? Dopey? Deb?"

Max stiffened noticeably as he interrupted. "I really don't want to talk about her. It's ancient history. I haven't seen her since she—"

But Harriet rolled on, not waiting for him to finish his sentence. "I met the most lovely young woman the other night at the *Down & Across* taping. I even introduced her to Gerry Orso as my niece." She looked up at the bright sky, now with a dreamy expression. "Too bad she's married, she'd be perfect for you. She was very pretty. Someone I would like to get to know a lot better."

"Thanks, Aunt Harriet."

"But then you know . . . Come to think of it, I was married to number three when I met your Uncle Harvey, and that didn't slow me down. Although Harv was huge a mistake in the long run, he's the only one of the five who wasn't worth a plugged nickel. Not even life insurance. I learned my lesson there—get that life insurance policy early."

Max removed two of the tumbled bricks from the pallet. "See, every one one looks entirely different, but they're all the same size, so they give you a very smooth, yet aged look."

"'Smooth but aged,' hmmm . . . That was Harvey, all right . . . You need a girlfriend, Maxie. Even if it's back to that tramp you used to be so stuck on."

"Can we just drop her, Harriet? Please?"

"The tramp? Sure, like she dropped you? I'll never forgive her for that . . . Of course if she came back, that would be—"

"That's not going to happen. She's with some guy in Malibu, living the high life. Now, can we just kill it?"

"Fine. Fine. But, that's Hollywood for you. These trampy actresses will always run off with the guy who's got the *in* with the studios, just like she did. Wait till you get your break, the ladies will be knocking your door down, too."

Max shook his head. "What about the tumbled bricks?"

"Well . . ." Harriet rolled the brick in her hands, inspecting all six sides. "They're very attractive." She picked up a second brick. "And no two seem the same . . . I like that, the lack of uniformity. And . . . And . . . I have an idea."

"Yes . . . ?"

"I have an idea how we're going to get you a writing job . . . And maybe a girlfriend at the same time."

"Let me worry about all that, okay, Aunt Harriet? Now, what about the bricks?"

She gave him a big smile. "Sure, Maxie, wrap 'em up"

"I need to measure your patio first to determine how

many I'll need. I'll take you home, and we can do it now, if you like."

"This all is very exciting."

As Max and Harriet exited the Garden Depot and crossed the parking lot toward his waiting pickup truck, a gray Toyota sedan zipped by them, honked twice and darted into a nearby parking space. The driver's door swung open, and a woman with bowl-cut hair stepped out, immediately locked the car, and began walking directly toward Harriet and Max.

"Goodness," Harriet said, "it's Wanda Jorcrof. Looks like we're not heading home quite yet. I need to talk to her."

CHAPTER

16

By seven-thirty Sunday evening, the silver crescent of the new moon had yet to appear on the eastern horizon. Its absence made Los Angeles glow, its vast parade of street lights, car lights, house lights, office complexes, and neon-bright strip malls in vivid contrast to the inky sky. Mile upon mile of pinpoint-sized sparks flashed on and off over the city and its spreading suburbs. And as their Continental Airlines Boeing 767 banked over Malibu on its final approach for landing at LAX, Sara and Rosco were treated to this spectacular, almost phosphorescent view. The cabin overheads had been dimmed; the night was a deep charcoal hue; and the ocean, vast and primeval, darker still. "Oh!" Sara murmured. "Perhaps, this is what paradise looks like. Paradise seen from above, that is."

"What would be above paradise?" Rosco asked with a smile.

"You've got a good point," was Sara's wry reply before a passing flight attendant reminded her that her seat belt wasn't fastened.

"Very bossy, these stewardesses are nowadays," Sara confided as the young woman walked toward the aircraft's aft section. The older lady deemed the term "flight attendant" too modern and vague, preferring the more nautical "steward" as if she were not aloft but aboard a transatlantic liner. Rosco held his tongue, opting not to mention that "bossy" might best describe Sara Crane Briephs—a trait that seemed to run in her family. Her brother, the senator, enjoyed the same reputation on Capitol Hill. The thought brought Rosco's mind full circle.

"Is Senator Crane still planning on being in Sacramento this week?"

"Oh, Hal and his 'energy crisis' investigations. Yes, indeed, he will be here. One would think one could travel across this grand country of ours and be able to escape the watchful eye of one's 'elder brother.' It makes me feel like I'm positively back in grade school."

Rosco laughed. "Los Angeles is a long way from Sacramento, Sara. Your visiting at the same time is purely coincidental. And if memory serves me, I believe the senator did plan his trip right after the recall count."

"Humph . . . So you say. Well, on with the show," Sara added. "My new career! Aging thespian! And a stranger in paradise!"

At a rented beach house directly below the path of the 767, the picture was not one remotely resembling paradise or even earthly contentment or peace. The rooms in Chick Darlessen's home were unlit, the silence inhospitable and grim. Having watched the Lakers's game with a number of sitcom writers up in the highlands of Pacific Palisades, Chick had consumed more than one too many Bloody Marys. Two or three too many, in fact. Then, absolutely blotto, he'd managed to climb behind the wheel of his new Porsche and had driven woozily home at 6 P.M.

Debra hadn't been on hand to great him, and he couldn't remember whether she had "spinning class" or yoga or step-aerobics—or whether she might have mentioned something about visiting friends. Alone, he'd breathed a sigh of relief at finding himself in a solitary state, then walked through the pitch-black sitting/dining area and entered his private office, where he'd immediately proceeded to pass out on the couch without bothering to flick on so much as his desk lamp. Now, at 7:30, the space was disorienting in its utter darkness, so the voice that roused him from his sodden sleep seemed to come from nowhere, almost like a ghost or a bad dream.

"We need to talk, Chickie."

"Who . . . ? Wha' the . . . ?" Darlessen thudded from the couch to the floor, and struggled to get his still-drunken bearings. Once he'd discovered where he was—home, in fact—he crouched there panting as a wave of nausea came and went.

"We need to talk—now," the voice repeated.

"Later . . ."

The unwanted visitor moved to the desk, depressing the button on the table lamp until a stream of yellow light spread across the desktop where the .38 revolver remained, having never been relocated to the kitchen as promised. Chick gazed at it briefly, then returned his concentration, such as it was, to the interloper's shoes. Queasy as he felt, it was remarkable how much energy he could expend in hating those particular shoes.

"What are ya tryin' to do? Give me a damn heart attack? Jumpin' in here . . . yellin'." Chick felt bile rising in his throat, as well as the unpleasant aftertaste of tomato juice, horseradish, Tabasco, and vodka.

"I'm not yelling. Far from it. There's no point in having the neighbors listening in. Besides, you're too drunk to be startled."

Darlessen grabbed at his throbbing head with both hands, then rubbed at his eye sockets with the tips of his fingers.

"Ha, ha . . . guess you're on the money about tha'—"

"We need to talk—"

Chick groaned. "Tomorrow . . . We can talk tomorrow. Monday. Can't you see I'm wasted?" He clambered back onto the couch, flopped face down and placed a pillow over his head.

But an angry hand grabbed the pillow, and flung it across the room. "Sit up, and look at me!"

"Uh-oh, somebody's in a foul mood . . . Again." The words were slurred; halfway along Darlessen started to laugh. It was a wheezy, helpless sound. "I suggest you—"

"We need to iron out a few details in this relationship of ours—"

Chick laughed louder. "What 'relationship'? Our so-called relationship's over . . . As of now." He rolled around and tried to sit up, but he kept sagging sideways. He wiped a drop of drool from his mouth with his shirttail, allowing his pale belly to hang out over the elastic waistband of his sweat pants.

"You look disgusting, Chick."

From his half-prone position, Darlessen belched loudly. "There, how's tha'? Give you somethin' extra to be disgusted about." A case of the hiccups was beginning to set in. "This may come as a . . . *hic* . . . big surprise to you, but I could not care less about you . . . and our *relationship* . . . I just want you the . . . *hic* . . . hell out of my space—"

"Sit up straight."

"How'd you get in here, anyway? I keep this room . . . *hic* . . . locked for a reason, you know . . ." Chick tried to think back. Hadn't he locked the door behind him when he returned? The turning of the key had become an almost Pavlovian response after he entered his workspace—his only haven of quiet and solitude in the whole damn house.

In response, his visitor sat on the edge of the desk, the nose of the .38 almost brushing a muscled thigh. "Your sanctuary, is that it? Your private retreat? No one's allowed in without the master's say-so." The tone was increasingly acidic; a hand began toying carelessly with the gun.

"Hey, watch that thing . . . *hic* . . . It goes off by accident, someone gets hurt . . ." Chick was finally able to sit up straight on the couch, but another wave on nausea started to move in. ". . . Here, give it to me . . ." He held out his hand, but his request was ignored.

"You haven't been square with me, Chickie . . . All those promises—"

"Wha' promises—?"

"I guess the concept of Chick Darlessen thinking of anyone other than Chick Darlessen is pretty damn remote, isn't it?"

"Wha' promises?" Darlessen repeated.

Again the question passed unnoticed while the pistol began casually passing from right hand to left hand and back again. The person holding it sighed in weariness and anger. "So, do I give you another chance? Or do I just fold this tent right here and now?"

"Fold your tent . . . *hic* . . . That's a great idea . . . And get the hell out . . . Which was my suggestion . . . *hic* . . . five minutes ago . . . And put down that damn . . . You know how dangerous—"

But the intruder suddenly stood, leveling the gun at Chick. "Things are going *my* way from now on. Not *yours*. Not yours anymore."

Frightened into soberness, Chick's face froze. "Get out" he managed to spit out, "or I'll call the cops and have you thrown out. So, help me, I will."

"*My* way—"

Darlessen lunged forward, while almost instantaneously, the .38 fired, sending a slug into his chest, passing through his heart and lodging in the wall behind him. As his dying body jerked reflexively backward, the remaining five bullets slammed into it while the shooter stared in horror at the growing pool of blood.

Five minutes later, a scream rose from the house, spilling in successive waves of urgency and fear as Debra Marcollo stumbled onto the deck, Darlessen's blood dripping from her hands. Then still wailing at the top of her lungs, she half-skidded and half-ran down the wooden steps and out to the beach where she was finally subdued by a passing off-duty lifeguard.

The Malibu police arrived at the scene less than seven minutes after that.

CHAPTER

17

Driving south from Thousand Oaks at 8:15 Monday morning, Lew Groslir could scarcely restrain himself from pounding the molded burl walnut dashboard of his Bentley or vehemently honking his horn. The heady array of expletives he permitted himself were yet another case—giving him ample means with which to vent his disgust, fury, and outrage over the sheer stupidity of some no-talent, bimbo girlfriend murdering a man only marginally more creative than she. "The no-account little witch," he spluttered and fumed. "Would I love to get my hands on her . . . What does she think . . . ? That she's gonna throw me off schedule because I didn't listen to the Chicken man and cast *her* as my lead actress? Slow down a Lew Groslir production? Fat chance!" It never occurred to his egocentric personality that the screenwriter's death might have had nothing whatsoever to do with him or the filming of *Anatomy of a Crossword,* although he did experience a momentary pang of concern over whether Chick had completed the final rewrites of the last three crucial scenes. Darlessen was—

scratch that, *had been*—a world-class sluggard when it came to work and bringing things in on time.

Barreling down the freeway, yelling into the leather-scented air of his Bentley Arnage T, Groslir began creating a list of potential Hollywood rewriters, down-and-out New York playwrights and mercenary novelists who could quickly take Chick Darlessen's miserable place. "I shouldn't have hired him in the first place," he groused. "I don't care *whose* idea the story was! That's what script doctors are for—to make the original guy's *concept* fly. I should have just bought the damn pitch and told Chickie to take a hike. Big mistake, Lew. Big mistake. You give a writer like him an ounce of power, you throw the whole Hollywood balance thing out of whack. It's like messing with the environment. This is a pyramid system . . . like food . . . ya gotta remember that, Lew. An empty carb—that's what Darlessen was . . . And how may empty carbs does a body need?"

But then the producer's brain suddenly veered in the opposite direction: Hollywood murders, and the major media ink they generated. The sorry tale began to look less like a potential problem and more like a probable gold mine. "On the other hand . . . maybe we're dealing with a PR bonanza here, Lew," Groslir almost cooed. "A dead writer? I like that. It's a hook, a good hook. And a sexy babe in a prison jumpsuit? I like that even better. This is beautiful. We're golden. This is money in the bank. And I'll betcha we can keep generating headlines till the show actually airs . . ."

A s Groslir dodged the BMWs, Miatas, and Mustangs on the inbound 101 Freeway and began plotting his next move in Culver City, the cast and crew of *Anatomy of a Crossword* blissfully and ignorantly hummed with unaccustomed contentment and a new-found verve. As yet, no one had heard the shocking news of Darlessen's death or Debra Marcollo's arrest. As a result, the first order of the morning's activities was the welcoming of Sara—the real Sara—whose keen and perceptive eye would help the movie's "Belle" and "Rosco" unveil the "murderer."

Ordinarily, the introduction of a replacement performer would have been a subdued affair, made tense and sometimes hostile by an overtaxed schedule, actors unwilling to reshoot scenes, costume refittings, and new lighting requirements as well as the hothouse camaraderie that exists in any theatrical venture. But from the onset, Sara was Sara, and her appearance among the falseness of stage "gilding" and "marble" had an eerily regal air, like Queen Elizabeth embarking on one of her famous "walkabouts."

"Oh, my," she said as she handed Dean Ivald her white-gloved and gracious hand. "You have perfectly recreated my cozy little nook back in Newcastle. You dear man! How very, very flattering! And that portrait of my great-great-grandfather? Why, no one could tell me I wasn't face-to-face with the genuine oil . . . It looks as much unlike him as the original."

No one interrupted as Sara paraded through her "sitting room," although a few eyebrows were raised behind her back. "A cozy little nook" would not have been the term on most on the onlookers' lips. And calling the director "a dear man" seemed tantamount to referring to the evil movie doll "Chuckie" as "Pinocchio."

Rosco and Belle remained in the background while Sara met her fellow actors as well as the grips and scripts girls, the makeup and wardrobe artists. "Isn't this simply lovely?" the grand old lady stated in her clear, patrician tone. "We'll be one enormous family all toiling about in this cavernous place. Like ants."

"And we all know ants have a queen . . ." Belle heard a voice behind her murmur. She turned and glimpsed Miso Lane in the background. To whom he was speaking, Belle couldn't see. "Didn't I tell you she was a dead ringer?"

Belle frowned, instantly cold, instantly wary and fearful for her friend's safety. *Death* and *Sara* were not words she wanted put in proximity. Belle pushed her way toward Miso. "What do you mean by 'dead ringer'?" If there was a more diplomatic method of opening the conversation or a more subtle way of discovering what Miso had meant by the term, Belle didn't stop to consider it.

The location scout/Polaroid junkie regarded her. "A ringer for the genuine article," he answered with a glib, dismissive shrug. "The real item."

"But she is the real person," Belle countered.

"That's what I'm saying."

"But you can only be a dead ringer if you're not authentic to start with," Belle persisted.

"Ah, the wordsmith splits hairs . . . Hey, she looks good," was Miso's less-than-illuminating reply. "She looks real good. It's just super to have her out here with us—her and everything that comes with her." Then he melted away as another bank of lights flashed on, revealing Sara in a different location on the sound stage.

"Rosco," Belle whispered as soon as she found her husband, "I really don't like this."

Rosco smiled and shook his head. He was enjoying watching Sara revel in the limelight. "She's having a great time, Belle, lighten up. Who wouldn't enjoy having a fling like this at her age?"

"But—"

"I know. You've got a hunch things here aren't all they seem to be—"

"It's more than a hunch."

He looked at her, his expression serious now. "You love Sara, and you're worried because she's not as young or spry or tough as she looks."

"That's not the problem."

"I promise you, there aren't any sinister types skulking around here or back at the hotel." He laughed in the hopes of sounding reassuring enough to banish her concerns. "And if there were . . . well, that's why they've flown in the Polycrates Agency—"

"But what if getting Sara to fly out here is part of a plot of some sort?"

"Plot?" Rosco wrapped an arm around his wife's shoulder. He was still smiling. "What exactly do you mean by, plot?"

Belle thought. Up to this moment, her worries had been too amorphous to name. "Well . . . kidnapping, for one . . . Sara's brother's an important U.S. senator, after all . . . and . . . and he does a lot of work in foreign relations . . . and he is here in California. Maybe it's an international—"

"Don't you think your alien cartel would have found it easier to nab Mrs. Sara Crane Briephs in her own home? After all, the stalwart Emma's hardly muscle man material. Though I'd guess she'd put up a better fight than most housekeepers."

Belle considered the suggestion. "Okay, then . . . Miso Lane and his buddies—or their confederates back East—rob White Caps while Sara's in California. All that silver and those antiques—"

"Al Lever's already on that, Belle. He's got a squad car patrolling Sara's neighborhood twenty-four-seven. And her house may be ancient, but she has a very sophisticated alarm system—only Tom Cruise would be able to get around it, or his stunt double."

"Ho, ho." Belle fell silent for a moment, then said, "I still have a bad feeling, Rosco . . ."

It was at that moment that Lew Groslir arrived and drew Dean Ivald aside. From the expressions on the men's faces, Belle and Rosco knew they weren't discussing camera angles or lighting design. After a brief consultation, Lew headed off to the production office, and Dean raised his voice so that he would be heard throughout the studio. "People, may I have your attention for a moment, please? Would you all please drop what you're doing and move into the Lawson's Diner set and take a seat? I'm afraid I have some unpleasant news to share."

CHAPTER

18

"S o?"

The word was said in almost perfect unison by Dean Ivald and Lew Groslir. They both laced it with the same amount of over-the-top incredulity while their faces conveyed a complementary measure of annoyance, agitation, and impatience. Following the general announcement concerning Darlessen's unfortunate demise, the two men had retreated, along with Belle—the focal point of this pointed exchange—to the production offices that overlooked the *Anatomy of a Crossword* set. Rosco had not been invited to join this intimate powwow, which had been deemed an "artistic discussion," meant only for the "creative family."

"Look, Belle, honey," Lew continued, "you don't throw two months of pre-production down the toilet just because you've got a dead writer. Do you have any idea how many writers there are in L.A.? We can replace Chick in twenty minutes if we need to."

"And that's the beauty of it, really," Dean added. "Because Chick managed to get his rewrites for those final scenes into my box over the weekend, we don't even *need* to replace him. We're set, we're ready to roll. If we have any questions, at all . . . well, that's what we hired you for, right?"

"It just . . . doesn't seem proper," Belle insisted. Like everyone else on the set, the news of Chick's murder had upset her, and understandably sent her into a mild state of shock.

"Who's to say what's *proper* and what isn't?" Lew responded as he began to pace in front of the one-way glass that separated the trio from the studio below, and the cast and crew who were now milling about in a funk. "Think about it for a minute, Belle. Do you think Chick would want us to pull the plug on this baby? *His* baby. His special project. No way, José. I mean, what began as merely another dynamite notion in his impressive repertoire has become Chick Darlessen's final—and maybe best—achievement, his swan song, if you will . . . Because in the long run, his death virtually guarantees him an Emmy nomination . . . And it's so quintessentially Hollywood—SCREENWRITER GUNNED DOWN BY GIRLFRIEND IN MALIBU BEACH HOUSE . . . What you have there is the full range . . . what's that word I'm looking for?" Lew rubbed the fingers of one hand together as if the elusive phrase were a bit of cloth he was plucking at. ". . . panoply! That's it! The full *panoply* of emotion. You have to love it."

Dean clapped his hands together. "Now that's the story we should be shooting, Lew—sex . . . violence . . . the Pacific Ocean, foamy and frothy . . . drugs . . . alcohol . . . buff lifeguard wrestles semi-nude, foxy lady to the ground on a Malibu beach. Talk about ratings."

"I'm not—" Belle started to protest, but Lew raised his arm like a traffic cop and silenced her.

"You're a genius, Dean, an absolute genius." Groslir grabbed the telephone and punched in a series of numbers. As soon as he was connected, he spoke so rapidly that Belle had difficulty following his words. "Tracy, sweetie, get me a writer, any writer, I don't care who, as long as he can spell the names right. I want a dramatic treatment drawn up on this Darlessen–Marcollo murder case today. And get it registered with the Writer's Guild by five o'clock this afternoon, before some other sleazeball beats me to it." Lew dropped the receiver into the cradle and took a deep breath. "Okay, now, where were we?"

"I don't think I can do this," Belle said, attempting to sound resolute and forceful. "And I also think both of you are asking for more trouble. Three people have been seriously injured already."

"Three? Three? Where the hell do you get three?" Lew demanded.

Belle counted off on her fingers. "Greg Trafeo, your first Rosco; Nan DeDero, and now Chick Darlessen."

Lew threw up his hands. "Oh, come off it, will ya, honey? For one thing, Trafeo was out on Sunset Boulevard when he had his accident . . . Stuff like this happens all the time in L.A. What am I? A damn babysitter all of a sudden? I've got to keep an eye on every employee on his day off? This is business, toots. Grow up, will ya?"

Belle stood. "I don't intend to sit here and have someone talk to me like that, I really don't." she began to walk toward the door.

"Hey," Lew said with a malevolent chuckle, "I'm the producer, sweetheart. I'll talk anyway I feel like talking— especially now that we don't have a 'creator' anymore. Now, sit back down, this meeting isn't over until I say it's over."

Belle turned back to Lew. She gave him an icy stare, then folded her arms across her chest; however, she remained standing. "Mr. Groslir, a friend of yours has just been murdered," she said. "I can't say I knew Chick well enough to call him more than an acquaintance, but that doesn't prevent me being saddened by his death . . . But I have to tell you that despite what you say about Greg Trafeo's accident, as well as Nan DeDero's, I now have very serious misgivings about having asked Mrs. Briephs to come out here, and at this point, I believe it would be best for us all to return to Massachusetts."

"Don't make me laugh. You have a contract, doll. And Mrs. Briephs has a contract, in case you haven't noticed. Even your damn husband has a contract thanks to Lee 'squeeze-blood-from-a-stone' Rennegor." Lew pointed his finger at Belle to emphasize his threat. "You take a hike on me, and I'll sue all three of you into the next universe . . . We've got a major weekly publication on board—all ramped up to publish that puzzle of yours to coincide with airdate. You welsh, and they'll have you in court before I can even *phone* my lawyer. You'll spend the rest of your days in a Boston breadline begging for a cup of watery broth. And I'll own White Caps lock, stock, and barrel by the time I'm done with Mrs. Briephs."

Dean could see that Lew's verbal abuse was getting him nowhere with Belle. "All right, all right, Lew," he said, "let's settle down." He rose and placed his long arm over Lew's shoulder. He was nearly a foot and a half taller than the producer, and standing in such proximity, they seemed to belong on a cartoon frame from the Mutt and Jeff comic strip. "Let me talk to Belle privately for a minute or two, okay? I think we can work something out." As he spoke, Dean walked Lew toward the exit. And without giving him a chance to reply, gently pushed him out, locked the door, and turned to face Belle.

"Why don't we sit down? And don't let Lew's bluster bother you, Belle. He's under a lot of pressure. He means well. That tough-guy stance? That's simply facade . . . Producers need to display a certain sangfroid if they're to stay in business. It's a cutthroat town. You don't get to the top by acting like a diplomat."

Belle dropped her hands to her sides and flopped back into the chair. She sighed. "I don't know, Dean, I would just die if anything happened to Sara."

"This has been a stressful day." Dean took his own deep breath, and released it slowly. "I mean, look at Lew. He never behaves like that." *What's a little white lie between friends?* Dean thought. *In reality, Lew is a notorious hatchet man.* "I've known him for twenty years, and I've never seen him this distressed, never known him to raise his voice like that. He's clearly upset about Chick . . . Of course, we all are . . . But he's right, Belle; Chick's death and Greg's auto accident had nothing to do with our operation here in Culver City. They're just a rather unfortunate set of events. And, after all, Chick's killer is in jail. Who can Debra Marcollo harm now?"

"I just have a very bad feeling about the future."

"Sara will be perfectly safe, Belle, and you have your husband here, on the set, to ensure that." Dean placed his hand on Belle's. "And, I'm afraid Lew's also right about the contracts, dear. He would look very, very foolish within the industry if this project were to fall though at this point in time . . . Now, I know it may sound mercenary to you, but Chick's death makes this show an absolute, guaranteed ratings bonanza. It could very well sweep the Emmy Awards. If Lew were to lose that kind momentum, that kind of prestige, he'd come after you—and Sara—with a legion of lawyers . . . And, I'm sorry to inform you, he'd win his case, hands down."

Belle sat quietly. She could think of nothing to say that might refute Dean Ivald's allegations. A look of complete defeat showed on her face.

"Belle," Dean said, patting her hand, "This will work out. Trust me." Belle remained silent, so he pushed on. "We've lost very little time with all these issues, and I see no reason why we won't be finished with Sara by week's end—as scheduled. I hope you don't feel like you're being forced into this."

"Yes, as a matter of fact, I do feel I'm being coerced, and I don't like it . . . But I also realize I don't have a choice . . ."

"No, I'm afraid you don't . . ." Dean took a long pause, then added, "Oh, and another thing, Belle, dear, I'd like you to do me the biggest favor . . ."

"Yes?"

"I don't think it would help Mrs. Briephs's performance if she sensed there was any . . . well, animosity or acrimony between you and Lew. Your friend needs to be relaxed; it's the only way to get a believable performance out of a non-professional. For her sake, I'd like you to put on an enthusiastic exterior—even if you're not feeling it inside. The show must go on."

Belle was again quiet. Finally, she said, "I don't know . . . I have to think this over. I'm not a liar. And I've never hidden anything from Sara."

"And that's laudable. A trait both you, and she, can be proud of." Dean stood. "But, remember, it's for her benefit . . . Now, why don't you take a few minutes to think things over while I step outside and give you a little privacy." He walked to the door. "Keep in mind, Belle, that everyone loses if you take Mrs. Briephs back to Massachusetts now. And most of all . . . Chick loses. He dies a forgotten man in the city he loved, if this show isn't aired."

Dean stepped from the production office and closed the door behind him. He strolled down the hall, and at the end he was nearly tackled by Lew Groslir.

"Well? Well? What'd she say? What'd she say?"

"Relax, Lew. What did I tell you earlier? Good cop–bad cop gets them every time. She's thinking it over, but she has no choice; she'll play right into our hands. Of course, she probably hates your guts."

"I know. I'm almost sorry we had to carry it out this way."

"Forget it, Lew, you're the producer . . . Everyone hates your guts."

The two men shared a pleased, complacent chuckle. Once again, Dean placed his arm over Lew's shoulder, and they headed back toward the office and Belle. But before opening the door, Dean said, "We have another slight problem, Lew . . . Now that Chick's out of the picture, so to speak, we're going to need Belle to stick around for the entire four-week shoot as an advisor. We can send her hubby and the old lady packing on Saturday, but Belle's got to stay behind. I suggest you have a little tête-à-tête with Lee Rennegor before we approach her with this. Lee may be greedy enough to lock her into something if it's fat enough—without running it by his client first."

"You know, Dean, for a director, you're pretty slimy. Have you ever thought of becoming a producer?"

CHAPTER

19

S hay Henlee was so weary and distracted that she left the studio without bothering to remove her "Belle" costume or blonde wig. It had been a long, weird day, and she felt the leaden claws of depression bearing relentlessly down upon her shoulders. Chick Darlessen was dead; his girlfriend, Debra, was behind bars; and a soundstage full of dispirited actors were murmuring innuendoes—Chick had been emotionally abusive; Debra was a dipso who still had the hots for Lance, her ex, whom Chick had all but blackballed from a part on *Anatomy* . . . it was enough to send any brain reeling. And the troubling part was that it was all true: every sordid, little, regurgitated detail.

Shay sighed, turned her car, by rote, toward her home in the hills near the Hollywood reservoir. It wasn't a chichi address like some of her fellow performers boasted, nor was it a big or lavish house that reflected her earning power, her ever-escalating "quote" as a rising film star. Unlike others in her category, Shay didn't have a live-in boyfriend, or girlfriend, or personal trainer, or private chef, or any of the entourage her current celebrity might have called for. She didn't entertain at home, either, or permit media shoots featuring her in her hillside cactus garden or sunbathing on her deck. The house on El Contento Drive, Shay felt, should be just that, a welcoming haven that remained separated from the hurly-burly of life in the entertainment business. And when she decided to go for a hike in nearby Griffith Park or take a picnic and encamp under the stars at the Hollywood Bowl, she needed to be anonymous, just another face in the crowd.

Her almost obsessive need for seclusion had nothing to do with the fact that Shay lived with her mother. All right, maybe it did a little. Okay, maybe more than a little. But if anyone *ever* queried her on why a thirty-something actress would even *consider* sharing a home with her mom, Shay would have countered with a swift, "Because she's my best friend, that's why—besides being the most terrific cook in the entire universe! And while you're fighting with your current squeeze about who forgot to buy milk or whose audition went better, or worse, I'll be happily ensconced with someone who has always loved me."

Leaving Cahuenga Boulevard (the actress' other peculiarity was a steady dislike of freeways) to begin following the twisting roads to home, San Marco to Deep Dell to Rinconia and El Contento, Shay considered what her mom's reaction to Chick's death would be, and what questions she'd ask about Debra Marcollo, and how, hopefully—under her wise and intuitive prodding—this horrible tragedy would begin to achieve some kind of perspective and maybe even a sense of peace.

Shay shivered, although the response wasn't due to the cooling air. *Poor Debra,* she thought. *What had driven her to shoot her boyfriend? Had she "snapped," as some people suggested? Was she drunk and therefore not fully in control of her actions? Or had Chick badgered, criticized, or belittled her until she was no longer capable of thinking rationally? Or was she justifiably steamed because Chick hadn't held his part of their bargain and cast her in* Anatomy? *What causes an apparently "normal" person to take another human being's life?*

But those questions were immediately overshadowed by her thoughts of *Poor Chick! A screenwriter on the cusp of fame, simply bursting with his sudden good fortune! New wheels, new home, new threads. Alive and at the top of your game one day, and the next—gone. Forever and ever and ever.*

Shay shivered again, then rolled down her window to feel the evening breeze and smell the fresh and pungent scent of the eucalyptus trees. As the night air blew into the car, her "blonde" locks lifted slightly, billowing upward in delicate strands, precisely the way the true Belle's hair moved. The wig was a good one; it looked and behaved exactly like living human hair, and Shay's reaction was to brush the hair away with the quick, impatient gesture of a pretty woman who has better things to do than spend time on her appearance. The action was a faithful copy of one Belle had used a thousand times.

The man in the vehicle following Shay's noted this replicated gesture. He'd been tailing the blonde woman since she'd left the studio parking lot, and this was the first time he was absolutely certain he'd been pursuing the right person. Her final destination was the only thing he found surprising.

As Shay distractedly opened and closed the electronic door of her garage, and her mother called out her habitually cheery words of greeting, the original Belle just as dispiritedly turned toward Sara with her own poor effort at an affable smile. The two women were ensconced in Sara's suite at their hotel in Santa Monica waiting for Rosco to return from his evening run before they ventured out to find some dinner. And Sara, never one to remain silent, was enthusing about her first day on the set and the "pivotal scene" she'd already shot.

". . . Oh, I believe I truly have found my métier, dear!" she gushed. "Dean says I'm a natural-born actress. Now, it's possible that he's simply being kind, but still . . ."

Belle's smile stretched wider and thinner. Not for anything in the world would she rain on Sara's parade, no matter what Lew Groslir had dictated concerning her dealings with the older lady.

"Imagine, at my age! A new career . . . Why, who knows what the future has in store? You know Dean—and that rather charming Lew Groslir fellow—were both mentioning the word *Emmy* . . . Well, more than mentioning, if the truth be told. The two men seem to feel our little vehicle may just be worthy of industry recognition, which would be a fitting reward for poor Mr. Darlessen." Sara cocked her head to one side as she studied Belle, noticing for the first time her unaccustomed reticence and unease. "Are you all right, dear?"

"Fine, Sara," Belle lied. "A little tired, that's all."

The older woman, chiding her gently, recommended vitamins, exercise, and a decent meal while Belle responded with a number of dutiful nods.

"And, no doubt you're upset over Mr. Darlessen's death. Everyone is," Sara continued. "Well, of course, it's a terrible, terrible shock. And that poor girl who killed him . . . What an awful tragedy."

Belle nodded again, then rallied. "Which scene was it Dean had you do today?"

Sara brightened immediately. "The one where I'm toying with the crossword while you and Rosco are upstairs examining the murder scene."

"You're sitting near the fireplace in the inn's main sitting area, the dead man's widow is fighting with his business partner's wife, and you're feigning disinterest—"

Sara's blue eyes sparkled with pleasure and pride. "All I did was look at the puzzle and pretend not to hear them squabbling . . . Dean said it was a 'brilliant and understated performance—quite remarkable in a novice'! Those were his exact words . . . I think both Carol Von Deney and Ginger Bradmin were miffed that I received so much praise. Although, I must admit, Belle, I owe some of my successful

faux concentration to you . . . all those Shakespearean references you wove into the crossword. I really did enjoy hunt-
ing for the clues."

Belle stared at her friend. "What Shakespearean references?"

"The ones from *As You Like It*." Sara reached into her
script bag and pulled out the puzzle. "Props said I could
keep this copy, as they'll be using fresh ones for subsequent
scenes."

Belle took the crossword. The grid was identical to the
one she'd created for the show, but like the word game that
had welcomed her to Los Angeles, the clues were entirely
different.

Across

1. Petites; abbr.
4. Greek letter
7. Later; abbr.
10. Tiny
13. Dose; med. abbr.
14. Mr. Torn
15. "... lend me your___"
16. "For Love of___"
17. Orlando's vehicle
20. "___no evil..."
21. Mr. Butler
22. Siouan
23. Polanski film
24. "... sans___ ...", re: 61—Across
26. Bat material
27. Mayday
28. Likely
29. Vegas lead-in
31. Shakespearean oath
34. Mr. Cassini
36. What's "Blowin' in the Wind"
37. ——Jima
40. "... the men and women merely___", re: 61—Across
42. ___—Cat
43. Sends a wire
45. Restaurant offering
46. Slacker
47. Deal memo; abbr.
48. Summer drink
51. Power group
52. Clear tables
54. The third age, re: 61—Across
56. Beineix film
58. Light filter
59. ___Man
60. Mr. Amin
61. The stage, in 17—Across
65. Classic car
66. 2001 computer
67. ___—Eyed Jacks
68. __the line
69. Sunbathe
70. Ms. Irving
71. Asner and Ames
72. Mr. Barrett, of Pink Floyd

Down

1. Laconian capital
2. Accident
3. Trickiest
4. Mr. Capote
5. Ache
6. News org.
7. "... sans___ ...", re: 61—Across
8. Scott of *Happy Days*
9. Mr. Carney
10. "Full of___and modern instances:", re: 61—Across
11. Arden and others
12. "... sans___ ...", re: 61—Across
18. Six-time home run champ
19. Delivers a ten count
23. Costumes
25. Romeo & Juliet
26. Lost
27. Arousing
30. ___*Well That Ends Well*
32. TV room
33. Sold out of seats; abbr.
35. Gold's arena?
36. Florence's river
37. Here in France
38. Tobacco ball
39. "... and mere___ ...", re: 61—Across
41. Slippery ones
44. Ms. Horne

IT'S JUST A STAGE

48. Turns away
49. Send out
50. Ate away
52. "In fair round___ . . . ", re: 61— Across
53. Maximum; abbr.
55. Spanish gold
56. What gossips dish
57. "What's the big___?"
58. Type of fan mag
61. Surprised reaction
62. Garden tool
63. *Howards*___
64. Mr. Craven

CHAPTER

20

"No, Rosco, I *didn't* explain to Sara that I hadn't created the *It's Just A Stage* crossword. How could I? Truthfully, I didn't know what to tell her—especially in light of Lew Groslir's diatribe and his insistence that I keep her in the dark." Belle's shoulders were hunched, and her spine curved with what looked to Rosco like a sign of defeat. She sighed, then seemed to sink deeper into unhappy meditation while beneath her the bed's quilted blue coverlet appeared equally depressed. Both person and object looked as if all the stuffing had been pummeled out of them.

Rosco walked across the hotel room. He sat beside his wife, took her hand, and said, "I think you need to put all of this junk out of her head. Relax and go with the flow. It's the L.A. way."

"I'm trying to, but everything seems to just keep *fwapping* back at me."

"*Fwapping? Fwapping?* That's a word?"

Belle smiled—barely. "You know what I mean . . . Just when I'm trying to deal with Chick's death, when we all are,

Groslir's *gross* vitriol comes along . . . And then I make nice, only to find that someone's tampering with the crossword Darlessen had me construct for the show."

"But *fwapping*'s not a real term?" Rosco persisted.

"No . . . well, I don't believe so."

Rosco let out a small laugh as he slipped his other arm around Belle's waist. "Since when don't you know if a word is or is not the genuine article? This is sounding like serious meltdown to me."

Belle tried to smile again, but the effort was curtailed as tears came to her eyes. "Maybe I just don't care anymore, or maybe words just don't seem that important right now . . ." She shook her head. "First Chick . . . and then this Lew business . . . and all those threats about contracts. This isn't fun, Rosco. I've never had someone fight with me like that."

"No, it isn't fun . . ." He held her close, and the two remained silent for some minutes.

Outside their window, Ocean Avenue was also devoid of human sound. Dinner between the threesome of Belle, Rosco, and Sara was long since past. The older woman, still glowing with excitement and newfound stardom, had been safely tucked into her neighboring suite while the light drizzle that had kicked up earlier as they'd strolled along the Third Street Promenade had turned into a full-fledged winter rain. The spattering of drops against the glass was a noise Belle ordinarily found comforting. Tonight it had the reverse effect. *The rainy season in L.A. Who knew there was such a thing?* she thought.

"No, it's not fun," Rosco reiterated at length. "And I'm sorry I wasn't there when Groslir started attacking you. I probably would have punched him in the nose."

"Which would have landed us in the middle of a lawsuit." Belle sighed afresh. " 'I'll sue your butt' seems to be the phrase of choice around Hollywood."

"Okay," Rosco said after another momentary lull. "Let's take a look at what's really going on here."

"One homicide, one overly aggressive movie producer, two weird crosswords, and two peculiar accidents."

"Leaving Chick, Groslir, and Nan aside for the moment," Rosco said as he kicked off his shoes and flipped them across the room, "why don't we start with the crosswords, which truthfully don't seem remotely sinister to me . . . Or, to be honest, even *connected* to the other situations. You had the *Greetings!* puzzle first, and then this Shakespeare deal that Sara was handed today, neither of which seem any more suspicious than regular fan mail . . . Given the fact that you're out here as a celebrity in your own right—"

"I know, they're legit expressions of respect, and I shouldn't worry." Although Belle's reply seemed in agreement with Rosco's suggestion, her tone indicated the opposite was true.

"I'm not saying don't worry about the other issues. I'm simply suggesting we separate the crosswords from anything else connected to *Anatomy*."

"Okay . . ."

"That didn't sound overly enthusiastic." Rosco's arms now held his wife tight.

She looked into his face, so close, so familiar, so loving and kind. "Okay."

"Better. Not *great* acting yet, but better . . . Maybe Dean can give you some coaching. Or maybe Sara. She seems to have come a long way in just one day." He kissed Belle, and she kissed him back, straightening her spine and lifting her chin.

"Okay." She allowed herself a gentle, self-deprecating laugh. "Two pieces of anonymous crossword fan mail."

"That's the spirit," Rosco said. "Now . . . let's start with Groslir . . . Much as I think the guy's a jerk for browbeating you, he does have three signed contracts and legal precedents on his side."

Belle's mood reverted instantaneously, and her body language followed suit. "If I'd known how potentially dangerous it was to be part of this movie, Rosco, I would never have allowed Sara to come out here. That's what's really bothering me."

"Hold on there . . . One: Sara's her own person; nothing— and I mean *nothing*—would have prevented her from grabbing this chance at some campy entertainment. Two: if you're referring to Nan's accident, that's all it was. Unfortunate? Sure. Scary for everyone involved? Absolutely. But accidents can happen, Belle."

"What about the original 'Rosco'?"

"I'll bet car crashes occur so often in Southern California that folks don't even blink an eye any longer . . . Maybe that's why most people out here own multiple vehicles— because one's always in the body shop."

Belle didn't respond immediately; when she did, it was clear that Rosco's argument had had little effect. "I just don't have a good feeling about this situation. And I'm not talking about the Chick and Debra disaster."

"Sara's not in danger, Belle." Rosco tried for a reassuring chuckle. "Heck, if I'd thought this set—or anything remotely involved with spending a week in Los Angeles—was potentially harmful, I wouldn't have let you come out here, let alone Sara."

Belle raised her eyebrows. "Didn't I hear you mention something earlier about people making their *own* decisions?" Then she shook her head. "Something weird's going on, Rosco . . . I don't know what, but it's not good."

"Well, I vote we put all concerns on the back burner till tomorrow. There's nothing to be gained by stewing over it tonight."

"You just want to get me into bed," Belle said with a small chuckle. For the first time since their conversation had begun, her tone was not only relaxed but relieved.

"Did I say that?" He glanced around the room as if looking for a nonexistent witness to support his claim. "I never said that."

"It's all in the translation." She chortled again, then rose and began turning down the bed. "I miss home."

"You miss Kit, that's what you miss . . . and having to fight for space in your own bed. Thank goodness we only have one dog, that's all I can say."

"It's her bed, too, Rosco, in case she hasn't made that abundantly clear."

Rosco smiled. "I imagine Kitty believes that *she's* allowing us to sleep on *her* bed." Then his smile turned serious. "It's only a week, Belle. It'll be over before you know it, so let's try to make it fun."

"I know."

"And we're in this together."

"I know that, too." Belle walked back toward him, but before she could put her arms around his neck, the phone rang. Rosco reflexively reached for the receiver.

"Polycrates," he said as he looked at the clock on the bedside table. It was twenty past ten.

Two minutes ensued during which time Rosco remained mostly silent, mumbling "Uh-huh," a few times while a male voice on the other end of the line did nearly all the talking. Belle, standing close, could hear the man's staccato and persistent tone, but couldn't make sense of the words.

As soon as Rosco hung up, she asked, "Who's calling at this late hour?"

"Jillian Mawbry."

"Who?"

"Debra Marcollo's defense attorney. He'd like to have a word with me."

CHAPTER

21

Rosco had never been a morning person, but 7:30 A.M. panned out to be the only time he had available for Jillian Mawbry. And since he was still rolling along on East Coast time, it wasn't all that bad; the rest of the day would be spent with Sara on the *Anatomy* set. Because of the early hour, Mawbry's offices in Westwood were not yet open, so they'd agreed to meet at his home on Paula Avenue, just over the Burbank line in Glendale. Rosco had little trouble locating the house. It was a nicely maintained three bedroom ranch-style home with a decent-size lawn, but the neighborhood was wedged between the meeting point of the number 5 Freeway and the 134. The noise from the cars, trucks, and Harley-Davidsons was close to deafening.

Rosco parked the Mustang behind a black-and-gold pickup truck and debated whether to raise the convertible's top as he studied the less-than-quiescent scene. Two laborers spoke in Spanish while trimming the bushes in front of Mawbry's house while another man stood on the property's side walkway staring into a green box that Rosco guessed was a sprinkler control panel. All three looked like honest men, so Rosco opted to leave the top down. He stepped from the car, glanced at the words painted on the truck's door, and smiled. MARQUIS DE SOD LANDSCAPING—LET ME WHIP YOUR LAWN INTO SHAPE!

Rosco walked up the brick path toward the front door but was stopped by the man near the sprinkler box.

"He's out back. It's easier to go around the side."

"Thanks," Rosco said, then added an affable: "You're working early."

"I take advantage of the mornings and evenings; when the sun's hot and high, I take a siesta. It's the only way to keep from frying your brains."

Rosco nodded toward the pickup truck. "Great name . . . Are you the 'Marquis'?"

He nodded. "What can I say, people notice it. A name like that . . . You'd be surprised how many people hire me just because they like the sound of it." He extended his hand to Rosco. "I'm Max, Max Chugorro . . . You're not a producer, are you?"

Rosco laughed. "No, 'fraid not. In fact, I don't know the first thing about the movie business." He glanced down at his trousers and shoes. "Do I look like a producer?"

"Come to think of it, no. You're a little too rumpled . . . maybe a little too casual . . . I'd say you looked more like 'talent' than a 'suit.'"

"'A suit'?"

"A studio exec . . . That's what I like call producers and business-types like that. A suit's what distinguishes them from us working stiffs."

"I see."

"Actually, I do a little screenwriting on the side, so I try not to let any opportunity pass me by, just in case you were in on the production end. You guys from the East Coast have a different way of dressing."

Rosco didn't bother to ask how Max Chugorro had pegged him as an outsider; the flat "A" of a his Massachusetts accent was hard to mistake.

The landscaper/screenwriter cocked his thumb over his shoulder. "Mr. Mawbry's in the back on the terrace . . . All that brickwork's mine." Max handed Rosco a business card. "Let me know if you need anything done. I've got dynamite references. If you're not into home hardscaping or landscaping, pass the card along. In fact, if you don't live here, pass it along to someone who does."

"Will do."

Rosco strolled down the walkway to the rear of the house. There was a substantial stretch of lawn out back as well, along with a ten-by-twenty-foot brick patio surrounded by a low wall covered with molded concrete planters. Jillian Mawbry sat in a metal chair in front of a matching table. A pot of hot coffee, two cups, and a plate of rolls and bagels were before him. He was speaking on a cordless telephone and waved for Rosco to join him and help himself to coffee.

The attorney was younger than Rosco had expected; possibly Belle's age, which was thirty-one, but his reddish-brown hair had already begun to thin, and his skin was a greenish and unhealthy white. Although as tall as Rosco, his pale pink Ralph Lauren polo shirt hung slackly from his shoulders, and his arms had no more muscle definition than copper tubing. After a moment, Mawbry disconnected his call and offered Rosco a surprisingly flaccid and indifferent hand. For a moment, Rosco wondered whether the man was ailing.

"Sorry . . . My sister's getting a divorce. Second one in as many years. I wish she'd have the good sense to find richer husbands if she's going to dump them so quick."

Rosco wasn't sure if he should laugh, smile, or look sympathetic, so he remained poker-faced and said nothing.

"I appreciate you driving all the way over to the Valley. I would have come to Santa Monica, but I had 'The Marquis' scheduled to do some sprinkler work, and he needed to get into the house and my breaker box. And Max has not been an easy man to book lately. Ya gotta grab him when you can."

"Not a problem," Rosco said, raising his voice above the freeway din. "I've got a nice rental car. I like to drive, see new places."

"I know, I know, the noise here is enough to make you crazy. I'm putting the house on the market in the spring. Moving to the other side of the hill. I was nuts to buy this place . . . Anyway, let's get to it, shall we? What do you know about Debra Marcollo?"

Rosco shrugged. "Nothing really . . . She's been arrested for murdering Chick Darlessen . . . And you're her lawyer. That's about it."

"Let me step back a bit. Why do you think I've taken on this case? And it's not for the bucks; Debra Marcollo doesn't have a plugged nickel, so scratch any big fat fee."

"I don't suppose *altruism* would be the answer you're looking for?" Rosco smiled for the first time. Mawbry didn't, so Rosco pushed on. "It's no different in New England . . . This case has notoriety. So my guess is you probably had to pull a few strings in order to be retained . . . The big guns with their mugs in the papers couldn't have been far behind."

Mawbry laughed. "Darlessen's murder is small potatoes for heavy-duty trial lawyers, but you're right on one count: I had to pull a few strings. A case like this could put me on the map. Right up there with your notorious 'big guns.'"

"And you want me to do some investigative work."

It was a statement, not a question, but Mawbry responded with a surprisingly decisive, "Right."

"I'm not licensed to work in California; I assume you're aware of that? Why not get a local P.I.?"

Jillian Mawbry laughed, but the sound had a hollow ring as if the man were practicing human vocal responses. "A license doesn't mean jack as far as I'm concerned. What's a license signify? That you get to carry a gun, right? You won't need a weapon, legal or not, to help me out . . . And, as far as a local investigator's concerned? Forget it; you're already here. You're on the *Anatomy* set. You're part of the furniture, for pete's sake . . . Look. A new guy snooping around only puts people on edge. You? You're a tourist. Your wife's under contract for the show. You and the old lady are under contract, too, which makes you just another curious dude asking a few innocent questions."

Rosco didn't ask how Mawbry had learned about his or Belle's or Sara's studio contracts. L.A. was clearly a smaller and tighter-knit community than he'd originally believed. Instead, he poured himself a second cup of coffee. "What exactly are you looking for, Mr. Mawbry?"

"Jillian, please."

"Jillian."

"The answer to that question is *anything*. All I need is something that I can use to plant a strong reasonable doubt into the minds of a jury."

"From what I've been hearing, it sounds like the cops have Debra Marcollo dead to rights . . . fingerprints on the gun and a confession to the lifeguard."

"So, Polycrates, you do know quite a bit, after all."

"The news was all over the radio on my way here." Rosco took a sip of coffee and added. "I gather you feel Debra's innocent?"

"Who cares? What's that got to do with the price of eggs? The trick is to drag out the trial as long as possible . . . Work the press . . . Get my name out there. But if it makes you feel any better, yeah I think there *is* reasonable doubt, and I don't intend to lose the case."

"But she confessed . . ."

Jillian Mawbry opened a leather case that was sitting on the table. He removed a sheet of yellow legal paper. "Here's exactly what she said when she ran into that off-duty lifeguard on the beach Sunday night. I'm quoting from the guard's statement. 'He's dead, he's dead. I don't know how it happened. The gun . . . just went off. I don't know. I don't know why I did it.' You can give those words any reading you want, Rosco, but unless, you were there, it's impossible to determine intent because you didn't hear Debra's voice and tone. The only stickler is the sentence, 'I don't know why I did it.', and she maintains she was referring to leaving the house. In other words, she's claiming she didn't know why she ran from the house."

"And the fingerprints on the gun?"

"Darlessen had taken her out a few days earlier to give her a lesson in shooting. That's why her prints are there."

"And she has witnesses to that?"

"No."

"You mean there was no one else present at the shooting range when she took her practice shots?"

"What shooting range? They fired the gun into the Pacific Ocean."

Rosco raised his eyebrows. "And no neighbors came out when they heard the shots?"

"In Malibu? What are you, crazy? If they heard anything at all, they probably jumped under their beds and waited for the sun to come up. Look, Polycrates, everything the cops have is circumstantial, as far as I'm concerned. Their case can be picked apart, but I need some alternative scenarios. I need some other motives. Maybe even some other suspects. I have nothing against framing someone else if it means getting my girl off."

Rosco drummed his fingers on the table for a moment, then said. "Like who? If Debra didn't kill Chick, who did?"

Mawbry lifted his hands in the air and said facetiously, "I bet it was Max Chugorro, my landscape guy . . . Yeesh, how the hell do I know who killed the poor sap? That's why I'm asking you to help me out here. The folks who knew Darlessen work on that *Anatomy* set. All I'm suggesting is that you nose around a little . . . undercover of course. I don't have to tell you that. If anyone realizes you're working for me, they'll clam up pronto."

Both men were silent for a minute, then Mawbry added, "Listen Rosco, I need your help here. I can't get in to talk to those people. I never met Darlessen, but he was a screenwriter, and a successful one. There must have been plenty of people who wanted him dead. Maybe he stole the script from someone. Happens all the time out here."

Again Rosco drummed his fingers. "I don't know how it works in California, but in some states the Bar Association doesn't look favorably on members who hire unlicensed P.I.s. It can become a real ethics issue, and bound to catch up to you later on."

"Ethics?" Mawbry shrugged. "I'll be putting you on as a consultant. You'll be giving me advice, that's all." He smiled; this time there was nothing forced about the expression, although it remained curiously devoid of either warmth or levity. "There's a way around everything."

Rosco glanced at his watch, downed what was left of his coffee, and stood. "I'm going to have to think about your proposal, Mr. Mawbry."

"What? Money? Is that it? I'll be taking care of you personally. Don't let Debra's bank account frighten you off. What's your quote? Because whatever you get in Massachusetts, I'll double it. How's that?" Mawbry pulled a checkbook from his leather case and scribbled a check for two thousand dollars quicker than most people can write their signature.

Rosco raised his hand. "Save it. I'll let you know by tomorrow afternoon. And to be frank with you, Mr. Mawbry—"

"Jillian, please."

"Jillian . . . I'm not about to dig up dirt to get a guilty person off the hook. That's not how I work."

"Well, why don't we just say that Debra's innocent until proven guilty. I think that's how the law reads."

"Right. It reads the same way in Massachusetts. I'll give it some serious thought and get back to you tomorrow."

"I've got time. Not too much, though."

"I'll bear that in mind."

Rosco walked back down the side of the house toward his car. Max was still working on the sprinkler control box. He had five or six multicolored wires stripped at the ends and was alternately touching them to a "hot" terminal, then watching to see which sprinkler heads popped up and shot water across the front lawn. Rosco stopped and observed him working for a minute.

"It's a microcosm," Max said without turning to face his visitor, "and I play God. This lawn lives or dies depending on when, and how much, water I give it. If I do it right, it'll live forever; but if I lose control, it'll start dying off piece by piece. The situation's all about control. If someone else mucks around with my box, things begin to die a slow death." He looked at Rosco. "That's a nice Mustang. What'd she set you back?"

"It's a rental."

"I thought so. So if you're not a producer, what are you?"

Rosco thought for a second, then realized, *What the heck, this is L.A., I can be anything I want to be.* "I play second base for the Red Sox," he said, then ambled over to the Mustang without waiting to see Max Chugorro's reaction.

CHAPTER

22

Belle and Rosco didn't have a single moment alone together throughout the remainder of the day. Immediately following his interview with Jillian Mawbry, Rosco
had returned to Santa Monica, picked up Sara and Belle,
and driven them to Culver City. The moment they arrived
at the studio, the production crew swallowed them like
barracudas after minnows. After wardrobe and makeup, a
half dozen of Sara's scenes were shot; episodes involving
Shay, Quint, Carol, Dan, Ginger, and Andy Hofren. The
work had necessitated so many takes, retakes, and set and
costume changes that both morning and afternoon had
been consumed without Rosco ever being able to fully explain to his wife what Mawbry had wanted. It wasn't until
the close of the shooting day, when Sara was being enter-
tained at dinner by Dean Ivald, before husband and wife
found time to confer. They decided a little distance would
be necessary to catch their breath and have a serious, unin-
terrupted conversation.

The beach in Malibu was the place they chose. A long
stretch of sand and the steady thump of waves breaking on

the shore had always featured in their weightier discussions; and although California wasn't coastal Massachusetts, it would do in a pinch. Especially in the dark of early evening, when the lights spreading oceanside might be mistaken as emanating from weathered New England shingle cottages and not from modern hot tub-equipped decks.

"What do you say we swing by Darlessen's house?" Rosco suggested as they made a left from the P.C.H. onto Malibu Cove.

"We won't be able to go in, will we?" Belle asked. "What I mean is, Mawbry didn't give you a heads-up on investigating the place, did he? Or keys?"

"I only told him I'd *consider* his request, Belle. Nothing more. Meaning: No keys. The police will have cordoned off the bungalow, but no one's going to stop us from taking a stroll on the beach below it. And since this is L.A., maybe we'll pick up some vibes."

"Sounds good to me—I think," Belle answered, then she released a small and rueful chuckle. "The scene of the crime. What a charming place for a date."

"Lucky we're already married."

Belle chortled briefly again. "And that you're such a romantic guy."

"Dude."

"What?"

"Dude. That's what I am out here. From what I've been able to pick up from Jillian Mawbry and others, no male is simply a *guy.* He's gotta be 'big guy.' Or he's a *dude,* a *hunk,* a *bod*—"

"A *bod?* Dream on, honey lamb."

"Thank you for your expression of support."

"Don't mention it. Don't worry, if I had any problems with your *bod,* you would have heard about it a long time ago."

This lighthearted moment ended abruptly as Chick Darlessen's and Debra Marcollo's home came into view. Yellow crime-scene tape festooned the cedar walls making the place look like a giant gift box wrapped in yard upon yard of a particularly garish ribbon. Rosco passed the house and parked farther along the sandy lane. Then he and Belle sat in silence before stepping onto the roadway.

"What a sad sight," Belle murmured as Rosco's professional gaze began assessing entrances, exits, approaches, the proximity of neighbors, and Mawbry's account of why only Debra Marcollo's prints had been found on the murder weapon.

"A 'reasonable doubt,'" he muttered under his breath, and Belle echoed the phrase. It was obvious that neither of them was comfortable with the present situation.

In the dim light, they instinctively reached their hands toward one another and they began moving toward the building where Chick Darlessen had been murdered. "I've got to tell you that I'm not at all happy about what you told me about this Jillian Mawbry character," Belle finally admitted. "He sounds like he's simply out to make a name for himself."

"You won't get any argument from me on that count."

"Meaning you could be 'consulting' on the part of the guilty person, Rosco. You'd be defending a murderer—"

"If she *did* kill Chick," Rosco repsonded. "That's the question . . . because if she *didn't* . . ."

Belle released a trouble sigh. "You've always been on the right side, Rosco. You've never willingly protected or abetted an unjust—"

"Right, but what if Debra's telling the truth, as Mawbry sort of seems to believe?"

"'Sort of seems to believe?' I think you're proving my point . . . And, 'I don't know why I did it,' sure sounds like a confession of homicide to me."

"Which is what the police believe and the prosecution will likely hammer home. And it's the lifeguard's interpretation."

Belle shook her head. "You heard the rumors that flew around the set yesterday, Rosco. Every one of them pointed to the fact that Debra had plenty of reasons to despise Chick."

"Rumors and hearsay are not the same as conclusive evidence when it comes to homicide."

"I realize that, but abused women often—"

"That story's circumstantial, Belle. Mawbry wasn't talking about an abusive situation."

She swiftly countered. "It sounds to me as if he spent most of his time discussing himself and his own motives for wanting this case, and how badly he needs it to succeed."

Rosco didn't respond for a moment. "*Succeed* was not one of Mawbry's words; *elongate* would be more like it. Look, I'm not suggesting Mawbry's an angel. In fact, I'd say he was more like a carrion bird, but I keep returning to this 'reasonable doubt' thing—"

"Which he said is only a tactic to sway the jury."

"That's right. That's what he told me . . . But he also alluded to the fact that he believed it to be a legitimate defense . . . Which brings me back full circle to the notion that Debra might be telling the truth."

"I don't know, Rosco. 'The gun . . . just went off' doesn't seem like a statement issued by an innocent person—"

"No, it doesn't . . . But our legal system is based on the premise of innocent until proven guilty, a point made by Mawbry."

Again, neither spoke for several long minutes. Around them, the sand continued to cool while the waves, lit here and there by high-wattage deck illumination, glowed an eerie and veiny green as they rose into the night sky and then crashed down upon the shore.

"It sounds as if you've decided to accept Jillian Mawbry's offer," Belle said at length, and Rosco's reply was equally slow in coming.

He shrugged. "Hey, you know me, I'm intrigued. I don't see how I can refuse."

"By saying, 'Thanks, but no thanks, Mr. Mawbry'?" Belle

quipped before reverting to her serious mode. "Well, if Debra didn't kill her boyfriend, then who did?"

"I guess that's what I'm going to attempt to discover." Rosco paused and looked up at Darlessen's dark and deserted house. "Unfortunately, if Debra *does* turn out to be the guilty party, then I'm stuck between a rock and a hard place."

"What do you mean?"

"If I discover conclusive proof that Debra did kill Chick, I'll be under a confidentiality agreement, and therefore, unable to take what I've learned to the police."

"Do you think that's what Mawbry has up his sleeve? He's only putting you on knowing you'd probably ask questions anyway? Do you think he's really trying to handcuff you? Trying to silence you?"

"I guess time will tell."

CHAPTER

23

By Wednesday morning, a sense of a new beginning had been established for the cast and crew of *Anatomy of a Crossword*. Having managed to make it through all of Tuesday without a single accident, death, or similar calamity befalling them, the players showed up bright and early with relatively uplifted and buoyant attitudes. No one spoke any longer about a "jinxed set," while Sara's performances of the previous two days had everyone wondering if the Nan DeDero "mishap" hadn't been a blessing in disguise: no more flubbed lines, no more temperamental outbursts, no more rude comments to "lowly" second assistant directors, no more sniping at the makeup women because of their own "tacky" hair styles and acrylic fingernails, and no more lengthy monologues consisting of every four letter word in the book. Even Lew Groslir had settled down and had opted to invite Belle and Rosco into his private studio office to present his version of an apology.

"I hope you're not upset with my little outburst on Monday," he began, but as neither Belle nor Rosco responded with anything more than minuscule shrugs, he continued

with a hurried and clearly rehearsed, "Of course, I was devastated by Chick's death, like everyone else—absolutely
devastated. I guess that's why you might have considered
my behavior somewhat . . . irrational. But that's the TV
business." He chuckled slightly. "The pressure can be astro-
nomical. Only the strong survive, that's what I like to say."
Lew directed his next round of statements at Belle. "I'm
sure you're feeling a lot of pressure as well, and I want to say
that as far as I'm concerned, you're handling it wonderfully.
You're very good at controlling your emotions, and I have
yet to hear one negative thing about you. Not one. Believe
it or not, people seem to like you."

"That's reassuring," Belle answered in a droll tone.

"I guess what I'm trying to say is that I'd like to see us all
on a little friendlier turf from here on out. I think it'll make
for a much smoother shoot."

"I have to tell you, Lew," Rosco said as his eyes narrowed,
"that I'm one of those husbands who gets—in your words—
'somewhat irrational' when people fail to treat his wife with
a certain amount of respect."

"And am I ever with you on that point, Rosco! Absolutely. I have no patience with rude behavior. None whatsoever. That's why I'm happy to see our cast and crew
getting along with Belle here. Hollywood can be a cruel
place if the powers that be take it into their minds to go after you . . . Well then . . ." Lew slapped the palms of his
hands on his thighs, glanced at his watch, and stood. "Now
that we've gotten that little problem straightened out, I'm
afraid I have a meeting in Burbank in half an hour. So I'll
leave you two love birds to enjoy the rest of the day's shoot.
Be sure to close the door when you leave." Lew turned and
walked out of the room.

Belle looked at Rosco, and said, "Gosh, I feel so much
better after all that. What a darling man."

Rosco laughed. "Shall we go back to the set and enjoy the
day's shoot?"

"Why not? That's an interesting choice of words: *shoot,*

especially since they're *shooting* the death scene today . . ." She stood, shaking her head as she glanced at the desk and chair Lew Groslir had just vacated. "Did I tell you they changed the script? I guess it was in Chick's final rewrites . . . Anyway, now Dan Millray's character, 'Edison,' is shot rather than suffocated with a pillow as things actually occurred back in Vermont."

Rosco raised an eyebrow. "Why would they change the real story?" he asked as the couple left Groslir's office and strolled toward the stairway.

"Dean explained it as 'shock value.' Blood sells better than a plain old blue face. 'Nothing like a quick bullet to the chest to wake folks up,' according to our director."

"But in the true incidence, we had the big 'cause of death' question . . . There was the issue of a potential poisoning with the recipe in the crossword, as well the brief possibility that the dead man had simply succumbed from natural causes."

"I guess *subtle* isn't what Dean is shooting for—"

"So to speak."

As Belle and Rosco disappeared into the stairwell, the key grip, Don Schruko, was huddled with the special effects coordinator, Bubba Screter, at a worktable outside the makeup room. Beside the table stood a clothing rack holding five identical pairs of pajamas. Each was blue silk paisley, and each had a small hole, the size of a dime, cut into the left breast pocket.

On the table in front of the two men sat five thin plastic packets filled with crimson "stage" blood.

"This shouldn't take me more than another ten minutes," the special effects coordinator said as he began rigging the blood packs with explosive charges that had been outfitted with tiny radio receivers. "All I need to do is focus the blood splatter so that it'll fly straight out of the breast pocket hole, then Velcro the packets into the pajamas and spot-paste these paisley dots back over the openings." He chortled. "Dean better be able to get this shot in five takes, because after that, we're out of clean pj's."

Schruko also laughed. "If this director can't kill Dan Millray in five takes, we'll have to get out the real bullets." He picked up one of the packets and examined the explosive charge. "What about blow-back, Bubba? If this thing fires inward, instead of out, our actor's going to have a nice little hole in his chest."

Bubba Screter took the packet from Schruko. "Sorry, buddy, nobody handles these but me. I don't want any screw-ups on my watch. To answer to your question, each blood pack will be backed with a sheet of aluminum, and I'll also be taping a Kevlar shield across Dan's chest under his pajamas. It'd never stop a real bullet, but your actor's got nothing to worry about."

"Sounds good to me. I'll be on the set. Let me know when you're ready for our 'dead man.'"

"Ten minutes, max."

Schruko returned to the set where he found Dean Ivald and Dan Millray discussing the murder scene. The stage had been dressed to resemble a third floor guest room in a Vermont country inn. The wall and "ceiling" adjacent to the dormer windows sloped inward, as if beneath the building's eaves, while the "view" of the "snowy fields" was lit with a bluish light intended to resemble deepest night in a secluded place. Lace curtains hung beside the glass panes. The lace motif was repeated in the canopy of the "antique" pine bed, a bureau scarf, and square doilies resting on the two night stands. Seating for this cozy "guest room" consisted of recessed window benches and a Queen Anne–style wing chair, while the backdrop walls were adorned with a subdued rose print paper. The only jarring element to this tranquil scene was a .38 caliber revolver. It sat on a prop table to the left of the set.

Schruko approached the director as the lighting designer walked across the elevated catwalk, making her final adjustments to the fixtures clamped onto the grid.

"Mr. Schruko, are we ready to shoot this sucker yet?" Ivald asked.

"Just waiting for the go-ahead from Bubba. Less than ten minutes." Schruko looked at Millray. "He's going to need to tape you, Dan, and suit you up. Bubba's over by makeup. If you're ready, maybe you should be in with him."

The actor ambled toward makeup, and Dean Ivald turned his attention to the principal camera where the cinematographer was in the midst of attaching a white tape measure to the lens in order to gauge the distance between the bed and film plane. Behind the camera, most of the cast and crew had arrived to watch the scene: Quinton Hanny, Ginger Bradmin, Shay Henlee, Carol Von Deney, Louis Gable, Miso Lane, Andy Hofren, Madeline Richter, and Jes Nadema were all there. Sara, Belle, and Rosco had joined them. Even Nils Spemick, the casting director, recently returned from San Francisco, had put in an appearance.

"Ahh," Dean said with a broad smile, "nothing like a bloody good murder to bring out the flock . . . Well, everyone get nice and comfy, and keep the chat down to a minimum, even though I'll be shooting this M.O.S."

Belle leaned toward Rosco and whispered, "M.O.S.?"

He shrugged. "Beats me?"

Shay Henlee, who was standing directly behind them, supplied the answer. "M.O.S. stands for without sound. Since no one has speaking lines, Dean will simply shoot the scene, and lay in the gunshot and ambient noises later."

"Not to appear overly dense, but shouldn't it be W.O.S. then?" Rosco asked.

"Legend has it that the term originated with a German director who continually pronounced the order *mit out sound* . . . so M.O.S. stuck in the business."

"If Dean's filming without sound," Belle wondered aloud, "why is he bothering to put blanks in the gun?"

"I imagine it's so that flame and smoke is seen coming out of the barrel, but I'm not sure."

"Okay people," Ivald shouted, "just because this is going to be M.O.S. doesn't mean we won't be firing the murder weapon, so plug your ears if you must. And no screaming, my nerves can't take it . . . Can I get Andy Hofren up here please?"

"Andy Hofren plays the killer," Belle whispered to Rosco.

"I can see why he needs to shoot Dan Millray instead of smothering him," Rosco observed with a chuckle. "He's half the guy's size. If Andy had to wrestle Millray with a pillow—as it really happened—it wouldn't be an easy task."

Dean Ivald and Andy Hofren moved to the prop table where the director picked up the .38 and handed it to the actor. "Ever fired a single action revolver before?"

"Oddly enough, no," Andy replied as he rolled the gun in his hands. "On my last film, we used Uzis and AK-47s. Before that, it was semiautomatics—Glocks mostly. On *New York Nightmare,* I carried a Beretta, but a few actors had .357s and 9mms. I shot a Tommy gun once. On *Death By A Mile,* it was a sniper's rifle, of course—a 30-06, a real beaut. And on *Range Wars,* because it was a Western, we had 30-30s and cap and ball .36s. Naturally, we were given M16s on—"

"Thanks, Andy," Dean interrupted as he retrieved the gun. "Now, you're not actually *in* this shot. Only your arm appears, and you'll be in the same shirt you're wearing when the cops nab you . . . All I want our audience to see is your hand coming into the frame with the pistol. It'll be a nice, tight shot. Quick. Clean . . . You'll have the .38 about seven feet from Dan's chest; on my cue, you'll fire. One shot only. Bubba Screter will be on the remote control and blow up the blood pack inside the pajamas at the same moment . . . You'll be firing blanks, of course, but I want to catch the flame as it emerges from the barrel. That, mixed with the flying blood, should give us a super visual."

"Sounds easy enough."

"We have five pairs of pajamas rigged, so I'll roll film,

then let Schruko get things cleaned up after each shot, and then we'll go again."

"We'll be doing all five takes?"

"Absolutely. I love this stuff . . . What's your preference, left or right?"

"I voted for Bush . . . both of them, actually."

Dean Ivald stared at him for what seemed like an eternity, then shook his head slowly. "No, no, are you left-handed or right-handed?"

"Oh. Right-handed."

"Good. Because I want the gun to come in on the left side of my frame, then fire, creating the illusion of the bullet traveling from left to right. The action should follow the same direction as the eye does when reading a book."

"No *problemo*. I like the literary reference, by the way."

Dean returned the gun to the prop table. "Also, make certain you're pointing directly at Millray's heart. He'll be wearing protection over his chest, but nowhere else. These blanks shoot a mean paper wad out the barrel, and I don't want to see him get hit in the eye with the damn thing. We've had enough problems already. And I also want that gun-barrel-to-heart angle perfect."

"The kill shot, right?" Andy said with a laugh.

Dean sighed. "Right, Andy." Then the director stepped back onto the set, and gazed up at the catwalk. "Can we start that snow falling outside the windows? And give me a full moon, too. I want to get a peek at it through the camera lens."

A voice from nowhere said, "Check," and Dean walked over to Belle and Rosco and said, with a fair amount of pride, "Well, folks, how's it looking?"

Belle replied, "Just like the real place."

"Miso and his Polaroid—the man's a genius. Well, you two are in for a real treat. Have you ever seen someone getting shot before?"

"A couple of times," was Rosco's quiet response. "When I was with the Newcastle Police Department. It's never a pretty sight. You don't realize how powerful a gun is until you see someone's flesh being ripped apart by a bullet. That's one reason I tend not to carry a gun. I prefer to see things done with minimal bloodshed."

Dean's jaw dropped open, and he remained speechless for a long moment. Finally he said, "No. No. I'm talking about the movies here, Rosco. Have you ever seen how we shoot someone on film? Not . . . not in real life."

"Nope, I never have."

The director sighed and shook his head again, then returned his concentration to the set. "What do you think of that snow? Makes you cold just looking at it, doesn't it?"

"I was going to ask about that," Belle said. "If you have a full moon, how can it be snowing?"

Ivald studied the scene. "Well, we have to light the 'exterior' somehow, otherwise we get black windows, glare from the stage lights . . ." He continued to gaze at the windows, then said, "No, I like it. I like the snow with the blue light. I like a full moon. I like the way it highlights each one of the snow flakes. We keep it. It works for me. You know what I call it?"

"No."

"Artistic license."

CHAPTER

24

Bubba Screter pulled what looked like a small portion of a flexible gladiator's breastplate out from under his special effects worktable and bent it around Dan Millray's exposed chest.

"Looks good," he said. "If you can hold it there, Dan, I'll tape it in place."

"Kevlar, huh? Is this the stuff the cops wear? Kind of thin, isn't it?"

"Oh, yeah, the cops' stuff is much thicker. This piece here will only protect you from possible blow-back from the blood pack and the paper wad from the blanks. It'd never stop a real bullet. Not a .38, that's for damn sure."

Bubba took a wide roll of white athletic tape and began securing the Kevlar to the actor's chest.

Dan laughed. "I haven't seen tape like that since I was a linebacker at Northwestern. Does it come off any easier nowadays, or does it still rip all the hair from your body?"

"It's no different. Do you want to shave your chest first?"

Dan rolled his eyes and groaned. "Thanks, Bubba, I'll take my chances."

After the Kevlar was fastened, Dan slipped into a pair of the silk pajamas. Bubba checked the positioning of his handiwork against the Kevlar. He double-checked the aluminum safety plate and the angle of the radio receiver's small antenna. When he was happy that everything looked perfect, he buttoned up the pajamas. "Okay, buddy-boy," he said, "time to meet the Grim Reaper."

The two men made a quick stop at the prop table, then stepped onto the set and checked in with Dean Ivald, as Bubba's assistant followed close behind with the clothes rack and the four remaining pairs of pajamas. Bubba carried the remote control box he would use to ignite the five blood packs; each charge was tuned to a different frequency.

The set had been transformed slightly to give it a "slept in" look. A pair of tweed trousers, rumpled shirt, bow tie, braces, shoes, socks, and a camel-hair sports jacket had been scattered across the floor. The quilt on the canopy bed had been pulled back and jumbled up to make it appear as if Dan had been sleeping restlessly. One of the pillows had also been tossed onto the floor and the alarm clock knocked over. Miso Lane was busy taking Polaroid photographs to make certain there was continuity between the five different takes.

"Okay, Danno," Ivald said, "let's have you on the bed, shall we?"

Millray crossed over to the bed, reclined on his back, and made himself comfortable. Bubba Screter followed and rechecked his blood pack to be certain it hadn't shifted in position now that the actor was lying down. A makeup man approached, mussed up Dan's hair, and lacquered it in place with hair spray. Miso Lane materialized once again, and snapped a Polaroid of Dan's new sleep-heavy and rumpled appearance.

"Now, Dan," Ivald continued, "remember that you drank far too much *vino* before going to bed. You left your wife stewing on the couch downstairs, and your sleep had been restless. We want to play up the poisoning subplot we established earlier in the film so that the audience is kept guessing as to how you'll be killed—right up to the moment Andy fires the gun." The director turned toward the camera and lights. "All right, people, let's settle down, we're going to rehearse this once." He turned back to Millray. "I may want to shoot this from more than one angle, Danno, so try to give me the same tossing and turning with each take, will you? It'll make life much more pleasant in the editing room."

Dan gave Ivald a thumbs up sign. The director stepped behind the camera and shouted, "Andy? Can I get Andy Hofren in here?"

Hofren arrived with the pistol gripped tightly in his right hand. Ivald looked down at him, scrutinized the height at which the cinematographer had selected for his camera, then shouted, "Mr. Schruko, can we get a box in here for Mr. Hofren?"

As if anticipating the director's every wish, the key grip was there in five seconds. He carried a foot-high wooden box and set it at Andy's feet. The actor stepped onto it, raising his right arm up to the same level as the camera's lens.

"All right," Ivald said, "now we're cooking. Andy, I want to let Dan have about fifteen seconds of tossing and turning. When I give you the word, you'll bring the gun into frame from the left side of the camera here. You'll hold it long enough to establish a menacing presence for the audience, and then on my cue, you'll fire it. Only once. I want this to look very clean . . . very premeditated. Remember your motivation . . . And don't fire the gun for the rehearsal. Lets save the fireworks for the actual takes, shall we?"

"You got it," Andy said.

"All right, people, can we settle down? We're rehearsing." Ivald waited for the background chatter to fade, then continued. "All set, Danno?"

"You bet."

"Okay, then. And . . . action!"

Dan rolled first to his left, then to his right. His eyes

were closed, but his brow was furrowed as though he were in the midst of a horrendous nightmare. His lips trembled and he began to mumble a string of incomprehensible words. Ivald allowed Dan to toss and turn for the fifteen seconds, occasionally saying, "Beautiful, Danno," or "I love it," or "Right on the money," while he checked the scene through a small video monitor that displayed exactly what the camera would record on film. And when the time was right Ivald said, "Okay, Andy, slowly bring the .38 into frame . . . That's it . . . a little farther . . . And . . . hold it right there . . . Perfect . . . And here we go . . . And . . . bang!" He clapped his hands together to simulate the gunshot.

"Beautiful. Andy, hold the gun there for a beat so we'll be able to see the smoke rising from the barrel . . . And . . . one thousand one, one thousand two . . . And . . . cut! Beautiful, people, beautiful. We're going to shoot this one."

Ivald then walked around the camera, crossed the set, and sat on the bed. "It looked super, Danno, but you're going to need to give me something when that bullet slams into your chest. You can't just lie there like nothing happened. Don't make it too large, but I do need a reaction."

"Absolutely. I'm saving my energy for the takes. I don't want to blow everything I've got on a rehearsal, do I?"

"Right." Ivald patted him on the leg. "Not too large or too long. Death should be almost instantaneous . . . Well, with that said . . . good night, sweet prince." The director returned to his place behind the camera. "Okay, this'll be picture, folks. Everyone back to one, please."

"Where's the .38?" Andy called out to Dean.

"What?"

"The gun. It's gone. I set it here on the camera dolly when I went over to get a drink of water, and now it's not there."

"Oh, honestly!" Ivald groaned, "What else can go wrong?" He turned to shout to cast and crew, but Don Schruko tapped him on the shoulder before he could speak.

"I have it right here, Dean," the grip said. His expression was tense and stern as he handed Andy the .38. "Safety first on my sets. I wanted to be sure the blanks were set properly before we start pointing guns at people."

"Good, fine, can we finally shoot this baby?" Ivald demanded, the impatience in his voice could be heard across the entire sound stage. Schruko stepped behind a lighting stand without responding and joined the crowd of actors and techies.

"All right, boys and girls . . . Here we go," Dean bellowed. "Roll camera."

"Rolling."

An assistant director stepped in front of the camera and held up a small black chalk board that read ANATOMY OF A CROSSWORD, SCENE NINETY-EIGHT, TAKE ONE, then retreated to his position behind the camera.

"Okay, Danno, die like a man," Dean said. "And here we go . . . And . . . action!"

Dan repeated his movements precisely as he had in the rehearsal; rolling first left then right, and grimacing his way through the nightmare. And again, when the time was right, Dean talked Andy through the firing of the gun.

"All right, Andy, bring the pistol into frame . . . Slowly . . . Slowly . . . Another inch or so . . . Perfect . . . Hold it right there . . . And on my signal . . . one thousand one . . . one thousand two . . . Fire!"

The explosion reverberated throughout the studio. The noise was deafening. Despite Ivald's orders, one of the make-up women screamed, then immediately covered her mouth in embarrassment while Bubba Screter triggered the blood pack in perfect synchronization. The thick red liquid spewed upward from Dan's chest, splattering the sheets and saturating the front of his silk pajamas while the actor's head shot back into the pillow. Then his eyes opened momentarily in shock and horror as his left hand stroked the front of the pajamas. He brought his bloodied palm up to eye level, surveyed the carnage, looked to the ceiling, and sank back motionless on the bloodied sheets.

"Okay . . . Hold it . . . Hold it . . ." Ivald said, elongating each word as the shot rolled on. "Zoom in closer, now . . . Andy, pull the gun slowly from the frame. That's it. Zoom in still closer on Dan. Give me a tight close-up on the dead man's face. And freeze it . . . And . . . And . . . cut! That was beautiful, people, absolutely beautiful. Mr. Schruko, get this mess cleaned up. We'll go again from one in ten minutes. On the money, Danno, on the money."

But Millray wasn't moving. And as stage hands began to re-dress the set, he remained completely motionless.

Ivald shouted, "Let's go, Danno, no sleeping on the job. Get yourself washed up and into a fresh set of pjs—PDQ."

Miso Lane took a quick Polaroid of Millray, then screeched, "O my God, he's not breathing! Dean! Dean, get over here! I think he's dead!"

Shay Henlee let out a bloodcurdling scream and whirled toward the costume room. Quinton hurried toward her. Everyone else stood frozen in shock.

Instinctively Rosco pushed his way past the actors and jogged over to the bed. When he got there, Dean and Miso were staring at the limp body.

"How could this happen?" Ivald mumbled. "Didn't Schruko say that he'd . . ."

Rosco wedged himself between the two men, grabbed Dan Millray's left wrist, and checked for a pulse. Then he let the arm drop.

"Strong as an ox," he said.

Dan's eyes popped open, and he sat up in the bed. "Hey, can't anyone around here take a joke?"

Miso laughed tenuously while Ivald gritted his teeth and released a weary sigh. "Actors . . . They'll be the death of me, yet . . . Get yourself cleaned up, Mr. Barrymore. Then we'll take it from the top."

The next four takes went smoothly, and without additional practical jokes. Dan died in an identical fashion from three different angles, and Ivald broke the cast and crew for lunch. But as Rosco and Belle began walking toward the studio door on their way to the commissary, the director called them back.

"Can I talk to you both in private?" he said, then led them toward a quiet corner of the studio where they were out of earshot of the departing cast members.

"What's up?" Rosco asked.

In answer, Dean Ivald pulled several objects from a shirt pocket and held them in his open palm. "I assume you recognize these."

Rosco nodded. "Slugs from a .38. The real thing, not blanks."

"Don Schruko just handed them to me. He found them in the pistol when he checked it before the first take."

"What?" Belle stammered. "Are you suggesting that someone was actually trying to kill Dan Millray?"

"I don't know what I'm suggesting, other than the fact that someone brought live ammunition onto my set and, I assume, intended to use it."

CHAPTER

25

Gerry Orso and Stan McKenet had every daily newspaper from Los Angeles, Ventura, Santa Barbara, and Orange counties spread across the surface of the round conference table in one of the second floor production rooms adjacent to the *Down & Across* set. Daily issues of *Variety* were there as well. The two men had been pouring over each page repeatedly for the last hour or so, as if they were terrified they'd miss something—which, in fact, they were.

"Nope," Orso announced at last. "Nada. Nothing. Zip."

"What about the obit pages?" McKenet demanded.

Gerry Orso gave the show's producer a look that indicated his displeasure at being taken for such a simpleton. "That's where I started, Stanley." He stretched the name out into two overly long syllables, Oliver Hardy fashion. "We have a dead man. We go to the obituaries. That's where we usually find our family histories. Next of loving kin . . ." The smile pasted across his tanned face was vulpine, almost evil, and it made his teeth look whiter and sharper than normal teeth. This less-than-cheery expression remained frozen in place for a second or two before vanishing into his beige-toned cheeks. The Gerry Orso of the big shmooze and the enthusiastic glad-to-see-all-my-happy-fans handshake was nowhere in evidence.

"Just asking," McKenet said sourly. "I like to be covered." As he spoke, he tapped a handmade loafer on the floor. The leather was a rich mahogany color and looked as thin and supple as the skins used to bind expensive books. The foot inside this pricey piece of apparel was surprisingly small and balletic for such corpulent man. McKenet tapped his foot again. The movement turned into a nervous tic.

"Well, don't ask," was Orso's acerbic response.

"Hey, am I the producer here or what?"

"In name, McKenet. In name only. Before you try to treat me like you do the rest of the staff, just keep in mind who owns what percentage of this show."

"As if you'd ever let me forget."

"*Down & Across* is successful because I make it a success, Stan." The tone was cold and clipped. "Because all the people out there in TV-Land love me. You bring in a clown like what's-his-name on *Million Dollar Mayhem*, just watch your ratings plummet."

"Yeah, yeah, if I hadn't taken a flyer and hired you as the show's replacement host, you'd still be down and out, believe me."

"Don't be too sure about that—"

"Down and out just like you howl at all the losers you take such pleasure in tossing off the show."

Gerry Orso's tight smile flickered across his face again. "Everyone loves beating up on eggheads, you know that, Stanley. It's as American as beating up on—" He looked at McKenet's busy foot. "Would you stop doing that? You're making *me* nervous."

"You? Ha!" McKenet was about to say more, but the door to the production room, the place "high in the heavens," as Harriet Tammalong liked to say, suddenly swung open, and Rolly Hoddal, the show's aging warm-up comic, appeared.

"Oh . . . say, sorry Mr. McKenet . . . Ger . . . I didn't . . . No one told me you were . . . I mean, wow, I thought . . ." The man swung there unsteadily, blinking rapidly as if trying to pull the producer and star into focus.

"Get out of here, Rolly," Orso and McKenet ordered in unison, and the comic backed away. Gerry followed it up with, "Yeah, take a hike, will ya?"

"Sure . . . I mean, I didn't know . . . Catch you later." He bumped hard into the wall as he exited.

"I wonder what controlled substance Rolly's into this time," Gerry said as he rose to lock the door.

"Who cares? The guy's cheap. Does his gig and doesn't ask questions . . . And he's loyal."

"I wonder why the hell he wanted to get into this room. Doesn't make sense."

That observation momentarily silenced McKenet. He frowned, then hastily began gathering up the newspapers as Gerry returned to the table. "Like he said, he didn't think the room was in use."

"You believe everything you hear, Stan? You start listening to people like Rolly Hoddal, you'll be in the funny farm before you know it."

"Look, Orso, I've got more on my plate than stewing over what that lousy comic's up to. He's probably got a bottle stashed in here somewhere." He stared down at the papers. "No relatives listed in any of the pieces on Darlessen, huh?"

"Only the bit about the poor Irish granny who raised little 'Chickie,' and how she started life working as a 'scullery maid' for a rich family back East . . . the rags-to-riches slant. Poor old crone, by heart bleeds . . . Brings tears to my eyes. She shoulda got herself on *Queen for a Day* . . . May she rest in peace." This time Orso grinned—a cat with a canary, a fox with a juicy dead hen. "Not one mention of Bartann Welner, which is a plus, and there aren't any little Chickie-Chickie Darlessens running around either. Meaning one

timely homicide is about to make two well-deserving producers a million bucks richer."

McKenet chuckled, and his nervous toes suddenly grew
still. "Here's to Debra Marcollo!"

"Couldn't have asked for a more perfect babe," Gerry
Orso agreed. "Here's to our fall-gal, Dipsy-Debbie."

"And another grateful nod to Bartann Welner and his
skunk of a nephew who are now both at last 'down' and very
much 'out.' "

Orso's smile suddenly disappeared. "We're forgetting
someone. A real potential thorn in our side, too."

McKenet chortled again. "Who?"

"We're forgetting Wanda Jorcrof. She's bound to resurface sooner or later."

McKenet paused for the briefest of seconds. "Not to
worry, Ger . . . She'll be a piece of cake."

Orso only stared at him.

"A piece of cake, Ger . . . like I said. I know how to silence Ms. Wanda Jorcrof . . . permanently. All I need to do
is find her. She was thrown out of her West Hollywood
joint. Went back on her rent's what I heard." Then McK-
enet's glance moved to the floor, momentarily resting on his
handsome shoes before drifting toward the other man's
footwear. "You know, Ger, those Guccis you've got on . . .
Well, how can I put it? They're kind of passé. You should
visit my shoemaker. He'll set you up, hand-stitch whatever
you want. When you're in the chips, you should dress the
part."

"I represent the common man, Stanley."

Stan McKenet threw back his wide head and laughed until he wept. "You kill me, Orso. You wouldn't be sitting in
this room with me right now if that were the case. The common man can drop dead as far as you're concerned."

"I'm the common man who just found himself five hundred grand richer than he thought." Then Gerry Orso's gaze
shifted from the producer's still-merry face to the door. "I

don't like it that Rolly Hoddal's skulking around up here. What's he up to?"

McKenet stood, stretching upward in his petite and well-shod feet. "You worry too much, Orso. I say, let's be grateful for what we got." He raised an invisible glass. "To Debra Marcollo's dearly departed boyfriend. What a terrible, terrible tragedy!"

Across

1. 60s grp.
4. Ms. Fabray, to friends
7. With 24-Across & 39-Down, Spacey flick
10. With 26-Across, Gibson flick
13. Fisherman's aid
14. Globe
15. Charged particle
16. *Where the Boys___*
17. With 54-Across, Curtis flick
20. Dealer's nemesis; abbr.
21. Gather up
22. Classic dictionary; abbr.
23. ___*Streets;* De Niro flick
24. See 7-Across
26. See 10-Across
27. Wire measure
28. Aug–Oct link
29. Normal school? abbr.
31. Stage whisper
34. Carmen___
36. "Under My Thumb" group, familiarly
37. CIA predecessor
40. *Ozzie &___*
42. She sheep
43. Reliable
45. 5-Down, e.g.
46. "A___ of Honey"
47. Summer at 5-Down
48. Hotel or cloth add-on
51. Bad review
52. Teary
54. See 17-Across
56. "___there, done that"
58. Lt.'s school
59. Tight
60. Mandela's grp.
61. Tracy flick
65. It's a dying company
66. Syr. neighbor
67. Ms. Grant
68. It can be slippery
69. Football scores; abbr.
70. Mr. Knotts
71. TV flick; abbr
72. Aves. & sts.

Down

1. Road blocks
2. Subdue
3. Agitate
4. Japanese drama
5. L'___ de Triomphe
6. Lakers org.
7. Mildew remover
8. Worked in the garden
9. *The___,* Reynolds flick
10. Ms. Kahn
11. Space
12. Mr. Jones
18. Hearst grp.
19. Deal memo; abbr.
23. Japanese soup
25. Take a load off
26. *The Ghost and Mrs.___*
27. Mr. Broderick
30. One-horse carriage
32. Morning wetness
33. Brooklyn or computer add-on
35. Mr. Parseghian
36. Religious group
37. Giant slugger
38. Spanish Mrs.
39. See 7-Across
41. Sore

WHAT'S IN A NAME?

44. Ollie's partner
48. More idiotic
49. Brought out
50. Honey badgers
52. Reason for revenge
53. "___ me no questions, . . ."
55. Week-glance connection

56. James "Maverick" role
57. Sir Geraint's wife
58. Italian bear
61. Bridge statement
62. It can be slippery
63. New prefix
64. Mr. Ayres

CHAPTER

26

The crossword puzzle had been burning a hole in Belle's purse almost since the moment she'd removed it from her in-box. It had been carefully tucked beneath a cast memo that she'd casually picked up after returning from lunch at the studio commissary. Rosco hadn't been with her; instead, he'd been watching rehearsals for another of Sara's scenes; Dan Millray's character had been successfully "murdered," the five takes subsequently "okayed," and here was Belle suddenly facing three crucial challenges.

One: No one other than she, Rosco, the director, the key grip, and the producer were aware that live ammunition had mysteriously appeared on the set that morning.

Two: She'd just been targeted with another crossword—this one filled with familiar names and a message that declared an ominous THE USUAL SUSPECTS.

And, three: As consultant to the film, and friend and adviser to Sara, Lew Groslir had warned Belle to act nonchalant, whether or not she had suspicions of foul play. Nonchalant!

No wonder she became a bundle of nervous energy for

the remainder of the workday. Her smile, when she passed Rosco or her elderly friend, felt so pushed and strained that she almost imagined she was undergoing extensive dental work. Dean Ivald, on the other hand, seemed preternaturally cool and focused. As he guided Sara through her afternoon scenes, Belle was struck by his ability to dissemble and pretend; it was as if nothing untoward had ever happened on the set.

When the workday finally ended, Belle fairly bounded into the Mustang, then jounced up and down edgily in the bucket seat while Rosco drove back toward Santa Monica. Sara rested regally behind the couple, describing in minutest detail the events of her hours spent on the *Anatomy* set, as if her companions had spent the day not among her fellow thespians but far away in Oxnard. It wasn't until Rosco handed the car keys to the hotel's valet parking attendant, and the older woman suggested she'd like a "bit of a lie-down before dinner" that Belle took a steadying breath. For the hour or two that Sara was resting in her rooms, Belle would finally be able to share her findings with her husband.

The endeavor wasn't as simple as she'd imagined. Rosco's first thought on reaching the hotel was to jump into the heated outdoor pool. Belle tried to protest that they needed to focus on what she considered a major breakthrough in the Darlessen situation, but then realized the best way to talk to her husband would be to just join him. So she slipped into her own bathing suit and grabbed a hotel-supplied terry cloth robe.

"But the names are all there, Rosco," she insisted as they left their suite and began heading for the elevators that would carry them downstairs. "LEW, SHAY, DEAN—"

"But the crossword lists DEAN as *Mr. Jones*."

"Naturally, the names have other references," Belle answered with some warmth. "That's what makes the puzzle so intriguing and so clever. NAN's clue is *Ms. Fabray, to friends,* though obviously it doesn't mean—"

"Give me twenty minutes, and then we'll discuss it. I need

to stretch some muscles if you want my brain to work. Who knew making movies required so much sitting on your duff?"

Belle sighed stagily.

Rosco smiled at her. "You know what your problem is?"

"I know . . . I know . . . I'm impatient."

"Twenty minutes, that's it."

"Honestly, Rosco, I don't understand how you can concentrate on something as mundane as swimming when—"

"We're not going to discover who killed Chick Darlessen by examining this crossword, Belle, even if it really wasn't Debra Marcollo. Besides, swimming is a form of meditation. Sound body, sound mind. It's very Zen."

Belle ground her teeth, but didn't otherwise respond.

The elevator carried them to the first floor where they crossed a flower-and-palm–lined patio. A white mist hovered above the azure blue of the long tiled pool, and exterior lights illuminated the trunks and fronds of the palm trees as well as the many terra-cotta pots that were filled with hibiscus and camellias, winter pansies, and feathery pale ornamental grasses, which shivered delicately in the evening breeze. Against this tropical backdrop, the sky was a clear, deep purple. The air felt almost too cold to swim.

"Are you sure you want to take a plunge?" Belle remarked meaningfully. "It's kind of chilly." The completed and folded crossword was still clenched in her hand.

But Rosco was already in the pool and churning his way down the lane reserved for laps. "Twenty minutes," was his watery reply, then he added, "You should, too . . . It'll loosen you up!" But the suggestion was lost in his splashing wake. Belle huddled in her robe, spread the puzzle on her lap, and stared intently at it. Her trusty red pen had not only filled in the solutions, but circled the crossword's many names. "SHAY," she said aloud. "MISO, LEE, MADELAINE . . ."

Rosco churned back in her direction. "Not coming in?"

She held the puzzle aloft.

"Might not . . . be . . . *Anatomy* cast . . ." she heard as her husband performed an expert turn against the pool's edge.

Belle's response was a nettled "Just because the clues list MISO as *Japanese soupy* and SHAY as a *One-horse carriage*, I'm supposed to be thrown off track? The puzzle uses the same grid as the one I constructed for the show, for Pete's sake! There's no way this is an accident, or even a practical joke like Dan's supposed-to-be-funny stunt this morning! Especially if you consider the bullets—"

But Rosco had already steamed away.

"Especially if you consider the *real* bullets that almost made an appearance in the *make-believe* murder scene," Belle continued explaining to the breeze. It was fortunate the couple were the only people enjoying the pool and garden; conversations concerning live ammunition and homicide were known to make the average hotel guest uneasy.

Belle returned to her contemplation of the crossword, frowning as she studied it. Her eyes grew so narrowed and focused they looked as though they were trying to bore holes through the paper in hopes of unlocking the truth hidden there. "LEW . . . DON . . . LANCE . . . And then there are the folks from *Down & Across* . . . STAN, which obviously refers to Stan McKenet rather than *Ollie's partner* . . . Gerry ORSO—"

". . . thought you said . . . clue for ORSO was *Italian bear* . . ." her husband tossed in as he made another turn.

"If you're not going to fully participate in this discussion, Rosco, then you can't lob snide comments. This isn't water polo."

He waved, or perhaps it was merely his arm pausing midstroke, before heading for the deep end of the pool once again. Belle's frown increased; this time, there was marked irritation in it. "That's not helpful," she called out. "What other ORSO would there be? And what about the reference to HARRIET? Or MATTHEW? Or to BART? Because that solution simply has to be the game show's Grand-Slam Winner Bartann Welner . . . I don't care if the clue is *James'*

Maverick role—or if the one for HARRIET is *Ozzie and* __."
She wrapped the robe tighter, her bare toes looked blue
against the sand-colored patio tiles. For a moment, she considered jumping into the water and warming up with a few
quick laps of her own, but her curiosity got the better of
her. "But who's MAX? And who on earth is WANDA?"

". . . met a MAX yesterday . . . working for Jillian Mawbry . . . He's a landscaper." Rosco offered before commencing another turn.

"What?" Belle jumped up as he began swimming in the
opposite direction. She scurried along the pool's stone coping as she called down toward the swimming figure. "Rosco,
what did you say?"

". . . MAX . . . Chugorro . . ." came the puffed response.
"Landscaper . . . owns a company called . . . Marquis de
Sod . . ."

"Aaarrrgghhh! This is no way to run an investigation,"
Belle all but shouted. She marched to the deep end of the
pool. "Is it twenty minutes, yet?"

"Not quite," was Rosco's teasing response as he flipped
into another turn.

"I suppose you're going to tell me you know a WANDA,
too," Belle called after him. Then she returned to her
lounge chair and stared at her husband as he sliced through
the blue water. He seemed impervious to everything except
the rhythmic movement of his body and his measured
swimmer's breaths. For a moment, she wished her own
brain was capable of such total disassociation and peace.
Her ability to multitask even affected her thought process,
making it impossible to focus on one subject.

"MATTHEW," she muttered. "HARRIET introduced
me to a MATTHEW. He's the key grip of *Down & Across,*
but what's she doing in the puzzle? And who on earth are
WANDA and ENID?"

As the questions hovered unanswered in the air, Belle became aware of footsteps padding toward her. "ENID?" she
heard Rosco repeat.

Belle glanced up. There stood her husband, toweling off as water puddled around his feet sending up miniature puffs of steam when it met the night-cooling ground.

"Are your 'twenty minutes' finished?"

"I took pity on you."

Belle cocked her head to one side. "This can wait, Rosco."

He laughed. "Oh, right, Miss No-time-like-the-present."

"I'm just not comfortable leaving problems unresolved."

"Or dishes in the sink. Or empty dog food cans in the refrigerator. Or beds unmade—"

"Those are housekeeping issues, Rosco. That behavior doesn't extend into the rest of my life. Eventually, the dishes disappear."

"Right. I wonder how that happens?" He sat beside her. "Okay, what's up?"

Belle wasn't immediately back on track. "We need to learn who WANDA and ENID are."

"I take it that you're assuming this crossword is connected to Chick Darlessen's death?" The tone was both teasing and serious.

"What other answer can there be, Rosco? *The Usual Suspects* . . . a list of names we recognize, except for the two. Someone's sending us a very definite message."

"And that is?"

"You don't believe me!"

"I didn't say that, Belle. I'm simply asking you what this mystery puzzler is trying to reveal."

Belle's shoulders slumped. "I don't know, other than the fact that we've got to track down these WANDA and ENID characters." Her speech grew faster and more forceful. "Look, we had a near fatality on the set today . . . Sunday, the film's screenwriter was shot dead—"

"By his girlfriend—"

"Or not, Rosco! Or not! What if Jillian Mawbry's right, and Debra's telling the truth about an intruder? Her name doesn't feature in the puzzle."

"But NAN does. So, following your logic—"

"Okay . . . okay . . . Well, maybe NAN isn't a suspect, but what about LANCE?" Belle stabbed at the paper in her hand, indicating the name at 61-Across. "After all, he used to be Debra's ex . . . then Quinton beat him out for the part, causing further ill will with Chick Darlessen . . . or . . . or the killer could have been LEW! Maybe Chick argued with him . . . wanted more money . . . I don't know—"

"This is sounding a tad far-fetched, Belle—"

"Perhaps, but weren't real bullets found on the set today?" Rosco didn't have time to reply before his wife barreled ahead. "Maybe Lew masterminded all the weird accidents; maybe he's trying to generate publicity . . . or he's secretly in debt and can't sustain the project . . . or . . . or the person who murdered Chick is gunning for an additional victim—"

"That's beginning to sound suspiciously like a conspiracy."

"And why not? You're the one who always says that where crime is concerned, there are no coincidences."

"So, someone's targeting Dan Millray?"

"Maybe. But maybe not . . . Because, what if the gun had been fired *accidentally* before Dan's murder scene was filmed. Think about that, Rosco. Think about how many 'accidents' have been associated with this project! To say nothing of trigger-happy Andy Hofren, who could easily have picked up the .38, aimed it while cataloging all his macho roles, then bang, the gun goes off—"

"Meaning a seemingly innocent bystander would have bitten the bullet."

"I'm being serious, Rosco! But yes, apart from that egregious pun, that's exactly what I mean. An actor, a member of the crew, *anyone* gathered to watch Dan's murder scene could have been shot, and the disaster chalked up to a tragic accident. And Andy's not the only one who could have been the perpetrator."

"And you're suggesting that whoever constructed this puzzle knows—"

"That's just it!" Belle gritted her teeth in frustration. "I have no idea what I'm suggesting! After all, there's a possibility these puzzles are being constructed by the person who actually killed Darlessen, which could suggest that the murderer's name doesn't appear in the puzzle, and our culprit created it to send us off on a wild-goose chase."

"Or the name *is* in the puzzle, also intended to trick us."

"All I know is that this is the third crossword that has mysteriously appeared on the set, and that all of them have used my original grid. My hunch, and it's a strong hunch, is that the constructor is onto something big, and that he or she is not the killer."

Rosco put his arm around her shoulders. "I take it you think I should accept Jillian Mawbry's offer."

But Belle was so focused on her own train of thought that she scarcely heard him. "Because if Debra's innocent, then who killed Darlessen?" Then her eyes grew bright, and her head snapped upward. "HARRIET," she announced. "I'll start with Harriet."

"Whoa . . . whoa . . . let's back up here. What do you mean by 'I'll start'? Aren't we in this together? More to the point, isn't Mawbry hiring *me*?"

Belle turned to gaze wonderingly into his face, her expression indicating her utter incomprehension at his question. "Of course we're together. But obviously, we'll have to divide our efforts if one of us is to stay with Sara all the time."

"I'm the one who was hired to be her 'bodyguard,' remember."

"Exactly. Which is why *you* take her to supper tonight while *I* go and hunt up Harriet Tammalong." Belle stood. "I better hurry and change. I need to get over to the Valley. I need to get in line for one of the general admission, last-minute tickets for *Down & Across*."

Rosco also stood. "Wait a minute, I'm not sure this is a good idea—"

"What choice do we have, Rosco?"

"Just say no?"

"Very amusing."

"I'm serious, Belle."

She stared at him in befuddled surprise.

"Look," he continued, "if you're correct about the 'accidents' on the set of *Anatomy* being arranged . . . and that someone had every intention of using the live ammo . . . then it stands to reason that there's a dangerous person on the loose."

"Exactly," was Belle's blithe response. "Which is why *you're* going to start investigating the folks at *Anatomy* first thing tomorrow morning, and why *I'm* driving to Burbank to watch the taping of *Down & Across* tonight."

Rosco's jaw tightened in frustration. "Belle, the name *Harriet* appears in the crossword. If you're correct about the puzzle being connected to Darlessen's death, what makes you think she's not involved? What makes you think she didn't shoot Chick?"

"She's a little old lady in orthopedic shoes, Rosco! And don't start telling me women like her are the most untrustworthy kind. Look at Sara."

"If you ever suggested that Newcastle's grande dame get fitted for orthopedic shoes, you'd be the next murder victim."

CHAPTER

27

L uck was on Belle's side. She located McKenet Studios without a hitch, and when she reached the *Down & Across* soundstage, tickets for that night's filming were still available. And the best part was that Harriet Tammalong was already mingling with the crowd inside. Immediately upon entering the studio, Belle saw the diminutive septuagenarian's white-pink hair and the carefully chosen and accessorized floral pants outfit, which seemed to be the older woman's stock in trade. It was as though a special spotlight had been aimed at Harriet and her gold-toned hoop earrings. The only jarring note was that Rolly Hoddal, the toupee-toting stand-up comic stood beside her, bending down in a private conversation that, at a distance, appeared almost conspiratorial. His pose was made more curious and awkward by his obvious difficulty at maintaining an upright and respectable posture.

Belle noticed Harriet's lips were drawn into a tight and unhappy line. The impression she gave, right down to the disapproving wrinkling of her nose, was that of wishing she were elsewhere. Then she glanced up the aisle, noticed her "niece," and trilled a joyous "Gale!," while Matthew, the stage manager, conducted Belle toward her "aunt."

"I'm just pleased as punch to see you again! And so very soon. Did that hubby of yours desert you and stay up in Minnesota longer than planned?"

Minnesota? Belle thought. It took her a second to recall the lie about Rosco being off on a fishing trip that she'd begun and that Harriet had then liberally embellished.

"Yup," Belle responded with the biggest grin she could muster. If words failed, sometimes the appearance of enthusiasm and goodwill served as an excellent substitute.

"Rolly, you haven't met my niece Gale Harmble, yet . . . She was here last week . . . her first time visiting *Down & Across*. She thought you were an absolute stitch in your warm-up act." Harriet smiled convivially while Belle caught her breath, curtailed the impulse to roll her eyes at the notion of the comedian being even remotely amusing, then decided to stop counting how many fibs she and the older lady had concocted between them.

Belle extended her hand. "Pleased to meet you, Mr. Hoddal."

The comic's rheumy eyes swiveled back toward Harriet. "I didn't know you had a niece. The only relative I've heard you mention is—"

"The things you don't know, Rolly, would fill *The Encyclopaedia Britannica* . . . Gale's from out of state . . . She's my sister's kid. She doesn't visit me near enough, do you Gale?"

Hoddal's gaze swept over Belle before returning to the older woman. "Gotta go. It's almost showtime, and Gerry's gonna be parading down the aisle before you know it . . . He doesn't like it if I mingle with the audience . . . Remember what I said, Harriet."

"Rolly, hon . . . words to the wise . . . Whatever, well, *substance* you're enjoying . . . I don't think it's helping you think straight—"

"Mark my words. There's trouble up there in heaven. I know what I heard." Rolly did an about-face while Harriet sighed, shook her head, and began leading the way toward her customary seat.

"I hope I didn't interrupt anything," Belle offered.

Harriet turned to face her, a sympathetic smile spreading over her creased and powdery cheeks. "Poor Rolly. You know those drugs can do terrible things to people's brains . . . make them invent weird stories and such . . . imagine folks around them are up to no good. It makes them paranoid, that's what I think. It's terrible, isn't it, what people will do to their bodies? And willingly, too! I tell you, Gale, the whole world's gonna go to hell in a handbasket if people keep sniffing and smoking that awful stuff." Harriet sat and patted the chair beside her. "I'm sure Matthew intended this for you." No further mention of Rolly Hoddal and his problems were made. "Now, I seem to remember you telling me you were only able to visit L.A. for a few days. Did you extend your stay?" Harriet's birdlike hand touched Belle's arm, and her tone turned concerned and worried. "I don't mean to pry, but I hope that doesn't indicate difficulties on the marital front."

From her third-row seat, Belle watched other members of the studio audience find their places while, on the stage, cameras were repositioned, lighting levels adjusted, and sound booms moved. As she gazed at the activity, Belle thought, and her deliberations turned to one Gale Harmble. The alias had been hastily chosen and insufficiently fleshed out. It was a name and nothing more, and the fact was causing problems— allowing Harriet to invent whatever story she chose while "Gale" was left playing catch-up. It was time, Belle decided, to take control. Given the current circumstances and what she hoped the evening might reveal, a better and bigger lie seemed called for. "I've got a confession to make, Harriet."

"Oh, dear . . . and I was so hoping you weren't having man troubles . . . It's never a good sign when husbands go off on vacations by themselves. And I should know, considering all the times I've been hitched. And ice fishing? What do you think really goes on in those little houses they roll out there on those frozen lakes—?"

"It's not about my husband. It's about me. I'm not exactly who I said I was."

Harriet turned a stricken face toward Belle. "You're not Gale Harmble?"

"Well, yes . . . Of course, I'm Gale . . . It's just that . . . well, I'm here on assignment . . . undercover, in a way. I'm . . . I'm doing a feature-length magazine article on America's fascination with crossword puzzles."

"Oh my."

"But I didn't want to tell you when we first met because I needed to have an unbiased view from a long-time fan of *Down & Across*."

Harriet eyed her companion. "You mean you singled me out on the studio bus?"

"No . . . that was pure luck, Harriet. Or maybe I sat beside you because you have such an honest face. However it happened, you were obviously the perfect person to give me a 'regular's' view of the show."

The older woman frowned. "So, you weren't telling the truth when you said you'd never seen *Down & Across* before?"

Belle shook her head. "I've been researching it—and the contestants and studio audience—for a some time now."

"And you aren't married? Because I have a nephew, a very charming—"

"Yes. I'm married. Sorry."

"Well, my goodness," Harriet clucked. "You certainly did a good job of pretending you knew nothing about Gerry or the others when you were here before." There was a sound of hurt in the older woman's voice, prompting Belle.

"I apologize for the ruse, Harriet, but I needed to—"

"Were you taping me on one of those 'lipstick' cameras?"

" 'Lipstick'?"

"I saw a TV special—an exposé, really—on women reporters who go undercover. They're equipped with cameras as small as lipstick wands. Sometimes, the gals hide them in little handbags or sew them into their shirts or jackets."

Belle pursed her lips in consternation. Ace journalist

Gale Harmble was proving as problematic a piece of fiction as Gale Harmble, out-of-town hick. "Did you know that more than forty million Americans do the crossword every day?" she offered in reply. The technique was one of Rosco's—pull out a list of facts when an investigation turns sticky. "Making those forty million plus *lexicographomaniacal*—crazy about crosswords."

"I never heard that term before," Harriet admitted. Her tone indicated a good deal of surprise.

"I'm considering entitling the story '*Exercise Your Hippocampus: Use It or Lose It.*'"

"*Hippocampus*," Harriet repeated. "There's a new one on me, too."

Belle decided that "Gale" was out of the woods. "You mentioned Bartann Welner when I was here before."

"But you must already know all about him, dearie. With your prior research on word games and everything."

No, Belle realized, *Gale's not in the clear yet.* "I'd like to hear his story from you, Harriet, as the most regular of the regulars at *Down & Across.*"

"Am I going to be in your article, too?"

Belle smiled. "Of course, if you wish to be. Or I can always cite you as one who spoke on condition of anonymity."

"Well, I don't know . . . Sometimes, fame has a funny way of courting disaster, doesn't it? Just look at what happened to poor Bart . . . Not that his death could be connected to being a Grand-Slam Winner, despite my little jest about Stan McKenet doing him in . . . Still, it does give you pause."

Belle was silent a moment. "I hope you're not seriously suggesting that Bartann Welner might have met with foul play?"

Harriet's brow creased. "Now, that's just an awful notion. I hadn't considered it seriously before. That would make two in one family—"

"Two?" Belle asked.

"Why, his nephew, Chick Darlessen. You must have read about it in the newspapers after you got here. It happened

Sunday. His live-in girlfriend shot him, in a beach house in Malibu."

Belle's surprise at this revelation was so great that she could hardly keep her voice steady. "Chick Darlessen was Bartann Welner's nephew?"

Harriet nodded, then tapped Belle's arm again. "The relationship wasn't mentioned in the obits." The old lady's frown deepened. ". . . Come to think of it, Gale, you probably know all about the film Chick was working on, on account of it being based on a true murder that was solved by clues planted in a crossword. I heard that famous puzzle gal is involved—"

"Yes," Belle interrupted. "I'll be visiting that set later this week."

Harriet studied her companion; her stare was disconcertingly probing. Belle felt it was time to add to her already gargantuan fib. "Due to the homicide, my editor and I had difficulties arranging interviews. Needless to say, the cast and crew were completely thrown off schedule by the tragedy . . . And, yes, I've been aware of the film's story line for some time. In fact, it was the coincidence of crosswords being featured in both a movie of the week and a game show that prompted my assignment. Crosswords and those devoted to them are obviously 'hot' all of a sudden."

Harriet continued to stare at Belle, who, in turn, continued to warn herself that the journalist "Gale Harmble" would be a complete professional during her various interviews, of which this was surely one. Belle pasted on what she hoped looked like a newsperson's encouraging but practical smile. "Does the name 'Wanda' mean anything to you, Harriet?"

"You mean Wanda Jorcrof?"

"Yes," Belle lied.

Harriet sighed. "That's just who Rolly Hoddal was jawing about when you came in. He claims—" Then the words abruptly ceased, and her lips pinched together in a sad and worried line.

" 'He claims'?" Belle prompted, increasing the 'trust-me' wattage in her wholesome face.

"I told you Rolly's into drugs, and whatever else he can find at a given moment. I've learned not to pay attention to his rantings. Wanda was a contestant on the show. A good contestant, too."

A noisy commotion at the back of the studio indicated that Gerry Orso was about to begin his promenade through the audience. Belle took an inward breath, and plunged ahead before she lost her momentum. "What about a Max? What can you tell me about him?"

Harriet's eyes narrowed. "Max?" she repeated.

"That's right. My sources tell me there was a Max who also appeared on the show—"

"I never heard of any Max," Harriet insisted. Then she turned away and began hollering Gerry Orso's name.

CHAPTER

28

The worst traffic in the world is in Boston, right? Rosco thought, then let out a aggrieved chuckle and shook his head as he reconsidered that foolhardy notion. *How could I have been so naive? Boston worse than L.A., or midtown Manhattan at lunch hour, or any "shore" location on a sunny summer weekend? Heck, I might as well have said the outskirts of Newcastle have serious "vehicular issues."* He stared at the 110 Freeway's five lanes of traffic. The morning rush had the cars lined up bumper to bumper like a parking lot at a World Series game. And not one of the vehicles had moved from their resting spot for the past eleven minutes, but who was counting? *I mean, what's the point of renting a Mustang?* he continued to grouse. *I could be moving faster on a tricycle—a rusted tricycle without tires.*

Rosco's intention, after completing his interview with Debra Marcollo, had been to take the 110 to the number 10 Freeway and be at the studio in Culver City by 9:30, well before Belle arrived with Sara. *Well, fat chance. Forget it. The hour had come and gone a lot longer than eleven minutes ago.*

While Rosco balefully studied the semis, pickups, SUVs,

luxury sedans, low-riders, and ordinary four-wheels-as-simple-transportation within his field of vision, he reflected on the Marcollo visit. He'd spent nearly an hour with her in the Los Angeles County Jail on Bauchet Street, and although their conversation hadn't shed much new light on who might have killed Chick Darlessen, Rosco was surprised at how calm and reasonable she'd appeared. Jillian Mawbry had painted her as potentially problematic, but Rosco's impression had been quite different. Perhaps three days in the cooler had given her time to reflect on things, or at least to get her act together.

Naturally, like everyone else incarcerated in the L.A. County Jail, she'd insisted she was innocent of all charges, and did a credible job of maintaining that the off-duty lifeguard had completely misinterpreted her when she'd sobbed, "I don't know why I did it." She'd also stated that the Malibu police had browbeaten her into making other remarks she hadn't intended—or that had then been taken out of context. Finally, she'd proceeded to run down a list of folks who'd had strained relationships with Darlessen: from Lance diRusa, her ex-boyfriend to Dan Millray, of all people. No one had been left out of the act.

Debra had also insisted—vehemently—that she'd been sound asleep when Chick had been killed, and that it was only the explosion of gunshots that had awakened her. She'd explained that Chick had deserted her for some of his Pacific Palisades buddies, and that in his absence, she'd polished off a bottle of wine, "maybe a little more", then locked herself in the bungalow's single bedroom where she'd fallen into a self-pitying and irate slumber. When the noise had assailed her troubled dreams, she hadn't been able to identify it at first. Then she'd grabbed her robe, rushed into Chick's office where she'd seen him lying in a pool of blood with the gun resting on the desk. Her only thought had been to escape from a murderer who she'd assumed was still lurking somewhere in the house. Debra had further described an incident with a prowler a few days earlier, which had been the motive for Chick supplying some rudimentary target practice, thus establishing her fingerprints on the pistol.

A lot of the tale sounded awfully convenient to Rosco, but all in all, he was inclined to believe Debra's story. For that reason alone, he considered his visit to the county jail to be worthwhile. But what seemed to clinch her protestation of innocence was this: Debra had maintained that Darlessen had opened a brand-new box of .38 caliber shells when he'd taken her down to the ocean for their practice session. He'd fired off a full cylinder and so had Debra, twelve rounds in all. The police report stated that five bullets had been retrieved from Chick's body, and one from the wall of his office, bringing the count to eighteen—which should have left another eighteen shells remaining in the box of thirty-six. However, the report also indicated that the forensic team found only twelve shells in the box. So if Debra was telling the truth about how much ammunition had been expended into the Malibu surf, then six .38 caliber shells were missing, a number that just happened to coincide with the amount found in Andy Hofren's prop gun.

A man in a large Mercedes-Benz, directly behind the Mustang, began leaning on the car's horn. The shrill noise cut into Rosco's eardrums and brought his mind leapfrogging back to the here and now. The traffic remained at a dead stop, and the piercing sound of the horn was having less than no effect on improving traffic flow. Surprise, surprise. However that didn't keep Mr. Impatient from continuing to express his dissatisfaction with the fact that life wasn't treating him with the appropriate deference and homage he expected, given the sticker price of his automobile.

Rosco stepped from the Mustang and walked back to the Mercedes.

"Would you mind not doing that? You're giving me a headache."

"You tell him, Pancho!" a squat and broad-shouldered man in a nearby Toyota shouted, and then laughed. "Give 'im hell!"

The Mercedes' driver reached under his seat and pulled out a .357 Magnum. It was a huge gun. "You want a headache? I'll give you a headache. Get back in that piece of junk Ford, you jerk."

Instinctively, Rosco raised his hands and took a couple of steps backward while a tall Hispanic man stepped from a pickup truck directly behind the Mercedes and ambled toward the open window. He noticed the driver was pointing a pistol at Rosco, so he eased his grass-stained canvas work vest away from his hip to reveal his own revolver and a gold LAPD detective's shield.

"Give me the gun, sir," the officer said in a tone that sounded as if he'd been weaned on the original *Dragnet*.

The man in the Mercedes began to stutter. "Hey . . . I mean . . . I mean . . . a man's . . . got a right to protect himself, right? I paid for this gun. It's mine."

"Give me the gun, sir."

"But . . . I . . ."

"Give me the gun, sir."

"He started it."

"Give me the gun, sir."

Rosco noted that the detective's inflection never varied. Nor did his stance. If the man decided on a sideline as an actor, each of his "takes" would have made a production's continuity department smile with relief.

The driver of the Mercedes swore under his breath, and reluctantly handed the .357 to the detective, who then looked at Rosco and said, "The traffic's beginning to move up ahead, sir. Please return to your vehicle. And please, sir, don't step out of a car on the freeway again." Following that stentorian directive, the detective refocused on the owner of the Mercedes and .357 Magnum. "Driver's license and registration, please, sir."

"Hey, a man's got a right to protect himself," he insisted as he handed over the documents. "That clown in the Mustang came after me. Didn't you hear his accent? He doesn't even live here. I'll bet that car's a rental. I got a right to protect myself. I own that gun. It's mine."

"When the traffic eases, sir, please pull your vehicle to the side of the highway . . . And please have your pistol permit ready for inspection."

"What? What are you talking about? What permit? You can't do this to me, you lousy—" He pulled out his cell phone. "I'm calling my lawyer."

"Just pull your vehicle off to the side of the highway, sir."

Rosco returned to the Mustang as the car in front of him began inching forward. When the congestion magically cleared, and he picked up speed, he could see Mr. Impatient in the mirror desperately punching numbers into his cell phone while steering his car to the side of the road. The sight brought a quick grin to Rosco's face. Being stuck in traffic definitely had its pluses on occasion.

The remainder of the ride to Culver City proved uneventful, and he pulled into the studio a little bit after 10:30. Sara and Belle had arrived forty-five minutes earlier.

"We were beginning to worry about you," Belle said. "Sara's already in make-up having her hair done, and Lew Groslir wants to have a word with us in his office."

"What's it all about this time?"

"One way to find out."

Don Schruko informed them that they wouldn't be "rolling film" on Sara for another fifteen minutes, so Belle and Rosco headed toward Lew's office, Rosco using the time to bring his wife up to speed on what he'd learned from Debra Marcollo.

Belle's response was a laconic, "That's quite a list of suspects she supplied . . . But at least we know Bart Welner didn't shoot his nephew. Dead people seldom commit murder nowadays."

"Lucky thing."

"Isn't it, though?"

During their conversation, Belle made no further reference to the previous evening's encounter with Harriet Tammalong as Rosco's reply to the Rolly Hoddal/Wanda Jorcrof information had been an expected, but no less irritating, "This is homicide we're dealing with, Belle. People who take it into their heads to kill other folks aren't always as nice or honest as they seem." *How could anyone respond to a fatuous observation like that? Belle thought. On the other hand, it was a point well worth remembering.*

"Wow, that was some scare, yesterday," Lew announced the moment the couple was seated in front of his desk. "Thank heavens Schruko kept it under his hat until Dean finished his takes. Otherwise, everyone would have freaked out."

"You're talking about the real bullets?" Rosco said in a tone that was half-question, half-statement.

"Yeah. That could have been a real disaster. And listen," Lew pointed a finger and wagged it meaningfully between Belle and Rosco, "let's keep this little dust-up between the three of us—and Ivald and Schruko, of course. It won't help morale if the entire set learns about it."

"How do you think those shells got there?"

"No telling, but all's well that ends well, that's what I say."

"I'd be a little concerned that something like this could occur again," Belle offered.

"What?" Lew replied with a forced chuckle. "The gun's been returned. We got the scene, we got the shot. The weapon's gone. End of story. No more bullets. Live or otherwise."

But Rosco wasn't so easily persuaded that the case had been resolved. "Who's authorized to handle firearms on a set like this?"

"What, am I talking to a wall here?" Lew snapped. "I said, 'end of story.' That's not what I brought you in here to talk about . . ." Groslir tapped his fingers on his desk and looked nervously from Belle to Rosco and back to Belle. "Okay, here's the situation. Because of Chick's death, we're going to need Belle to stay in L.A. for the entire four-week shoot. It's her story Darlessen adapted, so who better to fill in answers if we have questions? I mean a screenwriter can't do justice to the real deal." Lew held up his hand to prevent Belle from objecting. "I know what you're going to say—'You're not a writer.' Not to worry. Dean can handle additional dialogue if it's necessary . . . We just need you to make sure the project has a genuine look—and, also, in case any crossword-type problems arise."

Belle refrained from mentioning that "crossword-type problems" had already arisen. Instead, she responded with a determined "I can't do that. I want to go home."

"You have a contract, Belle—"

"Which says she finishes work tomorrow and leaves on Saturday," Rosco stated. He made no attempt to sound friendly or even polite.

Groslir grinned. It wasn't one of his more loving attempts. "Lee Rennegor agreed to the three week extension—a double salary for Belle. Rosco, you stay on as well. Mrs. Briephs is the only one who returns to Massachusetts on Saturday. Dean says he'll have all her stuff in the can by tomorrow at lunchtime."

"We never spoke to Lee about this," Belle stated.

The producer handed her a piece of paper. "Here's the deal memo Rennegor signed off on."

"Well, he never consulted me."

"That's between you and your agent, I'm afraid." Groslir leaned back in his chair, his smile had turned decidedly smug. "Look, Belle, this is a good deal. Nobody gets an offer like this any more. That's a hell of a lot of money that Rennegor weaseled out of me on your behalf, and you should be happy as a baby with clean diapers. What's an extra three weeks? Besides, what's it doing back there in Massachusetts? Snowing, right? The weather stinks back there. I saw it on the news last night. Snowplows all over the place."

"Maybe we like snow," Belle said.

"Where'd you get that? No one likes snow," was Groslir's dismissive response. "Well, skiers . . . but then, they're always breaking things . . . bones and things."

Rosco took the memo from Belle and perused it. "We have to think this over."

The producer sat up straight and laid his hands flat on the desktop. "Well, that's the point I'm trying to make here, Rosco. See, this situation is kinda set in stone. You can't back out without getting into some very unpleasant breach-of-contract problems. A deal memo's a deal memo. But, like I said the other day, it'd be nice if we could all just—get along. Now, I've offered you some very serious cash. Let's do the best we can for the next three weeks and depart as friends."

Belle and Rosco sat in stunned unhappy silence.

"See how easy that was?" Groslir continued. "I knew you two kids would see it my way."

Rosco stared back at him. "If I'm stuck here for another three weeks, I'm going to use my time productively and find out who put live ammo in Andy Hofren's .38."

"Maybe you didn't hear me earlier, Rosco. I said 'end of story' as far as that gun situation's concerned. If you want to push it, you can head back to the ice and snow and sleet this very afternoon."

Rosco handed the deal memo back to Groslir. "Hey, I've got a contract, Lew. I'll do whatever I want while I'm here. If you've got any problems, I suggest you talk them over with my agent."

CHAPTER
29

After they'd returned to the soundstage from their tête-à-tête with Lew Groslir, Belle decided to join Sara in makeup while Rosco took up a position on the catwalk above the Vermont Inn's "Parlor" set. Stagehands and prop people were busily dressing the furnishings below him. The metal walkway wasn't a terrific location if an emergency required immediate response, but it afforded Rosco a good view of the entire studio. Once the lights were kicked up, he could keep an eye on Sara, as well as everyone else. An added advantage was that the lamps' bright glare would keep anyone from seeing what *he* was doing. He hunkered down and commenced an all-too-familiar routine of watching and waiting.

However, given the events of the previous twenty-four hours, and the either accurate or spurious information he and Belle had gathered, it was difficult for Rosco to keep his brain plugged into only one issue; the mystery crosswords kept getting jumbled up with Belle's return visit to the taping of *Down & Across,* which, in turn, returned him to Darlessen's death, and then the .38 caliber shells that had originally been in Chick's possession. The shells that intuition told him might be the same ones Don Schruko had found in Andy Hofren's revolver.

The logical suspects in what might have been a major disaster had to be Don Schruko and Andy Hofren, since, as far as Rosco knew, they were the only two people who had actually handled the pistol. On the other hand, they were two of the most affable guys involved with the production. And he wondered, *Why would Don put real bullets in the gun just to remove them later?* On top of that, if Dan Millray had been a target for murder, Rosco could think of a heck of a lot more easier setups. Mistaken identity on a crowded freeway was the one that most readily came to mind.

As the stage lights advanced to their full wattage, Rosco kept one eye on Hofren and Schruko and another on Sara, although Rosco was beginning to question what potential danger could befall her in the busy studio. Like the loaded weapon, he could name other places where foul play would be more easily accomplished. A kidnapping on a quiet Santa Monica street was among them.

In typical Hollywood fashion, Dean Ivald was preparing to shoot one of the final scenes, although he was only a quarter of the way through the production schedule. Nearly the entire cast would be on the stage, Dan Millray being the notable exception since his character was now deader than a doornail. From his perch on the elevated walkway, Rosco felt the same perplexing sense of déjà vu that Belle had previously experienced. It was as though he'd died and been deposited in some metallic version of heaven where he was witnessing a flashback of his short time on Earth. He found it hard to ignore what was going one between the "Belle" and "Rosco" on the set, and at the same time, concentrate on Sara, Ginger Bradmin, Louis Gable, Carol Von Deney, and their attendant makeup artists and costume wizards. Trying to focus, Rosco shook his head vigorously but was only rewarded with a ringing in his ears.

The scene Ivald was filming was the one that implicated Andy Hofren's character of murder in the first degree, an accusation that the director wanted Hofren to greet with extreme nervous indignation. Being a good actor, the behavior made Andy appear guilty of every homicide in North America for the past ten years. While Don Schruko, the second suspect in the live ammo switch, spent his time doing what he always did during a take: restlessly pacing behind the cameras while trying to anticipate whatever obscure item Ivald might holler for next.

Watching this activity, Rosco realized he needed to return to the source. The key grip had been the one to discover the live ammunition. That was the person Rosco would talk to first.

Because of the number of performers involved, nearly three hours elapsed before the scene was finished. Angles were filmed and refilmed; reverse takes and actor's reactions were recorded; while toward the end, Ivald moved in for close-ups of his principals. Finally the director shouted, "Cut!" for the last time and glanced at his wristwatch. "All right, it's two o' clock people, let's everyone break for lunch, and be back here at three-thirty. We'll be going right into scene thirty-seven."

Rosco caught up with Don Schruko five minutes later, and the two men retreated to the now-empty electrician's workshop.

"I don't know if Lew Groslir told you," Rosco began, "but he'd like to keep this 'live ammo' business under wraps for fear of alarming the cast and crew."

"Yeah, he briefed me on that."

Rosco sat on a tall metal stool. He wanted to keep things light and conversational. If Schruko *were* guilty of exchanging real bullets for blanks, then the interview needed to be delicately handled. "I was just curious, but how could something like that happen?"

"You writing a book?"

Rosco laughed. "Hey, it's not a half-bad idea."

Don laughed as well and also sat. He then shook his head. "It's mind-boggling how something like this could happen. I have no idea. We don't keep any guns on the lot;

for insurance purposes, the studio doesn't own them. There's an outfit in Inglewood that rents firearms to production companies, so Mr. Groslir uses them. They also have a live firing range, so it is possible *they* left the real bullets in the gun. Although, those folks have an excellent safety record."

"Whose responsibility is it to make sure the gun's loaded with blanks?"

"It's one of those things that can fall through the cracks— and has—and did. On rare occasions, actors and crew members have actually been killed because of mistakes just like this. See, if a gun is fired off-camera, then it's the responsibility of someone on my team. A grip would have fired that gun, and I would have checked it out beforehand, personally. But once the pistol gets into the shot, then it becomes a prop. It's fired by an actor, so it's the prop department's look-out. It's a union thing. Once that gun and Andy's hand moved into the camera's frame, the .38 instantly became a prop. The mix-up factor's in here because according to the original script, the stage directions read 'off-camera gunshot,' which is why props obviously never bothered to check the gun."

"So, why did *you* check it if it was basically the prop department's job?"

Don frowned. Rosco noted the look of genuine consternation on his face. If directors felt ownership of their productions, key grips probably felt equally responsible for work running smoothly. "Dumb luck. As they were rehearsing the scene, I noticed the box of blanks on the prop table, and the seal hadn't been broken yet. My assumption was that props had just forgotten to load the dang thing, or didn't realize it was their job; so I went over to check it out."

"And you told no one until after Dean Ivald wrapped it up?"

"I have to agree with Mr. Groslir, this is the kind of situation that could ruin morale on a shoot, especially after the accident that put Nan out of commission and the original 'Rosco's' car crash . . . There's been too much yack about a

jinxed set, and we all know how superstitious actors can
be . . . The way I saw it, it was Dean's call as to when the
others were told; my decision was to stay mum until that
shot was in the can."

"But if the 'outfit in Inglewood' didn't leave the shells in
the .38, then as far as I can tell, you and Andy Hofren were
the only ones to handle it."

"I wish it were that easy, but the pistol sat on the prop
table, along with the box of blanks, from the time it arrived
on the set at 9:00 A.M. until Andy grabbed it for the shot.
Anyone could have fooled with it."

"Did Ivald return the shells to you?"

"No. He kept them . . . What's with all these questions?"

"Nothing, really," Rosco said, backtracking. He decided
that the "casual observer questions" had gone as far as they
could without arousing suspicion. "I'm just fascinated by
this business. I've been keeping a journal . . . Plus, as an ex-
cop, we always had concerns about munitions, station house
safety, and accountability." He glanced at his watch. "Say,
do you want to grab some lunch? I'm starved."

"Thanks, but I always bring mine. Some of the other grips
and me play a few hands of Hearts during the breaks. I'll ask
them if they saw anyone playing with that gun, but as much
as I hate to admit it, my guess is that the guys in Inglewood
screwed up big time."

"I guess Lew Groslir will have something to say about
that."

Don shrugged. "No telling."

By the time Rosco reached the commissary, Belle and
Sara had been joined by Louis Gable, Carol Von Deney,
Jes Nadema, and Madeline Richter, leaving no room for him
at their table, so he sat by himself, with his turkey sandwich
and coffee, and wondered if Don was right, and the bullets
had been accidentally left in the .38 by the 'outfit in Inglewood.' It seemed plausible. Horrific, but plausible.

"Ah, the loneliness of the celebrity's spouse," Dean Ivald said, looking down at Rosco. "May I join you, or are you into a Zen-turkey-sandwich thing that requires absolute solitude?"

"No. Please, have a seat."

Ivald placed his sandwich and bottle of designer water on the table and sat. "That scene we just completed worked like clockwork. Coordinating that many actors can be quite a headache. Your Mrs. Briephs is the find of the century. I do hope she's enjoying her time out here?"

"I think she is. I think she found you 'most charming' at dinner the other night."

"I could say the same about her. It almost makes me wish you and your lovely wife were playing your own parts, as well."

Rosco smiled and shook his head. "I have a reputation for being camera-shy. Remaining anonymous comes in handy in my line of work."

"Ever the detective. Mr. Plain Clothes, is that it?"

Rosco shrugged, then lowered his voice enough to keep the conversation private, but not to appear clandestine or too suspicious. "Let me ask you something, Dean. I realize Lew doesn't want the 'live ammo' situation made public, and that the near-miss was probably just that, but I'm still curious . . . How do you think real bullets found their way onto your set."

The director took a bite of his sandwich and a swig of water before answering. "I have no idea. But I'm very happy to tell you that the damn gun's gone back to it's rightful owners."

"Do you still have the shells?"

"I left them in my office. Why?"

"Well, as you just noted, I'm a P.I., which makes me curious by nature, I guess." Rosco bit into his own sandwich. "I'd like to have a look at them, if you don't mind. If we can establish the manufacturer, or some distinctive markings, maybe we can determine where they came from. We'd certainly learn if the pistol range had mistakenly left them in the gun. My guess is that they keep a record of all shells purchased and expended."

"I see your point. I'll get them for you after lunch, but I'd bet a good portion of my wages that the firing range did not leave bullets in the gun. I've worked with those people on a number of films. They take their business very seriously."

"Mistakes can happen, but I'm also inclined to believe that a professional range would check and double check a pistol before releasing it . . . Which brings us back to the possibility of attempted homicide. You know all of these people very well. Do any of them bear a grudge against Dan Millray?"

Ivald shook is head slowly. "I can't imagine that man has a single enemy."

"Let me take it a step further . . . If Millray had died, would it have closed down the set and put an end to *Anatomy of a Crossword?*"

Ivald released a cynical sigh. "No . . . You see, after viewing the rushes . . ." He looked at Rosco for a sign of comprehension, but found none. "Rushes are rough printouts of what was filmed on any given day. It's how we check our work before moving on. At any rate, after seeing the rushes that evening, I decided to go with my first take. So even if Dan had been killed during that initial shot, nothing would have stopped because I would have had all his work in the can. I'm not saying I would have used his actual death scene; there would have been ways to cut around it. I know I'm sounding incredibly hardhearted, but I'm also telling the truth . . . Actors do die during filming; it's an unfortunate situation, but it's also reality. The older ones can have heart attacks . . . There are accidents on location or at home, just like our original 'Rosco' who was very lucky to be merely banged up . . . But those situations, unhappy though they are, don't curtail production, especially this far into a shoot. Scenes are merely moved . . . body doubles hired . . ." Ivald leaned toward Rosco, and also lowered his voice. "Is that what you think's going on? Someone's trying to shut us down?"

"I don't know what to think," Rosco said, and then changed his approach. "How'd you get involved with this project, Dean? I mean, are you a crossword buff?"

Again, the director took a sip of water before responding. "I guess you could say that. None of these wimpy American puzzles, though. Strictly the *London Times,* for me. No offense, but the puzzles you Yanks create are child's play for an Oxford man."

"Have you ever tried to construct a puzzle on your own?"

Ivald chuckled heartily. "Oh, you clever boy . . . I've heard that your wife received a facsimile of her original crossword. Same grid, different clues and solutions. But I plead innocent to the dastardly deed."

Rosco popped the last remaining crust of his sandwich into his mouth and washed it down with coffee. "Actually, she's received three." He studied the director's reaction and added, "Your name appeared in the last one. A puzzle that also included the film title, *The Usual Suspects.*"

Ivald laughed again. "And how many other names appeared in this mysterious crossword of yours?"

"What if I were to tell you that yours was the only name?"

The director stood, picked up his empty plate and water bottle, said, "Then I would say you were lying," and walked out of the commissary.

CHAPTER

30

As Rosco, Belle, and Sara finished their lunches and reentered the still-brilliant afternoon sunshine to retrace the route from the studio commissary to the soundstage, far across the hills within the vast crisscross of streets that was downtown Burbank, two people were holding an emergency meeting. The place they'd chosen was a rear booth of Tori's Donuteria at the corner of Hollywood and Valhalla. Outside of the bakery/coffee shop, the air was heavy with car exhaust and the odors of pavement, grit, and grime; inside, the plummy scents of sugar, cinnamon, chocolate, vanilla cream, fruit jelly, and mocha icing wafted sweetly across the room. Even the glass carafes of coffee smelled candied and syrupy. The tones of the couple's voices, however, were far from honeyed or serene.

"I'm tellin' ya, Harriet. This situation looks bad for us. It looks real bad. We need to think about layin' low. I've been in jail. Three very long years. I never want to go back."

"Let's remember that we're in a public place, Rolly," was the steely and whispered response. "There's no reason to broadcast our concerns to all and sundry. A perfect crime requires perfect secrecy. And a certain sotto voce tone."

"I'm not as dumb as I look, you know," Hoddal shot back in his own subdued tone. He ran a hand across his head as he spoke. Minus the toupee he wore for "public appearances" he was almost completely bald; what little hair remained was a graying fringe that resembled a monk's tonsorial cut. Only Rolly's closest friends would have recognized him as the warm-up comedian from *Down & Across,* and even they might have been fooled. Oddly, his true self had become his best disguise. Hoddal repeated his latest complaint.

In answer, Harriet Tammalong merely gazed at him, and her silence made him more jittery, causing his shoulders to jounce up and down in swift, squirming spasms and his fingers, tip-tapping along the table's sticky surface, to clench and unclench as if he were a musician stretching his muscles before commencing to play. "That clown Rolly Hoddal . . . that's what everyone thinks. Like I haven't got a brain between my ears. Like I'm clueless or something. I mean, I know what Valhalla is. Not the street outside of this dump. Where we are, I mean. Where *you* insisted on meeting."

Harriet remained mute, but she did wrap her hands around the paper cup of coffee. The way she cradled it made it look as though she were cold.

"I mean, come on . . . How could I not learn junk like Valhalla and stuff? I've been doing the *Down & Across* gig for practically ever, ya know." The shoulders shivered; the face exploded in a series of tics and winks and ill-considered grins. "Valhalla—eight letters, Germanic myth. It means 'hall of the slain' . . . 'hall of the slain,' for Pete's sake! Okay, gods for four letters: Odin, wife Frigg . . . Thor, stepson Ullr—"

"No one's doubting your intelligence, Rolly," Harriet interrupted, but Hoddal was on a tear, and it wasn't caused by the caffeine in his untouched coffee or a sugar high induced by his two doughnuts from which he'd nibbled only the icing. He knocked a hand loudly against his head, not once but three times.

"And who did old Odin listen to? His two pet ravens, that's who. *Hugin,* that means thought, and *Munin*, meaning memory . . . And while we're on the subject of memory: *Mnemosyne,* Greek word; she was Mom of the Muses. Clio . . . four letters, represents history, Thalia, comedy, Erato, poetry—"

"Enough, Rolly!" Harriet ordered. Still maintaining her quiescent tone, the words became a hiss.

"The Muses' pop was Zeus . . . also four letters. Other, Greek gods . . . Four letters—"

Harriet Tammalong reached out one tiny hand and grabbed Rolly Hoddal's quivering arm. "I'm telling you to stop this gibberish right now! You're only attracting attention."

The suddenness of her action startled the words from his mouth, but not for long. "And I'm telling you I know who that dame is! The one you said was your 'niece'—"

"Yes. You told me already," the vehement hiss continued, "Belle Graham. *The* Belle Graham."

"Which you should have known, Harriet! The minute you spotted her! You being a crossword junkie and all."

Harriet raised a wry eyebrow. "Interesting turn of phrase for you, Rolly." Then she calmly changed the subject, leaning forward until her face was no more than a foot from Hoddal's. "Who's to say I didn't recognize her?"

"Your 'niece' is what you told Orso and Matthew—"

"Naughty me for telling a lie."

The comic's face clouded in confused and baffled thought. "So, you knew who she was?"

"From the moment I watched her board the studio bus Wednesday, a week ago . . . Gale Harmble was what she called herself. I found it convenient to play along, the same way I did last night."

Rolly waited for Harriet to say more, but she merely returned to her coffee, dipping a cruller daintily into the creamy surface and then taking petite bites of the warm, and soggy dough. "I don't know why you prefer those gooey, iced things, Rolly. You can't taste the doughnut for all the sugar. Me, I like the real goods."

"We're playin' with fire here, Harriet! Her hubby's a private eye, you know?"

Harriet Tammalong didn't respond; her half-smile remained inscrutable.

"And he's here in L.A., with her! And they're both working on crossword stuff, just like they did in—" Rolly's eyelids began to twitch so rapidly and skittishly, it was a wonder he could see past them. "Why didn't you tell me last week? Why didn't you warn me?"

Again, there was no reply from Harriet.

"It's too close for comfort, I'm tellin' ya . . . Why, before you know it—" The comic's words broke off again. He gazed morosely across the shop's narrow aisle and out the window. "Valhalla," he muttered under his breath. "Wednesday . . . So, you knew . . ." Then his voice grew more insistent—more panicky, too. "Besides, why did the Graham dame come back to see *Down & Across?*"

"Enjoyment?"

"Get real, Harriet."

"It's a very popular game show, Rolly. You know as well as I do that the ratings are—"

But Hoddal cut her off. "Me? Ya want to know what I think?"

"Of course I do. You're running this show, right?"

"I think someone's suspicious."

"Let's dispense with real names, why don't we, Rol?"

"Cuz they're going after Wanda!"

"Names."

"I heard it with my own ears, Harriet! Heard Stan telling—"

"Stop it at once!" Harriet made another swipe at Hoddal's arm, but he leapt backward in his seat while his flying sleeve made unfortunate contact with the white paper plate upon which his uneaten doughnuts rested. The plate and its contents went spinning toward the floor.

"Now, that's just a shame, Rolly. Wasting good food like that."

The comic stared at the linoleum squares nearest his chair as if trying to recall what the circular, brownish objects were while Harriet Tammalong regarded him. Her eyes narrowed, and her face took on a pinched and cunning look. "The husband—Rosco Polycrates—also met with Jillian Mawbry." Despite her prior command that Hoddal dispense with actual names, Harriet seemed to be getting true pleasure in producing hers.

Rolly's head jerked up. "Who's that? I know that name—"

"The lawyer, Jillian Mawbry. And the lawyer for Chick Darlessen's girlfriend, ex-girlfriend, I should say." Again, there was genuine relish in naming the screenwriter.

The comic turned bug-eyed. "How do you know that?"

"A little birdie told me."

"When?" Rolly demanded. "When did Mawbry—"

"Yesterday is what I heard."

Rolly Hoddal's neck seemed to shrink down into his shoulders until it all but disappeared. "I don't like this, Harriet. I don't like this one bit. Someone's onto us, for sure."

Harriet didn't reply immediately; instead, she dipped her cruller in her cooling coffee. "It's not possible, Rolly . . . And it's not *going* to be possible if we keep our wits about us. You came to me with this scheme, remember? Now, maybe you're right about a potential problem with Wanda; however, you had no cause to mention your concerns last night, especially considering our surprise visitor. Not to mention running the risk of having Orso or McKenet see us talking. Your behavior created a very awkward situation."

Rolly's response was an aggrieved: "I had my eye on Gerry and Stan, don't you worry about that, but I didn't know who your 'niece' was, then, did I?"

Harriet paused to think. "No, you didn't. But that still doesn't excuse you from blabbing—"

"I wasn't blabbing, Harriet! I was being subtle."

"Like a brick stuffed into a sock." Harriet's expression

turned more manipulative and mean, and with the change, her crafty smile broadened. "By the by, the Graham girl asked me if I knew who Wanda was."

Rolly yelped.

"Max, too."

"Oh, geez . . . oh, geez . . . She's onto—"

"Of course, I denied knowing anyone named Max . . . Wanda was another story—that I couldn't deny."

But Rolly, in his fear, was no longer listening. "What I was saying back then, Harriet . . . that's not gibberish, that Valhalla stuff . . . those gods and things, they're in crossword puzzles all the time. Odin . . . Woden, the guy was called, too. That's where we get our word Wednesday from . . . Woden's day—"

"Don't start losing it on me, Rolly. We need to keep steady here. We've got a lot at stake, and there's no reason we can't get away with it, especially if we keep it strictly to ourselves."

Debra's Real Deal
Killer Ginger Critters

Heat to the boiling point one half 61-ACROSS

Add one quarter 39-DOWN, three 17-ACROSS butter, and one 17-ACROSS milk.

Sift together two cups of 7-DOWN, one half 17-ACROSS each of baking soda, salt, and nutmeg, 10-DOWN, powdered cloves, and ginger. Then, 50-DOWN with a tiny pinch of 40-ACROSS

Combine both mixtures.

Use additional 7-DOWN, if necessary, to make dough thick enough to roll out.

With your favorite cookie cutter, trim dough into shapes.

Place cookies on buttered cookie sheet and bake at 350° for 5–7 minutes.

Serve warm or cold.

Across

1. Germany; abbr.
4. Capone and Franken
7. 31-Across St.
10. Policeman
13. Wide shoe size
14. 33-Down relative
15. Boy
16. Ailing
17. RECIPE PART
20. New, prefix
21. Mr. Kazan
22. Owed
23. White stuff
24. Fixed
26. The_____ of the Roses
27. IRT stop
28. Grads
29. King of France
31. Bucs' home
34. Nuts!, in cartoon talk
36. Greek specialties
37. Theater chain; abbr.
40. RECIPE PART
42. Take ten
43. Meeting
45. North Sea feeder
46. Toss out
47. Charge
48. Takes too much; abbr.
51. Red or Black
52. UFO crew
54. Robinson Crusoe penner
56. Also
58. Health care choice; abbr.
59. Speck
60. Joplin specialty
61. RECIPE PART
65. Ms. Gardner
66. Mr. Buchwald

67. Mr. Turner
68. Comedian, Jack——
69. Old salt
70. Grease
71. Kicker's asset
72. Ms. Landers

Down

1. Discourages
2. Man on deck?
3. Changed trump
4. Honest_____
5. _____Angeles
6. Syrup source
7. RECIPE PART
8. Superman role
9. Personals
10. RECIPE PART
11. Margarine
12. Remove snow
18. Lyric poem
19. Harem room
23. Guess
25. Lugosi role
26. Lean
27. Guided
30. Medieval coins
32. Org. for 10-Across
33. Nile nipper
35. King of Spain
36. Leg joint
37. Power serve
38. Ult
39. RECIPE PART
41. Overdraft letters
44. Fair grades
48. "The giants lay Pelion on top_____",
    Rabelais

THE REAL DEAL

49. Fawn over
50. RECIPE PART
52. "Half full, or half_____?"
53. Mr. Mix
55. Ice on the Elbe
56. _____fall

57. Etna output
58. Toss
61. Beanie
62. Giant Mel
63. Mr. Tolstoi
64. Lemon add-on

CHAPTER

31

"So, Belle, you and Mr. Cute-buns Hubby here, figured out who the murderer was just from analyzing the crossword with that gal's 'Ginger Critters' recipe in it?" Outfitted in flamingo pink and holding aloft a near-empty glass carafe of coffee, the waitress asking the question all but loomed over a formica table, whose surface was as vibrantly pink-hued as her uniform.

The response to her query was a lively chuckle. "'Killer Ginger Critters' was what she called them, Martha—"

"Can we please dispense with referring to my bozo ex-partner's tush for just one day, Martha? Can we do that? Please?" The request, grumpy but not implacable, came from the police detective seated at the other side of the banquette table. He was dressed in casual "civilian" attire, but the choice of clothing—chinos, and a zippered jacket bulky enough to conceal a service revolver—had "off-duty cop" written all over them. ". . . And how's a guy supposed to get a refill on java around here? Does everything in this joint fall apart just because a murderer's been nabbed? Where's Mr. Lawson? I want to file a complaint."

"Hold your horses there, Big Al, I want to know how Belle figured out who shot the guy." The starchy pink dress remained in place. There was no move to fetch more coffee.

"First off, it was Debra who constructed the crossword puzzle, Martha—"

"Debra?" The detective jiggled his empty cup but to no avail.

"Lay off the fries and pay attention, will ya, Big Al?" was the waitress' quick retort. "Belle already explained this to you; Debra was the dead guy's lady-love—"

"She created the crossword that contained the recipe, Al, as well as the secret 'Deb' message in the puzzle's diagonal. I guess she must have believed that only her lover would notice it—"

"I guess she was *dead* wrong about that!" The waitress chortled until her retro blonde beehive hairdo shook.

"You're a bundle of glee today, aren't you, Martha? Now, how's about that java?"

"It's coming. It's coming." Again the waitress failed to move from the tableside. "Go on, Belle."

"It was pretty simple, really. When the local police confronted the killer with what Rosco and I had discovered, he confessed to the entire crime . . . What else could he do? We had him dead to rights."

"And . . . CUT!" Dean Ivald patted his cameraman on the back and stepped onto the set. "That was super, kids. Just super . . . We're going to shoot it again from the top, but I've got a few notes here . . . Quinton, you were perfect, on the money; hang onto whatever you had working for you there. I liked your strong, silent 'Rosco' in this scene, so let's keep it; we don't want him too smug . . . Now, Madeline, you can be larger, more over the top with your 'Martha.' You and Big Al have a joking/teasing relationship going on, so really rib him . . . And the same for you, Jes; it's tit-for-tat with Madeline, so don't let her 'Martha' get the upper hand on your 'Big Al.' Okay, let's take ten, and we'll pick it up from first position."

As the four principal actors and the extras who'd been seated at neighboring "Lawson's" banquettes left the set and began to move off toward a soundstage table spread with rolls, bagels, fruit juice, water, and coffee, Dean reached out and took hold of Shay Henley's arm. "Can I talk with you for just one sec, Shay, darling?"

"Is something wrong?"

"Not wrong, exactly . . . but I feel I'm missing the famous 'Shay Henley breezy relaxation' in this scene, especially as this is one of 'Belle's' wrap-up conversations. The crime's been solved. She's back on home turf gabbing with her long-time buddies. Normalcy has prevailed . . . But you seem on edge, Shay. Is it because we have the real Belle Graham here? Watching? I can certainly have her step outside while we shoot this scene, although her presence hasn't seemed to bother you before."

The actress sighed and leaned her head on the director's shoulder. "Thanks, Dean. I'm fine. It's not Belle; it's been a stressful week all around. I'll get it together for the next take; I promise. I'm just dealing with a few personal issues."

"Anything you'd like to share?"

"No."

"You're certain?"

"I'm certain." Shay sighed, then changed the subject. "I was thinking, apropos of this scene we're working on . . . Since Chick Darlessen named a character after his girlfriend, and the real Debra then killed him, don't you think we should change the woman's name in the script? It makes me uncomfortable talking about a 'Debra,' who instigated a murder. The lines of truth and fiction keep blurring."

Ivald shook his head. "No can do, sweetheart. Too much reshooting would be involved at this point. Besides, Debra's name appears in that crossword, remember?"

Shay nodded. "Right . . . name in the puzzle . . . It was just a thought."

Dean kissed her lightly on the forehead and said, "Okay.

Let's take a little break, shall we, and we'll pick it up again in a few minutes."

The director walked over to the coffee urn, filled a Styrofoam cup, and added cream and sugar as the real Rosco approached him from behind and said, "Have you got a minute, Dean?"

Dean turned and smiled. "Sure. What can I do for you, 'Cute-buns'?"

Rosco laughed. "I've never heard that one before."

Dean's smile grew. "It was from your wife. She thought you'd get a chuckle if I dropped it into the script. So, what's up?"

"I was wondering if we could swing by your office for a minute and pick up those .38 slugs? I'd like to run them down to the range in Inglewood during the lunch break . . . see if the folks down there recognize them."

Dean looked to the studio's concrete floor and shuffled his feet for a second. "Ahhh, yes, well, we have a little problem there."

"Meaning?"

"Meaning . . . they're gone. Someone's taken them." Ivald raised his eyes to meet Rosco's. He shrugged. "Don't look so disappointed, old chap. It saves you from ruining your lunch hour by spending it mired in L.A. traffic. In the long run, you get the same blasted results. Clearly, somebody wanted the bullets back, and it certainly wasn't the pistol range in Inglewood."

Rosco made no attempt to hide the irritation he felt. He gritted his teeth and let out a low growl. "Were the shells hidden, at all? Didn't you lock them up? Keep them safe?"

The director shook his head. "They were in the center drawer of my desk. I never lock the office. There's nothing worth taking in there. Besides, we're all friends here, right?"

"And who could've known where they were?"

"Clearly, whoever put the bullets in the gun saw Don Schruko hand them to me, or me show them to you. I don't think it takes an Einstein to figure out what I did with them after that. My desk would be the first place anyone would look." Ivald downed what coffee remained in his Styrofoam cup. "I don't enjoy being pushed, Polycrates . . . Now, if you'll excuse me, I'm scheduled to do another take on this Lawson's coffee shop scene." He crushed the cup, tossed it into a trash can, and marched over to his cinematographer.

Rosco filled a cup with black coffee and returned to the the darkened Vermont-country-inn set where he'd left Belle and Sara. His face failed to conceal what he felt: annoyance, frustration, and the uneasiness of having too many questions without enough answers.

"Let me guess," Belle said after he flopped down beside her on the overstuffed couch. "Dean Ivald's lost the bullets?"

Rosco looked at his wife; he was obviously surprised by her willingness to ask the question in front of Sara. "Sara?" he said, "You know?"

"I had to tell her, Rosco," Belle acknowledged, taking his hand in hers. "I couldn't keep her in the dark any longer. I've just about had it with these endless Hollywood secrets and disingenuous behavior."

"Those value judgments aside," Sara said as she moved from a rocking chair and joined them on the couch. "Is your wife correct or incorrect in her assumption that our dear director has misplaced the ordnance in question?"

"Oh, the shells are gone. No doubt about it."

"Humph," Sara sniffed. "Isn't that convenient?"

"How did you know Dean had lost them?" Rosco asked Belle.

"It was Sara who guessed," Belle admitted. "When I told her what had occurred, she said it wouldn't surprise her if the bullets were never seen again."

"Who knew you were capable of such pessimism, Sara?"

The older woman sat up straight and gave Rosco a theatrical scowl. He responded by chuckling.

"Oh, laugh all you want, young man, but it seems to me that 'lost' isn't as appropriate a term for our missing bullets as 'stolen.' Knowing that one has possession of live ammunition that wrongly appeared on a movie set might be a fine inspiration for blackmail."

But Sara's theory was cut short as Miso Lane dashed into the darkened area. His voice was a high-pitched and terrified rasp. "Did you hear? Did you hear the news? Someone put real bullets in Andy's gun yesterday! If it wasn't for our key grip, Dan Millray would have been killed!"

CHAPTER

32

The meeting for the cast and crew that Lew Groslir and Dean Ivald had called was rife with hostility, fear, and a mounting spirit of rebelliousness. Belle could feel the stormy emotions surging around as though they were a physical presence, like gray and foam-flecked waves crashing onto a beach. The actors, grips, cameramen, make-up artists, props and wardrobe people, lighting designers, script girls, best boys, and still photographers were all crowded into the "White Caps" set, the largest gathering spot on the soundstage. Only Dan Millray, the potential victim of the live-ammunition-for-blanks accident, was missing; a circumstance, Belle decided, that the producer and director must have felt was a blessing indeed. Having released the actor when his scheduled filming was completed, they obviously had no desire to call him back for this messy debate. There were enough irate voices to deal with.

It was Louis Gable who led the charge. Perhaps his decision to be the first to speak was due to the fact that he played the innkeeper in the film, and therefore felt it incumbent to serve as the group's "host" and spokesperson, or perhaps the choice grew out of his many years in the business and a sturdy mistrust of all those who wore producer's caps. Whatever the actor's motives, his formerly congenial self was gone; in its place was a white-haired man whose ruddy cheeks were not due to the cold of a wintry, Vermont country inn, but to outrage, choler, and a fondness for single malt scotch. "And how long were you going to keep this nasty little secret quiet?" Gable's once-companionable gaze raked the producer and director. "Someone could have been killed!"

"Any one of us!" Ginger Bradmin added. Her voice was shrill. Her body all but quivered with fury. "Not just Dan, although, he was clearly—"

"Now, Ginger, what you're assuming isn't entirely—" Quinton began, but she spun tigerlike on him.

"You shut up! Just shut up! You have no idea what I was going to say—"

"That Dan was in the line of fire—"

"All of us were!" Ginger spat out.

"Your scene wasn't even—"

"We were all there for Millray's death scene, remember? Dean wanted us to be—"

"You can't blame our director for the fact that you—"

But she countered Quint's efforts with a swift and dismissive: "I don't know why you were hired for the part of Rosco anyway. Lance would have been far better."

"Now, boys and girls," Dean Ivald called above the din. "Let's not allow former marital relationships to get in the way of—"

"Butt out, Dean," Ginger hissed, "I'll talk to my ex in any fashion I choose. It's no concern of yours."

"Miss Diplomatic," Quint tossed in. "I hope you're not considering working in future Dean Ivald productions. Besides, the reason I was cast—and not lover-boy Lance—is that the role calls for an emotional quality and approach that's steady and perceptive, not hot-headed and hair-triggered."

"What you know about perceptive, Quint, could be written on the head of a pin."

It was Andy Hofren who succeeded in curtailing this spat between the former spouses. "And I could well have become a murderer in real life. That's very upsetting, Lew. If it wasn't for Don Schruko . . ."

Carol Von Deney turned to gaze at Andy—staring steadily down at him as she stood a good four or five inches taller. The witch of the show was either still in character, or her present caustic and arrogant demeanor belonged to the true Carol. "The point isn't that an actual homicide nearly occurred during the film's murder scene, Andy. Or that you might have become a real-life killer and Dan Millray a none-too-willing corpse. The point is that a weapon with live ammunition was left sitting casually—and carelessly—on the set. As Ginger has been trying to explain, anyone here could have picked it up, pointed it at any other person present, a script girl . . . one of the still photographers . . . my make-up man . . . anyone, and jokingly announced, 'Bang, you're dead!', and pulled the trigger—"

"That's absurd, Carol," Madeline Richter interjected. "No one here would be that foolhardy."

"No?" Carol parried as her sharp glance returned to Andy Hofren. "You don't think the trigger-happy clown who plays my charming husband isn't capable of an idiotic stunt like that?"

"I won't be spoken to in that fashion, Dean," Andy all but shouted at the director. "If you can't keep your cast—"

"Phone your agent if you've got a complaint, Andy," Carol countered. "I'll say anything I want."

"Gentlemen . . . ladies," Louis Gable ordered, "let's remember why we're here—"

Lew Groslir cut off the actor's words before he could expand on his insurrection motif. "That's right. Let's remember why we're here, everyone. Now, I admit this live ammo thing was an unfortunate mistake . . . but that's all it was: an accident—"

"Just like the other accidents?" a voice called out. Belle turned to see who was now openly challenging the producer, but whoever had spoken remained anonymous. The question, however, grew in strength and urgency, and was echoed by many members of both crew and cast.

Lew Groslir raised his hands as the words "accident" and "jinxed set" ricocheted around the vast and barnlike structure. The gesture, intended to be palliative, had a curiously worried appearance, as if the producer were the victim of an armed robbery. "If you're talking about the equipment that fell on Nan DeDero—"

"She complained on a number of occasions that she felt the set wasn't safe," Louis Gable argued.

"Probably because Gable was on site . . ." Belle heard a voice behind her mutter. The reply was very sotto voce:

"Oh, come on . . . Nan's been around the bend so many times, she probably forgot he was one of her castoffs."

"Not from what I witnessed," the first voice chortled. "Besides, don't you remember the stories that started circulating just after those two got hitched? Battery and everything . . . ?"

"You're kidding. From that harmless, old coot?"

"Scout's honor . . . What was that headline I liked so much . . . ? HAWAIIAN HONEYMOON WITH ADDED PUNCH. Besides, Louis Gable wasn't always old. Or paunchy . . . or Mr. Altruism as he is today."

Belle turned around to see who the gossips were, but the area was so packed with other concerned members of the *Anatomy* set that it was impossible to detect who the purveyors of those particular pieces of dirt might be.

There was a general stir of discontent while Lew Groslir fluttered his manicured hands, and Dean Ivald issued a stern "People . . . people . . . We need to wrap things up here. Unfortunate circumstances shouldn't make us forget that we're professionals here."

"Not all of us, Dean," another malcontent sang out. "You hired one actor who wasn't union when you cast her—"

"Who said that?" the director fumed. "Which one of you is daring to cast aspersions on Mrs. Briephs or her performance?"

No answer was forthcoming. Ivald pursued the question for another moment, before adding a cold and cautionary "That's an ungracious and mean-spirited comment, especially when I consider how pleasant and welcoming you've all been to Mrs. Briephs."

Belle glanced at Sara, who was standing beside Rosco. She seemed to be taking this newest controversy in stride. Her head was held high with pride. "Might I have a word, Dean?" she asked in her typically calm and blue-blood manner. Then she faced the group as if addressing a political rally of voters who were critical of her brother's senatorial leadership. "You all have been so very kind, and so very forgiving. If I had known that prior membership in the actors' unions was of such paramount importance, I certainly would not have accepted Dean's and Lew's invitation to join the cast."

No one responded to her statement. In fact, an awkward unease seemed to settle on the crowd. In the silence, Ivald forced a laugh, then continued in a louder and brighter tone. "We're all tired . . . I know that . . . And it's a strain working on such an emotional project. You can't have a film project about a jealous spouse and a dead rival without it taking its psychic toll . . . I tell you what . . . why don't we take a breather. It's Thursday afternoon . . ." He looked toward Lew Groslir who returned the glance with an almost imperceptible nod that Belle recognized as being part of their good cop–bad cop routine. ". . . What do you say, Lew? We take Friday off and resume filming our final scenes Monday? I think our boys and girls deserve a bit of respite, don't you?"

The producer gazed at the director as though he were carefully pondering a suggestion he hadn't previously considered. "You're the artist, Dean. If you feel we can afford the time—"

"I believe we can, Lew," Dean called cheerily back, "and I believe we should. No point in running these marvelous thespians ragged, or our devoted crew." He graced the group with a doting and parental smile. "Now, my hunch is that we've got a serious prankster among us—and maybe a joke that got more than a bit out of hand. After all, Dan himself, pulled quite a terrifying stunt during his death scene, and before we go any further, I think we should all give Mr. Schruko a nice round of applause for being on his toes and saving the day."

The cast and crew turned to face the key grip and gave him an enthusiastic ovation. He humbly waved his hand in an all-in-a-day's-work gesture.

"Now," Dean continued, "I'd like to give our prankster an opportunity to come forward. There'll be no repercussions; a joke's a joke. You all have my contact numbers: home, cell, car . . . If there's information you wish to share, or a suspicion, or even a confidential confession, call me . . . Or ring me up if you'd simply like to chat about other concerns. Perhaps you're having issues with a fellow performer or crew member, or you saw something you're troubled by . . . Perhaps you've heard rumors you don't like or understand. I'm here for you. I want the remaining days on *Anatomy* to go smoothly. Give me a jingle. We're in this thing together."

"Oh, please. Welcome home, Joe McCarthy." Belle heard a male voice mutter, but her search for this latest mystery cynic was curtailed as Lew Groslir took up where Dean Ivald had left off. The producer's words and tone took an entirely different tack, however. Where Ivald had been benign and encouraging, Groslir was now combative and demanding.

"And come Monday morning, I don't want to hear another gripe out of any of you. That goes for you, Gable, and for Carol, and Ginger, and Quint, too. Talk to Dean, fine. Bellyache, sure, go ahead. If you want to whine about an ex-hubby or a lover who jilted you, that's between you and Dean. But just remember who does the hiring and the firing in this town. Actors who earn reputations as being difficult to work with or overly political won't find it easy to get future jobs."

"Let's not be too hard on our happy, little band, Lew. Everyone needs to vent on occasion."

" 'Vent' all you want. Me, I save words like that for the guys who install air conditioners . . . I'm telling it like it is,

Dean. These people want to work, they don't make waves . . .
They don't even make a tiny splash. And that goes for the
crew, as well." With that, Groslir turned and marched away.
Ivald followed close behind.

No one moved; no one seemed to even draw a breath. In
the eerie stillness that gripped the soundstage, Belle became
aware that Shay Henlee was standing nearby, and looking at
her intently. "Can I talk to you?" she murmured in a nearly
inaudible voice. "In private?"

CHAPTER

33

Belle knocked on the door of Shay's private trailer, the actress' home away from home for the duration of the filming of *Anatomy*. The star opened it herself before Belle's knuckles had time to leave the metal. Shay was still outfitted in one of her "Belle" costumes, blonde wig included; and the effect of these two similarly clad women greeting one another was striking. The actress ran a quick hand through her hair, tossing it away from her face in a gesture that was a mirror image of Belle when hurried or distracted.

"Sorry, force of habit," Shay said with an apologetic smile. "When I'm working on a part, I try to inhabit the character completely—around the clock. That way I know I won't revert to 'Shay' when the cameras start rolling." She smiled more fully, but Belle could sense a definite unease, almost a sense of mistrust. "Call it brainwashing from my Actor's Studio days."

"You wanted to see me?" Belle asked.

Shay's response was to walk the length of the trailer's main room and pick up a stuffed teddy bear. There were a good many toy animals piled on the built-in, wrap-around sofas.

She then put it down and reached for another plush-covered creature. "My 'good luck gang' . . . Whenever I'm doing a shoot, someone inevitably discovers my collection and adds to it. The tradition began with my first role . . . Now I have to drag these guys with me wherever I go." She touched a moose with floppy, felt antlers and a crooked, oversized grin. "He's from *Ice House,* the story about the U.S. Women's Curling Team that made its first big win over Canada . . ."

Belle decided to keep quiet and let the actress choose when to bring the conversation to the situation that was troubling her.

". . . It was my mom, really, who started the whole idea of the menagerie . . . At least they're not *glass.*" Shay pursed her lips as if she'd said more than she wanted, then abruptly turned toward Belle. "A man followed me home. I didn't see him, but my mother did. I live with my mom . . . or she lives with me. Our place is perched on the side of a hill, and she was on the deck upstairs looking out for me because I was late . . . She does that."

Again, Belle sensed it was best to remain silent.

"I know it seems weird to live with your mother . . . No one is aware that I do . . . Well, my agent, but she . . . I mean, it's not that it's a secret, but . . . I suppose what I'm trying to say is that other performers in my position have significant others in their lives, and I have, well, Mom."

Belle smiled. "My mother died a long time ago. I think you're very lucky. Both of you."

Shay's eyes creased in empathy and regret. Belle realized the actress was struggling with a feeling of guilt for bringing up a potentially painful subject, so she returned the conversation to the stranger who had followed Shay home.

"Did your mother get a description of the man?"

Shay shook her head "no," then added a soft "I'm sorry about your loss."

"So am I," was Belle's quiet reply. "As I said, it was a long time ago, but I guess that's why I always like hearing happy stories that feature mothers and daughters."

"What about your dad?"

"He's gone, too." Belle's smile was pensive.

"Oh, dear. I guess I'm really putting my foot in my mouth this afternoon."

"It's okay . . . Well, that's not quite true. It's not easy losing both parents . . . But it does mean that I'm a grown-up living on my own terms."

Shay didn't respond for a long moment. "That's not a bad position to be in," she finally said.

"No, it's not," Belle agreed after another pause. "So . . . tell me about this mystery man."

The actress sighed and seemed to mentally shake herself out of Belle's world and back into her own. "All I know is that he was driving a pickup truck, which really narrows it down—there's only two million of them around. Like I said, Mom was out on the deck, and she saw my car climbing up the hill toward our home. It's a winding road and fairly free of traffic, so she was able to spot me when I was still at a distance. Right on my tail was another vehicle. She told me later she was surprised I hadn't noticed it." Shay hesitated. "I suppose I was distracted. This was Monday. The day we all learned that Chick had been murdered."

Belle nodded. "What happened when you reached the house?"

"I beeped myself into the garage as I usually do, then closed the door electronically and walked upstairs."

"And the truck?"

"Mom said it sat for a few seconds then sped off as the garage door settled back into place. We have exterior lights that are triggered when a car nears the house, so her assumption was that the driver didn't want to be identified . . . Look, I wouldn't mention this situation now if it weren't for today's problems—the live bullets and everything, and Dean asking for the offender to come forward . . . I've attracted my share of weirdos during my career, and I'd just assumed this was another oddball fan, maybe a guy who followed me from the studio parking

lot . . . I had to get a restraining order on one of these
creeps once."

"I gather your mother felt it was more serious."

The actress shrugged. "She's a worrywart, what can I say?
She's terrified that some nutcase will start stalking me again."

Belle thought. "Are you suggesting . . . no, that's too
strong a word . . . Are you beginning to suspect that there
may be a connection between the live ammunition and your
unwelcome visitor? Or even the situation with Chick?"

"I don't know what I'm thinking, Belle . . . but something feels very peculiar. I'm an intuitive person. I guess
that's what made me decide on an acting career. And I'm
starting to feel that these seemingly random and unrelated
incidents may, in fact, be linked. I was standing next to Nan
when part of the *Anatomy* set collapsed. A strange man followed me home. And now we have a dead writer and a prop
pistol filled with real bullets. As Ginger and Carol both said,
anyone could have picked up the gun and used it to commit
a murder, which would have looked like a tragic mistake."

Belle's brow furrowed in concentration. "Do you think
you could have been a target—a *potential* target?"

Shay shook her head, but there was uncertainty in her action. "All I know is that something isn't right."

Belle sat and looked around the cozy confines of the
trailer. The actress had made an otherwise sterile environment into a homey and ultrafeminine suite. There were floral-
patterned throw pillows, scented candles, a dressing table
lined with pastel-hued glass bottles, and the nondescript
wall-to-wall carpeting was dotted with vintage throw rugs.
"It's never an easy question to address, Shay, but do you
think you might have an enemy?"

"Me?" The actress was obviously nonplussed. She also
sat, but she did so with unaccustomed heaviness as if her
feet had been kicked out from under her.

"If these events are related in some fashion, then maybe
you're . . ." Belle paused. She didn't like frightening people,
but Shay had approached her, and was clearly seeking her

counsel. "What if that falling piece of scenery wasn't an accident? And what if Nan DeDero was not the intended target? What if it was meant to land on you?"

"Meaning that someone may also have intended to pick up the prop gun and take a potshot at me?" Shay interjected. "But then, where does this shadowy pickup truck factor in?"

"I don't know." Belle sighed while the actress crinkled her brow in concentration.

"I honestly don't believe I have an enemy in the world, Belle."

"Some of your fellow cast members wouldn't be able to make the same claim," Belle said with an effort at levity.

Shay's reaction was a small and world-weary chuckle. "You didn't see their best sides today, not by a long shot."

"No, I didn't," Belle agreed. "But what I did witness were people who appear quite disturbed about past relationships— and unable to let things drop."

"You mean Ginger and Quint? That's ancient history."

"Their anger toward each other seems very much alive."

"I think the issue is really Lance diRusa who was Quint's main contender for the 'Rosco' part and who, rumor has it, caused the break-up of Quint's marriage."

"So, Ginger and Lance are an item?"

Shay shook her head again. "Not any longer. He dumped her for Carol. And, somewhere along the line, Lance was also attached to Debra Marcollo."

Belle found her jaw hanging open. "One big, happy family."

Shay smiled fleetingly. "It was worse when Nan was still on the set. She and Louis Gable continue to behave like oil and water on occasion—"

"I heard mutterings to that effect just a few minutes ago." Belle frowned again. "What about Dan Millray?"

"Oh, Dan's a sweetheart! He wouldn't harm a flea."

"But someone almost did more than harm him," Belle replied. "Andy Hofren, in fact . . . whom Carol Von Deney seems to particularly dislike . . . Now, don't tell me those two were once a loving pair."

Shay was quick with her denial. "Not Andy," she stated. "He's not, well . . . He's not into girls."

"Sexual orientation has nothing to do with murder, but a spurned lover—of any sex—could try to turn Andy into an accidental killer . . . even attempt to shoot him with his own prop weapon."

"Andy's too much of a professional to let his private life interfere with his work."

"And Ginger, Quint, Carol, and Lance are not?"

"I see your point," Shay said. "In any good drama, passion can, and does, drive many a tragic character around the bend."

The two women sat in silence for a minute or two before Shay resumed speaking in a slow and deliberate tone. "I realize these relationships might seem a little, well, incestuous to an outsider, but they're not so very unusual for those of us in the business. Hollywood's a small place, and actors who have achieved a certain stature cross paths all the time. The ongoing joke is that 'a couple is madly in love until the show closes.' Well, the shows around here only run from four to eight weeks."

"What about you?" Belle asked. "Do you have skeletons in your closet, too?"

Shay stiffened, and Belle immediately regretted the query. Obviously, an actress who was loath to admit she lived with her mother would be reluctant to tell tales about her love life.

"I'm sorry, Shay, that was rude."

The actress either ignored or overlooked Belle's apology, instead stating a clear "You asked about professionalism. And I think that's a good point. Everyone here needs his or her job, either for the money or as a career move. In the long run, I don't believe any cast member would risk that security by committing murder, no matter how upset and disillusioned and hurt . . . This isn't the same as Debra shooting Chick."

Belle didn't respond. What was the point of creating new rumors and uncertainties? Instead, she said, "What do you want me to do with this information?"

"I really don't know . . . Maybe I just needed to talk to someone. Because if I tell my mother about the incident with the live ammunition, she'll call my agent and insist on a bodyguard, or worse—"

"Maybe a bodyguard's not a bad idea, Shay. At least for the time being."

"I hate calling attention to myself." The actress looked into Belle's face. "I know what you're thinking. Performers are supposed to have inflated egos, need a lot of stroking and public approval, but many of us simply want to disappear into our parts. We don't like standing out in a crowd. I guess it's because we're basically shy people . . ." Shay let her words trail off, then sighed. "I'll give your suggestion some thought." She stood. "I'm sorry to have called you in here in such a panicky mode. That meeting with Dean and Lew upset me more than it should have." She forced a smile. "'A grown-up living on my own terms' . . . I'm going to remember that."

Belle also stood. She walked toward the trailer door, but before reaching for the knob, she had a sudden inspiration. "Does the name Wanda mean anything to you?"

Shay cocked her head to one side, another perfect replica of Belle's behavior. "Just the movie, I guess."

"*A Fish Called Wanda?*"

"That's right. Why do you ask?"

"No reason. The name was in a crossword someone made me."

"A submission for your annual compendia? Or just a secret admirer?"

Belle chuckled. "You know a lot about my work habits, don't you?"

"That's my job, isn't it?"

CHAPTER

34

Santa Monica's Third Street Promenade had been closed to traffic years ago. In place of lines of moving or parked cars was a pedestrian walkway made festive with potted palm trees, fountains, and hanging baskets of flowers that bloomed, in true Southern California fashion, all year long. High-end shops lined the busy thoroughfare, and storefronts not offering up trendy merchandise had been refitted into restaurants featuring outdoor dining under large canvas umbrellas, the type found in open-air markets in Italian hill towns. The Promenade was a scenic and attractive gathering place; and even though the temperature had once again dipped into the sixties with the setting of the sun, it was no wonder that Sara Briephs insisted on eating her next to last California dinner *alfresco*.

"You see . . . it most definitely is not cold," Sara announced without much conviction as she rounded the corner of Wilshire Boulevard with Belle and Rosco on either arm. Belle's subconscious response was to slip free of Sara and work her arms into the sweater she'd draped over her shoulders. Sara followed suit. "Compared to Massachusetts, that is," she continued, "this is certifiably balmy."

"On February first?" Rosco said with a laugh. "I should hope so! We've got a foot of snow back home . . . and this certainly beats ice fishing in Minnesota."

"Don't be flippant with me, young man; this may be my last chance to have dinner under the stars until the flowers arrive in my garden in late May, and I have no intention of letting the moment pass me by."

"Carpe diem," Belle said with a shiver.

Rosco followed with, "Choose your poison, Sara, what'll it be? Sushi?" He pointed at a Japanese restaurant. "Italian? French? Maybe some seafood fresh from the Pacific?"

"I was thinking that a Mexican restaurant might be nice. I noticed one on the next block the other day. El Azteca, I believe it was, and I was intrigued by what in the world a chimichanga might be."

"There's only one way to find out."

Although it was a chilly Thursday night, the Promenade was bustling with people, and the restaurants were doing a lively business. Young street-musicians strummed their instruments and sang warmed-over Bob Dylan and Creedence Clearwater Revival songs from the sixties, positioning their open guitar cases at their feet in hopes of contributions from generous passersby. They couldn't have dreamed of a better mark than Sara Crane Briephs, who dutifully dropped a dollar bill into every open receptacle they passed on their way to the Mexican restaurant.

When they reached El Azteca, they were in luck. A group of four was just vacating a table in the front of the restaurant, and after the busboy had cleared it, they sat with a perfect view of the entire Promenade. Tall outdoor heaters had been strategically placed between the tables, raising the temperature to a comfortable seventy-plus degrees. Belle removed her sweater and draped it over the back of her chair.

"This is just perfect," she said. "Let's hope the food is as good as the ambience."

The waiter arrived and passed out menus, and Rosco said, "Margaritas all around?"

Sara sat straight up in her chair. "Well, I don't believe I've ever had a margarita . . . I guess there's a first time for everything."

But after the waiter trotted off, the fiesta atmosphere seemed to diminish, and the three sat quietly watching the pedestrians stroll by.

"This is certainly a mess," Sara sighed at last. Her statement needed no explanation. All three of them were still consumed by the past week's events. When Belle and Rosco failed to respond with anything more than slim smiles, Sara added, "I suppose it's entirely possible that Debra Marcollo is guilty, after all—"

"As always, it's a question of motive," Rosco said, "and to be honest, despite her presentation during my interview with her, Debra continues to be a major suspect. The evidence certainly points in her direction."

"But there's no way she could have put those bullets in the prop pistol the other day," Belle countered.

"Quite possibly the two issues are unrelated, dear," noted Sara.

Belle looked at her elderly friend. "I think they *are* related, Sara. The coincidence of six .38 caliber bullets going missing from Darlessen's beach house, and six bullets being found on the *Anatomy* set . . . well, it's a situation too obvious to ignore. And what about Nan's supposed accident, the one Shay is beginning to feel might have been intended for her? Or the mystery guy following her home? What about the hornets' nest that was stirred up when the cast and crew discovered live ammunition had been brought onto the set?"

"And what are your conclusions?" Sara asked.

Belle's glum face continued to regard her friend. "I have no idea." Then she sat up a bit straighter. "A lot of what

Shay told me this afternoon seems to revolve around Lance diRusa as a breaker of hearts and marriages."

"He apparently had ample reason to bear a grudge against Chick," Sara added.

"Enough for murder?" Rosco asked.

"Hear me out," Belle continued. "Now, obviously, Lance could have entered Chick's home, and he could probably have found a way to access the *Anatomy* set or even the pistol range in Inglewood where the prop revolver was rented. But something tells me that the evidence pointing to him as our guilty party is too easy—"

"The simplest solution is often the best," Rosco interjected.

"Let your wife finish, Rosco," Sara chided.

Belle gave her husband an arch and meaningful glance. "Thank you, Sara."

"We women have to stick together, dear."

"That we do."

The waiter arrived with their drinks, and the three fell silent until he moved away. Sara looked with some skepticism at the line of salt rimming her glass.

"Do I remove this or sip my margarita through it?"

"You do whatever you like," Rosco answered.

"But what is the correct mode?"

"To drink it through the salt."

Sara raised her glass and smiled, although the expression was still cautious. "Well, here's to my soon-to-be-embattled arteries."

Belle also smiled. "I don't think you need worry about health problems, Sara. Your arteries are probably a lot heartier than mine or Rosco's." Then Belle's face abruptly clouded, and her brow creased in concern. "However, if the accident that put Nan out of commission was, in fact, not a mishap, but staged—"

"Wait, back up," Rosco interrupted. "Are you talking about Shay's theory?"

"No," Belle answered slowly, "this one's my own." She paused for a brief moment before continuing; as she spoke, her speech gained speed and momentum. "What if Nan DeDero was the intended victim all along, meaning that someone needed her gone from the set, and what if, ultimately, her removal was simply a means to another end?"

"You've lost me, Belle," Rosco said.

But Belle scarcely heard her husband. "What happened after Nan was sent to the hospital? Sara was flown in as a replacement? And whose brainchild was that? Miso Lane's . . . whom I began to mistrust when I discovered he'd snapped all of those Polaroids back in Newcastle—"

"But where does Chick's death fit in?" Rosco asked.

"I don't know," Belle admitted, "but I *am* aware that Miso had access to the prop pistol . . . and I also strongly suspect he's fixated on Sara."

Sara laughed. "Not dear little Miso?"

"You see? That's exactly what I'm talking about, Sara! He has you completely buffaloed. He's up to no good, I'm sure of it."

Rosco looked at Sara, and then at Belle. "I don't see how this plays out. Are you thinking Miso Lane is connected to Chick Darlessen's death?"

"I don't know, Rosco. Maybe Chick discovered that Miso was intending to commit a very serious crime."

"Which would be what exactly?"

"Kidnap Sara? Hold her for ransom? Or her brother. Don't forget, the senator is up in Sacramento at this very moment."

"Well, actually, no," Sara said, "he'll be flying down here tomorrow to pay me a small visit. The coincidence of both of us being in California at the same moment seemed to warrant a meeting in the sun."

"See! See!" Belle said pointedly. "This all could be a plot by Miso."

"Oh, my dear," Sara said, "I'm very fond of you, and I must admit I've enjoyed being the center of so much attention, and

I'm thrilled to be able to spend a few moments with my 'very important' brother, but this theory of yours seems rather too inventive."

"Your brother's a distinguished senator, Sara. A statesman, really, with an international reputation. Perhaps this is part of a larger conspiracy. He's on the foreign relations committee, after all."

Sara laughed again. "What did they put in your margarita, dear?"

"I'm being serious!"

"That's what worries me," was the older lady's amused reply.

"Okay," Rosco said. "Let's leave Washington and international cartels where they are for the moment, and look at what we have: one dead screenwriter, a movie set that seems particularly accident-prone—"

"And my peculiar crosswords, especially the last one with all the names—"

Rosco shook his head. "I hate to say it, Belle, but I'm beginning to suspect those puzzles have no connection to the other incidents, other than the fact that I'd sure like to know who created them."

Belle stared at her husband. "You're kidding me."

"No, I'm not. I realize the latest mystery crossword has a potential name match-up—"

"More than potential," Belle countered with some heat.

Rosco took a measured sip of his drink. "Which sent you on a wild goose chase to the *Down & Across* set."

"Where I just happened to learn that Chick Darlessen was Bartann Welner's nephew," Belle argued.

"I think their relationship's completely circumstantial, Belle. Because from where I sit, we have a perfectly good homicide suspect in Lance diRusa. He had a motive for killing Chick, and a motive for wanting to throw a monkey wrench into the filming of *Anatomy*."

Belle swirled the liquid around in her glass. She didn't look happy. "Everything you're saying sounds very logical."

"Crimes often are," Rosco answered. "Even crimes of passion have a discernible pattern—"

"So you're convinced the crosswords have no part in Chick's death or the incidents on *Anatomy?*" Belle asked as she continued to gaze into her glass.

"I'm following logic again, Belle. If the mysterious constructor has information to share, why doesn't he or she come forward rather than supply a list of names that includes everyone under the sun? Except for Senator Crane, that is."

Belle frowned, then leaned back in her chair and released a long and weary sigh. "I understand what you're saying, Rosco, and you may well be correct . . . but I still would like to know who's creating those puzzles and why." Then she looked at her husband with a lop-sided grin. "Besides, I've never been a fan of logic."

As the chimichangas arrived, and Rosco—to Sara's surprise—requested another round of margaritas, a black-and-gold pickup truck was exiting Rinconia Drive in the Hollywood Hills and entering El Contento. When it neared Shay Henlee's hillside home, it stopped. Max Chugorro didn't want to risk triggering the sensors on the exterior lighting by driving too close, so he sat in the truck's cab and considered his options. *Words on paper,* he thought, *it's merely words on paper.* His brain repeated this soothing mantra a couple of times, then he picked up the package lying on the seat beside him, and eased open the cab door. The time was right for Max Chugorro to make his move on Shay Henlee.

Across

1. Dyer
4. Toupee
7. _____ and Mike
10. Command to Fido
13. Bat material
14. Garden tool
15. Dr.'s group
16. One-time link
17. LAST WORDS
20. But
21. Mr. Gooding
22. Roofing material
23. Cook book
24. LAST WORD
26. Head of the corp.
27. Mr. Chaney
28. Business letters
29. Computer technology; abbr.
31. Track shapes
34. Truck full
36. "_____ dead body!"
37. Laker's org.
40. LAST WORD
42. Thelma's connection to Louise
43. LAST WORDS
45. Deuce topper
46. *Gigi* star
47. Dye type
48. Vane reading
51. First lady
52. "I _____ Rhythm"
54. Mr. Sinclair
56. Great revue
58. Mr. Carney
59. Flounder
60. Tic-Tac-Toe loser
61. LAST WORDS
65. Ms. MacGraw

66. 100; abbr.
67. With 70-Across, LAST WORD
68. 28-Across relative
69. Nice eau
70. See 67—Across
71. Lauria of *The Wonder Years*
72. Type of trip

Down

1. Scamp
2. Tristram's beloved
3. Nickname for many a college athlete
4. _____ *Framed Roger Rabbit*
5. Debt; abbr.
6. Stage lighting filter
7. Veranda
8. LAST WORD
9. Roofing material
10. LAST WORD
11. List member
12. LAST WORDS
18. Cheer
19. Supped
23. Sheltered nook
25. LAST WORDS
26. LAST WORD
27. LAST WORDS
30. After a while
32. K—O link
33. NSW capital
35. Insecticide; abbr.
36. Court call?
37. B' Way's home
38. Feather stole
39. LAST WORDS
41. Imp
44. Worked a loom

FAMOUS LAST WORDS

48. Butt
49. LAST WORDS
50. Violinist Georges
52. Coffee option
53. Siouan
55. Tire fig.
56. Walk about
57. Wheel connector
58. Yemeni port
61. Mr. Ventura
62. Norm; abbr.
63. "Gotcha!"
64. Brando's first film; with
    The

CHAPTER

35

Rosco couldn't quite decide what was more unusual: the fact that Lance diRusa's theatrical agent had revealed the actor's home phone number without subjecting him to a barrage of questions, or the fact that Lance was willing to meet with Rosco at the drop of a hat. The issue of diRusa's Malibu house being only a quarter of a mile down the beach from Chick Darlessen's rental cottage was another phenomenon that came as a bit of a surprise.

Because of the astonishing ease with which these potential problems had been remedied, Rosco scooted out of the hotel without bothering to check with the front desk for messages—meaning that he missed the *Famous Last Words* crossword puzzle altogether. All he'd taken time for was a kiss from Belle and the standard warning, "Be careful, Rosco, Lance may be dangerous . . . and probably is."

At 10 A.M., the morning was already warm; close to eighty degrees, with bright sunshine reflecting off a lustrous blue ocean, it was a perfect day for a drive up the Pacific Coast Highway in a Mustang convertible. If anything, the ride was far too short, and Rosco spent the minutes enjoying the fresh air and wind, the sights of surfers combing the waves, and the pelicans riding the breeze rather than worrying if Lance diRusa really was a killer. It was possible he was simply a snubbed and disgruntled actor who seemed like a murderer. Why else would he agree to this meeting so readily?

Rosco exited the P.C.H., found Lance's driveway, and parked the Mustang near the actor's garage, beside an electric-green Dodge Viper. He was early. It was just 10:25, so he studied Lance's sports car for three or four minutes before ringing the doorbell. The heavy cedar door opened almost instantaneously, as if Lance had been perched there lying in wait for his visitor. "Like that Viper, huh?" he insisted with a cocky smile. "American muscle, just like me. A car needs to reflect its owner. That's something I like to tell the press. You see that Viper there, you see Lance diRusa. Special paint job. No one else has it."

In both size and weight, Lance was a near duplicate to Rosco, and he presented a similar confidence in stance and demeanor. But the actor's handshake and his boasting comments told Rosco he was dealing with someone far more arrogant, aggressive, and egoristical than he could ever be.

"Come on in," Lance said as his smile became less sincere and his voice took on a tone that was too loud for Rosco's liking. "It's a thrill to meet the real deal. I've been curious as to what the true Rosco Polycrates looked like. See, guys like me, in the industry that is, need to keep their mug in the papers, whereas the genuine article, like you, gotta do just the opposite. And I'm gonna respect that. I even turned off my security cameras . . . Yeah, I can't tell you how smoked I was when Darlessen screwed me out of playing *you* in *Anatomy*. I was really into that part . . . Brain and brawn . . . that's what I do best . . . my signature, you might say. Why don't we step out onto the back deck. It's more comfortable, and I've got a hell of a view of the ocean."

As the two men walked through the house, Lance made certain to point out his collection of Dali and Picasso prints, and with each one, Rosco was informed of the purchase price and estimated value in today's art market.

"Yeah," Lance said after they had settled into sleek black Italian lounge chairs on the deck, "I could've killed Darlessen for ruining that opportunity for me." This induced another laugh. "Of course, I didn't. But, like they say 'what goes around comes around.'"

Rosco paused for a moment, trying to ascertain the applicability of the remark. "Interesting," he finally said. "In fact, that's exactly why—"

Lance held his hand up, stopping Rosco in midsentence. "Hey. Hey. Who doesn't know why you're here? Why do you think I told my agent to cough up my phone number, PDQ? You could sell those seven digits of mine to any starlet in town for a fortune if you wanted. Hell, to be honest, I can't figure out why it took you so long to get out here."

"You were expecting me?"

"Sure. I was expecting you four days ago—you or the cops, and to be honest, I would have preferred LAPD. I would have liked to get a uniform out here. When I heard that Darlessen had been killed, I said, 'Man, the cops are going to be at my front door before I can finish my morning coffee.' Carpe diem, that's what I like to say."

"So does my wife."

"How about that . . . Anyway, whammo, next thing you know, they got Debra Marcollo locked up." Lance lit a cigarette, but rather than make him appear more macho, it made him seem weaker, less in control, and, to a certain extent, nervous.

"Weren't you and Debra dating at one time?" Rosco asked. He turned his face to look at the ocean's waves breaking on the beach rather than at Lance.

Lance laughed through his cigarette smoke. The sound was forced. "Hey, I've dated half the babes in Hollywood. If you're lookin' for a jealous lover angle, that ain't me. I can pick the women off the trees, anytime, anywhere. I can't tell you how many sweeties I've been through."

"So you're the one who dumped Debra, not the other way around?"

Lance inhaled deeply. "Is that what she told you? She said she dumped me?"

"I'd just like to hear your side of it." Rosco returned his gaze to diRusa's face.

"Yeah, well Debra's a liar. You can't believe anything she says. Sure she's gonna insist it was me who killed Darlessen. She's out to save her own neck." The actor gave his watch a nervous glance.

"Am I keeping you from something?" Rosco asked.

"No. No. I'm expecting someone. You want a beer or something? Tequila sunrise? Anything you want, I got."

"I'm fine. It's a little early for me—"

"Hey, sunup was a long, long time ago."

"Right." Rosco nodded, then got to the point. "When was the last time you were in Chick Darlessen's house?"

"A couple of—" Lance stopped in mid-sentence and flipped what was left of his cigarette out onto the beach. "How did you know I'd been in his house?"

"Debra told me," Rosco lied, then followed it with another falsehood. "Besides, the cops picked up a strange set of fingerprints at the house. I just figured they were yours."

"Hey, back off, I've never been printed. I've never been in the military. The FBI doesn't have any print records on me."

"I didn't say they were yours. I just put two and two together. I mean, you live right down the beach? So why were you in his house if you and Chick disliked each other so much?"

Lance reached for another cigarette but realized the move appeared self-conscious so he tossed the pack onto a long granite coffee table that looked almost purple in its blackness. "I'm trying to quit," he said to cover the move. "Look, that's my business why I was in Debra's house, okay? So drop it."

"But Darlessen was a real thorn in your side, right? He successfully barred you from the *Anatomy* set and stole your girlfriend."

"Darlessen didn't steal jack from me, I don't care what Debra says . . . Okay, hell, I was in his house because I was still
getting it on with her. I mean, why not, she's nearby, right?
She'd do in a pinch. And, yeah, she's got problems with
booze, but so what? Who doesn't? . . . Wait here." Lance
stood and walked back into the house. He returned in less
than a minute and tossed a key-ring to Rosco. "There. Those
are the keys to Darlessen's house. You don't believe me, walk
up there and give it a try. Who do you think gave those to
me? It sure as hell wasn't Chickie, I'll tell you that much."

Rosco studied the keys. "Why so many?"

"I don't know. That's what she gave me. The fat brass one
opens the beachside door, on the deck. I don't know what
the others are for."

"Do you want to go there now and find out?"

Again, Lance looked at his watch. "Nah, I told you, I'm
expecting someone. He shoulda been here by now."

"Forgive me for being blunt, Lance, but if you analyze the
facts of this case, you look guilty as sin. Darlessen steals your
girl, or borrows her, or whatever you want to term it. He
keeps you from greeting a lead role in a major TV film, you
live just south of him on the beach, you've got keys to his
house, your prints are obviously all over the place . . . And,
even if you didn't kill him, how can you sit here and do nothing and let your ex-girlfriend—or your sometime girlfriend—take the fall for a crime she didn't commit?"

Lance laughed. This time he seemed truly tickled. "That's
exactly what I told my agent on Monday! I mean, like almost
verbatim . . . But, hey, my prints aren't on that gun; Debra's
are. I don't know what kind of crock she's been feeding you,
but she pulled that trigger, you can bet on it. Me? I'm just
trying to make—" Lance was cut short by the ringing of the
doorbell. "I gotta get that. Take a gander at the view,
Rosco . . . stretch your legs . . . whatever . . . I'll be back in a
couple of minutes."

Rosco stood, but Lance returned almost immediately.
"Sorry about that . . . a little piece of business . . . Like I was

saying, I'm just trying to make the most of a situation. That's what you gotta do in my profession." He lit another cigarette, then said, "Now, I've got a little surprise for you . . . If you know what's good for you, don't turn around."

Naturally, Rosco began to swing his body around to see what Lance was looking at, but the actor growled, "I said, don't turn your head."

Rosco did as he was told.

"That's better. See, Rosco, I got some friends in high places. Some people who'd like to see my career really take off. And I don't mean just TV movies."

"I gather I've got someone behind me, ready to shoot, in order to make sure your career stays on track?"

"You're a smart guy. And that's exactly the way I was gonna play you. Quick-witted, clever, intuitive . . . Like I said earlier, I'm gonna respect what you've got to do. But you have to respect what I have to do. I'm just sorry you're not LAPD. It would make this a lot easier, and make a prettier picture . . . If you will."

Lance raised his hands slowly until they were level with his shoulders, as if Rosco had a gun pointed at him. "Just sit still, my friend, this'll be over in a second and you won't feel a thing." Lance looked past Rosco and added, "Are you all set, Carl?"

A voice said, "Ready when you are, Mr. diRusa."

Lance tightened his jaw and said, "Then, let's do it."

Rosco recognized the sound immediately, having heard it at crime scenes more times than he could remember. It was the whirring and clicking of a 35mm SLR camera with a motor drive attachment, most likely a Nikon. It went on for ten or fifteen seconds and abruptly stopped.

"Got it," the voice behind Rosco said.

"Great!" Lance stood and walked across the deck to Carl. "Can we get this in on Monday? That's what my agent's looking for. Maybe with a headline like, PRIVATE DICK SHAKES DOWN DIRUSA OVER DARLESSEN MURDER?"

"That's up to editorial, Mr. diRusa. I'm just the shooter."

"Yeah, well, thanks, Carl, I'll have my agent beam in with your editorial people."

Carl ambled up the side walkway of the house and Lance returned to his chair and said, *"Variety."*

"I gather you're not talking about the spice of life?"

Lance laughed once again. "I like that . . . 'variety is the . . . ' Good. That's good. Look, Rosco, I told you that my agent and PR people expected some major press out of this situation, and we haven't gotten even a squib in the *Toluca Times.* LAPD picks up Debra, and bang, it's all over in a week or two. Well, no way, José. We had to make a move. I said I'd respect you, right? And I did. We got the back of your head and that's it. We get my mug out there and you remain the mystery man. I respect what you do. You respect what I do. I'm a fair player."

"The problem I have with all this, Lance, is someone died last weekend, and a murderer is walking around free because the police have the wrong person locked up for it."

"Hey, you want to live in Fantasy Land, go down to Anaheim. I got work to do. I gave you a break here. End of interview."

Rosco stood, walked through Lance's house, and climbed into the Mustang without saying another word. He backed out onto the P.C.H. and headed north again. Anger at diRusa, at the whole publicity-hungry stunt made him strangely calm and focused. *At least I have the keys to Chick Darlessen's house,* he reminded himself over and over. *If I came away from this bogus interview with nothing else, at least I can return to square one without breaking and entering.*

Rosco left the P.C.H., relocated Darlessen's bungalow, and parked the Mustang on the road a hundred yards to the north of the house. Then he walked back along the beach where he climbed up to what had once been Chick's and Debra's second-story deck. Using the brass key, he unlocked the deck door and stepped inside into a central living/dining area with a galley kitchen at the rear. There was an open door revealing what had obviously been Chick and Debra's ocean-view bedroom, and another door, closed, that Rosco assumed led to Chick's small home office.

A cursory glance into the bedroom revealed little of interest, but the door to the second room was locked. Rosco tried the keys until he found the proper one, and swung the door open. There was a blood-splattered bullet hole on the wall; below it, on the couch, Darlessen's blood had dried into a dark-brown shade. More of it had stained the carpet. It resembled a thick coating of mud, but the odor was acrid and strong. The smell of death—there was no mistaking it.

Rosco sat on the edge of the desk and studied the scene as he tried to visualize what had happened on the night Chick Darlessen had died. *Did Darlessen catch Debra with Lance . . . or maybe someone else?* he wondered. *Did a fight ensue with either Debra or her lover wielding the murder weapon? Or was there some other issue at play? But then, why would the killer use Darlessen's pistol unless he or she came to the house unprepared, which seems like an unlikely scenario? Or, did the killer possess another weapon and opt not to use it in order to pin the blame on Debra? Or has she been the guilty party all along?*

Rosco groaned in frustration and leaned back on the desk where his left hand brushed against a brass cigarette box. He picked it up to read the engraving, "It's never too late to quit." He chuckled and shook the box. It made a rattling, metallic noise, nothing like the sound cigarettes make. He opened the box to find five weathered pebbles, each rubbed to a frosty sheen and nearly perfectly spherical in shape from years of tumbling through the Pacific surf. Rosco closed the box and set it back on the desk near Chick's answering machine. It had been disconnected from the wall jack, most likely by the police, Rosco guessed, after they'd listened to the messages. He tapped the play button and a computer generated voice indicated that there were three messages, all dated the previous Sunday afternoon—before Chick had been shot and killed. Rosco recognized Debra's voice on the first message:

"Hi, hon, I'm gonna be a little late. Gotta make a quick pit stop. See ya soon. Kisses."

The machine beeped and moved on to the second message:

"Hey, Chickie, it's me. I was hoping for a progress report. Where do we stand? Give me a ring."

The machine beeped for a third time:

"Chick, it's Stan, you there? Pick up if you are. Look, fella, we need to talk. This ain't chump-change . . . you know what I mean?"

CHAPTER

36

With her hand still clutching her favorite crossword-solving pen, Belle looked at Sara. "Putting aside logic for the moment—"

"Which I agree can be dramatically overrated, dear—"

"And Rosco's conclusion that the mystery puzzles have no connection to Darlessen's death—"

"Because, as you stated yesterday," Sara interjected, "if they're unrelated, how is it that the clues and solutions appear to have such uncanny bearing upon the case?"

To which Belle added a brief and gratified "Exactly!"

The two women were seated side by side on a beige ultra-suede love seat in Sara's hotel suite. A room service cart bearing two hearty breakfasts had been pushed aside, and the balcony doors were thrown wide open to the pleasant mid-morning sun. Sara momentarily glanced away from the crossword spread on the table before her to gaze through the doors. She was still clad in her dressing gown, a rather grand satin-trimmed affair she deemed appropriate for her new status as Hollywood diva. Belle was in her favorite jeans. The generation gap between these two friends was apparent only in their clothing; in all other ways, they behaved like peers—even to finishing one another's sentences. And sometimes each other's thoughts.

"*Famous Last Words,*" Sara mused. "An ominous title—"

"I couldn't agree more," Belle replied. "And look at 36-Across: '_____dead body'—"

"And ADIOS AMIGOS at 61-Across . . . especially in light of last night's dinner."

Belle's head jerked upward. "I know you think I'm crazy with my suspicions of international intrigue, Sara, but this crossword is full of foreign allusions . . . SAYONARA . . . ALOHA . . . CIAO . . . AU REVOIR—"

"The British TA TA at 12-Down—"

"I really don't like this, Sara. I don't like it one bit." Belle sighed in worried frustration. "Besides, the puzzle has a sort of teasing tone that makes me wonder if the constructor is playing a game of cat and mouse. And again, it's created on the same grid I used for *Anatomy*—just like the previous three." Belle leaned her troubled face into her hand. "What if someone *is* intent on kidnapping you? Some foreign group? Or . . . or maybe the senator?"

"I still fail to—"

"But it's possible, isn't it, Sara? Just admit that to me? That it is a possibility? And this puzzle constructor is literally scared to death to come forward."

"Well—"

"Wait! Let me get the other crosswords from my room. We'll lay them out side by side, and try to find connections. I won't be happy until we track down the constructor. Maybe I missed something in those earlier puzzles."

"But they appeared to be quite innocent offerings, didn't they, dear? Now, playing devil's advocate for a moment, what if the crosswords are intended as a jest of some type?"

"Well, I'm not laughing. And I don't believe you are, either. *Famous Last Words* doesn't sound remotely like a joke to me." Belle jumped up, spun toward the suite's main door, then suddenly turned back to the balcony, hurried over, slammed the French doors, and locked them. "Don't make a move till I get back. I'll just be a second. And, don't answer the door."

"Belle, dear—"

"Or the phone."

Sara laughed gently. "At the risk of sounding ungrateful . . . You're not a very large person if it came to alien abductors rappelling down the side of the building—"

"I'm fierce though," was Belle's swift reply. "And I can talk almost anyone into a comatose state."

As Belle and Sara huddled over the collection of mystery crosswords, Rosco was en route to Jillian Mawbry's home in Glendale. The attorney had felt the progress report Rosco planned to deliver was better handled at home, rather than in a public office building where their relationship could be compromised or unwanted questions might be asked. And besides, Mawbry had explained, since his property was undergoing a "major hardscaping," meeting with Rosco on Paula Avenue would afford him a chance to "keep an eye on the worker bees."

The first thing Rosco noticed as he turned off Fairfield onto Paula was the black-and-gold pickup truck with the sign that read MARQUIS DE SOD LANDSCAPING—LET ME WHIP YOUR LAWN INTO SHAPE! He smiled to himself when he spotted Max Chugorro and one of his assistants. They were unloading a pallet of aged and weathered brick. *Not a bad way to earn a living,* Rosco thought. *You were outside all day long, with different homes and different clients. And there was the creative side of it, too. Deciding which plants would thrive under what conditions, building a nurturing environment, working with your hands—to say nothing of the hours spent in hardware stores. That fact alone made the job appealing.*

Rosco parked on the opposite side of the street, and crossed to the pickup's tailgate where the two men were dealing with the bricks. Max glanced up, frowned, then returned his concentration to his task.

"Need any help?" Rosco asked. He was already rolling up his shirtsleeves in pleasant anticipation of using his muscles rather than a brain that seemed all-consumed with Chick Darlessen's death.

"Mr. Mawbry's not here."

"Not here?" Rosco's hands paused mid effort.

"That's what I said."

"He's expecting me."

"What can I say?"

"But—"

"Look, mister, I have a load of work to do. You got a cell phone? Give him a shout. Maybe he's on his way."

Rosco nodded to the air because Max had turned his back on him.

"I'll just try the doorbell—"

"I'm telling you Mawbry's not here."

But Rosco had already begun walking up the sidewalk toward the house, and as he did, he came abreast of the pickup truck's passenger seat. Sitting there, straight and quiet as a beanpole, was a small woman with pinkish-white hair. She was staring hard through the windshield; and Rosco had the distinct impression that something was wrong.

"Good morning," he said with a benign and noninvasive smile. "Nice day, isn't it?"

The woman didn't reply, although the corners of her eyes crinkled and her lips pursed in a tighter line making Rosco believe that she'd heard him.

He looked back at Max Chugorro, and wondered what the situation was; Max was watching his movements very closely. If it hadn't been for the sun, the warm skies, the presence of the landscaper's two assistants, and a neighborhood packed with comfortable homes, Rosco might have suspected some felonious activity. Maybe even an old woman held against her will. He tried the friendly ploy again.

"Back east, where I come from . . . Massachusetts, that is,

we've got a foot of snow on the ground . . . which makes this look like a real paradise—"

But Rosco's affable effort was curtailed when Jillian Mawbry's front door flew open, and the attorney himself barreled out. For such a physically frail specimen, he was moving with surprising determination and energy. His face was livid with anger. "You don't let me know you're here, Max? I'm sitting in the house watching C-SPAN for Pete's sake. I'm waiting and waiting, and you don't bother to inform me that you've finally returned with the right bricks, which I sincerely hope, this time around, are genuinely 'aged.' I told you from the beginning I didn't want new, and I told you I didn't want *facsimile* acid-aged or that tumbled junk, either." Mawbry merely nodded at Rosco. His concentration was wholly devoted to the landscaper.

"I didn't realize you were at home, Mr. Mawbry."

"What? You can't knock on the door like a normal person? You can't look in the garage?" Jillian nodded at Rosco. "I'm sitting in there twiddling my thumbs watching a bunch of D.C. hacks with comb-overs—and paying travel time for the Marquis, I might add. Maybe I should just start hanging out on the stoop like they do on the East Coast."

"Sorry, Mr. Mawbry," Max said. "I must have gotten my signals mixed. I thought you said you were driving home from the office."

"Which I was! Didn't we say you'd be here at 11 A.M.? Or was that my imagination? If you hadn't diddled away the morning, you would have been here long before me."

Max Chugorro's eyes hardened. "The traffic—"

"I don't want to hear about it." The attorney spun on his heel, barked a quick, "Okay Polycrates, tell me what you've got," then charged back toward the house.

Rosco glanced at Max and said, "Looks like we have an unhappy camper on our hands."

The landscaper merely shrugged, so Rosco followed Mawbry into the house, where he found him directing the remote toward the TV. The lawyer tapped the mute button,

silencing a balding defense department consultant but leaving on the screen his nervous, round, red face with its glued-
in-place hair. He appeared to be testifying in front of a senate
investigation panel.

"So much for that guy's pearls of wisdom. Don't you wish
it was that easy to shut up these clowns?" Mawbry said with
a world-weary sneer.

It took Rosco just over ten minutes to give the attorney his
verbal report. He opted to leave out any reference to Belle's
strange crosswords, as he felt they would be of no interest to
the lawyer. During the presentation, Mawbry interrupted
several times in order to toss in impatient comments: "I keep
telling you, I don't care who killed Darlessen . . ."; "I'm only
looking for reasonable doubt here . . ."; "You're not out to col-
lar a murderer, Polycrates; Leave that to the cops . . ."

When Rosco finished, Mawbry remained silent, nodding
to himself twice as if ticking off a private list but in all other
ways ignoring Rosco's presence and the information he'd
shared.

Then the attorney turned abruptly and accompanied his
visitor back to the front stoop. "Max is redoing the walkway
to the street, all in old brick," he said as if the previous conversation had already been stored in an internal file folder.
"That's what buyers want nowadays . . . What you see when
you approach a property is what counts. Nobody in L.A.
cares what's inside. That's what the realtors tell me, anyway."

Max Chugorro walked toward them. "Pauley and Sal-
vadore are going to frame out the job, Mr. Mawbry, while I
run over to Garden Depot and pick up some extra mortar.
I'll be back in twenty minutes."

Mawbry sighed in frustration. "I'll be gone by then."

"Yes, sir."

"Look . . . Max . . . try to make it *only* twenty minutes
this time, okay? I don't want your assistants making any
mistakes, here."

"You can count on me, sir." The word *sir* seemed to lack
the aura of respect normally attached to it.

While the landscaper returned to his pickup and his employer released another irritable sigh, Rosco asked, "I was wondering about the older woman sitting in Max's truck."

"You mean Harriet Tammalong?" was the attorney's distracted reply. "She's some relative of Chugorro's. I haven't seen her in a blue moon, but whenever she's around, you can write off the Marquis' day because you'll never get a lick of work out of him. She runs Max around like a puppet." Mawbry looked at the truck where Harriet still sat in frozen silence. "Maybe she's losing her hearing. Old folks get weird when their faculties start failing."

"That's not the impression I—" Rosco started to respond, but was interrupted by the buzzing of his cell phone. "Sorry," he said, "but I should take this."

"Keep me posted, Polycrates . . . And remember, reasonable doubt is all I need."

Mawbry hurried back to his house, Max and Harriet drove off, and Rosco answered his phone as he continued to walk toward the Mustang. It was Belle.

"Dan Millray's on his way to the hotel," she said. Rosco detected a surprising amount of nervousness in her voice.

"What does he want?"

"He wouldn't say."

"But he asked to see me?"

"You or me. He doesn't care . . . Rosco, he seemed highly agitated."

"Okay, I'm on my way. But I want you—and Sara—to go down to the lobby and wait for him there. Don't take him up to our suite or any other private spot. I'll be there in a half an hour."

"What's this about, Rosco?"

"I don't know, but stay in a public place until I get there."

CHAPTER

37

Rosco stepped off the wood-paneled elevator that had carried him upstairs from the hotel's subterranean parking garage and immediately spotted Sara and Belle sitting close together on the far side of the marble-floored lobby. They were perched on a long couch upholstered in blue and yellow and facing a matching highbacked chair. Neither of the women seemed to be talking, which was an oddity in itself. As Rosco approached them, he realized that Dan Millray had already arrived and was ensconced in the chair. He stood when he noticed Rosco, but the posture was neither casual nor relaxed.

"Sorry to drag you all the way back from the Valley, but there are a few issues I'd like to clear up . . . and then I'd like some answers."

The actor's gaze was more intense than Rosco remembered. Belle had been correct. Millray was agitated, all right.

Rosco nodded while he continued to regard the actor. "Have I missed anything?"

"No," Belle answered in a noncommittal tone, "Dan wanted to wait for you before he said anything—"

"I don't like having to repeat myself," the actor interrupted with some asperity, then forged ahead with a stern: "Here's the situation. Andy Hofren told me about the problem with the live ammunition. The issue came up this morning during one of our regular coffee and gab sessions. Andy assumed I knew. I didn't have a clue what he was referring to—"

"I would have imagined Dean Ivald or Lew Groslir would have informed you," Rosco said as a half question, half statement. "Sit down, why don't you?"

Dan returned to the chair, and let out a cynical chuckle. "Dean? Lew? I've been wrapped. Outta there, history, out-of-sight, out-of-mind. I'm the last person they'd call. Especially with bad news."

"I assume Andy also told you that the actors and crew confronted Lew and Dean?" Rosco asked as he sat beside his wife.

Dan nodded. "Indeed, he did . . . *And* the fact that everyone was given a day to 'cool off.'"

"If it weren't for Don Schruko checking that pistol—" Rosco began.

"Do I look like an idiot?" Dan snapped. "Do I look like an idiot to everyone on the *Anatomy* set? What do you people take me for?"

It was Belle who answered; her brow was furrowed in unhappy confusion. "What do you mean?"

Dan shot an irritable glance at Rosco. "Do you carry a gun, Polycrates?"

"For work sometimes. Not often, though. And not here. I'm not licensed in California."

The actor's voice became more severe. "I have a gun. It's a 9mm semiautomatic handgun. I keep it in a drawer in the nightstand beside my bed. The drawer is locked at all times, and the key is hidden in a secure spot . . . The ammunition clip is locked in another drawer on my wife's side of the bed. If someone broke into our house, we'd probably be dead long before I could get the damn weapon loaded and ready to fire, but I've arranged things in that fashion because I don't want my kids getting their hands on it. They don't even know I own a gun." Millray took a deep breath. "Where do you keep your weapon?"

Rosco wasn't certain what the actor's intentions were, so he answered with the truth, albeit hesitatingly. "We don't have any kids, so I'm somewhat less discriminating than you. It's in the closet out of sight hanging behind some old overcoats. When I travel, I put it in a gun vault."

"And if someone pointed a gun at you in jest," Dan continued in the same provoked tone, "what would you do?"

"I'd step out of the way, and ask the person to point it elsewhere. You never know when they're loaded."

"Now we're getting somewhere . . . And when you were in training to be a police officer, and an armed fellow officer approached you during an exercise, did you take his or her word that their weapon wasn't loaded?"

Finally recognizing Millray's argument, Rosco responded with a measured. "No . . . I always checked it out myself. That was policy at NPD."

"So, do I look like an idiot to you and everyone else connected with *Anatomy?*"

"You mean you had already examined the pistol?" Sara asked. "Prior to Mr. Hofren firing it during your death scene?"

"That's right, Mrs. Briephs. I took it from the prop table, and checked out all six chambers, and then personally handed the gun to Andy. And from that point on, I kept the weapon in my sight."

"Except for the moment when Don Schruko walked away with it to give it *his* safety check." Belle interjected.

Dan Millray shook his head. "In retrospect, I should have reexamined the pistol after Don returned with it, but I thought, *Why? What could be wrong with him making a second safety check?*"

"I don't mind admitting this," Belle said with a sigh, "but I'm very, very confused. How did live ammunition get into the gun between the time you gave it to Andy and when Schruko checked it? Unless Andy put it there?"

"Not Andy," Dan countered swiftly. "First of all, I've known Andy Hofren since we were at UCLA. We're good friends, and we work together on a regular basis. Second, he would have had to load the pistol right in front of the entire cast and crew. He never left the set."

"So . . ." Rosco said, thinking out loud, ". . . the bullets Schruko handed to Dean Ivald were never in the pistol, at all?"

"I know," Dan admitted, shaking his head. "It makes no sense."

The four sat quietly for several long minutes. Finally, Millray said, "I, for one, would like to have some answers."

"I think it's time I spoke with our key grip," Rosco suggested. "Have you mentioned this to him?"

"No," Millray answered. "Andy explained the scenario, and my first reaction was to come to you."

"Schruko told me that the reason he checked the pistol was because he noticed the seal on the box of blanks hadn't been broken, and he was concerned that the gun hadn't been loaded. Is that information consistent with what you saw on the prop table?"

Millray gave this question some thought, then shook his head. "I don't remember seeing a box of blanks. That's not to say it wasn't there, either sealed or unsealed . . . I just didn't pay any attention to that detail. I was focused on the pistol, removing all six blanks from the cylinder, double-checking them, and then reloading them."

Rosco leaned against the couch's back. "So the pistol was already loaded with blanks. Do you think it arrived that way from the rental company in Inglewood?"

"I doubt it. Even the paper wad in a blank can be dangerous if pointed at close range. I would guess they'd deliver an empty gun and a box of blanks with the seal intact, as Schruko said."

"Then logic would indicate that if the weapon had been loaded with the blanks, the seal on the box must have been broken."

Dan Millray reached into his shirt pocket, pulled out a slip of paper and handed it to Rosco. "Here's Don Schruko's home phone number. I'd like to hear his side of this story, and something tells me that you might be better at getting answers than I am."

CHAPTER

38

"So, what's up?" Don Schruko called out as he approached Rosco. The two men were at the far end of the Redondo Beach Sportfishing Pier where Rosco been been waiting for the key grip for a little over ten minutes. At Schruko's back, a number of fishermen had lines dangling in the water, parents and kids were out enjoying the warm afternoon air, and there was even a beat cop ambling slowly along the weather-worn wooden planks. It was an inviting, picture-perfect scene, full of comfort and homey tranquility, and Rosco was grateful Schruko had chosen it for their meeting. Or, he would have been, if his mind weren't so overwhelmingly distracted by his conversation with Dan Millray. In Rosco's opinion the key grip had some serious explaining to do.

It had taken almost an hour for Rosco to navigate the drive south to Redondo. He'd passed through communities he'd only read about or seen on postcards, and had repeatedly found himself wishing that he and Belle were vacationing rather than working. Venice Beach, Marina del Rey, El Segundo, Manhattan Beach, Hermosa Beach, and finally,

Redondo. It would have been fun to visit each one, stroll the boardwalk, sip iced cappuccinos, watch the antics of in-line skaters, open-air weight lifters, sleight-of-hand artists, the guy who supposedly juggled activated chainsaws.

Instead, he'd dutifully arrived in Redondo, parked the Mustang on Catalina Avenue, and walked to the International Boardwalk, determinedly bypassing its carnival-bright restaurants and anything-goes beach-gear shops, as well as the heady array of expensive watercraft bobbing peaceably in their slips.

"You wanted to see me?" Schruko asked again. He smiled, although it seemed to Rosco that the expression was less than amicable. The flip-side to the seemingly helpful and affable *Angelino* had bubbled to the surface.

"I'm going to level with you, Don. I've been pulling double duty on the *Anatomy* set . . . Debra Marcollo's attorney had asked me to do a little snooping around while I was ostensibly watching out for Mrs. Briephs."

"Yeah? So?"

"So . . . I've just had an interesting conversation with Dan Millray. He swears up and down that the pistol used in his death scene was filled with blanks from the very beginning. He told me he would never have allowed another actor to point a weapon at him without making certain it was clean."

Schruko shrugged. "Performers don't handle props until rehearsal starts or film is rolling. That's why we have unions."

"Maybe they're not *supposed* to, but Millray insisted he checked that pistol over and over again, and personally handed it to Andy Hofren, and then continued to monitor it until the moment you handled it, which is the only time he lost sight of it."

The key grip regarded Rosco. Gone completely was the genial, almost toadying, demeanor he habitually wore when working in the studio. "What can I say, buddy? All I know are the union rules. If Millray says different, that's his la-de-da." Schruko frowned. "Besides, what's this got to do with Debra Marcollo?"

"I was hoping maybe you could help me on that situation, too."

"What makes you think that?"

Rosco studied Schruko while his peripheral vision maintained a steady observance of the other inhabitants of the pier. The key grip was a big man, as Rosco was newly assessing; and his posture and stance appeared to be undergoing a metamorphosis. Aggression now seemed to mingle with latent rage.

"Well, one of the facts I picked up from Marcollo's attorney who got the information directly from LAPD, is that six .38 caliber bullets went missing from the house where she purportedly murdered Chick Darlessen . . . Next, we have six .38 slugs mysteriously appearing on the *Anatomy* set, which just as oddly disappear—"

Schruko shrugged his broad shoulders again. "All I can tell you about is what I pulled out of the prop pistol."

"Which Dan Millray refutes," Rosco stated. The key grip's ain't-got-nuthin-to-do-with-me attitude was beginning to wear thin. "Come on, Schruko. Let's quit playing games, here. You didn't *discover* live ammunition. You *planted* it. Which leads me to assume you had a motive for calling attention to the shells . . . Because, *if* they are the same bullets involved in Darlessen's death . . . *if* they came from the box of shells left in the Malibu house—and I'm going under the assumption that they are—*then* my guess is that you're into some type of extortion racket. Or worse yet, you personally took them from Darlessen's home, which clearly places you at the scene of the crime."

Schruko didn't respond, but he stared hard at Rosco. What he was thinking was impossible to determine. Reflexively, Rosco took a step or two farther away from the pier's iron railing. When dealing with suspected criminals it didn't make a lot of sense to put yourself in harm's way.

"Is that the deal, here?" Rosco continued. "You're sending a message to the killer indicating that you're aware of his or her identity?"

Again, Schruko didn't reply.

"That's a dangerous position to put yourself in, my friend: blackmailing a murderer . . . *if,* in fact, you didn't kill Darlessen yourself."

Rosco watched Schruko's mouth move, and his face tangle into a line of panicky knots. "I don't know anything about six .38 slugs missing from the crime scene," he said.

For a long moment, Rosco didn't respond; then he finally asked, "You're telling me that the live ammunition you planted on the *Anatomy* set wasn't removed from Chick's beach house?"

"I don't know anything about bullets missing from the murder site," Schruko reiterated. "Nothing. Nada."

Rosco thought. "But you admit you introduced six live shells onto the *Anatomy* set?"

The key grip's response to this query was to abruptly shift his focus toward the water and the distant greenish-blue line of the horizon.

"Which you then proceeded to 'find' and present to Dean Ivald?" Throughout this line of questioning, Rosco had noted the changing emotions racing across Schruko's face. "Is Ivald involved in Darlessen's death?"

"The bullets have nothing to do with Chick!" The words exploded from Schruko's mouth; his eyes swiveled back to glare at Rosco. "I'm telling you, I don't know anything about Darlessen or his murder!"

"If you and Ivald aren't involved," Rosco continued calmly, "what about Lew Groslir or someone else working on *Anatomy?*"

"Aren't you listening to me, Polycrates? The damn bullets have no connection to Chick!"

Rosco didn't reply. Instead, he continued staring at Schruko. He had a hunch the man had information he wanted to share, and he was right.

"Look . . . it's just a situation that got out of control, that's all." Schruko's words died off, but Rosco made no move to speak. "I mean, how was I to know what kind of weapon killed Darlessen? Don't you see, when it came time for Millray's death scene . . . and Andy Hofren got so fired up about his expertise with weapons . . . Look, Polycrates, all I wanted was a little respect around the set. Is that so hard to understand? No one was going to get hurt. How could they? The real bullets never went anywhere near the pistol . . . They never even got close to it."

"Respect?" Rosco asked cynically.

"Why not?" Schruko all but shouted. "Actors, producers, directors—they treat the grips like furniture. Like nothing. I wanted those self-centered prima donnas to realize that I was important. I was the man—a piece of glue that held the entire production together, and that if any of the grips weren't on the ball, if I let my guys slip up just a little, then the entire cast would be up a creek. I wanted some respect for me, and my guys . . . And we weren't getting it. Not from the actors. Not from Ivald or Groslir. Not from anyone."

"But Groslir and Ivald kept the incident under wraps, so you had to leak the story yourself. Is that how it played out?"

"Yeah . . . Well, I only had to tell Miso Lane; that's sorta like placing an ad in the *Los Angeles Times*." Schruko turned and squared off against Rosco. "Look, no one got hurt. Where's the harm? Stuff like this happens on sets all the time. It's casual but under control, like the stunt Millray pulled when Hofren shot him. I don't see anyone giving him the third degree. Look, Polycrates, it gives them all something to talk about next time they go to some trendy dive and 'do lunch.' "

"And Don Schruko comes off as the hero who saved the day?"

Don shrugged. "Sorta."

"And the piece of equipment that fell on Nan DeDero? Who saved the day there? Or did someone miss their cue?"

"No comment."

"No comment—that's cute, real cute." Rosco shook his

head and looked south toward the long breakwater. For the second time in one day, he was in danger of losing his temper. Schruko had run him around in circles, and he felt like pitching the man head first into the Pacific Ocean. If the key grip hadn't been so heavy, Rosco just might have done it. Instead, he returned his steely gaze to the grip's face. "So this is all just a big game with you? Hollywood high jinks. Stack the deck for kicks. It's just one more TV-Land fix, is that it?"

Schruko's head snapped toward Rosco's. There seemed to be a genuine sense of dread in his eyes. "What do you mean by that?" he demanded.

"Just what I said. There's no honesty in any of this, is there? Just fun and games."

"Yeah, but what did you mean by 'fix'?"

Rosco shook his head incredulously. "What do you think I meant? You're an adult. Figure it out."

Schruko squinted, his lips were white and tight. He didn't speak for several weighty moments. "But how did you find out about it?" he finally muttered in a strangled tone.

Rosco remained silent as Schruko raised his voice and repeated himself. The words all but quivered with anxiety. "How did you find out about it? The fix? Who told you? Where'd you get that?"

Rosco frowned in an effort to camouflage the confusion he felt. "It didn't take a genius to put two and two together."

"Well, then how the hell could you possibly suspect me of having any connection to Chick's death? He's the last person I'd want to see dead."

Rosco had no idea where this dialogue was heading, but he decided to bluff his way as far as he could. "Well, someone certainly wanted to see Darlessen out of the picture."

Schruko gazed moodily at the ocean. He seemed momentarily to have forgotten Rosco's presence. "It sure as hell wasn't me . . . Why else would I quit my job as key grip on *Down & Across* and take the *Anatomy* gig? To keep an eye on my investment, that's why. I wanted to have Darlessen where I could watch him . . . and then the creep went and croaked before coughing up the three hundred grand he owed me."

Rosco nodded in seeming empathy. Like Schruko, he opted to gaze seaward, although his motive was a concern that his befuddlement would betray him. "I heard the figure was a lot higher than three hundred grand."

"Okay, fine . . . three-thirty-three; I was in for a third. Who's nitpicking?"

"Hmmm." Rosco scratched his head, now choosing to appear baffled by the facts Schruko was presenting. "It seems my source told me quite a different story."

"Who have you been talking to? You're not listening to Rolly Hoddal, are you? Of course you are, who else could be that stupid?"

Rolly Hoddal? Rolly Hoddal? Rosco thought. *That's the* Down & Across *comic Belle mentioned.* "That's right," he said, "Apparently someone's putting pressure on him. He wants to talk."

While Schruko absorbed this latest lie, Rosco's mind raced to fit the pieces together. Clearly, there was some clandestine connection between *Down & Across* and *Anatomy of a Crossword,* and Schruko—along with Rolly Hoddal—seemed to be the ones who could explain it.

"Listen, Don, I'd like to help you out, but if Hoddal gets to tell his story first, you know who the fall-guy's gonna be: Y-O-U. If you never touched the money, maybe you have a legitimate out. Maybe it's Hoddal who should be going down for the fix?"

Don laughed. "*Nobody* touched any money. McKenet and Orso never paid a cent of it out."

"Take me back to the beginning, Don. Let's compare what I know—and what Hoddal's likely to admit to in public—to the actual truth . . . the truth from your perspective. I'd hate to see the wrong person take it on the chin, here."

Schruko let out a long and exhausted sigh. "I've gotta sit down." He walked over to a wooden bench and dropped his big frame onto it. He seemed truly worn out. Rosco moved over and joined him, creating a false mood of camaraderie.

"Okay . . ." Don started, ". . . I was the key grip on *Down & Across* until this new gig with *Anatomy*."

"Right," Rosco said. Then remembering the *What's in a Name* crossword, he added, "*Matthew* took over your position."

Don nodded in agreement. "The entire situation was Hoddal's doing. From the start, it was his idea. His baby. That's straight, no lie . . . Rolly discovered a way to sneak into McKenet's office and get the answers to the crossword puzzle grids on the afternoons prior to the tapings. He knew it would look fishy if he was caught sidling up to any of the contestants, so he needed a middleman. That's where I came in. I was supposed to select a likely player, a good actor, someone we could trust, someone who could handle the fix under pressure and make it look like the genuine article. Obviously, it was a six-month proposition; the contestant had to start at the bottom in the first round, go undefeated, then wait for McKenet to schedule a Grand-Slam show. But once we got our boy there, and he won, we'd split the million dollars three ways—"

"So you found Bartann Welner."

"He was perfect. You never saw a guy with that much cool. He was like Gary Cooper posing as your great-grandfather. Not in a million years would anyone suspect that he was in on a fix. It worked like a charm."

"But then he died on you."

Don laughed with the irony of it. "Right. The best laid plans of mice and men . . ."

"Leaving Chick Darlessen with his uncle's million bucks."

"Grand-Slam Winners don't cash out till the show airs . . . but, yeah, that's the basic scenario."

"And Darlessen was willing to split his uncle's take?"

"Rolly worked that out somehow, not me. Maybe he had something on Darlessen. As you know, Hoddal's a pretty slippery guy. Whatever happened, I was just happy to learn that I hadn't lost out on my cut altogether. But now with Chick dead . . ."

"And no heirs, from what I understand."

"Yep. And Orso and McKenet won't air the show if there's no one screaming for a payoff. Why take a chance that some distant cousin might pop out of the woodwork? They'll just hit the erase button, adios Bart, pocket the million bucks, and move on."

Rosco nodded. "When did Orso and McKenet get wise to the fix?"

"If they knew it went down, this is the first I heard of it. I always assumed those two were in the dark, but I never trusted either one of them farther than I could throw them."

Rosco considered how best to respond. Since he was inventing the story of a game show under possible criminal investigation, further theories about the producer and star were probably better avoided; McKenet and Orso were two people he knew less about than Rolly Hoddal. "So, all the players are dead and gone?" he asked at last.

"Yep."

"Except there's someone who lost the Grand-Slam prize to Bartann Welner."

"Oh, yeah. I almost forgot about her . . . Wanda something." Schruko pondered this information for a few seconds. "You're right, she gets screwed out of her twenty-five grand consolation prize if McKenet doesn't air that show." Don leaned back on the bench, looked up at the bright blue sky, and let the hot sun warm his face. He remained motionless for a long time. Finally, he said, "Oh, man, I don't know why I signed on for this. I don't know what I was thinking of." He then looked at Rosco. "No one got hurt with this situation. No money ever changed hands. I swear it. I can't believe that cruddy comedian wants to blab about this. There'd be no proof of any wrongdoing if he'd just keep his damn mouth shut."

"I don't know who's after him, but I'm guessing he's not good under pressure."

"You can say that again. He was a pool of sweat when old Bart nailed that last answer to pick up the million." Schruko gazed at Rosco; appeal was written all over his face. "Can you help me out here, Polycrates? Tell Rolly to curtail his free-speech activities? He won't pay attention to me if he's trying to save his own skin, but he's obviously listening to you . . ." The words faded as Rosco stood and turned toward the pier entrance.

"It all depends on who's pressuring him to talk . . . and why."

"I don't know . . . I just don't get it. Why's he coming to you?"

"That's what I intend to find out."

Don dropped his head into his hands. "Try to keep Rolly quiet, will ya? It's just like the bullets on the set—nobody got hurt with this fix. Tell Hoddal to let it pass. Why bring it out now? The money's gone. Tell him to kiss it goodbye and keep his mouth shut."

While Rosco had Schruko in a talkative mood, he decided to look for one more answer. "Belle's received a number of strange crossword puzzles. Do you know anything about them?"

Schruko looked Rosco dead in the eye, then after a beat mumbled, "I might."

"One of the puzzles lists names from both *Anatomy* and *Down & Across*. You're the only person who's worked both of those sets."

"It wasn't me."

"Then who?"

Sensing a small victory, Schruko smiled. "I'll make a deal with you, Polycrates. You see if you can talk some sense into

Rolly Hoddal, and I'll tell you what I know about those puzzles."

"I'm not in the mood to play any more games, Don."

"You talk to Rolly for me, and then we'll have another chat."

CHAPTER

39

When Rosco returned to Santa Monica shortly after 3 P.M., a yellow Volkswagen dune buggy was in the midst of vacating a parking spot on the street in front of the hotel. He backed the Mustang into the space, turned on the alarm, and began walking toward the entrance's revolving door. None of his activities had been missed by the watchful eye of Belle, who'd been anxiously sitting in the lobby for twenty minutes waiting for him. She jumped up and hurried to the door, reaching it at the exact moment he did. They spun around on opposite sides of the glass panels twice before Belle jumped out on the sidewalk and waited for him to join her.

"Boy, have I got a news flash for you," she blurted out. The excitement in her voice made it bubble.

"And I learned some pretty startling information from Don Schruko." He kissed her, but Belle reciprocated with no more than a distracted peck.

"Me first," she insisted while her feet did a little tap dance of impatience.

Rosco laughed. "Not if I don't get a more enthusiastic greeting than that.

"Rosco! This is important!"

"And our marriage isn't?"

"Okay, okay . . ."

They kissed again.

"Better," Rosco said with another chuckle. "Not perfect yet, but—"

"Rosco!"

"Let's try it one more time."

Belle couldn't help but laugh. "You're too much."

"Just what I like to hear."

They kissed a third time. When their bodies pulled away, Rosco studied his wife. "That was a definite improvement . . . Okay, shoot."

"Shoot?"

"Tell me what got you so fired-up you forgot how to smooch."

"Oh, right . . . right . . .! The game show! Bartann Welner fixed it! The show was rigged! He never won the million dollars—at least not legally. Not honestly." Belle halted her rapidly escalating stream of words long enough to grab Rosco's arm and begin pulling him toward the Mustang. "Come on. Let's go. Harriet Tammalong knows who I am. She always has. She's been lying from the very first moment we met! And I thought she was such a sweetheart."

"Whoa, whoa, whoa." Rosco raised his hands and stood his ground. "Back up a second, will you? Let's start at the beginning. How do *you* know the show was rigged?"

"Harriet called me. She told me. She's an absolute wreck. She wants to talk, but not over the phone."

"Ahh, now I see . . . We're going to the San Fernando Valley to chat to the deceitful Harriet Tammalong, is that it?"

"Of course, Rosco, don't be so dense. What did you think I was talking about? Let's get a move on. I told her we'd get there by four."

"So, that nice little embrace back there's not going to lead to anything more *substantial*?"

"Rosco!"

"I know . . . I know. I'm 'too much.' "

"But in a good way."

"That's a relief. I'd hate to be compared to some of the less than 'good' folks we've been dealing with." Rosco smiled, shook his head, and the two of them crossed the pavement to the Mustang. But before reaching the car, he suddenly stopped. "What about Sara?"

"What about her?" Belle demanded.

"All your concerns about her safety . . . the clique of international felons . . ."

"Oh, she's fine," was Belle's airy reply. "The senator's chief-of-staff arrived in person to escort her to their lunch date. He had a driver and another aide in the car with him. They were both huge."

"And you decided to trust these guys?"

"Rosco, are we going to Harriet's or not? Of course, I trust them. The aide's been with the senator for years . . . Now, let's move!"

"Let it not be said that you lack patience."

"A virtue grossly overrated."

"According to you."

"Rosco, come on!"

His grin grew as he slid behind the wheel and started the car. "So . . . Harriet told you the game show was rigged. And on what startling new development does she base that fantastic notion?"

"It's not fantastic, Rosco; it's the truth. Apparently something you said to Don Schruko must have really struck a nerve. The minute you two split up, Don called Rolly Hoddal; he's the comic at *Down & Across*—"

"Thank you, Miss Information Booth," Rosco tossed out.

"What? I didn't know if you remembered that or not."

"I remembered." Rosco pulled a U-turn on Ocean Boulevard and headed down the California Incline toward the P.C.H.

"How come you never get caught making U-turns. It's not fair. Everyone gets caught but you."

"You'd rather Erik Estrada came up on his *CHiPs* cycle and gave me a ticket right now?" He spun the Mustang onto the P.C.H., screeching the tires slightly, and took off south toward the number 10 Freeway. "I assume you have her address?"

"Who?" Belle asked as she was rocketed back in her seat.

Rosco didn't bother to answer, but as the g-forces subsided, Belle said, "Oh, Harriet, yes, she lives in Encino, on Delano Street . . . We're not in that much of a hurry, you know. Erik and his buddies could be lurking around any corner."

Rosco eased off the gas a little. "Okay, so Don Schruko called Rolly Hoddal . . . And . . .?"

"And Rolly immediately phoned Harriet."

"And told her that *Down & Across* was fixed?"

"Well . . ." Belle admitted haltingly. "I'm not sure *what* Rolly said now that I think about it . . . All Harriet mentioned was that he'd called in a panic, that the show was rigged, and that she needed to talk to us in person. She didn't actually repeat Rolly's exact words."

"But she did tell you that she'd known your identity all along."

"Right! She said that, too . . . Well, I had to ask her because I was so startled to get a call from someone I believed knew me as Gale Harmble, journalism's jewel. Logically, she would have had to ask the front desk for Belle Graham, right? It's very suspicious, don't you think?"

Rosco responded with a sardonic. "Gee, I don't know, what makes you say that?"

She slapped his shoulder with the road map. "I'm being serious."

"So am I . . . But don't let anyone see that I have a map in the car. I'd hate to ruin my reputation."

"Hah. I'm going to open it up and wave it at everyone on the freeway and yell, 'It's his. The wimp in the red Mustang convertible needs a road map!' "

As they continued their drive to the San Fernando Valley, Rosco explained what he'd learned from Don Schruko. With each piece of information, Belle gasped, then murmured a stunned "Wow . . . Everyone's in on this thing . . ."

"And," Rosco concluded fifteen minutes later as they exited the 101 Freeway at White Oak Avenue, "apparently Schruko also knows who's been creating the crosswords you've received. But he's playing coy and refusing to divulge the name unless we can somehow squelch this business about *Down & Across* being rigged. It seems everybody is all of a sudden looking out for themselves. The rats are fleeing the sinking ship."

They arrived at Harriet's house on Delano Street just in time to see Max Chugorro's pickup truck disappear around the corner onto Zelzah Street. Harriet was still standing on her small concrete entry porch when Rosco pulled to a stop and parked.

"Wait a minute, you're the man who was at Mr. Mawbry's today," Harriet said as the couple approached her. "What's going on, Belle? I specifically said I would only to talk to you and your husband."

"This *is* my husband, Harriet. This is Rosco."

The older woman gave them a distrustful glare, but nevertheless opened her front door and asked them to join her inside. The small house was tastefully decorated, the furniture so well cared for it appeared brand new. Harriet was clearly attracted to Asian art. Japanese scrolls adorned the walls, and a collection of Chinese porcelain sat on glass shelves that were supported by wires hanging from the ceiling. She caught Rosco staring at the display and said, "Earthquakes. The shelves swing when the ground shakes and nothing falls off—just like at the Getty Museum. I didn't lose a single piece with the Northridge quake, and the epicenter was right up the street. My friends laughed at me. Well, ha-ha on them, look who still has her china . . . Please, sit, both of you."

Belle and Rosco sat on a camelback love seat, and Harriet

dropped into a small slipper chair. Her hands shook slightly, and her eyes blinked rapidly with what appeared to be a nervous twitch.

"I didn't do anything wrong," she announced with some force. "I want to make that clear from the start. It was all Rolly Hoddal—"

"That's pretty much what Don Schruko said to me this afternoon," Rosco replied. "Hoddal must talk a good game . . . Either that, or he's everyone's number one sap and fall guy."

Harriet ignored him. "And I never met Bartann Welner— face-to-face, that is. I only saw him from the audience. I never spoke to him." The shaking in Harriet's thin hands and fingers began to increase. "But I admit that I was a teensy bit suspicious of his success . . . It seemed too easy for Welner. He was a millisecond too fast on that buzzer . . . each and every time. It wasn't logical that a man of his age could piece the words together that quickly . . . And to completely shut out Wanda Jorcrof? That seemed fishy, too . . . But he seemed so dear, such a lovely old gentleman, who would have suspected that he was cheating?"

"But if you had nothing to do with rigging the show, how did you figure it out?" Belle asked. "And why the need to see us all of a sudden?"

In a flash, a layer of fog lifted for Rosco. The puzzle was finally falling into place. "Rolly Hoddal was trying to set up another fix, wasn't he . . . ? He didn't get his money so he wanted to give it another shot. And he wanted you to play Bartann Welner's part."

"Rolly's very persuasive. He . . . He . . ." Harriet looked to Belle, but Belle merely continued to examine her.

"But I thought you mentioned he had problems with substance abuse," she said dryly.

"Well, you see . . ." Harriet began, her fingers knit and unknit themselves.

"And why would you agree to participate in such a thing?"

Belle persisted. "You certainly don't need the money. Or were the five husbands a lie, too?"

Harriet released a long sigh, then reached for a tissue and dabbed showily at her eyes. But Rosco saw no sign of tears.

"Were you and Rolly going to cut Don Schruko out of the game this time" he asked, "or was he still expecting his take when he finished up with the *Anatomy* shoot?"

"I'm not part of anything illegal! That's what I'm trying to tell you! Yes, Rolly *suggested* I might be a contestant. And, yes, perhaps, *initially,* I gave him . . . well, the wrong idea about my interest . . . I admit, the excitement was flattering for an old woman like me . . . But I swear to you I told him in no uncertain terms that I would never participate in his nefarious schemes. Never! And that's why I asked you two to come here. To explain that I had nothing to do with rigging *Down & Across.* Not now or in the past . . . In fact, just yesterday, Rolly and I met, and I tried and tried to persuade him to give up the idea of rigging the show. I told him it would never work a second time."

Rosco studied Harriet. Her protestations seemed too practiced to be real. "So you're stating that you rejected Hoddal's proposal from the start?"

"Yes."

"Meaning that your decision was to put an end to his entire scheme?"

"Unless Rolly's ignoring my advice and considering a contestant I know nothing about. I don't know what he's up to. He was fit to be tied when he never received a dime from the first fix." Again, Harriet glanced at Belle and again dabbed at her still-dry eyes. Rosco decided it was time to change tactics. He looked toward his wife, exchanging a private message of complicity.

"Are you sure it was *Rolly* who called off the fix?" he barked at her. "On *your* advice? I can't buy that, Harriet, because from what Don Schruko told me—"

"Rosco," Belle interrupted. "Can't you see she's upset? There's no need to be harsh—"

"Harsh? These people have perpetrated a million-dollar fraud, and you think I'm being too harsh?" He returned his concentration to Harriet and tried to catch her off guard. "My wife's been receiving anonymous crosswords. One of them includes the names of everyone on the *Down & Across* set." Rosco counted off names on his fingers as he raised his voice. "Stan, Bart, Orso, Matthew, Wanda, Max, and you, Harriet, right in the center of the grid. What can you tell me about that?"

"Rosco . . .?" Belle repeated as a gentle warning while Rosco abruptly stood.

"I'm annoyed by these people, Belle, I really am." He glowered down at Harriet. "What can you tell me about those crosswords. And don't even consider lying. I'm through with that."

"I . . . don't know anything," Harriet quavered.

"But you recognized my wife the moment you saw her. You're obviously a puzzle expert. You lied to Belle. You've been lying all along. Why? What are you up to? You and Max? How does Max fit into all this?"

"Maxie isn't involved. You have to believe me."

"Why? Why should I believe you, Harriet? Tell me one iota of truth that's come from your mouth. Just one!"

That was all Harriet could take. She broke down in earnest and sobbed into her tissue. Belle crossed over and place an arm around the older woman. "I don't know what's gotten into him, Harriet."

"I'm not finished with her, Belle. She knows a lot more than she's letting on."

"No . . . No," Harriet whimpered. "That's all there is . . . And I swear I've done nothing illegal. Maybe I shouldn't have listened to Rolly . . . or . . . or I should have gone to Stan McKenet right away—"

"Nothing?" Rosco almost shouted. "A man has been murdered, and the wrong person locked up for it. Do you know what that means, Harriet? It means that a killer is walking around free. And that killer is somehow involved with both *Down & Across* and *Anatomy*—*if* you give any credence to that crossword. And you know what, Harriet? I've got a little bug inside of me; and that little bug is saying, 'Harriet Tammalong knows exactly who killed Chick Darlessen.'"

"It's Rolly who knows!" she whined. "He found out. It has nothing to do with me! Nothing!"

Belle removed her arm from Harriet's shoulder, stepped in front of her and looked down at the old lady's tear-stained face. "Who killed Darlessen?"

"Stanley . . . Stan McKenet did."

Rosco stared at Harriet. "The producer? Why? Because he didn't want to make the million dollar pay-off? Is that your theory? Which would mean that he might have killed Bartann Welner on top of it."

"No . . . Rolly . . . This is all Rolly's reasoning . . . He's certain Stan didn't kill Bartann because if that had been the case, he would never have attempted to rig the show a second time. He would have been far too frightened . . . Rolly feels Welner died of natural causes, but that the incident prompted Stanley's decision to eliminate Chick Darlessen as well."

"Why would Rolly believe such nonsense?" Rosco demanded. "McKenet's a businessman. He makes those sizable payments to every Grand-Slam Winner. It's part of his show's budget. I don't buy greed as a motive."

Harriet shook her head. "I know . . . It does seem unusual. That's why I didn't believe Rolly when he first mentioned it. I thought he was just being his usual paranoid self. But people get into financial scrapes all the time. Maybe Stanley's a gambler and lost a bunch at a casino . . ." She shook her head again. "All I can tell you is that Rolly has a key to the production office. That's how he steals the answers to the contests . . . And he swears he heard Stanley gloating over Darlessen's death—and pledging to remove Wanda, as well."

"Wanda Jorcrof?" Belle asked. "Why?"

"Because she's been pushing Stan to air the Grand-Slam show she lost to Bartann Welner. She has no money, and she desperately needs her twenty-five thousand dollar consolation prize. But Stanley wants to bury the segment. He's afraid another Welner relative will appear on the scene. Rolly insists Stanley is going to silence Wanda." Harriet took a deep breath.

"I assume Rolly has warned Wanda," Belle said.

"He did," Harriet replied in a thin and weary voice. "But she refused to believe him. Insisted his brain cells were misfiring . . . which is one of Rolly's problems. He does tend to see little green men with crazy hairdos on occasion . . ."

This time Belle sighed. "Why didn't you tell me you knew I was Belle Graham? Why did you propagate all those lies?"

"You're the one who started it," Harriet countered swiftly. Her tone was edgy and combative.

Rosco stared hard at the older woman. "I'm not getting a good read on this story of yours, Harriet—"

"Fine. Don't believe me. But if you want to learn who killed Chick Darlessen, it's Rolly Hoddal you should be talking to."

A stalemate fell upon the room until Harriet suddenly burst out with an anxious, "And now Rolly's private address book's been stolen from his dressing room. That's why he phoned me. He's beyond paranoid—"

"I thought he called you because I spoke to Don Schruko," Rosco interjected.

"That, too," Harriet countered. "But this other situation's more important . . . Because, Rolly's certain Stan McKenet took the address book, which lists Wanda's current residence out at Zuma Beach. See, she had to move because Stan wasn't coming up with her payment and she fell way behind on her West Hollywood rental. Rolly was the only one who had her present information. I should have never given it to him. She asked me not to pass it on to anyone, but Rolly wanted to send her a card. He wanted to send her some money."

Belle and Rosco looked at each other. Harriet's tall tale wasn't sitting well with either of them. "And why are you telling us this?" Belle asked.

"Because Wanda's in danger."

"And why should *we* believe that," Belle persevered, "when Wanda's evidently willing to shake it all off?"

"Don't then!" Harriet all but screamed. "Don't believe a word I'm saying! It's no skin off my nose, is it? Let another person die. Who cares? But don't say I didn't do my duty and warn the only folks who could help her."

"What folks might those be?" Belle asked.

"Why, you two, obviously. That's what you do, isn't it? Investigate criminal cases. That's why you met with Jillian Mawbry."

"And where is Ms. Jorcrof hiding?" Rosco asked. His tone was beleaguered, but it also held a modicum of cynical amusement, as if he were suddenly willing to follow Harriet Tammalong's lead.

"I have the address right here. She's out by Zuma Beach." Harriet handed Belle a slip of paper while maintaining a steady disregard of Rosco. "You'll be saving a life, Belle," she said.

B ack in the Mustang and driving west on the 101 Freeway, Belle turned to Rosco. "Do you think we should reconsider roaring off in hot pursuit of Wanda . . . because of what Harriet said Rolly said? What I mean is, do you think we're putting ourselves in jeopardy? Neither one of us quite believed Harriet's protestations of innocence back there."

"No, we didn't," Rosco interjected slowly. "But she's a smart cookie. I'd say she knows a lot more about rigging *Down & Across* than she's sharing. But I think she's far too savvy, and long in the tooth, to get mixed up in a murder— or try to set us up for one."

"But whoever stole Rolly's address book may very well be

on his way to Wanda's right now. And if that's who killed Chick—"

"Then that person's dangerous. No question about it. But I still don't believe Harriet's setting us up."

"So her motive for having us hunt up Wanda Jorcrof is altruism, just like she said?" Belle asked.

"Now see, that's the Grand-Slam million-dollar question, isn't it?" was Rosco's reply. "Down . . . and across."

CHAPTER

40

The drive to Zuma Beach and Wanda Jorcrof's one-room rental above a detached garage took Rosco and Belle west on the 101 Freeway to Malibu Canyon Road, which led them to the Pacific Coast Highway and the ocean. They followed the P.C.H. north for eleven miles until they turned briefly inland to a tiny surf-worshipping community that sat across the highway from Zuma's broad stretch of sand.

By the time they arrived at 6262 Ebbtide Way, the sun was already low in the sky, bathing the roadway, houses, and distant mountaintops in a heavy golden glow. As they pulled up to the curb, they were greeted by the sight of a teenage boy washing a late-model brown Volvo station wagon in the driveway fronting the garage. His surfboard leaned against a nearby wooden gate and had clearly been hosed down long before he'd decided to tackle the car. Rosco and Belle stepped from the Mustang as the kid looked up. "Nice 'stang, dude," he said with genuine admiration. "What're ya running, five-point-oh?"

"Running?" Rosco asked.

The boy craned his neck to look around Belle at the car—or more specifically, the chrome emblem attached to the front fender. "Yeah, runnin', dude. Like in engine? Displacement? Horsies? Where're you from, outer space?"

"No. Massachusetts." Rosco said a little more sternly than he needed to, but his intensity seemed to elude the young man.

"Yeah, dude, that's the kinda wheels I need. I'm tired of this wagon my old man bought me. Safety, that's what he's always yammerin' about, but this thing makes me look like I'm, like, twenty-five, or something."

"Ancient. Yeah, I can dig that," Rosco said as Belle interrupted in a tone that sounded inadvertently schoolmarmish and prim.

"We're looking for a Ms. Jorcrof."

"Oh, yeah, Wanda . . . Like, what's up with her anyways? Like, everybody's tryin' to find Wanda today."

"Everybody?

"Yeah, like, some dude in a suit was just here—drivin', like, a black Jag . . . Not a roadster, but, like, one of those sedans my granny has—and she's like, fifty, dude."

"What'd this guy in the Jag look like?" Rosco asked, wincing slightly as he said the final word.

"Like? I don't know . . . like, he looked like a guy in a suit, like an agent, maybe."

"A theatrical agent?"

"No, dude, like the *X-Files*. Like a suit and tie agent."

Since the Jaguar, which was clearly Stan McKenet's, was nowhere in sight, Rosco surmised that Wanda Jorcrof probably wasn't around either. "I gather Wanda's not here. Do you know where she went?"

"Yeah, like, I told the other dude, she, like, took Gabby over to the beach."

"Gabby?" Belle asked.

"Like, her dog, dude?"

Belle wasn't exactly sure that she qualified as a "dude," but she let the comment pass. "What kind of dog is Gabby?"

Her assumption, at this point, was that the boy might be better qualified to describe a dog than a woman or man.

"She's like, kind of, like, a poodle mixed with something else. Gray fur that's kinda curly and matted. Looks like a Rastafarian on a bad hair day."

"Big?"

"Nah, small . . . like, thirty pounds, max."

"Thanks," Rosco said, and turned back to the Mustang.

"Hey, you dudes can, like, get to the beach by walking down that little road over there." The boy pointed to his right. "I mean, like, that's how Wanda goes, so, maybe you'd, like, run into her. Besides, it's faster. The guy in the Jag wouldn't take my word for it—figured I was gonna like rip off his car or something. A sedan? Get real. Like, dude, who would want it?"

"Great. Thank you."

Figuring the Mustang was Hertz's problem and not theirs, Belle and Rosco opted to walk. After about fifty yards, the lane dead-ended at the P.C.H. They jogged across the highway, and entered a large, empty parking lot. The winter winds had coated the surface with a layer of sand, and shallow drifts had formed against the curbs and the concrete road barriers. In summer, there wouldn't be a parking space available, but now, in February, at the close of the day, it was an eerie, empty slate. Standing in the extended dark shadow of the facility's deserted ticket booth, Belle and Rosco scanned the area, but both pavement and beach appeared devoid of human life. Stretching for miles in both directions, sand and sea were no longer the rosy gold of sunset but a soft pewter color that would soon turn leaden and chilly.

"I'd feel a whole lot better if you went back to the Mustang and waited," Rosco said in a quiet tone. "You can talk to your new buddy—*dude*."

"Why? I don't think we, *like,* have much in common."

Rosco smiled, but his mouth was tight and worried. "We've got a killer around here somewhere, Belle. It's getting dark, and I'd rather you didn't get into the line of fire when he pops up."

"And what about you? Don't I get to worry about you?"

"Worry all you *like,* but do it back at the Mustang . . . I'm a professional. I can handle McKenet."

"I don't doubt that, but you've never seen him, Rosco. You can't identify him. I can—"

Belle's protest was curtailed as a compact gray dog darted down the beach toward a long, low-slung cinder block picnic/changing/restroom facility at the far end of the parking area. In the animal's wake was a woman who appeared to be in her late fifties. Her hair was a chopped, dark gray, and she was clad in a gray sweatshirt with gray sweatpants. In the waning light, her skin also appeared gray. She hurried after the dog shouting, "Gabby! Gabby! Come! Bad girl! Bad girl!"

Belle mouthed a hushed.

"Wanda."

Gabby was clearly into a game of *chase;* she continued to race along the beach, a blur of fur flying along, seemingly suspended a foot above the surface of the sand. Gray Wanda was no match for her pet; she ran and stumbled after the dog, entreating Gabby to return, but the dog seemed intent upon reaching the empty building. Despite its ghostly appearance, it must have contained some remnant of beach-food pleasures that had arrested the animal's keen sense of smell.

"That must be him!" Belle suddenly gasped as she pointed toward a Jaguar sedan that was rolling slowly into the lot. Invisible within the shadow of the wooden ticket office, the couple watched the driver silently emerge from his car. "It's McKenet."

At that moment, Gabby, barking loudly, barreled through an open door of the beach facility while Wanda, clearly winded, reached its broad concrete deck, and McKenet spotted his prey. He called out Wanda's name, but the sound of the dog's echoing yaps and yips drowned out his words. Oblivious to McKenet's presence, Wanda proceeded into the building; and the producer in his gleaming two-toned wingtips and expertly tailored suit hurried after her.

"Wait here," Rosco said as he handed Belle his cell phone, "and call the cops. McKenet's probably armed . . . be sure to tell them that."

"But——" Belle began.

"I know what I'm doing, Belle. I'll be careful." Then he took off in swift pursuit of McKenet and Wanda.

As Rosco entered the nearly night-dark facility, the noise of the dog combined with Wanda's numerous entreaties almost, but not quite, drowned out McKenet's angry shouts. Then there was a pause, not in Gabby's insistent barks, but in Wanda's pleas to her wayward pet. McKenet's voice filled the void with Wanda suddenly arguing back. What the two were fighting about, Rosco couldn't discern—the words disappeared beneath Gabby's now quite-anxious yelps. Rosco followed the sounds, circling through the empty rooms in the hopes of taking McKenet unaware. The few windows and doors that hadn't been boarded up against winter storms provided the sole illumination for his search, but it was scant.

When Rosco finally spotted the pair, they were still separated by one long concrete hallway. McKenet's back was to the entry of a small changing area. Through the blackness, Rosco could make out that Gabby was now on a leash and bucking and straining and lunging at the producer, her pointed white teeth reflecting what little light there was. Wanda seemed unaware that a third person was approaching. She held the dog back with one hand while the other gesticulated wildly toward McKenet. A stalemate appeared to have been reached. Rosco moved stealthily forward, all the while trying to adjust his eyes to the ever-darkening air.

When he was within eight feet of the doorway and McKenet, Rosco saw the producer begin to reach inside his jacket for what he believed was a weapon. In an instant, Rosco shot forward, propelling himself toward McKenet like a linebacker making a last-gasp tackle on a scoring half-back. He wrapped an arm around McKenet's shoulders and slammed his body into the steel door jamb. A gasp of air escaped from Stan's lungs, and a sound of fear echoed from his mouth as he tumbled onto the concrete. Felled by the speed and surprise of Rosco's attack, McKenet lay on the gritty floor, his face in the dirt, his arms pinned to his sides, while Rosco knelt above him.

The producer winced in pain. Anger had replaced his initial sense of terror. "Who the hell are you?" he demanded. "What do you want?"

"Take it easy, McKenet. The cops are on their way. It's over. You'll be charged for the murder of Chick Darlessen."

"Are you crazy?" was the stuttered reply. McKenet raised his head just enough to glower at Wanda. "She killed Darlessen. Didn't you hear her? I have it recorded on my Digital Voice Recorder. Who the hell are you?"

In his confusion, Rosco looked from McKenet to Wanda, back to McKenet, and then back again to Wanda who suddenly dropped her dog's leash. This time Gabby made no effort to escape.

"Who are you?" McKenet demanded for the third time.

Rosco released McKenet, and both men clambered to their feet. "Rosco Polycrates . . . I'm a private investigator." He paused again and studied the other two for a moment. "I was hired by Debra Marcollo's lawyer to look into the Darlessen murder."

"And you thought I killed him?" Stan said incredulously. "Where would you get such an inane idea?"

Seeing no evidence of the gun he believed the man possessed, Rosco ignored McKenet and turned to Wanda. "You shot Darlessen?"

Wanda's response was a stricken lowering of her head. "I just went there to talk, that's all . . . talk some sense into him. I needed that money. I didn't mean to . . . I just lost it." Then she raised her chin defiantly. "Chick was a pig! He knew I was broke . . . He was making big money . . . And he knew what I was going through—that I'd have to give up my house if I didn't get my share of the winnings . . . He could have pressured McKenet." She pointed at the producer. "And he did nothing. Nothing!"

Rosco looked at McKenet for corroboration while Wanda continued her tirade.

"Why couldn't you air the show, Stanley? I needed that money to survive. You and that creep Orso. You get your jollies stepping on the little people, don't you? Orso taunting me at the end of the show, digging it in . . . 'Looks like you're *Down & Out,* Wanda . . .' Then you both make me beg for my loser's share? Come groveling for what amounts to lunch money for you two? You should all rot!"

Stan McKenet raised his right hand. In it was a crumpled envelope. He opened it, removed a cashier's check, and handed it to Rosco. "I was trying to give this to her. It's a check for her twenty-five thousand dollars. The consolation prize she would have won if the show was aired. I just wanted her off my back." He shook his head. "And you thought I was pulling a gun, is that it?"

"It looked like that from the rear. I wasn't about to stop and ask questions."

McKenet dusted the grit from his handsome suit, then glanced in dismay at his ruined wingtips. "I'm going to be honest with you here, fella. I have no intention of airing that blessed show—ever. Why should I? Why should I pay out a million bucks to some distant relative of Bartann Welner's who wouldn't know a crossword puzzle from a checkered flag? They don't deserve jack. Neither did Darlessen, as far as that goes, and I don't mind saying it . . . Look, I was here to dispose of Wanda once and for all, okay? Call it hush money if you want, I don't care. But she's the only person who could make my life miserable for not airing that show, so I decided to buy her off . . . I don't need my life being any more miserable than it already is." Stan pulled a small Sony recording device from his breast pocket. "I have all of this on my DVR. I record everything anyone says to me. This is L.A., fella, I cover myself. Like you, I like to hang onto evidence."

Rosco nodded slowly. "Right . . . Did you know the Bartann Welner shows were rigged?" he asked after a moment.

McKenet stared at him in disbelief mixed with horror. He quickly turned off his Digital Voice Recorder. "What?" he demanded. The word wobbled in his throat. "What do you mean, *rigged*? *Down & Across* has never been *rigged*. Never. Don't make accusations you can't back up. I'll have a lawyer down your throat before you know it."

"Rolly Hoddal stole the correct answers from your office. He teamed up with Bartann Welner and Don Schruko, and they fixed the shows."

"I knew it! I knew it!" Wanda began to rant again. She turned toward McKenet with hate in her eyes. "There's no way that old coot could have beaten me. I didn't win a single round in the Grand-Slam. It had to be fixed. I want my money! I want the whole million. He didn't beat me. I was cheated!"

But the sound of police sirens broke in on her outburst; and with the blaring wail moving ever closer, Wanda began to sob, as her frightened dog whimpered beside her.

C rossing the pavement under police escort, Wanda noticed Belle standing beside one of the cruisers. "You're Annabella Graham, aren't you?" she asked in surprise. "You're the crossword editor . . ."

When Belle nodded, Wanda glanced back at Rosco who was walking beside Stan McKenet. In Rosco's left hand was a dog leash, at his feet was a confused and shivering Gabby. "And he's . . ." Wanda began, then stopped herself. "Yeah, I've read about you two . . . And . . . you've got a dog, don't you?"

As Belle again nodded, Wanda pointed toward Gabby. "See that she gets a good home. Could you do that for me? Please?"

CHAPTER

41

"Sadie Hawkins Day. That's what we called February twenty-ninth when I was a kid, Big Al," Martha Leonetti pronounced as she approached the booth while balancing an armload of four steaming platters. This was the real Martha speaking—not an actress pretending to be Martha—meaning that "Big Al" and the rest of the Breakfast Bunch were each the genuine article: laugh lines, frown lines, a few unwanted, extra pounds, and all. While Lawson's coffee shop-cum-diner-cum-all-around-local-hangout was the original—in all its homey and unglamorous glory. "It's the one day, every four years, when a woman gets to ask a man to marry her," she continued. "You lookin' to get lucky tomorrow?" The place was bustling, the business as brisk as the Massachusetts weather, and that was despite the five inches of freshly fallen snow that sat atop the three feet that wouldn't be melting until sometime in April.

"Whoa, hold on there, Martha," Al Lever protested, "You gotta clear any marriage proposals you're aiming at me with the wife I already have."

"I don't see where anybody's asking *you,* Al. Just giving you a little history lesson, that's all." With a flourish, she placed the plates of goodies in front of her patrons and made her customary proclamations: "Poached egg with rye toast, no butter, for Mrs. Briephs; waffles with extra blueberry sauce and double whipped cream for the Puzzle Gal; Spanish omelette and french fries—extra order and extra crispy—for Big Al; grilled cheese and bacon for Mr. Cute-buns, Rosco."

Rosco raised his hands as the others exploded in convivial laughter. "I had nothing to do with that line in the movie, Martha," he said. "It was all my charming wife's doing. A real comedienne, she is."

"But Ivald told Belle he was keeping it in his final cut, right?" Martha countered. She raised an eyebrow as she spoke. An authority when it came to expressions of arch disbelief, her blonde beehive also appeared to rise to new heights of skepticism.

Rosco made a mock grimace. "Yeah, well . . ."

"So, Cute-buns, you'll remain."

"Better you than me, buddy," Al Lever chortled as he speared a forkful of home fries.

"You keep munchin' that stuff, Al, you're gonna' get your own nickname, and *cute*'s gonna have nothin' to do with it."

"We shouldn't have told you about that line," Belle said, still chuckling. "We should have waited until the show airs next month. That way it would have been a big surprise."

"What other *surprises* do you three have in store?" Al asked suspiciously. "Besides the Hollywood tans you're all flaunting in our wintry faces?"

"I guess you'll have to wait and see, won't you?" Belle answered with a mischievous grin.

"That's what I'm afraid of. That I'm going to be the laughingstock of the Newcastle Police Department—if not the entire town."

"Oh, Albert, you mustn't mind Belle," Sara soothed. "Jes Nadema played your character very respectfully, and with a deft touch that portrayed a sensitive but turbulent inner-life. Don't you agree, Rosco?"

"Right, Sara . . . Except for the 'fat-suit,' the costume gang made you look huge, Al. Pretty unattractive, actually."

"What?" Lever's voice rose in indignation. "Jes Nadema wore a 'fat-suit'? He played me in a 'fat-suit'?"

"Rosco!" Belle chided. "Don't say that . . . That's not true, Al; Jes wasn't given any additional padding."

"Well, they didn't need to," Rosco tossed in. "Have you seen that guy lately, Al? You know how these ex-wrestlers blow up once they stop working out. Man, he looks like a moose now." Rosco was laughing in spite of himself.

"Stop it, Rosco. Leave Al alone. None of that's true, and you know it. Jes is still in great shape. No one in town's going to tease you when they see the movie, Al. In fact, they're going to be impressed."

Martha returned with a pot of coffee and filled the four cups. "So it was Shay Henley who was constructing those puzzles, all along . . . Did she ever tell you why?"

It was Sara who answered. Her tone had not yet fully abandoned its haughty, Hollywood-diva quality. "Her behavior is consistent with the Actor's Studio approach, Martha. Professional performers go to great lengths in order to assume the shape and color of their roles—to make the characters truly live. In fact, Shay shared the technique with me. I found it an enormous help in preparing my own part . . . Of course, I was playing myself."

"What's the technique?" Al asked, "making up crosswords?"

"Goodness, no Albert! You misunderstood, entirely! You see, in order to create a believable character, one must 'inhabit' the role. One must literally 'become' that person; in Miss Henley's case, that would be Belle. So, in doing her her 'homework,' if you will, Shay attempted to turn herself into a crossword constructor, hoping that the activity would help her better understand her—or Belle's—motivations in certain scenes. Shay went so far as to visit the *Down & Across* tapings, incognito naturally, for two weeks prior to our filming of *Anatomy*."

"Unfortunately," Belle added, "Shay had a difficult time creating new grids; as a result, she decided to use the one I constructed and insert new words."

"But why didn't she tell you what she was up to?" Martha asked.

Rosco shook his head as he replied. "One reason is that we never point-blank asked her . . . She also told us she wanted to see how long it would take us to figure it out. Just another case of Hollywood high jinks. In fact, the *What's In A Name?* crossword that had Belle champing at the bit was pure coincidence . . . The ENID that my dear wife believed was a major mystery player turned out to be Shay's mom—as well as *Sir Geraint's wife*."

"But she let Don Schruko in on her secret, right?" Al wondered aloud.

Belle smiled ruefully as she nodded. "She told nearly everybody! The entire cast was in on the joke! And since everyone knew the puzzles were harmless, they were just waiting to see how long it would take for me to catch on."

"But they had no idea how serious and pertinent you believed the crosswords were." Martha finished Belle's thought. "And now . . . Shay and Max Chugorro are an item . . . I can't wait to see how the movie mags handle that juicy tidbit."

"I'm sure he'll be listed as an up-and-coming screenwriter, and not the 'Marquis de Sod.'"

"Wait. Wait," Al protested, "I didn't hear anything about this Max person and Shay Henley. When did all that happen?"

"If you'd show up on time for breakfast once in a while," Rosco joked, "you wouldn't miss half our conversation . . . Max Chugorro was the guy Shay believed was stalking her, but, in fact, all he wanted to do was get his latest screenplay into her hands. When he followed her home, he was trying to find out where she lived."

"Screenplay?"

"It's a biopic about one of Pancho Villa's mistresses. Max figured if he could get a star like Shay Henley to agree to do the lead, he'd get a studio deal in a flash."

Martha let out with a hearty chuckle. "Old Maxie didn't realize he was going to get Ms. Henley's bod in the bargain."

"Well, she fell in love with the script," was Belle's diplomatic response.

"Hah! She fell in love with something . . . Only time will tell if it was the script or not." Martha walked over to the cash register to take another customer's money, then immediately returned. "And the Nan DeDero 'accident'?"

"As far as anyone can tell, that's all it was," Belle answered. "As of now, Don Schruko isn't admitting to foul play."

"Of course, if Schruko did arrange Nan's accident, he needed to have assistance," Rosco said, directing the comment toward Al Lever. "As it stands, the Los Angeles County District Attorney has become very interested in the rigging of *Down & Across,* so we'll have to wait and see what comes out of that investigation. Apparently, Rolly Hoddal's talking up a storm in an effort to save his own skin—which, naturally, means implicating Schruko . . . If things get too hot, whoever was aiding and abetting on *Anatomy* may come out of the woodwork."

"And what about poor Harriet Tammalong? Is she in the clear?" Lever asked.

"Poor Harriet?" Belle said with a small laugh. "Al, she was in the middle of perpetrating a million-dollar fraud."

Rosco polished off a healthy bite of grilled cheese sandwich. "It does look as if Harriet's going to dodge the bullet, though, Al. It's up to Stan McKenet and Gerry Orso to push a case against her, but right now, the less publicity the better as far as they're concerned. The show is on very thin ice with the sponsors as it is."

Lever pointed one of his french fries at Rosco. "Speaking of dodging bullets, Poly-crates, what happened to the six

.38 rounds that were missing from Darlessen's box of shells?"

"Apparently, Wanda believed she and Chick were alone in the house when she decided to confront him. As soon as she heard Debra in the other room, she reloaded the gun and hid behind a filing cabinet—meaning that if Debra had discovered the murderer still on the property . . . Well, who knows what might have happened. Obviously, Wanda wasn't thinking too lucidly at that point . . . At any rate, the police report placed the gun and the box with the twelve remaining shells on their evidence list. No mention was made of the weapon being reloaded; and I had no access to the LAPD evidence room. Any official files I saw came through Mawbry, but LAPD considered him nothing more than a sleazy ambulance chaser, so the details they supplied were sketchy, at best."

"Well, he did save Marcollo's bacon," Al observed.

Sara suddenly and unexpectedly sighed. "A sad story, all around, if you consider the number of lives affected."

"That's what murder cases are about," was Lever's sobering response.

"And so much conniving," Sara continued, "and selfishness. And greed."

"The chance to snag a million dollars can bring out the worst in some folks," Al concluded in the same pensive tone.

"But there was a good deal of kindness, too," Belle added gently. "Shay and Dan . . . they're fine people. And there were many, many others."

It was Martha who dispelled the impending gloom as she again returned from the cash register. "So, how's that new pooch of yours working out?"

"Gabby? Oh, she and Kit are establishing their own routine," Belle said with a small smile. "But they're having a little trouble determining who's going to be the alpha dog. Rosco seems reluctant to give up the position."

"Ho, ho. One trip to the 'coast' and my wife sees herself as the next Jerry Seinfeld."

"Actually, they're getting along really well, Martha. I guess it's just a matter of Gabby adjusting to a life that's no longer in the fast lane."

"I could give her some pointers," was Martha's pithy reply.

Across

1. Zoological body
5. 100 yrs.
8. "Porgy and_____"
12. Former Russian ruler
13. Former capital of Bolivia
16. Mr. Estrada
17. DON SCHRUKO
19. *The_____Vanishes*
20. India_____
21. India Pale_____
22. Holler
24. Movie goof
26. Unruly audience missile
29. Like many plants or pens
31. Alumnus
33. CAR or DAQ lead-in
34. Some H.S. Courses
36. _____-Rooter
37. Restaurant list
39. Victory or peace sign
40. Ger. neighbor
41. Was indebted
42. Competitor
43. Druggist's deg.
44. Measured
46. Bernhardt & Miles
49. Saunter
50. TV control
52. Rom or fin ending
53. Roman 2,050
54. _____*Max*
55. Stereo predecessor
58. DAN MILLRAY
61. Press
62. Chilled
63. Killer whale
64. License plates
65. Some Greek letters
66. Fires

Down

1. Backdrop
2. Type of ether
3. STAN McKENET
4. Noah's craft
5. Grand_____Dam
6. Brünhilde's mother
7. Some Greek letters
8. GALE HARMBLE
9. Koufax stat.
10. Mr. Caesar
11. Pie in the_____
14. GERRY ORSO
15. Ryan & Tatum
18. Transports
23. Concern for 5-Down; abbr.
25. LANCE diRUSA
27. MAX CHUGORRO
28. Roscoes
30. DEAN IVALD
32. On the_____
35. Ms. Grant
37. May honoree
38. Lambs' 37-Down
42. Fastener
43. Green shampoo
45. Silver or Wood
47. Battle groups
48. Position
51. Icelandic sagas
53. Roman 2,101
55. Smash
56. Certain savings acct.
57. Low clouds
59. Pound sound
60. Mauna_____

POST SCRIPT—"THE NAME GAME"

Anagrams from "Anna Graham"

After completing the Post Script, puzzle you've obviously discovered that some characters' names are anagrams of famous personalities from the past (except our own Belle Graham).

Max Chugorro	=	Groucho Marx
Lance diRusa	=	Claude Rains
Gale Harmble	=	Belle Graham
Dean Ivald	=	David Lean
Stan McKenet	=	Mack Sennett
Dan Millray	=	Ray Milland
Gerry Orso	=	Roy Rogers
Don Schruko	=	Rock Hudson

But these aren't the only ones! Here are some more anagrams that appeared in *Anatomy of a Crossword* Hint—they're all performers except one famous writer (W) and one famous lawyer (L)

Ginger Bradmin
Chick Darlessen (W)
Nan Dedero
Louis Gable
Lew Groslir
Quinton Hanny
Shay Henlee
Rolly Hoddal
Andy Hofren
Wanda Jorcrof
Miso Lane

Debra Marcollo
Jillian Mawbry (L)
Jes Nadema
Lee Rennegor
Madeline Richter
Bubba Screter
Nils Spemick
Harriet Tammalong
Greg Trafeo
Carol Von Deney
Bartann Welner

The Answers

GREETINGS!

M¹	G²	A³		A⁴	T⁵	E⁶		C⁷	H⁸	E⁹		F¹⁰	A¹¹	N¹²
Y¹³	U	L		D¹⁴	I	N		L¹⁵	O	T		A¹⁶	S	A
W¹⁷	E	L	C¹⁸	O	M	E	T¹⁹	O	L	A		M²⁰	A	P
I²¹	R	M	A			O²²	U	T		S²³	I	P	A	
F²⁴	R	A	N	K²⁵		E²⁶	M	T		E²⁷	E	L		
E²⁸	E	N		L²⁹	T³⁰	D			D³¹	R	I	N	K³²	K³³
			U³⁴	R	I	S³⁵		G³⁶	O	B	A	C	K	
A³⁷	F³⁸	I³⁹		G⁴⁰	E	T	A⁴¹	T	A	N		R⁴²	O	K
D⁴³	A	N	G⁴⁴	M	E		E⁴⁵	R	I	E				
T⁴⁶	A	K	E	A			A⁴⁷	L	I		A⁴⁸	G⁴⁹	E⁵⁰	
		L⁵¹	O	N		G⁵²	A⁵³	P		L⁵⁴	A⁵⁵	V	E	D
S⁵⁶	W⁵⁷	I	M		S⁵⁸	I	R		M⁵⁹	E	O	W		
T⁶⁰	E	N		W⁶¹	H	A	T	M⁶²	E⁶³	W⁶⁴	O	R	R	Y
E⁶⁵	E	G		H⁶⁶	E	N		A⁶⁷	G	O		T⁶⁸	G	N
M⁶⁹	D	S		O⁷⁰	A	T		E⁷¹	G	O		S⁷²	E	N

IT'S JUST A STAGE

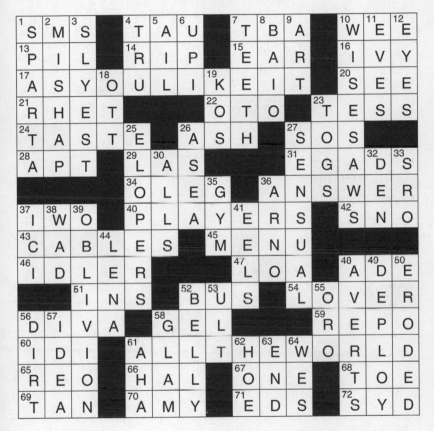

WHAT'S IN A NAME?

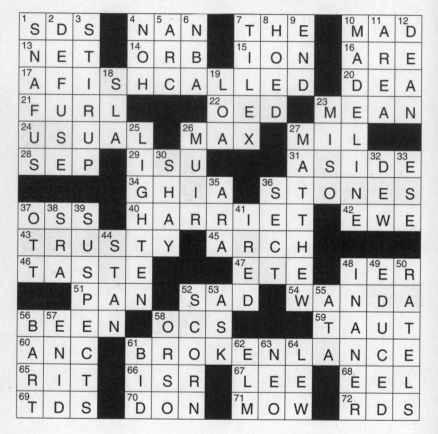

S¹	D²	S³		N⁴	A⁵	N⁶		T⁷	H⁸	E⁹		M¹⁰	A¹¹	D¹²
N¹³	E	T		O¹⁴	R	B		I¹⁵	O	N		A¹⁶	R	E
A¹⁷	F	I	S¹⁸	H	C	A	L¹⁹	L	E	D		D²⁰	E	A
F²¹	U	R	L			O²²	E	D		M²³	E	A	N	
U²⁴	S	U	A	L²⁵		M²⁶	A	X		M²⁷	I	L		
S²⁸	E	P		I²⁹	S³⁰	U			A³¹	S	I	D	E³²	E³³
			G³⁴	H	I	A	A³⁵		S³⁶	T	O	N	E	S
O³⁷	S³⁸	S³⁹	H⁴⁰	A	R	R	I	E⁴¹	T		E⁴²	W	E	
T⁴³	R	U	S⁴⁴	T	Y		A⁴⁵	R	C	H				
T⁴⁶	A	S	T	E			E⁴⁷	T	E		I⁴⁸	E⁴⁹	R⁵⁰	
		P⁵¹	A	N		S⁵²	A	D⁵³		W⁵⁴	A	N⁵⁵	D	A
B⁵⁶	E⁵⁷	E	N		O⁵⁸	C	S			T⁵⁹	A	U	T	
A⁶⁰	N	C		B⁶¹	R	O	K	E⁶²	N⁶³	L⁶⁴	A	N	C	E
R⁶⁵	I	T		I⁶⁶	S	R		L⁶⁷	E	E		E⁶⁸	E	L
T⁶⁹	D	S		D⁷⁰	O	N		M⁷¹	O	W		R⁷²	D	S

THE REAL DEAL

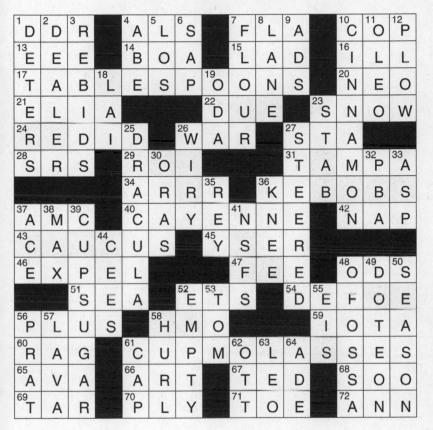

FAMOUS LAST WORDS

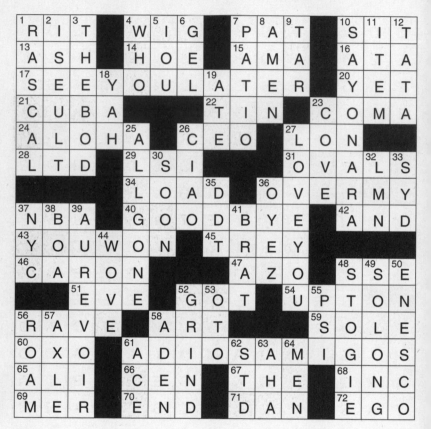

POST SCRIPT—"THE NAME GAME"

Anagram Answers

Ginger Bradmin	=	Ingrid Bergman
Max Chugorro	=	Groucho Marx
Chick Darlessen	=	Charles Dickens
Nan DeDero	=	Donna Reed
Lance diRusa	=	Claude Rains
Louis Gable	=	Bela Lugosi
Lew Groslir	=	Will Rogers
Quinton Hanny	=	Anthony Quinn
Gale Harmble	=	Belle Graham
Shay Henlee	=	Helen Hayes
Rolly Hoddal	=	Harold Lloyd
Andy Hofren	=	Henry Fonda
Dean Ivald	=	David Lean
Wanda Jorcrof	=	Joan Crawford
Miso Lane	=	Sal Mineo
Debra Marcollo	=	Carole Lombard
Jillian Mawbry	=	William J. Bryan
Stan McKenet	=	Mack Sennett
Dan Millray	=	Ray Milland
Jes Nadema	=	James Dean
Gerry Orso	=	Roy Rogers
Lee Rennegor	=	Lorne Greene
Madeline Richter	=	Marlene Dietrich
Don Schruko	=	Rock Hudson
Bubba Screter	=	Buster Crabbe
Nils Spemick	=	Slim Pickens
Harriet Tammalong	=	Margaret Hamilton
Greg Trafeo	=	George Raft
Carol Von Deney	=	Yvonne De Carlo
Bartann Welner	=	Walter Brennan